The
Cygnet Prince

The Tudor Rose Murders Series

Book Three

G J Williams

Legend Press Ltd, 51 Gower Street, London, WC1E 6HJ
info@legendtimesgroup.co.uk | www.legendpress.co.uk

Contents © G J Williams 2025
The right of the above author to be identified as the author of this work has been asserted in accordance with the Copyright, Designs and Patents Act 1988. British Library Cataloguing in Publication Data available.

Print ISBN 9781917163484
Ebook ISBN 9781917163491
Set in Times.
Cover design by Sarah Whittaker | www.whittakerbookdesign.com

All characters, other than those clearly in the public domain, and place names, other than those well-established such as towns and cities, are fictitious and any resemblance is purely coincidental.

All rights reserved. No part of this publication may be reproduced, stored in or introduced into a retrieval system, or transmitted, in any form, or by any means electronic, mechanical, photocopying, recording or otherwise, without the prior permission of the publisher. Any person who commits any unauthorised act in relation to this publication may be liable to criminal prosecution and civil claims for damages.

Dr G J Williams, like John Dee, is Welsh but raised in England. After an idyllic childhood in Somerset, where history, story-telling and adventure were part of life, a career of psychology, first in academia and then international consulting, beckoned. It was some years before the love of writing returned to the forefront of life.

G J Williams now lives between Somerset and London and is often found writing on the train next to a grumpy cat and a cup of tea.

When not writing, life is a muddle of researching, travelling to historic sites or plotting while sailing the blue seas on the beloved boat bequeathed by a father who always taught that history gives the gift of prediction.

The first book in The Tudor Rose Murders series, *The Conjuror's Apprentice*, was published by Legend Press in 2023, and the sequel, *The Wolf's Shadow*, was published in 2024.

Follow G J on Twitter
@gjwilliams92

and Instagram
@gjwilliams92

Visit
www.gjwilliamsauthor.com

The Cygnet Prince is dedicated to my dear friend and first reader, Christine (Chris) Cook.

Like the lovely Anne of Cleves, Chris bore all her own life-trials with grace and created joy with what she had. Her love for her husband, children and grandchildren shone on them and her warm support, wit and intelligence shone on those of us lucky enough to call her friend.

Her last words to me were that she was proud of me – words that sustain me and make me so proud to call her my friend. Thank you, Chris.

Cast of Characters

The St Dunstan's Household

John Dee – scholar, astronomer, theologian, physician, conjurer
Margaretta Morgan – John Dee's apprentice disguised as his servant and scribe
Master Constable – householder and merchant
Katherine Constable – lady of the house and wife to the merchant, Master Constable
Huw – Margaretta's brother

The McFadden Household

Angus McFadden – vintner
Susan McFadden – sister to Margaretta and wife of Angus
Little Jack and Maria – their children
Grace – servant

The Cecil Household

Sir William Cecil – lawyer, politician and advisor/friend to Princess Elizabeth
Lady Mildred Cecil – Cecil's wife and one of the most educated women in England

Court

Elizabeth I – Tudor Queen of England
Robert Dudley – master of the Horse and favourite of Elizabeth
Blanche ap Harri – gentlewoman and keeper of books and jewels

Kat Astley – chief gentlewoman
Henry Carey – cousin to Elizabeth
Beatrice ap Rhys – launderess
Bishop Alvaro de la Quadra – Spanish Ambassador
Doctor Burcot – physician to Henry Carey and then Elizabeth

Germany – Solingen, Witzhelden and Cologne

Peter Albrecht – guide and translator for John Dee and Margaretta
Amalia of Cleves – sister of Anne of Cleves
Gilda – baker
Otho van Wylich – illegitimate son of Otto van Wylich
Ursula – daughter of Caspar Vopel (deceased)

The retinue of Anne of Cleves on her journey to England, 1539

Nicholas Wooton – churchman, ambassador and negotiator of the marriage to Henry
Otto van Wylich (deceased) – guardian and friend of Anne's father
Mrs Gylman (deceased) – née Susannah Hornebolt, limner sent to teach Anne English language and manners
Thomas Seymour (deceased) – one of the reception party at Calais

Ladies in waiting to Anne of Cleves' ladies in 1540

Margaret Douglas – niece of Henry VIII
Catherine Carey – cousin of Elizabeth and sister to Henry Carey
Katherine Willoughby, Duchess of Suffolk – life-long friend

Lincolns Inn

Will Fleetwood – lawyer, merchant, and favoured by Cecil
David Owens – pupil and nephew of Beatrice ap Rhys

Other characters

Siôn Jenkins – former archer, vagrant, servant
Captain Neerman (deceased) – captain of *The Mariella*
Tom Chapman – owner of Anne of Cleves' former home in Norfolk
Sam – friend of Margaretta and their carriage driver/wherryman
William Pudding – minister of St Mary's Church, Norfolk

Prologue

The figure shrank back into the filthy alley, ignoring the stink of piss and rats that seeped through the oiled cotton veil across their face. The sailors ran past, shouting, and pulling the wailing cabin boy as they charged up the gangplank. Now it was safe to step forward and lower the material to better see. The figure smiled and nodded.

One sailor leaned over the gunnels, sweeping a pitch torch across the dark and filthy water. 'There he be.'

They used hooks to drag the body to the quayside, face down, the leather jerkin on the man's back making his body look like a huge black turtle in the detritus. The cabin boy whimpered as the younger sailor ran down the water steps, reached out to grasp the hair, then shook his head and called up, 'No life.'

Back in the alley, the figure pulled their hood forward, tightened the veil and walked away. There was no sound of footsteps. Just a rasping whisper – 'Thy will be done.'

Part One

Chapter One

September, 1562. London

'The son of a virgin and man who could not abide to lie with her? Hah.'

'Yes, Doctor Dee.' The messenger gulped and glanced at the door to ensure he could not be heard. 'He claims to be the trueborn son of King Henry and Lady Anne of Cleves.'

'Fie. Does he also claim to be the second coming?' Dee chuckled at his own jest, then grumbled as he looked back to the manuscript spread across his cluttered desk.

'No, sir.'

'Well, that is surely a mercy for England. If the Lord comes among us, we do not want him a madman.'

The servant bit his lip and shot a pleading look to Margaretta. She looked to her master. 'Come, Doctor. The last time you worked for Sir Cecil, it served you well.'

'Pah. William Cecil did nothing for me. It was Robert Dudley who pulled me back into the light of Court... and into the eyes of Queen Elizabeth... when he asked me to calculate the most auspicious day for her coronation.'

Margaretta dropped her voice to that of a mother coaxing a difficult child. 'But Doctor, think of the challenge—'

'I need no challenge. I simply have my place at Court to maintain.' John Dee bent over his papers. 'Why does Cecil always want my attention when there is a manuscript to write.'

He tapped hard on the parchment. 'My most important work yet. The Kabbalah and the cypher of universal knowledge.'

'But Sir Cecil says this plot could destroy Court,' bleated the messenger. 'This man is claiming he has a greater blood line to the throne than our Queen. He has items.'

'Items?'

'Jewellery and letters which connect him directly to Anne of Cleves. He insists he has all proof required.'

'Foolery. Last time Cecil had me investigate a threat to our Queen, he insisted a man came back from the dead to be hanged in an oak. There were *items* then too. He was wrong then and is again.'

'But this time it is the Queen who calls for you, sir.'

Dee froze, then stood, eyes brightening in excitement as he pointed a finger towards the door and barked, 'Why did you not say, boy?' He snatched up his book and a quill. A grab at his cloak which was thrown over his shoulder and he was darting to the door. 'Margaretta, come.'

'But you have not yet broken your fast.'

'No time to eat, girl. Destiny calls.'

Chapter Two

Huw stood at the door, staring at the floor as Doctor Dee rushed through, followed by the relieved messenger who was chattering about where they must go for instructions. Margaretta held back until the door was closed. '*Huw. Dere gyda fi.* Huw. Come with me.'

Brother and sister scuttled to the kitchen, taking care to tip-toe past the chamber where Katherine Constable, lady of the house and baleful admirer of her lodger, John Dee, would be supping her way through her first jug of Malmsey wine. By midday she would become either loud and demanding or quiet and bitter. It was never predictable which – only that one of her harsh sides would emerge from the dark, drink-fed thoughts.

Huw went straight to the log-pile – his favourite place – and started to nudge each piece so that every outer edge was perfectly aligned. Margaret pulled on her cloak as she gave instructions in their mother tongue of Welsh. 'I have to go out with the doctor, Huw. It seems we have another mystery to chase.' She nodded back towards the hallway. 'You need to lay the table for break of fast. Then, the midday meal. Stay close for the day and, if the mistress calls, then you take her some more wine and do not try to correct anything she says – you know what happens.'

Huw started to step from foot to foot, shaking his head.

'But she says foolery. She says I am her brother reborn.' The stepping increased. 'I am Huw... Huw.'

Margaretta sighed and bent towards her little brother only to make him take two steps back and avert his face. 'I won't touch you Huw. But when I'm away you must do all you can to keep her happy... the poor woman.'

'She is rich. Not poor.'

'Maybe in her pocket, brother. But her heart is quite empty. Stuck between a husband who would swap her for a glass of port-wine and her unnoticed love for her lodger who only has eyes for the magic of his learning. Years she has yearned for a little attention. Even her cat preferred to sit on Mam's lap.' She stepped to the chair their mother once sat in and ruffled the animal's ears. 'And give Cadi-Cat some milk.'

'I miss Mam.'

Oh, little brother, so do I. But I keep these thoughts to myself. Every day I recall her voice, her eyes, her face. Sometimes the memory is sad; sometimes angry. All those years she wasted in misery and anger. All those harsh words and cruel jibes when all I did was care for her. But... and I thank God... there were the few months before she passed that we had her back as she was – the kind and good mother who raised us. Thanks to a woman called Clarissa and a maid called Grace.

Huw frowned. 'Go see Clarissa and Spot.'

Margaretta gasped. 'How did you know what I was thinking, Huw?'

The boy grinned. 'Colour changed. Huw like Margaretta. See things, feel things. Margaretta know thoughts. Huw know people's colour.'

'What are you saying?'

Huw looked away, biting his lower lip as the foot shifting started again. 'See colours round people. Light colour, good soul. Dark colour, dark soul. Clarissa is yellow like sun. Good.'

'When did it start?'

'Always.' He shrugged. 'I thought all people see colours.

Then Mam say, "No. Be quiet. People think you moonstruck... bad."'

His sister smiled and whispered. 'Well, it's our secret. And I'm glad I'm not alone. And what colour is our dear sister, Susan?'

Huw scowled. 'Dark grey when with you. Blue with Little Jack and Baby Maria.'

Margaretta huffed, 'That make's sense – I think she only has a heart for those children. For the rest of us she has a swinging stone in her breast. What about her husband?'

'Black. All round him.'

Margaretta laughed. 'That is all the proof I need, brother.' She bent her head so that he could see her smile at him and ignored the way he closed his eyes. 'Who else has a good colour?'

'Grace is violet like flower.'

'Susan's maid? Well, she is a sweet girl.' *Do I see a little red come into your cheek?*

Then Huw blurted, 'Little Jack same colour as me.'

Margaretta laughed. 'Well, that's good. Better he has a soul like yours and not like his father's.' *Why do you seem so bothered that Susan's firstborn has the same colour as you? I feel worry. No point asking, you will tell me in time.* 'Now I must away and pretend to be the doctor's servant again. There to feel the thoughts of all around me and feed him those nuggets which he then presents back as his own brilliance.' She went to the table to cut a slice of bread to hide in her pocket. 'But it keeps us off the streets and our bellies full.' She turned to the door, then looked back and pointed at the tabby cat sitting on the chair by the fire. 'And keep Cadi-Cat here in the kitchen on Mam's chair. The mistress is still afeared of her claws.' She smiled as Huw giggled in delight.

She left just as Katherine Constable called for her honey tea... and wine.

Chapter Three

John Dee was striding up and down the cobble path, pulling at his beard. 'Come, Margaretta. Why does a girl take so long putting on a cloak? We could be half-way there by now.'

'Because the girl has to make sure the house is seen to while you are away so that you do not return to find your bed thrown out in the street by your landlord.'

Dee frowned. 'You are getting quick tongued for a servant.' He turned and stepped into the waiting carriage.

Margaretta checked he was looking away and quickly dropped the slice of bread into the three fingers of the crooked-nosed beggar who leaned against the wall. She then followed through the carriage door emblazoned with Sir Cecil's coat of arms and sat down opposite her master. 'Because you and I know I am no servant, Doctor. I am your apprentice and weapon. You use me to hear, feel, sense and pry into the minds of others.' She gave him a playful grin. 'And I keep Mistress Constable up to her cups in Malmsey to keep her from bending your ear to her desires.'

Dee sighed and slumped back in his seat. 'It is true, Margaretta.' The horseman cracked the whip and the wheels lurched. 'Indeed, you are nearly a better student than Christopher was. Braver in accepting the power beyond the veil. Quicker in understanding the crystals and cards.' Silence. His eyes flicked to his companion and he reached out to pat her hand.

'Oh, I am sorry. I did not mean to... cause pain. That was thoughtless of me.'

Margaretta stared out of the window failing to stop the tears gathering. She gulped down a sob and whispered, 'I still see Clara in the market, carrying their child. He is flaxen haired like his father.'

'You must try to feel some pity for her,' said Dee gently.

'Why should I feel pity for a foul bizzem?'

Dee sighed again. 'Because she is a widow with a small boy who will never recall his father. Come, Margaretta. Christopher is dead a year now. He has spoken to us through the cards and is comforted by the angels. Do not weep for him.'

Margaretta turned her head quickly to glare at her master, green eyes flashing anger. 'I weep for myself, Doctor. For Clara *had* him, the angels *have* him and I only ever knew to *want* him.' She swiped away the tears. 'First Mam, then Christopher. It's too much.'

'And I have been much away with my travels and studies. You have been all alone through all this.' He paused and pressed a smile onto his face. 'But you have studied hard and learned everything I asked of you. You are much advanced as my apprentice.'

'Strange cards and cold crystals do not give the comfort of another's love, Doctor.'

'There may be another,' ventured Dee, his voice feigning hope.

'I do not want another. Better to stay alone in this world; for then the hurt of love will never scar your heart.'

Dee frowned sadly but nodded and sat back. 'We are both sole travellers through life, Margaretta. Let us focus on helping another like us. We will help Elizabeth.'

The carriage rattled down a strangely empty Cannon Street into Ludgate Hill. The few pedestrians held pomanders to their noses and scuttled quickly, avoiding any stopping to converse. Pamphlets nailed to doors pronounced the horrors of the smallpox and proclaimed that God was sending a plague to add to the misery of three bad harvests. A church bell tolled another death. Only a few peddlers called out their wares as they passed by, and the usual grubby hands of orphans and poor imps reached up pleading for a morsel of food. Margaretta wiped the last tear from her cheek announcing that for all her woes she did not know hunger and pulled an apple from her pocket to push through the window into lucky fingers. 'Poor little mites,' she muttered. Then she looked to Dee. 'Are we going to Sir Cecil's new house on The Strand?'

'We are certainly going to The Strand, but Cecil has given instruction that we are to go to Dudley House to collect Robert and then take the barge. He will tell me… us… everything on the way.'

'On the way where?'

'Hampton Court Palace… where I will have an audience with the Queen.' Dee gave a self-satisfied smile. 'In keeping with my position as her astronomer and philosopher. We will start at the very throne this mad pretender wishes to snatch.' Dee smiled again. 'And when I have uncovered his falsity, my standing in that glorious seat will be even higher.' The carriage slowed and Dee readied to alight. 'Here we are. Get ready to feel, Margaretta.'

The carriage had halted outside a large house built of brick and timber with high arch windows and steps leading up to a large door. A liveried servant opened the carriage door bowing in greeting. 'We are expecting you, Doctor Dee. Master Dudley is waiting in the rooms by the riverside lawns while the barge is readied.' He looked at Margaretta. 'I will take your servant to the kitchens.'

'No. She is my assistant. She stays.' Dee just walked on.

Margaretta smiled at the servant, bobbing her head in greeting. With his look of disdain, she did not need to feel his thoughts – but they came through anyway.

Ah, and here we are again. A man looking at a maid and

wondering how she could possibly have the right to walk with a scholar like my master. Wondering what I do to have such rank when you may only open the door. And now you wonder if... damn you.

'No, sir. I lift his books and papers – nothing less seemly.'

The startled servant reddened. There was no time to deny his thoughts before Margaretta turned on her heel and stamped up the steps after Dee.

'My old tutor. I am much pleased you could come so quickly.' Robert Dudley, now Master of the Horse and dressed to show his riches and rank, strode across the room, his face lighting with genuine pleasure.

Dee greeted with equal warmth and prodded him in the chest. 'Are you any better at your number lessons, Robert? Or do you only seek to count horses and coins these days?'

Dudley gave an exaggerated bow. 'And I count them so well because of your schooling.' He noticed Margaretta. 'Ah, you bring the mysterious maid with you.'

'Good day, sir.' Margaretta kept her gaze steady this time as he surveyed her from shoulder to foot, lingering on her breasts. The first time she was perused by this man was four years ago when she had to visit him in connection with the body in the oak. She had blushed then. But now her heart had hardened. He may be favoured, but like all men, he was ruled more by his stick than good sense. Anyway, there was so much rumour about him and Queen Elizabeth that lesser women were sure to be quite safe. Only a year ago the pamphlets were claiming she was with his child and he would soon be on the throne as king. 'I hope you are in good health.' *Your health is good, but your mood is not.*

His face darkened and he looked to John Dee lowering his voice. 'I am. But Elizabeth is very upset. We must avert anything which may affect her humours.'

'Tell me about—'

Dee was stayed with a hiss from Dudley who raised his finger to his lips and then pointed towards a door at the end of the room. Then he whispered, 'de la Quadra is in residence,' as he pulled at one ear. 'I think his strange, veiled apple bringer has just left.'

Dee tilted his head on one side like a bird listening for a worm. 'The Spanish Ambassador?'

In an instant, the door opened and a short, lean, dark-haired man stepped through. Dark, deep-set eyes in a square face the colour of light tanned leather were bright under a heavy brow. If he smiled, it was hidden under a beard as black as coal. 'Did I hear my name?' The voice was soft and precise and with the lilt of a high-born Spaniard. He was passing a bright red apple from hand to hand as if it were a toy.

Dudley forced a smile that was more like a grimace. 'Ah, Señor... oh, my apologies, I forget your closeness to God... *Bishop* de la Quadra. You must meet my dear friend and former tutor, Doctor John Dee.' Then the voice hardened. 'Though I am sure you know more about him than me.'

De la Quadra ignored the sarcasm and gave a short bow to Dee, glanced at Margaretta and then looked to Dudley. 'Did I hear that your dear Queen suffers with her humours?' A wry smile. 'I must visit Court and pay my respects.'

'Gad, de la Quadra. Do you hide the ears of a rabbit under those Spanish locks?' Dudley's irritation seemed to simmer up in his throat. 'Queen Elizabeth has the strength of a lion, sir. It is merely that the rain has fallen for two weeks and curtailed our daily hunting.' Now a sardonic grin. 'With your Spanish humours only powered by the warmth of a Spanish sun, maybe best you stay away from the chill of Court.'

The atmosphere tensed as the two men stared at each other. The Spaniard raised one eyebrow. 'If your dear Queen would only put herself in the warm embrace of a husband, Master Dudley – a royal husband, touched by God – she would have no fear of rain and the fact that she cannot ride her servant.'

He gave a little smirk. 'Apologies for my weakness of English, sir. I meant to say that she cannot ride *with* her servant'.

This was the touch paper. Dudley raised a finger to an inch from the other man's face. 'Do not hide sneering behind language. Your English is as good as any at Court.' He turned on his heel and walked to the window snapping over his shoulder, 'and Elizabeth will marry the man of *her* choice... not yours.'

De la Quadra gave an oily smile. 'Then it would seem the man of her choice has yet to be identified.' Without waiting for a response, he looked at the apple, turned, nodded to Dee then left the room leaving Robert Dudley balling his hands into fists.

Margaretta stayed in the shadows. *My, the rage inside you. Not only with the Spanish priest. Everything you want is slipping away. Also, bitterness and disappointment towards him. Now fear. You think of Elizabeth. Love. Now the name, Amy. Your dead wife. If it were not for Amy. Resentment. The word 'killer'.*

Dee cleared his throat. 'My, my, Robert. I think you have an enemy there.'

'Men you once believed friends are always the most bitter of foes, good Doctor.'

'Friend?'

Alarm. You have said too much.

Dudley pointed through the window. 'That discussion can wait. See, the barge is here. My man, Tamworth, is waving for us. We must go.' He gestured to the door. 'The wind is behind us and so will carry our words away from the oarsmen.'

The barge was long and well-appointed with a small cabin in the bow to give shelter from the weather. Inside, polished wooden seats, smelling of beeswax and softened with velvet cushions surrounded a table laden with wine vessels, goblets and plates of marchpane. Dee pulled off his cloak, shook off the raindrops, settled himself onto a soft cushion and gestured to Margaretta to sit near the door. 'Take a cushion there and make sure no oarsman shows any sign of hearing our talk.'

Robert Dudley looked a little bemused at a servant being given a comfortable seat but shrugged and sat close to Dee. A nod to the helmsman and the barge was pushed away from the bank and the rhythmic slap of wood on water began. He sighed as his shoulders slumped. 'We are only just finished with the Douglas plot and now we face this.'

Dee leaned forward, his eyes bright with anticipation of learning more gossip. 'Margaret Douglas, again?'

'If ever there was a demon in damask it is her.' Dudley lowered his voice. 'Mary Queen of Scots has only been on Scottish soil a year and Margaret Douglas is reigniting her determination to get a Catholic on the throne. She has been plotting to have her vile, milksop son, Henry Darnley, married to Mary and so combine the royal blood lines. Both Darnley and Mary are direct descendants of Mary Tudor, King Henry's sister. Both of royal blood and both believe they have a claim to the throne. Married – they combine the threats.'

'I am sure Cecil will have managed the situation.'

'True. He used his network to find that Margaret was sending messages to that villain, de la Quadra, who was then seeking the assistance of Philip of Spain. It was quickly stamped upon. Margaret Douglas is held at Sheen Castle and her weak-headed husband in the Tower blubbering at the walls every day. Their messenger, one Francis Yaxley, is in the Tower too.'

'Where is the boy, Darnley?'

'Slipped the net in York while being brought south from their Yorkshire estates. We think he escaped to France.'

'And the consequences for Bishop de la Quadra?'

'Elizabeth's fury and we all watch him closely.' Robert pointed back down the river. 'Never travel with him or answer his questions.' He turned to look at Dee. 'And now this upstart from Cleves arrives with no warning. Another dark shadow, Doctor. A strange and worrisome threat.'

'I hear he claims to be the love-child of Henry and Anne of Cleves,' snorted Dee. 'Madness.'

Dudley frowned. 'But he raises the old scandal. Worse, he has a worrying amount of evidence to support his claim.'

'Go on.'

'First a gold locket, engraved with Anne of Cleves' swan emblem and the words on her wedding ring to King Henry: *God send me well to keep*. Cecil has named him "The Cygnet Prince".'

Dee chuckled, then shook his head. 'Europe has many a good goldsmith.'

'But inside a lock of copper hair. The same as Henry's portraits.'

'Oh, for goodness sake, Robert. Many people have copper hair.' Dee pointed at Margaretta. 'Under that coif is a tumble of fox-red curls. A quick snip of a scissors and she could fill a hundred lockets.'

Dudley raised a hand to stop John Dee. 'He also brings letters which were sent to his aunt – the woman who raised him – giving instructions on how he must be raised to fulfil his destiny as King of England.'

'From Anne of Cleves?'

'No. From a friend of Anne – an intermediary – as Anne was constantly under watch. Cecil says the pen-name is sinister and covers someone. Something about bad deeds.'

Dee leaned back looking thoughtful. 'It was well known that King Henry kept a close eye on his ex-wife through her servants. Though no bad deeds were ever connected to her.'

'Maybe because she was careful to never send letters in her own hand,' sighed Dudley. 'But the most worrying evidence is what you see. Stand this man next to any portrait of young King Henry, and I would defy you to tell them apart. Same stance, same shape of face, same small eyes and mouth and the same muscular body and good legs that Henry sported before life and despair took him to monstrous fattening.'

Dee raised his eyebrows. 'His hair?'

'Copper.' Dudley turned to Margaretta and spoke harshly. 'Make sure you keep that pretty mouth well buttoned. I will not have any gossip spilt in—'

'That's enough, Robert,' cut in Dee. He raised a finger. 'Margaretta helped me in the case of the body in the oak. You took enough accolade.' The finger moved to point to Margaretta. 'And it was her following my instructions that saved Elizabeth's reputation.'

Dudley looked chastened and turned to look at Margaretta, his face puzzled.

Well, well. For the first time in seven years, you have publicly named me as your helper, John Dee. A big step for you, my teacher. Or was it a slip because Robert Dudley was over-stepping his power and thinking he had master-ship over your servants? And you, Robert Dudley? You fear this young man with a swan-signed locket. He is more than a threat to Elizabeth. He is a threat to the future you crave. He could slice through your dreams. 'Do not fear, sir. I know my place.' *It is to make my master look good and, in so doing, keep my brother safe and fed.*

Dee began a list of questions. They learned that this man had arrived in Dover just days ago. He had known where to go – straight to Bishop de la Quadra, the Spanish Ambassador – and made his claim for the throne of England. The Bishop, in a show of being helpful, had taken him to William Cecil, now Queen Elizabeth's secretary and foremost advisor. Having made his case, he had insisted on going to Hever Castle, claiming it to be his mother's favourite residence. He would stay there while they made their arrangements for everything to be put before Parliament and make way for him to ascend the throne. 'So, he knows what he is doing,' said Dudley. 'He is audacious and knows where to make a power base.'

Dee raised a hand in question.

'Hever is now owned by the Waldegraves and occasional home to young Charles and the widow. But she is staunch Catholic and so no friend of Elizabeth.'

'Did you speak to him… get a sense of his nature?'

Dudley reddened. 'I took him for a friendly walk in the grounds. Tried to explain to him the folly of his claims.'

'You mean you threatened him.'

Dudley gave a short nod. 'He is a confident pup. He laughed at me and said he had all he needed to prove the truth of his lineage and kingship. The arrogant little bastard.'

Dee raised his brow. 'But, if we cannot prove him false, we face the worst of all fates – the rise of the Catholic faction who see Elizabeth as an illegitimate pretender to the throne.'

Dudley nodded. 'And they will rise together to bring about Elizabeth's downfall. With that we will see the end of the Tudor dynasty, find ourselves ruled by a king more loyal to Europe than England and, more than that, a king who will haul us back into Catholicism and the influence of Rome.' He closed his eyes below a furrowed brow. 'Court is already seeing omens. Last year the storm took the steeple off St Pauls. This year so many strange births. Did you see the dead-born babe with the ruff of skin and feet of a toad brought to Court? Then the terrible predictions of Nostradamus and John Prestall are putting people in fear of Elizabeth's life, and—'

'Fie, Robert. You see more in the supernatural than even I can imagine – and I am a reader of the heavens. Storms are part of nature and Nostradamus is a charlatan by nature, and Prestall a Catholic schemer who will say anything to get attention and undermine my standing at Court. The man is a muddlehead of the worst kind.'

'But now the omens have reached inside the walls of Court.'

'What?'

'One of the royal dogs went mad the day the Cygnet Prince left Court. Bit a lump of flesh from the groom's leg. Horrible. We had to shoot it.'

'Any dog can turn vicious.'

'Not this one. I picked it from the litter myself as a gift and selected the gentle one. It was Elizabeth's pet.'

Chapter Four

Hampton Court Palace loomed up as the barge rounded the river bend. The helmsman shouted orders and steered them into the gaily decorated pier as Tudor Green clad servants, badged with the Tudor rose, ran to take the lines. Dudley led the way and commanded a man called Will Scarlet to have the boat cleaned and turned in readiness for taking Doctor Dee back to St Dunstan's when the tide turned. Scarlett bent his head and obeyed, but his mouth was set straight. Other servants averted their eyes.

Oh, you are not popular here, Master Dudley. Your handsome face and strong bearing does not impress these men. I feel their disdain. I hear the word killer.

There was a shout from a man striding across the lawns, arm raised in a greeting. 'Cecil,' murmured Dee, lifting his hand in response. 'Let us see if there are further developments.'

Cecil nodded at Dudley and held his hand out to John Dee. 'Greetings, John. I am glad to see you.' His eyes slid to Margaretta. 'Ah, the servant who is more than a servant.'

Dee ignored the comment and started to walk towards the palace. 'No time for chatter. Her Majesty will be awaiting me.'

'Not so fast, John,' cut in Cecil. 'The Queen is out riding. She will be away an hour or more.'

Dudley reacted as if Cecil had hit him. 'Riding? Without me?'

Cecil forced a smile. 'Do not be offended, Robert. She

was much agitated this morning. I thought fresh air would do her good.'

'Who is with her?'

'Blanche ap Harri and a groom of the stables who I told to follow and not too close.'

A flash of anger and now relief from Master Dudley. Like a child who has been left out of a game then finds it was not deliberate. But there is something else from you, Sir Cecil. Deep dislike. Anger. Resentment. Distrust. Yet you hold a friendly smile on your face. You cover your feelings very well. Dudley has no idea.

They turned towards the palace, Margaretta walking behind the men in a display of being the servant. Cecil steered them towards a tree with a wooden seat below it. 'Let us speak here. The oaks have no ears.'

They gathered under the leaves. Dee nodded to Margaretta to stand at a distance. She knew the game. She would stand just close enough to hear and to feel.

I hate this. As if I had no worth. Yet you cannot do your investigating without me, Doctor John Dee. You need me more than you need your cards and crystals. Without me, your brilliant mind would have to work without the feelings and thoughts that I pick up and bring to you. Without me you would have to ask more questions and make more assumptions. With me, they think you are more brilliant than all the men in all the universities of the world. But the world is such that I must stand apart and keep my head down in subservience. Damn this.

Cecil spoke with a low voice. 'As if his arrival here is not enough, it seems bad luck follows this Cygnet Prince.' He sighed. 'First a mad dog. Now the captain of *The Mariella* – the ship that gave him passage. A dutchman called Neerman. Found floating in St Katherine's dock this morning. Dead.'

Margaretta flinched. *I hear howling.*

Dudley shrugged. 'Do your spies not tell you how sailors drink? We are always fishing them from the water full of rum.'

A surge of bitterness. You resent the way this young man

talks to you as if you are an old fool. Yet you bend your head in respect, Sir Cecil.

'But Captain Neerman was not a man for drinking. He called it the Devil's brew. More than that, unlike most sailors, he could swim.'

'Are there any witnesses?' asked Dee.

'Only the cabin boy. Frightened out of his wits, claiming he heard the howl of Satan before the captain started raving. The rest of the crew were in the taverns. He ran for help and they returned to find their captain floating.' Cecil looked sharply at Dee. 'You will need to go and investigate. It might be a coincidence – but if there is anything suspicious, we need to raise security around the Queen.

Fear. I feel it strongly. But it is not just you. It is me. The doctor will make me look on the body. Oh, God.

Chapter Five

They approached the huge west door of the palace. Cecil turned to Margaretta. 'Maybe you would feel more comfortable in the servant's quarters, my dear.'

John Dee went to object, but Margaretta was quick. 'Yes, Sir Cecil. I would like that.' *For you do not know that your wife smuggled me in here seven years ago and I made a friend of the laundry woman. If she is still here, I will use our mother tongue to find out more than you think possible.* She gave a reassuring nod to John Dee. He well knew her gestures by now. But it was all one way. He remained the only one she could not read. Cecil pointed to a path going to the rear of the palace and she walked away in a pretence of meekness.

The kitchens were just as she remembered. A hell of heat, smoke and the constant clamour of clanking pots and shouting chefs. Serving boys scooted along the outer corridor, trays of roasted meats and bread held above their heads. The looks started but not the bawdy jokes levelled at her last time. But back then she was just eighteen. Now she was a woman of twenty-five and young lads would assume her a married woman. *It should have been so. I had a flash of happiness... snatched away. A pox on that girl.* Margaretta quickly made the sign of the cross across her breast to ask forgiveness for her dark thoughts and then stopped a lad running with an empty tray. 'Does Beatrice ap Rhys still work here?'

The boy nodded. 'Old Beatie? Ay. She'll be out in the laundry.' He pointed at the side door. 'Through there and follow your right hand to the rosemary bushes. The washing house is just beyond.'

Through clouds of steam drifted the lilting tones of the launderer. Margaretta found the woman sitting on a chair pointing at various tubs of hot water and shouting orders. '*Beatrice. Margaretta Morgan ydw i. Cwrddais i gyda ti…* Beatrice. I am Margaretta Morgan. I met you…'

'*Wel, yr Arglwydd mawr.* Well, great heaven.' Beatrice's eyes opened wide and a warm smile spread across her face. '*Dw i'n dy gofio di'n dda.* I remember you well.' She struggled to raise herself, pushing down on a stick she had not needed seven years ago. She was still built like a barrel, through the breasts seemed to have grown more than her belly. She shuffled towards Margaretta and took her shoulders. '*Mor bert ag erioed.* Pretty as ever.' She winked. 'And can you still curtsy like a taught you?'

Margaretta made a play of curtsying low, making the old woman chortle and clap her hands. In seconds, she was back to the chattering, as before, in Welsh.

Beatrice pointed towards the entrance. 'Come. We can talk outside where the air is better for breathing. I will be glad to be away from the dread of those damn stockings.'

'What are stockings?'

'The death of me – that's what they are.' She laughed. 'Mistress Montagu, the royal silk-maker has found a way to knit silk into the finest stockings for our Queen. Six years it took her. And she has made us a fine mess.'

Margaretta raised her hands in confusion. 'But what is a stocking?'

'Long socks that shine like the moon. So, when our Queen

lifts her hem to dance the Galliard with her Sweet Robin, she shows a pretty ankle.' Beatrice shook her head. 'Our Queen was much taken and swore, "I will wear no more cloth stockings." So now we have to launder the precious hose of silk and we live in fear of a snag. Pah, it would be faster to craft another crown than knit another pair.' She made slow progress forward, the stick clicking on the stone floor and her other hand holding Margaretta's arm for steadiness as she huffed herself into the open air. 'There is a seat over there by the drying bushes.' In the light, the ageing of the laundress was more obvious. But the eyes were as bright and young as they had ever been. She took a deep breath, looked up at the sky. 'I am so blessed.'

'Blessed? Sitting in steam all day and worrying about stockings?'

Beatrice chortled. 'When Elizabeth arrived here, I thought I was on my way to the Alms House. But Blanche ap Harri heard me giving orders in the linen rooms and spoke well of me. A good woman is Blanche. Keeps her word.'

And I know that she keeps secrets too. 'I have heard she is very loyal to Elizabeth.'

'Loyal as a dog, and full of good sense and the wisdom of the books she has read. Not like the other one.'

'The other one?' *I know exactly whose name you will say.*

'Mistress Astley. Or Mama Kat as the Queen calls her.' Beatrice raised her eyes to heaven and put her hands in prayer. 'Thank the Lord she is beyond the years of childbirth. She would have raised monsters.'

Margaretta gave an encouraging laugh and the old woman was cheered into spilling more. 'She spoils Elizabeth. Will not say a thing even though Court is awash with enough scandal to fill my great wash-tubs.' She stiffened. 'But I must not be a gossip. It is dangerous.'

Margaretta leaned in conspiratorially. 'Do you remember when I disobeyed you and looked into Queen Mary's birthing chamber? I have never told a soul.'

Beatrice gave a short laugh. 'I should have boxed your ears, girl.' A kindly look. 'But you remind me of my younger self. Full of hope and ideas.' A sigh. 'Who knew I would be married only to a wash-dolly all my life.'

Sadness. Regret. But then you think of a young man. 'Do you not have family?'

'My sister's son is all I have. David Owens. But I look on him as kindly as any boy I could have born. A good boy he is. Doing well, too. He worked hard and earned a pupillage at Lincoln's Inn. A lawyer he will be.' Beatrice stopped, looked sideways, eyes wide. 'And he has no sweetheart.'

No, no, no. I am not having my heart pulled by another man. I gave up the first I loved to my friend Lottie and lost the second. This heart is as cold as a grave. Margaretta nudged Beatrice's arm. 'Tell me about Mama Kat.'

The old woman folded her arm across her voluminous breasts in a display of indignation and lowered her voice to a whisper. 'Kat Astley turned a blind eye when Elizabeth was in Robert Dudley's privy rooms and he in hers... alone. They are almost sewn together.' She shook her head. 'You must have heard the rumours.'

I feel gloating. This makes no sense. You are a loyal woman. I hear a rustle. What was that? Margaretta looked around. Nothing. Just the rosemary and lavender bushes grown to dry the royal clothes. She was being foolish. 'I've seen pamphlets papering the streets of London saying that Dudley was soon to be king. And cruel ones too saying the Queen was heavy with his child.'

'Pah. All gutter talk. There is to be no birthing in this palace. I should know.'

'How?'

'Think girl. I do the laundry. I know every stain and spillage. And I know when menses come and go.' Beatrice turned to look at Margaretta and laughed. 'Why do you redden, girl? You are old enough to know what happens in a bed. Though it may have been true if Amy Dudley had

36

not cast a cold hand from her grave to quell the Queen's passion.'

'People in the London alleys say she was killed.'

'They said it here too. Every corridor rattled with accusations. Even when the officials sent a report saying her neck was broken by a fall down the stairs, people muttered about it being a plot to open the path for a royal marriage.'

That is why I hear the word 'killer' mixed with his fear.

Beatrice shuffled to sit closer. 'It was only because of Blanche that Elizabeth saw sense. My, there was a row. Kat screaming. Blanche hissing.'

Margaretta leaned in. 'Go on.'

'Out here it was. In the drying ground. That's why I heard... though they don't know. Blanche was like a tigress with Kat. Telling her she was a prattle-tongued fool... allowing Elizabeth to walk into the dangers she faced before when an ill-suited man played with her heart.'

'What did Kat say?'

'Oh, she was haughty, as she always is with Blanche. Thinks she is above her in every way. She is English, the governess, and the one called Mama Kat. I remember her words. "I am her mother in every way except birthing. I know how to protect her."' Beatrice shook her head slowly. 'And I will never forget the ice in Blanche's voice when she spat back, "You were no mother when you let Seymour in her room and you are no mother now – letting Robert Dudley smear her virtue with his ambitions." That stopped Kat's squawking. She started crying and ran inside. The very next day we heard she had gone on her knees to beg Elizabeth to curb her passion for Dudley.'

And I recall Blanche in a kitchen in Hatfield declaring she would protect Elizabeth's reputation to the grave and beyond. You are enjoying this conversation, Beatrice. But can I get more from you? Just a little white lie. 'I saw another pamphlet yesterday. It said a true king of England has arrived from abroad. A Catholic king.'

Beatrice stiffened. 'They are whispering about it in the great hall. The young fool claims he was born the son of Anne of Cleves and old King Henry. Impossible.'

'How do you know? You were in Mary's household, miles away.'

'Because we laundresses are terrible talkers. I knew the laundress for Anne of Cleves. Elyn Tyrpyn. A bit bawdy she was.' A chuckle and Beatrice turned to English, mimicking a woman with a strong Midlands accent. 'I'm telling you true. The only seed old Henry ever planted in our linens were the caraway seeds he flicked from his beard after eating Anne's German cakes. And the only thing his stick entered was his codpiece – and there were plenty of room for it.' She bent over and hooted with laughter.

Bitter satisfaction and a desire to do harm. This makes no sense. That cannot be you, Beatrice. You are too kind. Another rustle. Not the sound of feelings but a dress through bushes. 'Hush, Beatrice. I heard something… someone.'

Beatrice gulped and Margaretta stood, looking round. At the far edge of the garden a black cloaked figure flitted through a gate. Margaretta ran, skidded through the gap in the wall and looked down a pathway leading back to the palace. Empty. *Oh, Lord, I feel fear. My own fear. I think we were listened upon.*

She looked around to see she was in a small orchard. At the far end was a woman, bent over, gathering apples into her apron. Margaretta ran over. 'Mistress, did you see a person in a black cloak?' The women stood but kept her veiled face averted. She coiled the brown apron around her hands to stop the apples falling and shook her head.

You are frightened of me. I feel your anxiety. 'But they came this way. Surely…'

Another shake of head and the woman bent back down to the apples.

Chapter Six

'Margaretta, come. I need you to take notes.' It was John Dee shouting from the edge of the drying grounds.

Margaretta had returned to the bench to sit with Beatrice who told her that the woman in the orchard was a strange one kept here as a charity while her husband was away. The veil hid scars and she spoke only to her crucifix. The fear that they might have been overheard had dissipated as they agreed that everything they had said was in Welsh except the words of Anne's laundress. 'I must go, Beatrice. My master is quick to complain if I am not doing his bidding.'

The older women peered over to him. 'Is that the man they call the great conjuror? The one who read the stars to define Elizabeth's coronation day?'

'The very one. When Robert Dudley called on him to do the task, I think light came back into his world. He has been a regular visitor to Court since.'

Margaretta ran across to Dee while Beatrice lumbered to the laundry house. Dee was frowning. 'Where have you been, girl? I am about to speak with Cecil alone and I need your senses. You should not be gossiping with servants.' He turned and started marching back to the palace entrance.

'Not gossiping – investigating. I already have a witness that there could be no child of Henry and Anne.'

Dee stopped short and turned to her, eyes wide. 'What?'

Margaretta tapped the side of her nose. 'Never underestimate what is seen and known by those who wash the dirty linen of the powerful.'

'Go on.'

Margaretta looked around. No-one in earshot. *I will not mention the cloaked figure. It was nothing.* 'You need to summon the laundress to Anne of Cleves. She can attest that there was no bedding between Henry and Anne.'

Dee nodded, smiled. 'Good. Very good.' He pointed to the door. 'We see Cecil in his rooms. So back to servant, Margaretta.'

Damn you. 'Yes, Doctor.'

He picked up on the irritation and spoke low and cold. 'That is our agreement, girl. I teach you and you help me. In doing that we both get our wishes – you for a roof over your head, me for respect at Court. We both win as long as we play the game.'

'But can I not have a little thanks for what I do?'

He stopped, turned, glared. Then a finger to his own chest. 'Recognition.' The finger turned to her. 'Roof.' The set of the mouth. 'Be grateful.'

Damn you. All you can think about is your own standing. You need me. You use my gifts. But like all men you think they are yours to use by right of you being born a man. 'Yes, Doctor.'

Cecil was standing at the window of his office, staring across the lawns. The slight twitch of his head showed he had heard John Dee and Margaretta enter but did not turn. 'All this could be lost if you cannot give us proof, John.' Then he turned, gestured to the chairs in front of his desk and walked over to sit behind it. He was pale and those grey eyes leaked his worry.

John Dee sat, pulled parchment from his bag and handed it to Margaretta. 'Notes, girl, and no speaking.'

You old scut.

Cecil pinched the bridge of his nose and closed his eyes, the gesture he always made when his mind was in turmoil. 'What are your thoughts, John?'

Dee leaned back and put his hands together, fingers pointing up to show he was thinking. 'We must unravel this young man's claims. We will gather sufficient voices to state his story is a myth and then smear his name with the death of the captain. A hint of witchcraft around your person is never a good thing in this land.' He made a cynical smile. 'For your friends soon disappear.'

Oh, well done, Doctor. Another jab at Cecil for leaving you to face the Tower seven years ago. But should you really prod the man who can promote you in Court?

Cecil glowered but did not rise to the bait. 'And where do you plan to find these voices, John? He is making claims about events over twenty years ago – events which were hushed up then and have stayed silenced.' He tapped on a bundle of parchments, bound with a ribbon on his desk.

John Dee nodded. 'Ah. The scandal that never was – that Anne of Cleves birthed a fair child by Henry in 1541. What are the details?'

Cecil glanced at Margaretta. 'I trust you can keep quiet, girl.' Before she could answer he warned, 'Do not write this down. Some notes are not for making.' He pulled at the ribbon; his face drawn. 'After King Henry divorced Anne of Cleves, he was expecting her to fall into gloom. After all, she had been cast aside for a girl of seventeen and her lady-maid at that. But, no. Anne entered a period of gaiety. New clothes, entertaining, receiving guests. She was a regular visitor at Court and even danced with young Kathryn Howard, already the king's new wife. Far from despairing, Anne appeared delighted with life. Henry became very fond of her and would visit when he wanted the calm of an understanding ear. He went on a progress with Queen Kathryn in early 1541. Then in that same spring, Anne went on a progress. Where she went is a mystery.'

'Surely her papers were retained. They will give her whereabouts.'

'That's the strange thing. When she died in 1557, her entire estate was appendixed before sale. Her papers were retained for Court filing and assets put up for auction. Indeed, Mildred spent a small fortune on her dresses. One hundred pounds for God's sake.'

You have a hopeful smile Sir Cecil, but when you speak of Mildred you feel deep worry.

'Well, look in the records,' cut in Dee sounding exasperated.

'I am trying to tell you, John. We have no record of where she went or why. Nothing. But the rumours began in the late autumn. A woman called Jane Rattsay claimed she had seen Anne in a bed nursing a fair child. Then others furthered the rumour.' He opened the file and flicked through the papers. 'One Frances Lilgrave, a woman of her household and also Richard Taverner, a member of the signet office. Such was the concern that the Privy Council – the highest council in the land – were involved and arrested them for interrogation. They were sent to the Tower – only used for the most threatening of royal problems.'

'But the rumours were unfounded,' broke in Dee, pointing at the file. 'It will say in there.'

'Of course, it does,' snapped Cecil. 'For God's sake, John. It was no time to be embarrassing Henry. He was an old man facing the ridicule of Europe by divorcing Anne claiming he could not abide to bed her and was fawning... no, lusting... over a wife of just seventeen who all Court knew was secreting young Thomas Culpepper into her bed. No man dared tell him that he had not only made a mistake but that he had made a bastard of the one thing he wanted most in life – another son.'

Dee leaned forward. 'Are you saying a son was born?'

'I am saying we have no proof that a son was *not* born. That is our weakness. We have no records. Nothing between March, 1541 and March, 1542 when Anne returned to

Richmond with an ague and King Henry had his doctors put at her service. That is the leverage that this Cygnet Prince brings to our door.'

Dee paused in a display of thinking deeply. 'So, we need proof of Anne remaining a maid all her life.'

'And you cannot fail, John. This pretender is dangerous to Queen and country.'

'Fie. It will take more than a young man with dubious proof of parentage to topple Elizabeth. She is loved by the people. And my calculating of the coronation day...'

Cecil banged the desk and gave a low snarl. 'Do not be naive. She is loved by the Protestant people. But a large Catholic faction plot and plan her downfall every day. They already have a willing queen in Mary Queen of Scots, who lurks over the border insisting she is the rightful queen of England. If they have a Catholic king on our throne then they have the perfect marriage to snatch this country from the Tudor dynasty and put us back in the clutches of Rome.' He groaned and pinched the bridge of his nose. 'This man is more than a pretender, John. He is a rallying call for those who would destroy Elizabeth and all those around her.' He looked up and stared at John Dee. 'And that includes you.'

A clever move, Sir Cecil. Threaten John Dee with loss of standing – going back to the dark days of being the son of a Court outcast – and you will get anything out of him. He will move mountains to help you now. And I feel your fear too. It is deep in your gut. You believe this man just might be telling the truth and your whole world could collapse at your feet. You not only care for Elizabeth, you depend on her power for your own. Oh, you will slither and snipe at those you call friend if it suits you. But not her. Never her.

Doctor Dee's agitation was evident. There was even a tremble in his voice. 'Then we must move quickly. I want a list of people around Anne at the time. As I said, we will start with the lowly before we prod the wasp nest of the powerful.

We will speak with the laundress. She will know, if anyone, if Henry spilled his seed in his former wife's bed and if her monthly courses stopped.'

'Clever,' purred Cecil. 'I will have her found.'

Dee gave a self-satisfied nod and seemed to calm.

Damn you, John Dee. That was my investigating. Not your brilliance of mind.

Doctor Dee rose. 'I also want a list of the women close to Anne of Cleves – her ladies in waiting. Just in case the laundress cannot close this case.'

Cecil nodded, picked up the bundle of parchments and stood. 'I will have the laundress found by the morrow. Also, a list of the others.'

Just as Dee stood, the door opened. Robert Dudley entered looking as puffed as a peacock. 'Elizabeth has returned from hunting.'

'I think you mean Her Majesty,' snapped Cecil but was ignored.

'She wants to see you, Doctor Dee. And the strangest of things. She says to bring your little maid.' He made a pompous chuckle. 'Maybe she wants to know why her advisor of the stars always has a lowling tugging at his hem.'

Damn you, Robert Dudley. I'm not such a lowling when you are staring at my breasts. It seems Elizabeth's affection has swelled your self-importance to the level of a sneer-pot.

Robert frowned. 'Are you glaring at me, girl?'

'No, sir. I do not see well. It sometimes looks as if I am angry.' *And I have my fingers crossed against the lie. My eyes are as strong as your arrogance.*

Chapter Seven

John Dee was almost tripping on the heels of the green-clad servant such was his eagerness to be in Elizabeth's company. Dudley kept abreast of him giving advice on her mood. Apparently, Blanche ap Harri had warned against a hard gallop on wet ground so her mood was less than sunny. Even worse, she has mislaid her pearl encrusted looking-glass. Mislaying was a common occurrence but always a drama. They went up a flight of stairs into a gallery.

This is where I curtsied with Beatrice. This is where I heard poor Kathryn Howard's screaming through the centuries. I feel her still and it makes my legs tremble.

At the end of the gallery a black-gowned woman stood outside a large oak door. It was Blanche ap Harri looking just as before with a few more creases around her eyes. She peered through the dim light. 'Is that you, Doctor Dee?'

'It is, cousin. I understand Her Majesty is in want of my presence.'

An icy silence. Then, 'We are not cousins, John Dee.' The tone was of a mother to a disobedient child. As they approached, she looked behind Dee and then smiled. '*Croeso, Margaretta.* Welcome, Margaretta. *Wyt ti'n iawn?* Are you well?'

'*Iawn, diolch, Meistres Blanche. A chithau hefyd gobeithio.* Very good, thank you, Mistress Blanche. And you too I hope.'

Dudley tutted. 'And what are you jabbering about?'

Blanche turned her cold grey eyes on the younger man and almost spat. 'We speak pure language, Master Dudley. Not the thin mish-mash you call English.' They glared at each other and for a second the air went cold.

Dudley was the first to break. 'I will take John inside.' He nodded to the two door-guards to make way. Blanche stepped forward giving him no option other than to follow her or shove her aside. He gave a low snarl.

Inside the room was a hum-drum of activity. Sitting in the middle, on a high-backed throne, looking annoyed, was Elizabeth. She was magnificent. Flame-red hair fell over her shoulders and framed a face of ivory translucence. The lips were berry-stained crimson, contrasting a gown of deep green velvet and, around her neck, a string of pearls so big they would pass for mistletoe berries. Margaretta was struck by her hands – long, white with perfect nails that plucked sugared plums from a deep dish at her side. Around her the ladies of the chamber were chattering and discussing their samplers. Kat Astley turned and stared at John Dee with no measure of warmth.

'Ah, my good Doctor. How do you fare today? Do the stars shine well on us?' Elizabeth's voice was strong, melodic and intelligent.

Dee bowed low and Margaretta dropped to a curtsy. 'The sun, moon and stars are all bedazzled by you, Your Majesty.'

She laughed out loud. 'Gad, Doctor John. You use prettier words than the Prince Erik they sent to woo me. And he thought himself a poet.' She made a little frown. 'Though I sense he is much disturbed of his mind.' She shot a hard look towards Kat who put her head down.

I feel your warmth. You like my master both as a scholar but also as a man. You are close in age, though he looks older than you. You feel safe with him.

Elizabeth clapped her hands towards the women who fell silent. 'Leave us. Seek my looking-glass.'

In an instant there was a scraping of chairs, rustling of gowns and patter of feet as they all made for the door, like a scurry of mice fleeing a cat. Kat Astley took Margaretta's arm. 'This way, young woman. This is not a place for you.' But she was stayed by a bark from Elizabeth. 'Blanche has introduced her, Mama Kat. She will stay.'

Kat Astley turned with a look of horror and then shot a look of pure venom at Blanche who stood by the door, staring ahead, refusing to meet her gaze. She released Margaretta's arm with a huff and stomped to the door, still glaring at Blanche.

Elizabeth looked at Dudley. 'I will see Doctor John alone, Two-Eyes.' When he started to object, she leaned forward and smiled before stating slowly and low, 'Alone, Sweet Robin. Be gone.'

Robert Dudley stamped out like a thwarted child and Blanche left quietly after him, a small smile on her face.

The room quiet, Elizabeth relaxed. 'Sit, Doctor. Let us converse in comfort now that the sparrows have stopped their twittering.' She pointed at a seat at the side of hers. Then she looked at Margaretta and smiled. '*Mae Blanche yn dweud dy fod di'n ddibynadwy.* Blanche says you are dependable.'

She is speaking my tongue as if she was raised in the village next to me. What do I say? My words are stuck in my throat. 'Ydw... Mawrhydi. Yes, Majesty.' Oh Lord, I can feel the red rising in my cheeks.

Elizabeth laughed. '*Rwyt ti'n synnu fy mod i'n siarad iaith y Nefoedd.* I surprise you that I speak the language of Heaven?'

'*Ydy.* Yes.'

'*Ces I fy magu gan Lady Troy ac wedyn Blanche.* I was raised by Lady Troy and then Blanche. *Gwarchodon nhw fy ngwaed Tuduraidd.* They protected my Tudor blood.'

'*Dw i'n mor bles.* I am so pleased. *Dywedodd Myrddin y byddai'r Gymraeg yn rheoli'r tir un diwrnod.* Merlin said the Welsh would one day rule the lands.' Seeing Elizabeth look perplexed she stammered, '*Darllenes i amdano fo yn llyfrgell Doctor Dee.* I read about him in Doctor Dee's library.'

'*Felly, rwyt ti'n ddibynadwy ac yn ysgolhaig, hefyd.* So, you are dependable and a scholar too.'

Margaretta glanced at John Dee who was looking irritated at being excluded from the conversation though he understood every word. *I am taking your thunder and you are becoming annoyed. I cannot feel you, but the jut of your chin tells me all. I will respond in English.* 'No, Your Majesty. I am no more than a useful servant and scribe.'

Elizabeth smiled and turned her face to John Dee.

Was that a wink she made at me?

'Do the stars predict a swan's cygnet coming to take my crown, Doctor John? Were the planets lying when they gave you my coronation date?

'No. The stars do not lie. I will cast another horoscope this very evening to confirm.' He smiled kindly. 'Sir Cecil and I are quite determined to make him a stubble-goose and have him back on a boat to Germany with his tail-feathers between his legs. And Robert Dudley will assist us. Do not fear.'

Elizabeth smiled then sighed. 'Oh, it is not the Cygnet Prince I fear – but those who would use him to bring about my downfall.' She bit into another sugar plum. 'I have enemies, Doctor John. People who would haul us back to the horrors of my sister's reign. Not even the ever-seeing eyes of my Spirit Cecil and the protection of my Sweet Robin can stop the Catholic nobles once they smell blood. My blood.'

Fear and anger. It is deep. You are lonely. Surrounded by people every moment of your day and yet so alone. I also sense love. It is for Dudley who you call Sweet Robin and Two-Eyes. When you use those names, your voice softens. Yet there is sadness in the voice too. As if you are talking to a lover who will always be behind a wall. Inside that magnificent façade is a woman who wants to be held and loved.

'You must have faith in the destiny that has been set out for you. You will reign long and well. The horoscope predicted a golden age in which the eyes of Englishmen will be opened to the world and all its riches. I will write a treaty to gladden your heart. I have ideas…'

Elizabeth quelled Dee's talk with a tap on the back of his hand that she then took in her own. 'It is not ideas I want, good Doctor. It is peace of mind and to stop the Catholic clamour for my crown.' She bit her lip. 'I know my father was no saint. We all knew of my half-brother, Henry Fitzroy, born to Bessie Blount. He was raised as much a royal child as were Mary, Edward and I. But I cannot believe my father would sire a son and leave him in the shadows. Nor do I believe that Anne of Cleves, the good and kind woman that she was, would deceive us. Anne would have made a good mother. But not of my brother.'

The touch of her hand made him glow. He gently squeezed it in return. 'There will be no peace in my heart until yours is quietened of this worry.' Dee smiled. 'Rest well with the fact that you are loved by the good.'

She nodded and slumped back in her chair. 'I tire. Go do your best.' Then those dark eyes opened wide as her voice betrayed the fear and anger in her. 'No. Do more than your best. Save my throne, Doctor. Rid me of this swan's bastard cygnet.'

Chapter Eight

The barge took them down the Thames to St Dunstan's parish, the barge men treating them as befitting an advisor to the Queen and wherries flitting out of their way. Dee lounged on the cushions, a smile on his face but the eyes narrow, showing that he was deep in thought. 'We need to move quickly, Margaretta. Starting tonight. First home for you to ensure our landlady is happy, then we scry, then to St Katherine's dock.'

'But it is late afternoon, doctor. The light will soon be fading. Oh, God. A body decaying, dim light, the heat of a boat that has sat in the sun all day. I cannot bear the thought of it. Dead bodies are bad enough, but a body in heat is more than I can bear.'

John Dee scowled. 'No wailing, girl. We must have something to say to Cecil tomorrow.' Then he looked back into the wake of the barge. 'We will be doing much moving up and down this river. And on road to. We cannot trust strangers. Where is that lad who wherried you some years ago – the one married to your friend?'

Are you trying to torture me? The first man I lost – or I let get away. The man I pushed to my friend, Lottie. 'Oh, he is very busy, Doctor. I hardly visit any more. He and his wife are consumed with his work and raising a little one.'

'Then a regular income for a few weeks will be welcome.

Send message that I will retain his services for ten pennies a day.'

'But I can get another—'

'No,' was the bark. 'I want someone trustworthy and lip-sealed.' He turned away and stared across the river at the melee of boats, wherries, swans and detritus. A dead rat swirled away in the wake of the barge and the rowers frequently cursed as floating rubbish caught in their oars and the flow of their pulling was halted to shake it off. When they slowed, the stink was worse.

At Dycekey steps they were helped like nobility, to Dee's further delight. He dropped a penny into the man's hand and failed to see the look of disdained disappointment. No doubt, nobles tipped more from their pockets.

They walked up the bank and parted. Dee going to the front of the house and Margaretta to the servant's door at the back in their ritual display of being master and servant. Inside, all was quiet. Huw was sitting at his normal seat, his wooden alphabet before him on the desk. He did not look up but kept muttering to himself and rocking.

'*Beth sy'n bod arnat ti, Huw?* What's wrong with you, Huw?'

He shrugged and shook his head. Margaretta dropped her voice to coaxing and sat opposite, taking care not to look directly into his face as that was punishment and would only make him run to the woodhouse. Though, with the shortage of wood these days, there was little there for him to chop. She spoke in their mother tongue of Welsh. 'Come, Huw. I know your moods. Something has happened.'

First silence. Then more rocking. 'Angus came. Susan too.'

'So, our sister and her featherheaded husband. What did they want? And why lower themselves to come through this door? Susan has not visited since Mam passed through the veil.'

'Say I will live with them. Go soon.'

Damn you, Susan. You ran away from our brother when

we were growing. You have fluttered your way into the home of a wealthy vintner and only ever summon Huw when you are short of a servant. Then he is thrown back to me. What is your game? For it will not be for our brother's well-being.

'No, Huw. You are staying with me. You don't want to go, do you?'

Huw rocked harder and rapidly arranged his letters. 'Snip-tongue.'

Margaretta laughed. 'Yes, she is. But never let her know we call her that.'

The letters were arranged again. '*Dyn o'r duwch.*'

'Man of blackness? Angus?'

Huw nodded. 'Black all round him. Means bad for Huw.'

'Don't you worry. I will speak to Susan and stop her silly ideas.' Margaretta went to continue, but there was a long, wavering call from the mistress. She looked at Huw who made pretence of drinking deep from an imaginary cup. 'Oh, Lord. Has she been on the Malmsey all day?'

Katherine Constable wobbled, her eyes blinking as she tried to focus on Margaretta. 'Where have you been?' she hiccupped.

'Carrying for Doctor Dee, mistress. He was called to the palace.'

'And you went?' The indignation was only heighted by her slurring.

'I talked with the laundress while the Doctor held meetings with Sir Cecil. The Doctor was also summoned to see the Queen.' *And you do not need to know that I was present. One fact is sufficient. Why hurt you with the whole truth?* 'His standing is surely rising, mistress.'

A look of delight and a hiccup. 'Your sister visited me today and her charming husband too.'

'And why were they bothering you, mistress?'

'Oh, no bother,' trilled Katherine as she slumped back on the chair. 'Said they had a proposition. Said they wanted Huw to have a trade and be a man able to manage in the world.' She stared at the window. 'They were very sympathetic about my brother and said they would ensure Huw has the chances he did not.' Her mouth set in a line as she held back the pain.

Damn that bitch I call sister. Huw has obviously told her you insist he is your poor dead brother come back to earth. 'My sister can appear much kinder than she truly is. I think Huw is better here with me.'

The other woman frowned. 'No, no. Susan said how much she loved him. Angus did too. They said he would come to nothing if he stays here chopping logs for you.' A self-convincing nod. 'Yes. They can give him a trade and independence.'

'But, Mistress—'

'No, Margaretta. As Susan said, you cannot keep Huw here like a pet to do your chores. We have made our agreement. Away now. Bring our evening meal.' She turned to close the conversation.

Damn you to hell and back, Susan McFadden. And damn your husband even further into hell. I will fight you. You will not take Huw to be your slave. 'Yes, mistress.'

'Psssst.'

Margaretta jumped and looked up the stairs. 'What is it, Doctor?'

He beckoned her upstairs. Margaretta quietly pulled the door and crept up to John Dee's office.

'Look at this.' He pointed to cards laid in the shape of a cross on his messy desk. His tarot deck. Used by others simply as playing cards, to him they were the symbols and messages that helped him unravel the people and connections within his cases. And for seven years, Margaretta had been learning the craft. Always in the secrecy of his room for this was no game. It was conjuring. And conjuring meant death – even if it is for the Queen. 'The cards are beginning to reveal the key players.' He tapped the central card. 'Remember this?'

'Queen of swords. An independent and intelligent woman. Always alone. In each of our cases it represents Elizabeth.'

'Quite right. Now this one. It represents the influence from the past, or the genesis of the issue.'

'The strength card. Major Arcana, so a powerful card. A woman with her hand in the mouth of a lion but smiling. She has tamed it.' Margaretta looked up. 'I am not sure. But I think this represents a strong woman.'

'Go on. Think girl. The lion is the king of the animals. Who had a king tamed?'

'From what Cecil said, I think this is Anne of Cleves.'

'Very good, you are making connections. Anne of Cleves, like the woman in this card was kind, caring and strong. The only wife to navigate Henry's curse of killing wives – except Katherine Parr who only survived because she had wit enough to talk him out of signing her death warrant. He called Anne "sister" and put her above all women in the land save his pretty little wife, Kathryn Howard.'

Dee tapped on the card to the right of the queen of swords. 'Current influences.'

'There are four cards here.'

'The cards always speak. When I pulled the top one, the others fell from the deck. So, the top card hides the under cards.'

Margaretta picked up the top card and studied it. 'Minor Arcana. King of wands. I know these less well. But a king, haughty in looks, alone. He holds a sprouting wand indicating future promise – real or aspired.' She looked up at Dee. 'Who is this?'

He shrugged. 'We need to find out, but the card underneath is the knight of wands – so linked by family or patronage to the king. A young man. Ambitious, adventurous, athletic. A knight does the bidding of a king.' He tapped the next card. 'And below that the page of wands – a messenger.'

Margaretta turned the fourth card and shuddered. 'A person staring at seven cups, each holding something. There are riches, evil creatures, wishes. This depicts someone who wants everything, but notice that the cups are just out of reach.'

Dee gave a satisfied grunt. 'Good. You are learning to interpret the cards well. I see you have kept up your studies while I have been away.' His eyes moved to the bottom card of his spread. 'Future influences.' He turned it slowly. 'This filled me with dread.'

'Oh, God.' Margaretta clasped a hand over her mouth. 'The death card. And the bringer of death holds a flag with a Tudor Rose.' She looked up at Dee. 'Does this mean the end of Elizabeth?'

'Death comes in many guises – the end of eras, ideas, lives, hopes, dreams. But look into the card. Tell me what you see.'

'In the background a boat as if bringing someone ashore. Then a bishop, Catholic by his garb, pleading or bargaining with death. Below the horse, a dead man and a boy child. Also, a woman.' Margaretta's eyes opened wide. 'The same woman. Look. It is the same woman as in the strength card. White robed with flowers in her hair. Is it Anne of Cleves?'

'Possibly. Look at how she holds the child's hand but does not see him. Strange.' Dee leaned back. His face looking drawn in the candle light. 'Then I asked for more information on the Cygnet Prince. I almost wish I had not.' He turned over two more cards.

'Dear God. The Devil and the two of wands,' Margaretta looked at him in alarm. 'I recall from our previous investigations the Devil brings the worst of tidings.'

Dee nodded. 'It represents a person wracked with anger, obsession and violence. The worst of enemies for they are secreted away.'

'But is the two of wands evil? It looks sad rather than threatening. Just a man staring from a castle across the land.' Margaretta looked ashamed. 'I have not spent so much time on the Minor Arcana.'

Dee smiled. 'It takes years to learn them all, girl. You are doing well. So, listen and learn.' He turned the card for her to see. 'Indeed. It is a wise man and usually an indication of a new beginning. He is looking back at his past… or somewhere… with sadness. But about what? Or who?' Dee banged his hand on the desk making Margaretta jump. 'Damn this. The cards are throwing information at us, but nothing makes sense.'

Margaretta gulped. 'We are certain of Elizabeth and Anne of Cleves, but the rest are a mystery. And they are hurtling us towards death and danger.'

Dee rubbed tired eyes. 'We have no time to waste. Make the evening meal and we will journey to St Katherine's dock.' As Margaretta walked to the door he added, 'And send a note to that wherry-lad. Don't think I didn't notice you redden when I asked you before. We have no time for the heart, Margaretta. We have a Queen to protect and my standing to improve.'

I do not think you have a heart, Doctor. I think a stone swings in that breast of yours.

Chapter Nine

The carriage pulled to a halt as dusk darkened the sky. Dee jumped out and asked a passing sailor which ship was *The Mariella*. Margaretta followed, the bile rising in her throat. 'Do you really need me, Doctor?'

'Damn it, girl. With me seven years and still you quail at the sight of a body. It is but a shell – and a shell full of stories.' The sailor made the sign of the cross as John Dee marched away along the quayside. *The Mariella* was quiet, and a man, better dressed than most sailors, sat in the stern, looking through papers. He lifted his head when hailed by John Dee and walked to the narrow plank that bridged the ship from the quayside. 'You must be Doctor Dee. I'm bosun Adams. I had a message that you would be arriving.' He grimaced. 'Good thing too. The ice has but a day before it is all melted and then we will not be able to abide the stink.'

Margaretta groaned. Dee stepped onto the plank making little greeting but asking to be taken straight to the body. Then he would have questions. The surly sailor frowned. 'I can only tell you what I have picked up from the men. I'm replacing the previous bosun. He jumped ship.' Dee seemed not to hear and was already making his way below, calling to Margaretta to hurry up. The sailor gave her a look of sympathy but shouted down the steps. 'Go astern. You will find Captain Neerman in his cabin.'

By the time Margaretta stepped in, the white linen was

already stripped from the body and the sweet, cloying smell of death filled the stuffy cabin. Margaretta retched only to get a look of warning from Dee. 'Breathe through your mouth. Concentrate on what you see, not what you smell.' He leaned over and prodded at the grey, swelling skin as he walked around the body. 'No sign of bruising or cuts.' He moved to the face and lifted an eyelid. 'Bloodshot. Seems he struggled in his final minutes. But that would be true of a drowning.' He took the man's shoulder and heaved him over. 'Look at his back. Any wounds?'

Margaretta opened her eyes and scanned quickly. 'Nothing. Just scars from the pustules boys get as they turn to man. No cuts. No bruises.' She looked away again.

The body thumped onto its back and the head lolled sideways, making Margaretta cry out. Dee tutted. 'Get a candle, girl. I can see something on the face.' He held the candle close and turned down his mouth in disgust. 'Teeth marks. The rats have been at the body.' He looked up at Margaretta. 'Can you tune into him?'

She closed her eyes. *What happened? Please tell me quickly. Help me get out of here. I feel so very sick.* Then the feelings. 'Pain. Panic. A shadowed face. I can only see the mouth. I feel stumbling, falling. I see water. I think it will stop the pain. Now I am going down. The pain. Oh, I cannot bear... black it is all...'

'Alright stop.' Dee had her by the shoulders. 'Come back to the room. Look at me. This is not your pain. Breathe.' He patted her shoulder. 'Well done.' He turned back to the body. 'So, someone caused him pain before he went into the water.' He pointed to the door. 'Go and call that man down from the deck.'

The surly bosun stood at the door, refusing to step over the threshold. 'I will not share space with a drowned sailor. Their soul seeks another home. I do not want his torture.'

Dee span round. 'How do you know he was tortured?'

'The cabin boy found him raving on deck, screaming to the stars that he had unleashed a devil. Then he jumped.'

'Where is the cabin boy?'

'Ran in fright. No-one has seen him since that night.' The man shook his head. 'The poor lad fetched help but by the time they were back the captain was cold in the water. Probably thought he would be blamed.'

John Dee growled and went back to the body. 'What else do you know?'

'That Satan entered the ship before he died.'

Dee and Margaretta turned and stared. 'What?' asked Dee.

'The cabin boy – he heard the howl of Satan just before the captain was possessed of his soul. A terrible sound coming from the bowels of the boat.' The man shuddered. 'I have a priest coming tomorrow to bless and cleanse her or no sailor will sign up and we need to be trading by end of week.' He nodded towards a corner. 'Even the rats are dying on this death-ship'.

Margaretta looked around. There was a dead rat on the cabin floor. Then she spied another under the captain's table. *I feel your concern. You think there is witchcraft here. Something is bothering you but you do not know what it is. The dead rat scares you.* 'Do rats normally die so readily?'

'No. And if they do the others eat them. We just have bodies.'

John Dee stood up straight. 'This howl of Satan. Tell me more.'

'It came from within. A terrible sound – so the men reported.'

Dee clicked his fingers. 'Get a lamp. We will go to the bowels and see what is there.'

The boson froze. 'You will not get me down there before the priest has trodden before me. No, not I.'

'Then get me a lamp, man. I have no time for superstition.'

The smell was terrible as flies buzzed into their faces and the air seemed thick. Hammocks swung in the heat making strange shadows. They made their way astern saying nothing, Dee holding the lamp high and stopping every few paces to look around. Nothing. Even the eating table was cleared. A few kit bags were stowed on hammocks but nothing alive could be seen. They reached a door carved with 'Rope'. Flies crawled across the polished wood. Dee pushed the iron handle but it was tight shut. 'Hold this. I will have to pull it.'

Margaretta took the lamp and stood back, trying to stop the tremble in her hand make the shadows worse. Dee put both hands to the handle and tugged. Nothing. Again, this time with his foot on the door jam. There was a scrape, then a thud and he clattered back with a yell. Margaretta screamed as a cloud of black flies swarmed out. Then the stench hit them. She managed to put the lamp down before falling to her knees, hands to her face to keep the insects from her eyes as she retched again. The next thing she felt was John Dee, pulling on her arm. 'Up, girl.'

'I can't. I want to be sick. Please, let me…'

'Don't be a fool. There is something dead in here. It's not Satan. And, if it is, we will be the toast of every bishop in the land. Get up.'

'But I am…'

'Being a weakling. Facing that which scares the powerful is our path to fortune and standing. Up. Follow me.' He grasped the lamp and stepped through the door, then stopped and held it high, batting flies away with the other hand. 'There it is.'

'What is it?'

'Cannot tell. Come in and hold the lamp.' A few steps in and holding his hand over his mouth and nose to quell the stink, he bent over. 'It's a dog. Days dead from the number of maggots eating it. Bring the light closer.'

Margaretta stepped forward and gave out a little cry. 'The poor thing. Its face is covered in blood. Who would do that to a poor animal?'

Dee was on his knees now, his face close to the dog's

muzzle. 'Blood is around the mouth, tongue out and the claws extended. Look.' He pulled up the animal's paw and tiny maggots tumbled out. 'This happens when an animal dies in pain. More evident in a cat. But dogs do it too.' He looked around. 'Dead rats here as well.' He sat back on his haunches. 'This dog died of poison. The rats around him have bitten the dead body and died too.'

'So, the sound of Satan was this poor creature howling in pain.'

'Or madness. The boson said the captain was raving.'

'You think they were both poisoned?'

'We will soon find out.' Dee pulled himself up and pointed to the door. 'Come, girl. Let's get out of this hell hole and test that body.'

Oh, God.

The boson looked shocked when told that his Satanic howling was no more than a dog dying, but he could not explain how the dog was in the rope locker. He was instructed to get the dog removed and burned, not buried. Without another word, Dee beckoned to Margaretta to follow to the captain's cabin.

The linen was pulled back again. 'We will start here.' He moved to the head, prised open the mouth and peered inside. 'Bring the lamp.' He looked up, eyes hard. 'No, weakness, girl. Hold it close so I may see.'

Margaretta took a deep breath and stepped forward trying not to look at the grey bloated face of a once handsome man.

'The tongue is black and there is blood on the teeth.' Dee opened another eye. 'Bloodshot in both eyes. This could be from the body trying to expel poison as well as drowning. There is only one way to tell if this man died of inhaling water. We see if there is water in his lungs.'

'No. Tell me you are not going to cut him open. I will not watch. I cannot. It is more than I can…'

'Stop your whining, Margaretta. I have no time for this

weakling speak.' He glared at her. 'Get the sharp knife from my bag. The one I use to open seals.'

Why, why are you so very hard on me? You know this part of our work is terrible for me and no matter how many times I look on death, still I feel the horror of it. Why do you suddenly become so very harsh and cruel? If I could feel you as I feel others I might understand. But I can never reach your mind so I must react only to your words. Sometimes I hate you, John Dee. 'Here it is, Doctor.'

'Now watch what I do. This is a good lesson for you.'

'Yes, Doctor.' *I feel I might faint.*

Dee leaned over the left side of the body and started to feel up the torso, counting the ribs as he went. Stopping at six, he took up the knife and started to push it through the bloated grey flesh, ignoring a small mew from Margaretta. He pressed hard until the knife suddenly stopped, then a hard shove and the knife was up to the hilt in the body. 'Now watch the wound when I pull it out. We are looking for water.' He slowly withdrew the knife. Nothing. Not even blood. 'This man was dead as he hit the water. If he had drowned, the lungs would be full of dock-brine. They are dry.'

'But he has been here two days or more.'

'Lying prone with nowhere for the water to go.' Dee looked up at Margaretta. 'This man and the ship's dog died of a terrible poison which first sent them mad and then quickly to their death.'

Dee pulled himself up to full height. 'I think hemlock.' He looked around the room. 'Get the lamp, girl. Look for clues.'

Margaretta picked up the oil lamp, the smell of it making her stomach heave more. There was nothing strange. Just the table, papers, a sextant and in the corner a bed neatly made. Behind her, John Dee was muttering about clues. 'Come spirits. Help me. Where do I look?' Then her eyes went back to the table. At the side was a basket with red apples and small cakes with baked apples atop them. She walked over and recoiled.

John Dee was at her side in seconds. 'A dead rat and only one cake half-eaten.' He gave a satisfied smile. 'If they were safe, the rats would have devoured them. But they are clever creatures. They see a fellow animal dead and run away.' He looked around for a bag and handed it to Margaretta. 'Use this to gather the apples and cakes, but do not touch them to your skin.'

Suddenly he froze. 'What did Robert say about that royal dog?'

Margaretta gulped. 'It went mad and bit the groom.'

Dee's eyes opened wide. 'Jesu.' He turned to look at Margaretta. 'There may be poison in the palace.'

Chapter Ten

They arrived back at St Dunstan's before seven of the clock. Dee had told the bosun to have the sailors and the cabin boy found and ready for questioning in the morning. Then, he had voiced his plans as they trundled through the falling evening light. From outside came the din of hawkers packing their wares into baskets. Sailors fell from tavern doors shouting to doxies who sat in windows calling lewd offers to the street below. Old women sat in doorways holding out frail hands for a little charity and street urchins dived through legs trying to spot any fallen food or, better, a dropped coin. 'We must send a letter in haste to Cecil. Then I will calculate another horoscope. Tomorrow, we find out more about Captain Neerman, then go to Cecil to speak to Anne's launderess and get our list of voices. The carriage stopped at their door. Dee grumbled that Katherine Constable would no doubt be waiting for some company. 'Damn the woman,' he growled.

'That is harsh, Doctor. You owe her much. Who was it who negotiated your office being held while you were in the house of Bishop Bonner escaping a witchery charge? Who was the woman holding your hand when you faced the gates of heaven four years ago? Who has kept me, Huw and Mam – while she lived – with a roof over our heads as you trawled Europe for books?' *For the love of God, can you not see how her heart is yours for the taking? She sits in that chamber all day, ignored by a husband who has lost his soul to the bottle and pining for just a little kindness from you.* 'Would it hurt to just share a glass of wine with her. If she were a sick patient, you would.'

'She is not sick,' snapped Dee.

'She is sick of her life, Doctor. There is no harsher affliction.'

He grunted and went silent. Margaretta crossed her fingers and hoped it had worked. Maybe a little pity in his heart would help both her and Katherine. 'Very well. One glass. Then I must conjure.' But there was a small smile on his face.

'Just tell her you must do a report for Cecil. That will have her showing you the door. There is no greater supporter of your rise to rank.' Margaretta waited a few seconds, took a breath and asked, 'As you will be talking to Mistress Constable and then conjuring a horoscope, may I go to my sister's this evening? I must see her on urgent family business.'

Dee narrowed his eyes. 'Have I just been played, girl?'

'No, Doctor.' *Fingers crossed behind my back again.*

'First get a messenger for my letter. Then you may go. Be back by nine of the clock.'

The house of Susan and Angus McFadden had been improved in the last few years. There were now more outbuildings and the front extended to include a terrace that Susan insisted was in the style of a French palace. Margaretta jumped down from the cart, paid a penny fare to the young driver and turned to walk up the path through well-manicured lawns and neatly clipped hedges.

So here you are Susan in your even more perfect house and your perfect children and perfect garden. Let's see what you are planning for our brother. I have a feeling this will not a be a warm, sisterly discussion.

Grace, the maid, answered the door, her face lighting up on seeing Margaretta. 'Hello Miss. It brings sun to my soul to see you.' She stepped back to allow entry. 'Is Mistress Susan expecting you?'

My word, Grace. You have hardly aged a day in all these years. Still like a child with a heart of gold. I can never thank you enough for reminding my mother what it was like to be kind to a young girl. You will never know what a gift you gave me. 'She is not, Grace. So be ready with a bucket of water to douse the flames coming from her forked tongue.'

As ever, Grace bent double in chortling and put her hands to her mouth to stifle the sound. 'I think she is playing Primero with Master Angus, now that the children are abed.'

'Really? But Primero takes quick wit and the ability to count.' Margaretta winked. 'When we were on the farm, Susan was never allowed to count the new chicks. She used to count their legs and beaks and always gave our Dada three times more than could ever come from eggs.'

This was a titbit that Grace craved – old stories, much exaggerated, of her mistress' humble beginnings on a farm in Wales. She muffled her laugh and led the way to the main living chamber.

Margaretta did not wait for a call to enter when Grace knocked on the door. She stepped in, thanking Grace for her time and stood looking on the domestic scene. Unsurprisingly, Angus McFadden was well into his cups and slumped on a chair at the table opposite his wife. Susan was trussed into an expensive dress, a stomacher tight and hips exaggerated by a farthingale in the new style. Her coif was of velvet – not the linen that covered Margaretta's head. By the fire, staring at the flames was old Master McFadden. He turned his head slowly and smiled, a flicker of recognition in those eyes, but the terrible scar now on his face from the barrel that dropped from a crane and broke his skull just a year ago. *You poor old thing. Working all those years to build up a good business only to be crushed by the very thing that had made you. So, now your business and your fortune are in the hands of your stupid, vile, womanising son – Angus McFadden. You sit and stare and understand little of the world around you. Sometimes life is so very unfair. I will greet you first.* 'Good evening, Master McFadden.' Margaretta crossed the room and took his hand in hers. He squeezed it back and gave a watery smile. 'You are looking fine and well today.' *Just a nod. You do not understand, but I feel your warmth and just a little pleasure that a face smiles at you and you feel the touch of another.*

'What are you doing here, sister?' Susan was on her feet now. 'I do not recall receiving a note to warn us of your arrival.'

'Warn you? You need warning, Susan? What alarms you about a sisterly visit?'

Susan looked to her husband for support, but he was leering at Margaretta's breasts as usual. He made a small hiccup and then a sickly smile. 'Well, it's our comely little kinswoman. Come sit with us.'

'I have no need or time to sit, Angus.' She turned to Susan. 'Why did you come to St Dunstan's – without warning – and talk to Mistress Constable about Huw?'

Susan made a dismissive bat of her hand. 'Huw needs a trade. Now that Angus is running the family business, he can teach him.' She made a sickly smile. 'Little Jack is too young and Baby Maria will not learn trade – she will marry well. We need to fill the gap until Jack is of age to enter the trade.'

Your eyes are flicking side to side. You think of our home. What game are you playing?

A small laugh from Angus as he stood and made a lop-sided step to his wife's side. 'Yes, dog-boy needs to earn his keep in the world. He can be useful in The Vintry. He's strong enough to heave barrels and can count. It's a start for him.'

Margaretta turned on Angus. 'He is not a dog-boy. He is special. And you are not going to use him as a cheap dock-worker to keep money in your pocket.' She turned to Susan, her voice rising in anger. 'You have never done a kindness for Huw. You ran away from him when the other children threw sticks. Now you turn away while your greedy husband uses him as cheap labour. You will not have him. He needs love and care, not a quay-side lash.'

Susan paused before answering. 'You are being a sentimental fool, Margaretta. Huw does not understand love and care. He understands orders. He needs help with everything and all he has.'

'Rubbish. Orders may be all you are capable of giving, Susan. But it does not make it right.' Margaretta raised her hands in placation. 'For the love of God, he is still mourning Mam. He needs me.'

Angus snorted. 'Dog-boy does not feel. He just does.'

Damn you. I will not stand here listening to an oaf with nothing to fill his head except vile thoughts. Angus yelled as the shove in his chest sent him barrelling back, his chair over-tipping and spilling him on the floor. In seconds, Susan was running at her sister, grabbing her arm and pulling her round. 'Don't you dare attack my husband, you little—'

'Little what, Susan? Little sister who looks after Huw? Little daughter who cared for Mam? Little wise woman who had to get you medicines? Little holder of all your secrets?'

Susan's face was white with anger. 'You think you are so very goodly, don't you? You think you are such a good daughter and sister. You are not.'

Margaretta lowered her voice to a low snarl. 'No. I'm not perfect, Susan. But nor am I cruel, spiteful, a liar, a user and a woman who turns her back on an inconvenient family. Where were you when Mam was groaning her way into heaven, the canker in her breast making her call out in anguish for the end to come? Where were you when Huw and I were holding her close all night? Where were you when we wrapped her in the winding cloth and wept? You were here, Susan, in your perfect house with your far from perfect husband. Huw and I faced it together and we will do the same for the rest of our lives.' *Damn. I feel the tears hot on my cheek. I do not want to give her the satisfaction of seeing me weep with the pain of it all. I will turn away and leave.*

As she reached the door, Angus clambered to his feet and stood unsteadily. 'Too late, little sister. The deal is done.'

You are thinking of our home too. I feel greed.

Margaretta ran to the hallway, not waiting for a servant to be called to show her out. There at the bottom of the stairs was Little Jack in his sleeping shirt, staring.

Margaretta stopped and forced herself to speak in a kind voice. 'Jack. How is my young nephew?' No response. 'Will you not look at your aunt, Jack? You are staring at the wall.' No answer. 'Come, Jack. You are seven years old now. You may say hello.' Nothing. 'Did the shouting frighten you, *cariad*?'

Margaretta bent down to smile at the child. Jack shook his head, closed his eyes and started stepping foot to foot.

Chapter Eleven

Dee looked up as Margaretta slipped through the door of his office. 'You are back early. You can look at this horoscope and check the calculations. A good lesson for you.' He frowned. 'What has happened?'

'Susan and Angus want to take Huw to work in The Vintry. They are up to something.'

Dee sat back. 'Maybe that would be a good job for him. Counting, checking, writing notes of receipt. It might be a trade.'

'How can you think that anything Susan and Angus want can be good for Huw? How can you even imagine that they have a scrap of good will in their hearts? They would steal a bone from a stray dog if…' *Steal. That word felt like a knife in my heart.*

'Stop squawking, Margaretta. Remember your place.' He pointed at the desk. 'We have a murder to investigate. Your sister can be managed another day. Go dry your eyes and come back ready to learn.'

Damn you. I hate you. 'Yes, Doctor.'

The bread kneaded for the early bake, Margaretta returned to the office. John Dee was staring at the full moon shining through the window. He did not turn, but beckoned over his shoulder then pointed at the parchment on his desk. It was etched with a square divided into sections, each with a symbol and calculations. 'Look at that and give me your analysis.'

Margaretta sat, pulled the candle close and scanned the document. 'This is a horoscope for Elizabeth. You have her birth constellation in the centre – the seventh day of September in the year 1533, making her Virgo. But she has Libra rising and Aquarius in her house of emotion. So, calm on the outside but easily swayed by strong passions and she has a deep sense of justice.' She pointed to the upper quadrant. 'Mars is rising in the house of status and position. This will bring her a period of challenge and maybe a battle.'

'Good. You are learning well. Keep going.' His voice was softening.

'Here in the left quadrant, Venus is transiting. This is the house of emotion, love, intimacy.' She paused. 'Robert Dudley and his influence?'

Dee tapped on the next section. 'Look at what is coming up behind.'

Margaretta shook her head. 'Saturn. That is about hard lessons and restriction. So, her love will not reach fruition. She has already tasted unkindness over Amy Dudley, has she not?'

'She has indeed. And so has Robert. But these two are not fated to be together. Though they are yet to realise this and Elizabeth remains blinded.'

Margaretta looked back at the parchment. 'The sun is in her house of family and home. So, this is good. It means positive action. Illumination. Truth.' She traced her finger across. 'But the other planets, the moon, Mercury and Jupiter are all clustered here in the house of money.' She looked up puzzled. 'Is this good?'

Her master shook his head. 'It means many hidden ideas, ambitions, emotions, ideas, communications. It is a muddle as the three planets pull from each other. The largest planet is Jupiter – the planet of ambition. This is the web of intrigues we are trying to untangle. It means Elizabeth is facing hidden ambitions and communications.'

'It seems our Queen has challenges coming in all her houses except the one of family – so those who are of her household will gather around her.' She looked at Dee. 'But can they protect her?'

'I have sent warning to the palace, but I worry.' He looked again at the moon. 'Get the garnet crystal. We have a few minutes of moon left.'

Margaretta jumped up and went to the book that hid the precious red stone and brought it back to the desk. She knew what to do and placed it in the middle of the horoscope.

'Tell us. Show us,' whispered Dee. A cloud cleared from the moon and the room was suddenly bathed in silver light. Shards of red spread across the parchment. 'Look, there it is. The strongest beam is falling on the house of money and status. A bad omen.'

'Why?'

'That is where the trouble lies – the ambitions. That is where the people depicted by the king of wands, the knight of wands, the page of wands, and the seven of cups are lurking.' Dee picked up the stone and stared at the parchment. 'We need to work quickly. Early tomorrow we start at the ship and then go immediately to Cecil. Tell Huw he must mind the house all day.' Then a grunt and a softening of the voice. 'We must keep him here where he is wanted.'

So, you do have a heart.

Chapter Twelve

A chill wind lifted the waves to slap against the quayside. The surly boson was waiting at the top of the gangplank. 'I have two for you. Waiting on the crew deck. Cost me a whole shilling to keep them here until you arrived.'

Dee waved a hand in dismissal. 'Did you find the cabin boy?'

'No. He sailed yesterday with a Dutch trader.'

'Then I will not repay your shilling.' Dee ignored the grumble and marched along the deck towards the captain's cabin, Margaretta running after him with the bag of parchment, quills and an ink horn.

Two sailors sat at the table, both red eyed and stinking of rum. One had a black eye and a smear of blood on his face. They were quaffing small beer to slake their thirst.

'My name is Doctor Dee. I understand you sailed with Captain Neerman from Antwerp with a German passenger.'

The bruise-eyed sailor nodded. 'Well, we didn't know we were bringing bad luck to English shores. Or we would have jumped ship before she sailed.'

'Yes, yes,' replied Dee. 'Now tell me what you know of the captain's last night.'

'All we know is from young Zach. Poor little bastard had the fright of his life. First the angel of death arrived and within an hour the howl of Satan came from the bilges. Next thing he knew, the captain was rolling around like a ship with no keel and raving like a man possessed.'

Dee sat up like a bolt hearing the name of his fascination. 'Angel? What angel?'

'Caped. Hood up. No face to be seen. Gloved hands.'

'Man or woman?' demanded Dee.

'Must be man. Women are not allowed on a ship.' The sailor turned to glower at Margaretta. He shrugged. 'Asked for the captain. Stayed but a few minutes. Soon after, the captain was a mad man.'

'Did Zach say what he was raving about?'

'Nah. It were in Dutch. Something about a "fair gift".' The sailor frowned and shuddered. 'Then he jumped in the water and started trying to climb a ladder which were not there. That's when young Zach ran for us. By the time we were found, the captain was face down in the water. Gone to his maker.'

Dee turned to Margaretta. 'Do you have all that noted down?' She nodded. The bruised sailor spoke again. 'Why are you bringing a woman aboard? Bad luck they are.' His companion nodded and glared.

'Yes, yes. Now, the captain's dog.' Dee pointed at the door at the end of the crew deck. 'I am told it was often in there. Why might that be?'

The sailors looked confused. 'Only at eating times,' began the quieter man slowly. 'The captain spoiled him as a pup. Giving him food from the hand at table. The creature would jump up to beg food. So, every meal time, he were given a scrap from the captain's plate and then put in the rope locker to stop him a stealing from us.' The man shrugged 'We ain't seen the animal since the captain passed.'

Silence. So, you are deciding not to tell these men the dog was poisoned. No doubt to stop any rumour-making. I bet you will change the subject quickly to avoid questions.

Dee looked at the quiet man. 'You. Tell me about the German passenger.'

'Trouble from the start,' he declared in a broad West Country accent.

'Seemed to think he were some kind of fucking Prince.' He made no apology for his cursing to either Dee or Margaretta and took another slurp of beer that dribbled down his chin. 'And we don't like crucifix chanters.'

Dee cocked his head on one side. 'What do you mean?'

The sailor leaned forward and spoke low and slow. 'I mean men who wail at the cross when the waves come up. We might as well have had a woman the whole passage for all the snivelling we had. Seemed to think we were meant to keep the ship flat for his comfort, the fucking fool.' He took another deep quaff of ale.

First you laughed. Then anger. All of you muttering. Shouting. You are recalling your captain shouting. 'Maen nhw'n cofio'r Capten yn sgrechian.'

The bruise-eyed sailor twisted round to stare at her. 'My mother was a Welsh woman. How did you know about the shouting?' He stood, his chair falling back with a clatter and he stared at the cabin door as if checking he had an escape.

'The bosun mentioned it,' she lied.

He picked up his chair and sat, though keeping a wary eye on her. 'Tis true. It started well. Then on the second day out of Antwerp there was some kind of disagreement.'

'Do you know what it was about?'

The sailor shrugged. 'Was all in foreign tongue. But they did not speak for the rest of the crossing. No dinners at the captain's table.'

The other sailor cut in. 'Jan understood it. One of the top-sail men. Gone this morning. He said something about them shouting about the Queen and destiny.' He pulled his forelock. 'If that little fucker had any bad feeling towards our good Queen Elizabeth, I wish the pox upon him.' The other grunted his agreement.

Margaretta scribbled and Dee sat back thoughtfully. 'Did he say anything to the crew?'

'Spoke hardly a word to us – unless he were complaining that the sails made the ship heel and disturb his comfort. Fucker.'

A book. I see a book. 'Would the captain write a book, sirs?'

The sailor refused to look at her but spoke to Dee. 'There will be a log of the journey. But that is only to record tide and time. Not our business.'

Dee nodded. 'Is there anything else you can tell us... me. I want to find out who harmed your captain.'

The sailors were silent and then shook their heads. 'Say true, sir. If there were more, we would spill everything. Neerman were a good man. Been a captain across this channel for more than twenty-five years. Paid on time and in full he did. Rarely used the lash and only when deserved. We sailed with him seven years. Will be hard to find better.'

Dee nodded. 'I understand.' He went to his pocket and put two half-shillings on the table. 'I thank you on behalf of Her Majesty.' Then he rose, his smile showing delight in the amazement on the two men's faces.

Oh, how you love to glow in the glory of Court. The feeling of being important is like milk to a babe. It nourishes you.

The sailors were glad to leave the cabin and Dee turned. 'Well done, girl. Your abilities are getting stronger. Come.'

'They thought I was a devil in a dress.'

'Yes, yes. Superstition is a sailor's religion. We must find that log.'

The smell in the captain's cabin was even more rank than before and the wetness on the floor showed the ice had completely melted. Margaretta groaned and clasped both hands over her face. Though she thanked God the linen was covering the body. Dee went straight to the table and rummaged through the papers. In seconds, he pulled a leather-bound book and opened it. 'This is it.' He flicked through the pages. 'I can see numbers and navigation points. But the notes are in Dutch. Not a language I know.' He handed it to Margaretta. 'Put this in the bag. Cecil will have someone in his network who can interpret.' He started to walk out of the cabin. 'Oh, and write down "fair gift". We need to know what Neerman was shouting.'

Minutes later they were out in the light, Margaretta gulping in fresh air. Dee called to the bosun to have the body removed and buried quickly and then to get the priest for blessing. He walked away ignoring the man's complaints about the shilling.

Chapter Thirteen

'Sam!' Margaretta beckoned him in. The sun was already warming the mid-morning air. It should have gladdened her heart, but it meant that the smell of piss and worse was rising from the streets. As the autumn days shortened people did not have to get up so early to sneak their chamber pots out to the gutters before light, so the stench was new and acrid.

'Well, Missy Margaretta. It is months since you came to visit our house and then a note to say I am employed.' Sam made an exaggerated bow as if to a queen.

'Stop your cheek, Sam. It is Doctor Dee's request. We need a wherry man and carriage driver who can keep a still tongue.'

Another bow. 'Then I am your humble, silent servant, Missy.' He turned and winked at Huw now understanding that he would have no look back. Only a giggle.

Margaretta cuffed his shoulder. 'Hush yourself. How is my little friend Lottie?'

'Like a ripe fruit about to burst.' He grinned. 'Our second is due any day.' Then his face darkened. 'I hope it is less painful than before. Broke my heart to hear her cries.'

'Do not worry. A second child is always easier. The body knows what to do. Your third will come like a pea from a pod. The fourth she will not notice.'

Sam laughed and Huw joined in.

Oh, Sam, you are a good man. But I pushed you away into Lottie's arms. Now I walk into the warmth of your home and wish I were there and part of it. 'How are Master and Goodwife Tovey and their Tilly?'

'All good, Missy. Tilly passed her twelfth birthday last month and is doing well at her lessons. She is learning the book keeping from Goodwife Tovey so that they keep the business in the family.'

'And what about you, Sam? Last time we met, Master Tovey was saying you were due some rank in the business.'

Sam pulled back his shoulders and smiled. 'I have been made chief builder and given a share of the business. All the wherry boys are under my command, but I do a few hours a day to keep my hand in and know what is happening on the river.'

'Going up in the world.'

'Up in experience and trust, Missy. That is good for me. To learn from a good man each day is a privilege indeed.'

Oh, I feel the same. I learn too. But Doctor Dee is a strange teacher. Every day he is here I have to navigate his moods and the swing from cold to kind. Then he leaves on another search for books and wisdom and I am left to fend alone with only a list of studies to further during his absence. 'I am glad to hear it, Sam.'

Sam leaned towards her. 'If you came a visiting more often, Missy, you would have fewer questions. It must be more than half a year since you graced our home.'

Because it hurts to see the love among you all when I have to come here to a cold kitchen and only a brother to love who will not even look in my eye when I speak. Your happy home makes me so lonely. 'I will come soon, Sam. It has been so very busy. Now, let us talk business. As my note said, you will be on retainer. We need to go to Hampton Court this morning. Can you do that?'

Sam grinned. 'Suits me well on all counts, Missy. Money in my pocket for my family and fond company while I earn it.' Another wink at Huw, rewarded with a nod and a smile.

Do not be kind to me. It hurts. When I hear your softness, I recall both you and Christopher. Two good men lost to my past, never to return.

'Why do you look so sudden sad, Missy?' Sam ducked his head to look into her eyes. 'I think you still sadden after the young man who died. Lottie was sore worried about you.'

'I do, Sam. But he was not my man.'

'Lottie will not tell me the story but…' He patted her shoulder. 'If he were not your man, then he died less happy than he could have been.'

Stop, stop, stop. 'Hush you, Sam. I will see you back here in an hour.' Margaretta moved to the door. 'And give my friend a kiss from me.'

Margaretta took a deep breath, sucked in the pain and lifted her head to see Huw pointing at her. 'Grey. Margaretta sad. Christopher grey too.'

His sister frowned. 'Christopher was sad? How do you know?'

'Saw him in market with fat girl and baby. Asked for you and a little blue showed. Faded when I said you well. Grey. Dark grey. Had been blue before. Then more grey. Then died.'

'Why didn't you tell me, Huw?'

'Mam said "no". Make you cry.' The boy shifted from foot to foot and shook his head, anxiety rising. 'Huw not unkind.'

Margaretta softened her voice. 'No. You are a good and kind brother, Huw. That is why I want you here and not with Susan.'

He gave a small grin. 'Make you pink again.'

Yes, Huw. For I will surely be grey if they take you from me. You are all I have. Except that damn cat. Though I suppose that animal feels like a little bit of Mam in my life still.

The door to the office creaked. Dee looked up and put a finger to his mouth and whispered. 'Katherine has just been here. Upset we are going out again.' Dee beckoned her in. On his desk was a single card. Margaretta shuddered. It was the Devil again. 'I asked the cards to help us with the captain's death. This was the card I pulled. And then...' He pulled the next card from the deck. 'Look at what was underneath it again.'

'The page of wands.' Margaretta looked at her master. 'I think a page represents a messenger or servant.'

Dee nodded and tapped the next card on the deck. 'Very good. So now we have the king of wands, his knight and the page or servant. And this was below the page of wands.' He turned the next card that depicted a man toiling under the weight of ten wooden wands, his face and hands hidden. 'Each card is supported by the previous – so this suggests the page of wands is helped by the ten of wands... and they are both somehow linked to the Devil.'

There was a bang as the window flew open and wind gusted in, fluttering the cards from the desk. Dee cursed and jumped up to stem the draft. He turned back and stopped still, staring at the floor. 'Look.'

Margaretta walked around the desk. Every card had landed face down except one. 'The king of wands.' She looked to Dee. 'The king of wands is working with the Devil, isn't he?'

Dee nodded slowly. 'And a king in league with the Devil is a terrible thing indeed.'

Chapter Fourteen

The morning was grey with dark clouds threatening to soak all below. Dee stepped over the nose-skewed beggar. Margaretta followed, dipped into her pocket and again dropped a slice of bread into his lap without looking in his face as Katherine had forbidden her to encourage him. What Katherine did not know was that the man was an old archer from North Wales, and Margaretta and Huw were slipping food to him every day. It was understood. If alone, they spoke in their own tongue. If not, they acted as cold strangers.

Sam, splicing a rope to pass the time, looked up with a grin. 'Fine morning, Doctor Dee, and fear of ague has cleared our lanes. I'll have you where you belong – in Her Majesty's company – within the hour.'

Well done, Sam. You can see the doctor's chest puffing out already. You give him the importance he craves and he will keep you paid. Simple.

Dee stepped aboard and settled himself, then looked to Sam. 'Young man, I trust Margaretta has told you that anything you hear on our journeying is never to be mentioned to anyone else. Is that understood?'

Sam assumed a serious face and nodded. 'Missy has made it very clear, sir. You do important business and my mouth must be sewed shut.'

Ugh. Don't say that. It reminds me of that awful sight seven years ago.

Sam leaned forward as if in a conspiracy. 'I understand I am not even to tell people that I wherry or carriage you, sir. Such is the secrecy of your work.'

Dee nodded with a self-important smile cracking his face.

Well done, Sam. Your retainer has just been firmly secured.

Half a mile from Hampton Court, the road was thick with waiting carts. Sam called down to ask why the delay to be told that soldiers were searching every load of goods and food at the gate. Dee yelled out of the window that he was on Queen's business and had to be given clear passage. Grumpy waggoners pulled their vehicles onto the verge, scowling as Sam pulled past. At the gates, two guards crossed their halberds and refused entry until Dee had given his name and word was sent to Cecil to request admission. Dee was pacing in agitation and insisting they should know his face, but they just stared ahead, sending him to boiling fury.

Cecil was at his desk, his face drawn. To the side, a pile of files, each tied with red cord. He rose when John Dee entered. 'Good morning, John.'

Dee went to vent his anger, then stopped short, for sitting by the window was Bishop de la Quadra. 'We meet again, Doctor Dee.' Instantly, he shot a suspicious look at Margaretta. 'With your unusual assistant.' He passed a red apple between his hands.

'Just a trusted servant, with ability to take notes. Nothing more,' was Dee's acid dismissal.

You old scut. You rely on me more and more as I learn my lessons. I am seven years an apprentice now and can read the cards, position stones, write all your notes and even check your calculating. And that is on top of my gift to hear the unsaid. This Spanish bishop is suspicious of me. I feel it and see it. But you will never reveal your need of me.

Dee looked between Cecil and the bishop. The silence almost crackled. Cecil rose. 'The Bishop and I were just finishing our conversation.' He turned and bowed to the Spaniard. 'I am sure you have matters to attend to, sir.'

The other man rose with a look of irritation and made a cursory nod of his head, then strode across the floor. He pulled the door closed after him, very softly, and Cecil turned to Dee. 'Tell me all.'

'I could have told you an hour ago if I had not had to navigate a mile of carts which—'

'—Are being searched in response to your warning letter,' snapped Cecil, picking up a parchment of Dee's scrawling hand. He lowered his voice to a warning growl. 'Not a single berry will enter these walls which has not been searched. The palace is on danger-watch.'

'Good,' said Dee, his mood warming at the importance given to his words. 'But if the royal dog was poisoned, then the evil is already within.'

Cecil nodded. 'And every corner of every room is being systematically searched. Your advice has been taken very seriously, John. Now, I hope you bring news to help us.'

Dee pulled off his cloak, dropped it over a stool and sat on the comfortable chair by the desk. He took out the notes Margaretta had written on the ship and made a display of placing them in order across the desk. Then the log book was placed above them. 'Before I give our findings, what do we know of this Cygnet Prince's nature?'

'I found him a man of good nature and gentle manners. Well-educated with extensive knowledge of England, our history and political events. A little arrogant about his standing. But he is also kind in words about Mary, Queen of Scots.' Cecil's voice was hard, bitter.

'Hmm. Interesting. The sailors on *The Mariella* hated him and there was loud disagreement with the captain. Such was the tension that our Cygnet Prince did not dine at the captain's table after the first night.'

I feel strong interest. It must be you, Sir Cecil. But why do I feel satisfaction?

'Do we know the basis of the disagreement?'

'No. But the words "Queen and destiny" were heard.' Dee paused then bent to his bag and pulled out another parchment covered in circles and scribbles. Each circle had a name in it. He spread it out on the desk saying, 'This is all our evidence and the key players.' He tapped on the central circle. 'Our Cygnet Prince. We know he is linked to an aunt in Cleves and has contacted Bishop de la Quadra here and stays peacefully at the Waldegraves' in Hever. He also claimed lineage from a king and a former queen of England.' Dee tapped on two other circles with the names Henry and Anne. 'He is also linked to Captain Neerman. The Cygnet Prince had harsh words with him and days later he is visited by a cloaked, basket-carrying figure and poisoned along with his dog.' Dee turned to Margaretta. 'Get the cakes and apples.' When handed to him, Dee put the bag on the desk with a thump. 'I think you will find these are the source. We found a dead rat in the bowl and nothing eaten. I suspect hemlock – first madness, then death.'

Cecil nodded to Margaretta. 'Put them in the corner. I will have them tested with rats from the cellars.' He narrowed his eyes. 'How are you linking this to the royal dog?'

Dee gave a satisfied smile. 'It was a gift from Robert Dudley. Robert Dudley told the Cygnet Prince he was false. More harsh words. The dog of gentle nature went mad and attacked... sounds like hemlock again.' Dee tapped on the circle named Dudley.

'So why not poison Dudley?'

'Difficult. Elizabeth has elevated him to the highest of rank. So, his food is tasted.' Dee leaned back. 'I surmise the dog was either a warning or simply practice.'

Cecil pinched his nose. 'Are you saying this Clevian pretender is a poisoner?'

Dee shook his head. 'Unlikely. My analysis indicates he is assisted by people in power. Royal connections and their aides... and an evil influence.'

Cecil learned across the desk. 'Analysis? What evidence is behind this analysis?'

Dee said nothing and stared at the parchment.

Cecil pulled it away and pointed at Dee. 'Are you conjuring with those damned playing cards again?'

Dee avoided Cecil's eyes. 'It is simply calculing of the mind. My intelligence... cleverness.' He picked up the log book. 'There may be clues in here about the argument, but it is in Dutch. Also, the captain shouted "fair gift" before he died. Might shed some light on what happened. Do you have a friendly, Low Country spy who can translate?'

Cecil looked irritated and then took the book. 'Leave it with me.'

Dee relaxed. 'And see what else you can find out about Captain Neerman.'

Cecil nodded and spoke slowly. 'You will keep to real evidence, John. Facts. Not your unholy conjuring.' He lifted the top file. 'I have the list you want. We cannot start with the lowly as you suggested. The laundress to Anne of Cleves was taken with the sweating sickness over five years ago now.'

Dee gave a start.

So, Doctor. Your pretence of thinking so cleverly has been thwarted. So how are you going to bring Beatrice into the room without admitting that I gave you the information? I see your panic though I feel nothing from you. 'Excuse me, sirs.' Margaretta stepped forward. 'Launderesses are known gossips. Would anyone in the laundry have been working at that time?'

Dee turned to Margaretta. 'Hush girl. I was just about to demand the same.'

Liar.

Cecil grunted and rose. He stepped towards the door. Only then did Margaretta notice he was in stockinged feet. He opened the door and gave a start. 'Bishop de la Quadra?'

The Spaniard's alarm quickly melted into a smile. 'Sir Cecil. I was just passing and thought I would see if your audience with Doctor Dee was finished.' He nodded through the door at Dee and gave a small bow. 'I see not. Excuse me.'

You. I was feeling you earlier – not Sir Cecil. Interest and satisfaction. You were eavesdropping.

Cecil called to a servant and gave instructions to get the eldest woman from the laundry.

A few minutes later, they heard the click-clump of Beatrice ap Rhys lumbering along the corridor, heavy breathing showing the effort it took. Margaretta stood. 'It sounds like a woman hard of walking. I will go and help her.'

Dee gave a nod. *Yes, because you know I will tell her to say nothing of our conversations and you will get the credit.*

Outside, Margaretta walked to Beatrice who was looking alarmed and red in the face. '*Peidiwch â dweud dim am y sgwrs ddoe. Ond dywedwch bobeth rydych chi wedi dweud wrtha i.* Say nothing of the conversation yesterday. But say everything you said to me.'

Inside the office the old woman pulled herself up straight and looked at Cecil, then Dee. 'Beatrice ap Rhys, sirs. Laundress for forty years.'

Dee made a respectful bow of his head. 'Goodwife ap Rhys. A woman of my own land.' He made one of his charming smiles – the one rarely seen.

Beatrice nodded and looked around, wide-eyed. Cecil gestured to a chair. 'Please sit, Goodwife Rhys. We want your help and prefer you to be comfortable.'

John Dee took over the questioning first instructing Margaretta to take notes. 'Goodwife ap Rhys. I understand you have laundered many years.'

'Every year of my working days, sir. I started with Queen Mary when she was just a babe.' Beatrice shook her head in sadness. 'God rest her troubled soul.'

'So, you would have been laundering when Anne of Cleves was queen and then the king's favoured sister.'

'I was indeed.'

'Did you know the laundress to Anne of Cleves?'

'Yes. Elyn Tyrpyn. From the Midlands. A terrible gossip.' Then put a hand to her mouth as if the words had tumbled out and her eyes darted between the two men.

Cecil stepped in. 'Beatrice. We will not be angry if you heard gossip. But you could assist us in helping our Queen if you would share anything said to you.' He gave an encouraging smile. 'I know you are taught to never speak of your monarchs, but sometimes a rule bent is a ruler saved.'

Beatrice looked over to Margaretta who gave an indiscernible nod. 'Well, it is not words I would ever use, sir. A bit bawdy was Elyn.'

'Go on. Tell us exactly what she said.'

Beatrice took a breath and repeated, complete with Midlands accent, the words she had shared with Margaretta in the drying grounds. 'I'm telling you true. The only seed old Henry ever planted in our linens were the caraway seeds he flicked from his beard after eating Anne's German cakes. And the only thing his stick entered was his codpiece – and there were plenty of room for it.'

The room was silent. The woman gulped. Put her hands to her throat and stuttered, 'Mayhap I should have stopped after the seeds, sir.'

Cecil raised his eyebrows, nodded at Beatrice and then snapped at Margaretta. 'Do not write that last sentence. Some words need no noting.' Then he turned back to Beatrice. 'Are you quite sure that is what she said?'

'As sure as I am Beatrice ap Rhys.'

He picked up a piece of parchment for himself and dipped

a long goose quill. 'Did she speak of Anne of Cleves' menses being constant?'

Beatrice's hands fluttered further up to her face as she reddened. 'Why, sir, we have no need to speak of such things.' Then she frowned and looked into the middle distance, contemplating. 'But Elyn was a true slip-tongue, so she would have spoken of it if they had stopped.'

Cecil's eyes gleamed like a magpie spotting a gem. 'So, we can assume that Anne of Cleves had her normal courses through the years after she was divorced of the king.'

'Oh, I cannot confirm that. For the Lady Anne did go on a progress in the country in the summer of forty-one and Elyn went with her. To tell truth, I did not see Elyn again.'

Cecil looked up with a look of concern. 'Do you retain contact with anyone else who worked in the laundry of Lady Anne?'

'No, sir. They scattered to the wind.'

The gleam in Cecil's eye dulled.

Beatrice gulped. 'Have I said something amiss?'

Cecil put his hand to the bridge of his nose. 'No, mistress. You have told truth. And the words of Elyn Tyrpyn are of help.' He gave a weak smile to calm the woman. 'That is all for now.'

Margaretta stood to walk Beatrice out after she was thanked again and given stern warning not to repeat a word of the conversation. She had nodded her nervous assurance and was evidently relieved to be dismissed. As they stepped out, a black-cloaked figure moved in the shadows at the end of the corridor and disappeared round a corner. *Satisfaction. Even delight. Who are you? I'm sure that's the same black cloak I saw in the drying garden.* She ran the length of the corridor but when she reached the bend there was no-one there. She returned to Beatrice. 'Who walks around in a black cloak?'

The other woman huffed and answered in Welsh. 'People

with money enough to pay for good cloth and the black dyes.'
She patted Margaretta's arm. 'That's half of Court, *cariad*.'
She patted again and lumbered back towards the laundry, muttering about having to 'wash those damn stockings.'

Strange, I felt satisfaction. And not a kind satisfaction.

Back in the office, both men were in a dark mood. Dee was reading a file and muttering the names. He glanced up. 'Get ready to write, girl. William has created a list of women around Anne of Cleves.'

Cecil frowned in irritation at his title being dropped in favour of his Christian name but picked up the paper on his desk. 'There were many, but only three still alive – Catherine Carey, the Duchess of Suffolk and Margaret Douglas. God knows why so many have departed this life.'

It was Dee's turn to be irritated. 'Mayhap because it is more than twenty years and because we have been beset by four years of the Spanish ague. You might recall I nearly *departed* this life the first year of it.' He pointed at Margaretta. 'You were lucky I was able to guide my servant to get you the evidence you needed to save Elizabeth from losing her queenship.'

Cecil raised his hand in placation. 'Indeed, John. I have not forgotten your great efforts from your sick bed. Nor has Elizabeth. But the vague memories of three women are not going to give us what we need.'

Dee frowned. 'Why? They are alive, well and will have memory.'

Cecil gave a small groan. 'Catherine Carey is in the depths of despair after losing her last possible child. Her sixteenth issue and the only one to die a babe. Rumour has it she has not spoken in weeks.'

Dee huffed. 'We cannot allow niceties to inhibit our investigation. Catherine Carey is a close and loyal supporter of Queen Elizabeth. I will be kind in…'

'No kindness can cut through the darkness of a child's death,' snapped Cecil.

Oh, you poor man. You are recalling little Francesca. Only days old when you held her cold little hand and wept your goodbyes. Then two little boys, both called William to carry on your name. Gone in months. A deep pain that you hide rises like bile in your gut. I feel a dread. You think Tommy will be your only son and heir. But you think of Lady Mildred and a sudden spark of hope.

Dee persisted. 'And Catherine is much loved by the Queen so will want to assist.'

Cecil looked back at the list. 'The Duchess of Suffolk was a good friend. Indeed, Anne left her a diamond ring in her will. But the Duchess must be kept away from any bad news. She is a good friend and still trying to settle the Willoughby Inheritance. Any scandal will not further her cause.' Cecil sighed. 'That leaves only Margaret Douglas.'

'She may welcome an opportunity to get back in favour.'

'Hah,' barked Cecil. 'That serpent in cloth of gold. She would sell her soul to put her son, Darnley, on the throne. She plans to marry the little imp to Mary Queen of Scots, and create a Catholic dynasty.' Cecil rose and started to pace, smacking one hand into the other. 'If she knew of the Cygnet Prince, we would see the sparks on her heels as she ran to his cause. We are facing the peril of the Tudor dynasty, John. God help us.'

'But the Cygnet Prince would thwart her plans for her son.'

Cecil gave a cynical laugh. 'Any sniff of a Catholic plot will have her slavering like a hungry dog. We cannot allow her knowledge of this. Gad, that women plagues me with letters every day demanding freedom for her and her wailing husband. If she knows we need her help… it gives her power.'

Dee's mouth was set. 'Well, we cannot tarry. I will start with Catherine Carey with her brother's help. Henry Carey owes us much favour after the case of the wolf in the Hatfield oak.'

Cecil gave a resigned nod and looked back to the window.

So much pain. You worry about your wife, Mildred, and how she cries every night holding her children's booties, though no-one else sees her despair. Hard on the outside and as soft as butter inside. Little wonder some call her a crab in a kirtle. But that dart of hope again.

Chapter Fifteen

'Why the fuck do you want to bother my sister? Have you not heard the sadness she endures?' Henry Carey turned to bluster back down the tapestried corridor but turned back, coming close to John Dee, the smell of expensive wine on his breath. 'Don't you bother her with your mad conjuring.'

Dee stood still, his eyes fixed on Henry's in a display of moral strength. 'My intention is to prevent distress – the distress of having to uproot her children yet again to flee from a Catholic queen.'

Henry Carey stopped short, his eyes narrowing with concern. He was a Tudor in all but name. Red hair, a strong face, small mouth, long fingers and a love of good clothes. His brocade glistened as much as the anger in his dark eyes. No wonder they rumoured he was really Elizabeth's half-brother. Apparently, she could curse like a sailor too when her ire was raised. He spoke slowly. 'What are you saying?'

Dee looked along the corridor and lowered his voice. 'I am sure you have heard about the German pretender.' Henry nodded. 'Well, I am tasked with proving that his story is as empty as a hatched egg. I am saving your cousin's throne – just as I did in fifty-eight.' A quizzical raise of the eyebrows. 'Do you recall the mummers?'

Henry made a sharp intake of breath. 'What has it to do

with Catherine? She was only in service to Anne of Cleves for a few months before the divorce.'

'And then she went to Court where she was much trusted. If there was any rumour, she would have heard it.' Dee raised a hand in response to Henry starting to argue. 'And she is one of only three women who can assist right now. The others are dead.' He paused while Henry calmed. 'I understand she is in deep mourning. That is why I ask you to help me in speaking to her... just as I helped you.'

Henry gave a small snarl and nodded. 'When?'

'This afternoon. I understand she is in her London residence.'

The other man nodded again and then looked behind John Dee. 'The same strange maid is with you. Do you not have the lad in tow this time? The one with the same name as my own.'

Margaretta suppressed a small cry. *This is like a knife in my heart.* 'I think you speak of Christopher Careye, sir.'

'That's the one. A fine young man. How goes he?'

'Gone to his maker,' cut in Dee with a small shake of his head and a glance towards Margaretta. 'Just over a year now.'

Henry Carey grunted and mumbled, 'God takes the young and the good.' He turned and walked away, calling back that he will be in the courtyard at twelve of the clock.

John Dee patted Margaretta's arm and pointed down the corridor. 'Come, let us get air and think about our questions for our visits.'

Visits? But we are only going to one person. Or are we?

Good to his word, Henry Carey was in the courtyard talking to Sam about the horses when they emerged at midday. The journey into London was spent with the two men in conversation – the Cygnet, or 'Little Bastard' as Henry called him, the improvement in coinage, the beggars on the streets created by their land being set over for sheep and the wool trade, shortage of trees for firewood. Margaretta held the door and pushed her face out of the window in a vain attempt to stop the sickness in her stomach and hearing the misery of the conversation. As they reached the outskirts of London she held on tighter as the smells of too many people living in close quarters began to assault her nose. Dung, rotting meat, the wares of hawkers, the stench of a dead chicken in a gutter. Henry Carey looked out and growled again. 'These city villains are charged with cleaning the pave and roads in front of their houses and stores. Not one of the fuckers does his job.'

Dee pointed at Margaretta in an attempt to get Carey to curb his cussing, but the other man did not even notice the gesture. Instead, he pushed his head out of the window and shouted at Sam to 'stop driving like a girl skirting a mouse,' and to 'run the wheels over any guttersnipe getting in our way.'

A solemn-faced servant showed the trio to a room at the front of the house. Henry stepped ahead, telling Dee and Margaretta to hold back while he spoke first to his sister. Through the partly open door, they could hear a low conversation. Henry's voice was low, soft, kind.

Love. I feel the affection you have for your sister and also worry. You have never seen her like this. Frightened, yes. You recall fear when she had to flee mad Queen Mary, but this is something you cannot assuage in her. I feel your helplessness.

Carey opened the door. 'Come in. But Catherine is very tired.'

Dee nodded and went forward to bow to the woman who was lying on a long seat by the window that looked out over the Thames. Like her brother she was copper-headed, ivory skinned, long of face. But she did not have his vigour. Any beauty was masked by the tight lines drawing down her mouth and the dark shadows like smudges beneath her eyes. She was like a snuffed candle. She gave a wan smile and a token nod back. 'Doctor Dee. The last I saw of you was at Court when you showed Her Majesty your globes.'

'Indeed, Lady Catherine. The planetary globes fashioned

by my true friend Gerardus Mercator. He is now working on a map of—'

'No dallying, Dee,' growled Henry.

Dee stopped short and turned to Margaretta. 'This is my servant and scribe. She will write and never open her mouth.' He waited for a nod and continued, 'I have only a few questions my lady. But questions which are critical for the safety of your cousin's throne.'

Catherine looked at Margaretta, her face giving away no thought. *But I feel your pain, mistress. It is like a weight in your breast. Hard, heavy and hurting. You wake every morning and for a few seconds wonder where you are and then the terrible sadness hits you like a punch in the gut. I hear a baby wailing. Oh, God, he died in the grip of pain. You begged your God for mercy. It never came. He screamed, then silence and he was gone.* 'You shed tears like me, girl.' The voice trembled.

'I am so sorry for your loss, my lady.'

Catherine gave a watery smile and she looked back to Dee while Margaretta pulled out paper, an ink horn and quill. 'How do I help my cousin, Doctor?'

'I ask you to take your mind back to your time in the household of Anne of Cleves. More accurately, the months after the agreement to divorce.'

Catherine frowned. 'Good Lord, Doctor Dee. I was only eighteen years when Lady Anne arrived. I was with her but five months, though I recall those days as happy indeed.'

'And after the divorce… What was the atmosphere between her and King Henry?'

'Indeed, warm. He was, I think, much surprised and relieved at her rapid agreement.'

'Was there affection?'

There was a sudden bang as Henry Carey hit the desk. 'God's blood, Dee. Stop skirting. Catherine is tiring.' He looked at his sister, worry in his eyes. 'Dee just needs to know if the old king swived the maid of Cleves. Did she drop him a son?'

Catherine closed her eyes and shook her head. 'Brother. When will you learn prettier manners?' She tutted and raised a finger to silence him before looking back at John. 'In truth, Doctor, it was a joy to see her so happy. As if relief had put a light into her heart. Mrs Gylman had improved her English and she was kindly to King Henry, but so was she to Queen Kathryn Howard. And Lady Anne was not a woman of two faces. She would not be so gracious with the queen if she was dallying with the king.'

'Mrs Gylman?'

'The Court illustrator sent to Cleves to prepare Anne in speaking some English. She journeyed back with Anne and then stayed in her household as a tutor.' Catherine made a small smile. 'A good woman but loose-tongued.'

Dee nodded and turned to ensure Margaretta was taking everything down. 'On the subject of loose tongues, you must have heard the unfortunate rumours in late forty-one... of a fair, male child being seen in Lady Anne's arms.'

Catherine Carey suddenly looked bereft. 'She loved the warmth of a helpless little soul in her arms.' She looked away as her lips pursed, trying to hold in a cry. 'Doctor Dee, though I am keeping distance from society, I know the claims of this pretender prince. I will swear on a Bible that I do not believe, nor did I see any sign of Anne of Cleves bearing a Tudor prince. She looked towards Margaretta. 'Have the fair copy of my exact words written, including my oath and I will sign it gladly.' With that she bowed her head and fell into silence.

You are not telling the whole truth, my lady. But you're loyal. There was something said, something believed. And why do you emphasise 'a Tudor prince' and not 'a child'?

Dee rose, bowed and waited for Margaretta to put away the paper and pens, then they all left, Henry Carey making sure the door was close shut before snarling. 'You have everything you need, Dee. Now do not bother my sister again, or, as God is my witness, I will fucking...' He stopped short and bent his head. His voice rose high as if strangled. 'Would that I could take her pain away.' He stood up straight. 'I will tarry here a while and see if she needs any company.'

Dee nodded. 'I will have the statement sent for quiet signing and ask that you witness it.' He turned to Margaretta. 'Add Mrs Gylman to our list.'

Chapter Sixteen

Dee walked down the steps to the carriage and looked up at Sam. 'The Duchess of Suffolk has a residence in the Barbican. Take us there if you please, young sir.'

'Are you taking your friend?' Sam grinned. 'He can clear the streets for us with his cussing.'

'Thank heavens no, Sam. Margaretta's ears will need a washing with any more.' Dee clambered into the seat and settled back.

Margaretta climbed after him. 'Sir Cecil forbade any interview of this lady.'

Dee put on his imperious voice. 'As ever the snake protects his friends. I will seek forgiveness, which is easier found than permission.'

My, how your confidence has grown, Doctor. When Robert Dudley asked you to use your skills to calculate the most auspicious date for our Queen's coronation, your chest puffed up with pride and has never gone down. And as your star rises so does your delight in defying Cecil. 'Yes, Doctor. Who do we say I am?'

'Same as ever. My scribe and bag carrier. Nothing more. You must be invisible.'

Damn you.

The Duchess of Suffolk raised her face from a Bible. Her ivory skin made her look younger than her years but a long nose, small mouth and high arched brows over dark eyes gave her a look of perpetual disdain. She was not amused at her afternoon being disturbed. She was even less impressed when Doctor John Dee ignored her complaint that she was awaiting an invited visitor, kissed her a greeting as if he were familiar and sat himself down. The atmosphere only iced further when he gestured to Margaretta to sit and take notes. The snort of indignation from the Duchess was intentionally loud. She clicked her fingers at an old pug dog under a table. 'Gardiner, heel.' She smiled cynically at Dee who was looking bemused. 'Named after that pariah, Bishop Gardiner, lapdog to Queen Mary. It pleases me to call him to heel.' Then a cold stare. 'I will give you an audience of a few minutes.'

'Good, good,' smiled Dee. 'Then let us get straight to the heart of the matter. I understand you were in the household of Anne of Cleves.'

The response was clipped. 'Formally, yes. But I was also a married woman with my own household.' She sat up. 'Let us be frank, Doctor Dee. You are seeking information linked to this little German sop who has arrived on our shores claiming England's throne.'

'Indeed. I am charged by Sir Cecil to—'

'I know with what you are charged, Doctor.' The voice was more of a bark. 'And I know Cecil... William... said I was not to be annoyed with this foolery.'

My, you are angry, madam. You think of a will. You are in a fight. The doctor poses a threat. If you are dragged into any public scandal, your enemies will use it. You just want us to go. I need to ensure the doctor does not tarry or we will be shown the door forever. 'Bydd yn gyflym. Be quick.'

The Duchess shot a hard look at Margaretta. 'What rogue tongue does this woman speak? Not only do you bring a low servant to my sitting room, but one with a lack of manners too.'

Dee gave a conciliatory smile. 'Forgive her, my lady. She can scribe but her speaking is ignorant. I find it helpful in ensuring secrecy. She cannot repeat any words.'

You arse.

It worked. The Duchess relaxed. 'Very well. All you need to know is that my first husband and I greeted and hosted Anne of Cleves when she arrived from Calais. Days later she was married.' She looked towards the window and her voice softened. 'We all felt the king's disappointment. Poor thing. She was a sweet woman.'

So, beneath that hard exterior you have a warm soul. You liked Anne of Cleves. You recall her with pity.

Dee nodded. 'And her mood when she was cast aside?'

The Duchess frowned. 'Strangely joyous. Within a few months she was wearing the most fashionable of clothes, holding the best of celebrations at her residences of Hever and Chelsea and even dancing at Court. She became beloved of all who met her... including King Henry.'

Dee straightened his back as if preparing for bad news. 'Beloved? Is there any chance...'

The duchess made a harsh, cynical laugh. 'Henry had already accused Anne of being so foul to him that his manhood would not respond.'

'So can you attest and swear that he did not sire a son with Anne of Cleves.'

The Duchess tutted. 'I can attest I believe it to be impossible, Doctor. But I cannot swear it. After the divorce, most of her ladies, including me, were moved to the household of the new queen. Only a few had any sight into the house of Anne of Cleves.'

Dee nodded. 'I see.'

You are not listening. She has said "most of the ladies", "only a few". '*Pwy welodd nhw?* Who saw them?'

Dee jolted and made pretence of turning and shushing Margaretta as if she were an irritating fool. Then he turned back with that smile. 'So, which few ladies did have sight my lady?'

'Well, the German ladies who were not sent back after the marriage, and a few German servants. Mrs Gylman stayed close to assist with language… and then, of course, that meddler, Margaret Douglas.'

'And why did Margaret Douglas stay close?'

'Hah, Doctor. If you knew Margaret you would not have to ask. She saw advantage. Anne's reputation with the king was rising and so it was good to hold her coat tails. And Anne, though raised in a Protestant country, had kept the Catholic faith.' She gave another snort. 'Of course, Margaret Douglas would take her under her wing.'

'Yet you were the closer friend, my lady. Cecil says you were bequeathed a ring.'

'Our close friendship developed in later years.' She frowned and made a small shake of her head. 'I was sad not to have that ring.'

Dee looked quizzical. 'Why did you not?'

The woman raised her brow. 'It was lost when Anne's assets were collected. Hah. Probably lost into someone's pocket.' Dee went to ask another question but was stayed by a raise of the Duchess' hand.

'Enough questions, Doctor Dee. All I can say is that Anne did not birth a Tudor prince. But, if you want absolute testimony that Anne of Cleves was a maid, then you need to speak with Margaret Douglas as she was closer.' The duchess stood and pointed to the door. 'I thank you to give me time to prepare for invited guests.' The emphasis on 'invited' was like acid.

Dee rose, bowed and thanked the woman for her time. He gained a terse agreement to sign the notes of their meeting and then turned to shoo Margaretta towards the door. By the time they passed through, the Duchess of Suffolk had turned her back.

Back in the carriage, Margaretta was sullen, though Dee showed no sign of noticing. Having asked Sam to take them to the house of Robert Dudley, he was surveying her notes, grunting at each line.

Seven years I have tolerated your poor manners. Seven years when I had to keep quiet for fear of losing protection for my family. But Mam is gone and it seems Huw is being taken from me. It is only me. What can I lose? 'Do not ever treat me like a dog who carries your bag again.'

Dee did not look up, but raised a finger towards her as he kept reading in a silent warning to mind her place.

'And do not treat me like a child.'

Silence. Another wag of the finger.

'You are a cruel master.'

This was the trigger. Dee slammed down the papers and raised angry eyes. 'Watch your tongue, girl. I started my learning at seven years old. At fourteen I was at Cambridge studying every hour of the day but for four hours sleep and my prayers. I have been to the great learning houses of Europe and conversed with the most brilliant of minds. I understand the Earth, the stars, the elements and the body.' He jabbed a finger at her. 'When I found you, you were a seventeen-year-old washerwoman with nothing but the ability to feel and to hear the unsaid. Both skills raw and un-honed. Do not think you are my equal in seven short years. You are an apprentice. Nothing more.' He picked up the papers and went back to his reading.

Margaretta swallowed hard and shut her eyes to try to stop the tears streaming. It did not work and she looked out of the carriage window to hide her face.

Then softer words. 'We will do your horoscope later. Good learning for you. I think you might find Mars transiting the seventh house.'

She pulled her face away from the window. 'Meaning what?'

'That you will be in strife and argue over contracts—'

'But, I—'

He raised the finger once again, though without the angry jabbing. 'The planets rule our minds and bodies, Margaretta. The quicker you accept that the better you will manage your humours.'

'Maybe my humours are more affected by other people than by the moon or Mercury, Doctor.' She bent her head and tried to stem the tears again.

He patted her knee. 'Your sister? Hmmm. She is ruled by celestial movements too, my dear. Our power is understanding them.' He sat up straight as the carriage began to slow. 'Here we are. Dry those tears. We do not want Robert thinking I am a harsh master. I was once his tutor, you know. Yes, I was trusted with the young minds of the greatest families in England. The Dudleys, the Herberts, even sent learnings to King Edward…' His voice trailed off as he climbed out and walked to the steps.

And what planets make the muddle that is you?

Margaretta jumped down after him and looked up at Sam whose smile slid into a frown. 'Has he made you cry? I'll speak my mind if—'

'No, Sam. My own worries make me tender these days. My sister…'

Sam raised his eyes to heaven and sighed. 'Is she still a sow in silk?'

'She is indeed. And trying to take Huw away.' Margaretta looked down as the tears started again.

Sam jumped down from his seat and took her shoulders. 'She is a bizzem, true, Missy. Why don't you come and see Lottie and the family? We will cheer you.'

Oh, Sam. You are a good man. I wish I could say yes, but every time I see you with Lottie I think of Christopher and all we could have had together. To walk into what I will never have – love and a family – is more than I can bear. But I will lie to save your feelings. 'Thank you, Sam. I will certainly try to visit when this investigation is at an end. It will cheer me to see you all so happy.' She smiled, wiped her tears and made her way up the steps.

Chapter Seventeen

Robert Dudley was staring out of a window, rapping his fingers against the glass as if drumming his frustration. The room, filled with signs of wealth – tapestries, plate, fine crystal from the continent – was tense with his mood. He spoke over his shoulder as they entered. 'I hope you bring good news, Doctor.' He looked towards the door and walked across to close it shut. 'We do not want those Spanish rabbit ears listening to our talking.'

'The Bishop is here again?'

Dudley nodded, his face clouding further. 'He has been given leave to use this house as a base. He returned from Court but an hour ago.' He sighed. 'My own fault I suppose. I offered this when I thought it good to keep Philip of Spain close and friendly to Court.'

Oh, there is more to this. You are recalling secret conversations. Plotting. A hint of guilt. What did you agree with the bishop? And why do you so resent him now? Something to tell the doctor later.

Dee sat himself down and poured a glass of deep red wine without being invited. Then filled another for Dudley. 'We are making progress, Robert. So far, we have a laundress reporting the physical impossibility of a Tudor birth in 1541 and two high-ladies of Court willing to testify that they are sure there was no birthing of a Tudor prince.' He sat back, looking self-satisfied. 'I find ignoring the instructions of Cecil is getting us further and faster. Though he is useful in organising his spies to give assistance. We will have the log book of Captain Neerman translated from Dutch. And, hopefully, his last utterances.'

Robert began to pace. 'Good work, Doctor. But with Court the midden of gossip and fear that it is, we need absolute proof. They are already muttering that there is no accession after Elizabeth. What are your plans?'

'We step in closer to the household of Lady Anne. I will next speak with Lady Margaret Douglas and request that Cecil finds Lady Anne's English tutor – a Mistress Gylman. I believe they will corroborate the story that Anne remained a maid.' He took a deep gulp of wine. 'Then we confront this Cygnet Prince with the impossibility of his claims.'

Robert smiled and his shoulders relaxed. 'You do well, sir. We will soon be back on our path.'

You think of marriage. Does your ambition have any bounds, Master Dudley? Damn, you have seen the surprise on my face. You are looking straight at me, your face imperious. I look down. It works. To you I am nothing but a body to survey. But I feel you, Dudley, and you hide something. You fear it being known.

Dudley poured more wine and started to raise it in salute to his old tutor, when there was a hammering at the door and a green-liveried messenger barged in.

Dudley reacted. 'Damn it, sirrah. What do you mean by—'

'Apologies, master. But I seek Doctor Dee and Sir Cecil said to come here if he was not at his abode.' The servant turned to Dee and handed over a wax-sealed message. 'You must attend Court in haste, sir.'

Dee stood, took the package and broke it open. He read briefly and looked up, his face taut with shock. 'Beatrice ap Rhys lies dying. They suspect poison.'

Chapter Eighteen

The horses were sweating as they clattered into the courtyard of Hampton Court. Dudley had insisted they ride instead of using Sam's carriage. Cecil was waiting, his face drawn. He pointed to an archway. 'This way.'

The room was hot and dank. The smell of sweat and a full chamber pot filled the air. A young girl was standing by a trestle bed, mopping the glistening brow of old Beatrice. She turned to Cecil. 'Still no words from her, sir. And her breathing worsens.'

Dee stepped forward, pushing Cecil and Dudley aside. 'Tell me every detail. What happened?'

'Beatie went to her room. Next we knew, she came out raving and grabbing at her throat. She was pointing at something. Sissy got her to the piss-pot but then down she went... like a sack of stones. Twitching she was and kicking. Terrible to see, sir.'

'Did she say anything?'

'Not that we could understand. It was in another tongue.'

She was speaking in our tongue. 'What did it sound like, miss?'

'Anngaldee,' came a voice from the corner. They turned to see another laundry girl in the shadows. 'I heard her in her room. First a little cry as if happy. Then silence. Then she kept screaming, "anngaldee", over and over. Still screaming it when she ran out. Pointing at someone not there.'

Margaretta nodded and looked to Dee. 'Black Angel.'

Cecil groaned and nodded at the girls. 'Leave us and take that stinking chamber pot out of here. Say nothing of this and tell the other maids to keep silent or you are all out on the streets.' He waited for them to scuttle out and shut the door before he stepped over to stand by Dee. 'We have a poisoner within, don't we?'

Dee nodded. 'The same pattern as the captain of *The Mariella*. The cabin boy spoke of a black angel. First raving, then collapse. Same as the dogs.' He turned to look at Dudley. 'Who feeds the royal dogs?'

Dudley shook his head. 'They roam the grounds. People are always giving them titbits. I have told Elizabeth…'

'So that does not help us,' replied Cecil. He nodded at Beatrice. 'We need her to live and tell us who it is.'

Dee nodded. 'I do not have huge knowledge of poisoning. Does the Queen's physician have skill?'

'He may, but he also has a mouth like a holed bucket.'

Margaretta stepped forward. 'Clarissa. The herb woman of Southwark. She knows everything – causes and cures.'

Dee turned quickly. 'Yes. And keeps a closed mouth.' He looked back to Cecil. 'Get a trusted servant here. When… if she revives at all, give her warm milk to calm the stomach. We will get the herb woman to bring a remedy.' He turned to the door. 'But first we go to her rooms to seek clues.'

They stepped across the small yard to Beatrice's quarters. Inside it was neat and simple – a trestle bed, a desk, a coffer for her clothes and a painting of a young man on the wall. *That must be David Owens. A handsome boy indeed.* On the coffer was a plate with sugared plums, two sweet cakes and crumbs.

Dee snatched the plate and sniffed the red shiny fruits. 'Crumbs suggest one cake was eaten. I think these are poisoned. They are exactly like those on *The Mariella*.'

Dudley was agitated. 'I will interrogate every person in this place.' He banged his hand on the table. 'Damn them to hell.'

'Curb your shouting, Master Robert,' snapped Cecil. He pointed to the door. 'We must suppress this evidence, not scream about it.' For a few moments the men stared at each other in fury, until Dudley looked away muttering about wanting only to protect Elizabeth.

Dee ignored the tension and picked up a kerchief into which he scooped the cakes. The corners tied, he handed it to Margaretta. 'Take this to the herb woman. She may be able to discern the poison within and bring the better remedy.' He spoke to Dudley. 'Find your best horse and a trusted servant to clear the way. Also, another horse to bring the woman. We need to make haste if there is any chance to save the launderess and get our evidence.'

Cecil was staring at the floor. 'Someone has ears in my office.'

Chapter Nineteen

'Spot. You are turning into a fine young man.' Margaretta held out her hands as the boy grinned and stepped forward. 'And hardly a sign of your limp.'

'Mother has healed me well, Miss Margaretta.' He took her arm and planted the customary kiss of friendship on her lips. 'We have not seen you in months. What brings you... just a visit, I hope. Mother will be—'

'No, Spot.' Margaretta noticed the slight frown. 'Forgive me, *Simon*. I must not use that old name you used when a street child. I come in urgency for your mother's help. A great secret. Is she here?'

The boy nodded. 'She is in the herb garden. We are trying to grow a new plant from the Eastern lands. It needs much care.' He moved quickly to the back of the shop where he called into the dark corridor leading to the back of the house.

Seconds later, Clarissa emerged, wiping her hands on a linen apron over a plain dress. She was the same as ever. Beautiful chestnut skin, black hair and eyes of amber. There was no sign of the passing years. Her face brightened on seeing Margaretta. 'A good day it is the day you come through our door.' She put her arm around Simon's shoulders. 'Do you see how my boy grows?'

'I do. Forgive me, but I have no time for conversation, Clarissa. I... we... need your urgent help.' Margaretta looked to the door where the royal servant stood outside. 'It is something to be kept quiet.'

Clarissa nodded and pointed to the door at the rear of the shop. 'Come into the living quarters.' Once inside she pulled a curtain across and lit a taper candle. 'Is it your sister again?'

'No. A situation at Court. Poisoning. Doctor Dee is doing an investigation and a woman who gave evidence became gravely ill this morning. A man went the same way a few days ago on a ship. He died.' Margaretta pulled the wrap of cakes. 'These were given to her and also to the ship's captain.'

Clarissa bent over, sniffed, then broke a cake in half as she picked out a sliver of leaf. 'Symptoms?'

'First raving. Madness. Then—'

Clarissa raised a hand. 'Did they appear to see something?'

'Yes. Then agony in the belly and flux from mouth and...'

Clarissa nodded and looked her in the eye. 'Then falling down with the limbs twitching?'

'We know that of the woman, yes. The man fell in the Thames.'

Clarissa held the cakes before Simon's nose. 'A lesson for you. Tell me what you smell.'

The boy bent, sniffed, frowned. 'Like a flower. Maybe a field flower for the smell is strong.' He straightened. 'So, it comes from a green plant, not a mushroom or grain.' He looked closely. 'Specks of green. A leaf.'

'Good. Now move to the injuries.'

'Bad humours affecting the stomach and moving first to mind then limbs. So, it is carried through the water of the body and not the phlegm. No gasping, but flux. So not a poison of the lungs. The body will die by the inner guts dying.'

'Good. Very good.' Clarissa seemed to grow with pride. 'You learn well, my son. Can you guess the poison?'

'Henbane?'

'Good thinking. But the flux is the difference.' Clarissa turned to Margaretta. 'This is herba belladonna. So named by Andrea Matthioli in his great works of living plants. The evillest of poison. I expect she is sleeping and cannot be woken now?'

'Yes.' Margaretta said as she wiped away tears. 'I think it is my fault. I heard someone when we spoke. I should have listened to my feelings. I—'

'No time for regrets, my friend. We need to do our best.' Clarissa turned to Simon. 'Get the charcoal and the powder of marshmallow. Pack it in paper while I get my cloak.'

Within minutes, two women were racing their horses through the streets of London with the servant shouting for clear passage ahead of them. Margaretta prayed.

God get us there in time. Save that old woman and my soul for not protecting her.

Chapter Twenty

'Go to the kitchens and bring me a funnel and a length of calf gut... cleaned out.'

The laundry girl looked aghast at Clarissa. 'Gut?'

Those amber eyes burned. 'Do you want to save Goodwife Beatrice?'

The girl ran and came back with a bowl of slithering gut. Clarissa picked it up, lay it along Beatrice's chest and cut a length with a sharp knife from her belt. 'Now boiled water. I need a quart in a clean jug. And make sure you have none of your lye or soap in it. Then go to the gardens and bring me a thin sapling about the length of your arm – it needs to be firm but bendable.' The girl ran again.

'What are we going to do?' asked Margaretta, her voice betraying anxiety.

'Flush out the evil,' answered Clarissa as she opened the package wrapped by Simon. She smiled. 'Ah, my boy is going to be a good physician. She picked up a dried root. 'He also thought of ginger which will calm her stomach and quell the sickness if she survives.' She turned back to Beatrice. 'We need to put pillows under her shoulders so that her head falls back. She is big. Can you lift her?' With great effort, they pulled the old woman up and eased a well stuffed bolster under her shoulders. Immediately the head fell back and Beatrice started snoring. Hearing footsteps, Clarissa went to the door and took the jug and water from the girl, then told her to go back to the laundry as this was 'not for a tickle-stomached child'. She came back to the bed. 'You need to hold her head so that her chin is in line with her chest. I need a clear run down her throat. She might fight.' She looked hard at Margaretta. 'Fight back. Her life depends on it.'

Margaretta took a deep breath and waited while Clarissa poured the contents of one paper into the water, tested the temperature with her finger. A strong smell of charcoal wafted around the room. Then she took the cane and pushed it down the gut making a loose knot at the end. She put the funnel by the bed and nodded. 'We are ready. Pull her head back and keep it still.'

Margaretta almost cried out as Clarissa slowly, determinedly pushed the gut-covered sapling into Beatrice's mouth and down her throat. Then the moaning started and the old woman tried to struggle through her stupor. Gargled screams were useless as Margaretta held her head tight, pulling back to keep the chin in line and Clarissa pressed on, down and down. Then she stopped and pressed on the top of the belly. 'Hold tight. There will be a sudden shove as I break the gut at the end. She hit the wood and a terrible moan came from Beatrice. In seconds, the sapling was whipped out and the other end of the gut slipped over the base of the funnel. Holding it high, Clarissa poured a steady stream of black liquid into Beatrice's stomach. Every few seconds she would press on her belly and rub in small circles. The moaning had moved to pitiful squeals but there was no stopping until the jug was empty. Clarissa moved fast. Rubbing Beatrice's belly in small circles and murmuring prayers. 'You need to be ready. The body will expel this mixture in a few minutes. As soon as she heaves, you need to grab that gut and pull it out fast.'

'Oh, God. I—'

'No time for being weak,' snapped Clarissa.

Minutes passed then they felt Beatrice's chest tense and the mouth opened wide.

'Pull the gut now. Fast.'

Margaretta grabbed the vile tube and yanked. At first it felt stuck, then another pull and it slithered upwards into her hands. Clarissa grabbed the old woman's arm and heaved her sideways, only just missing the stream of black water which spewed out onto the floor. Beatrice heaved three times and then whimpered. But her eyes half-opened. Clarissa gently rolled her back and signalled to Margaretta to help remove the pillow. As it was pulled from under the patient, they heard a whispered, '*Diolch i Ddyw.* Thanks to God.'

'The next phase will be a fever while the body burns out the poison. We will need cool water for her brow and more boiled and cooled to warm for the root of marshmallow. Leave the door open. The stench in here is terrible.'

Margaretta fetched the water and in silence helped the herb woman mix the root and fill a beaker. They mopped her brow and lifted her head to encourage little sips of the drink. Clarissa kept her eyes on the flushed face. 'I am sorry I was hard on you, Margaretta. I was frightened.'

Margaretta made a small smile. 'So was I. Will she live?'

Clarissa patted Beatrice's belly. 'These pounds of flesh will have protected the body and we kept the charcoal inside for a good time. If we can nourish her with the marshmallow and sooth her inside, she has a chance. Though recovery will take weeks.'

'Doctor John is bound to ask me when she might speak.'

'Tell your good doctor he must await until the morrow at least… and that's only if she lives.' Clarissa looked around. 'And we need to clear out these bad humours. The belladonna in her stomach is now on the floor. Can you get buckets of hot water and lime? We will wash the floor and then our shoes.'

As they rose, there was a moan from Beatrice and she opened her eyes. '*Clogyn du, dwylo du, wyneb du,*' came a hoarse whisper.

'Black cloak, black hands, black face,' whispered Margaretta. 'And I am in trouble.'

Chapter Twenty-One

'What the hell do you mean? You did not think?' Dee stamped up and down the tapestried room, every footstep on the polished wooden floor echoing in the high ceiling. 'Your fucking lack of thought might have cost my whole reputation.' He turned on his apprentice. 'I might have the killer in shackles by now.'

'It was only when Beatrice mentioned a black cloak that I put it all together – the person in the garden, the person on the ship, the person in the corridor who may have heard Beatrice again and then... the fact she said "black cloak".' Margaretta lowered her head. 'I did not see the significance.'

Dee narrowed his eyes. 'Are you telling me you did not feel anything in their presence?'

Oh, God. I am caught. Do I lie? No. You always know. 'A strange mix – joy, suspicion, anger, urgency.' She shrugged. 'Nothing that made sense.'

Dee smacked his hand on his brow in a show of incredulity. 'Joy at hearing something, suspicion of who is speaking, anger at their protection of the Queen and urgency to act on the information – whether that is passing information or killing. And which part of that makes "no sense"?' His voice had moved to sneering.

'I am sorry.'

'You might well have been seeing the poisoner. Or maybe

it is their servant. Whichever it was, we have lost our chances to know.' Dee wagged a hand at the door. 'Ask the stables if you can borrow a horse and go home. I will rest here and think. I do not want to see you. See if you can do better being a maid and keeping our landlord happy.' Then, as she was leaving the room, 'And return in the morning – early. With a better head on your shoulders and hopefully weakened Mercury in your seventh house.' And with that, Dee turned his back on her.

In St Dunstan's the dusk was settling and shadows lengthened on walls. The streets were clearing of hawkers and traders and behind them the usual wake of detritus and mess. Even worse, the pungent smell of piss from corners where men had sought quick relief rather than move to the tavern middens. Margaretta opened the back door. It was eerily quiet. The only tiny sound was a mew from Cadi the cat who uncurled and stretched before padding over for a ruffle of her head.

You poor thing. You miss Mam, don't you? You miss the love you had and the arms around you. As do I. But you are lucky, cat. You had it all your life. I lost it for years, though I thank you for softening her. Then there was Clarissa, who saved the doctor's life and my sanity by telling Mam to find her soul. 'Where is Huw, Cadi? Hmmmm? Where is he? Here – a titbit of cheese for you. Where is Huw?'

She opened the door to the main house. Silence. '*Huw, ble wyt ti?* Huw, where are you?' She went out into the yard and called again. Nothing. As she walked up the stairs to the doctor's office her stomach began to tighten. Surely, she was being foolish. He must be here. She looked at the closed door of Katherine Constable's sitting room. She would be asleep in her cups, but she might know.

There was no point in knocking, the snoring was loud enough to frighten the mice. 'Mistress Constable.' Louder. 'Mistress Constable.'

A snort and Katherine opened bleary eyes. 'What is wrong? Who is shouting?'

'I cannot find Huw, mistress. Have you seen him?'

The other woman heaved herself upright and made a shaky grab for the dregs in the glass of Malmsey. 'Susan came. He starts with Angus tomorrow.'

'What? You let them take him?'

Katherine frowned. 'Do not raise your voice at me, girl. He is being given an advantage in life.'

'And when was slavery an advantage, mistress?'

Katherine Constable reddened in fury. 'How dare you question my intention. Huw is like my—'

'Brother. Yes, mistress. You have said before. But would you have sent your little brother into bondage?'

'Get out.'

Oh, God. My world is falling apart. Mam. Where are you? I'm frightened.

Chapter Twenty-Two

The wide-eyed maid called through the crack in the door. 'Who is it? Why the hammering?'

'It is me, Grace. Margaretta. Here to see my... my vile sister.'

The door opened and Grace stepped back. 'I have never seen you so angry, Miss Margaretta. Your sister is eating with Master Angus.'

'Then let me give them indigestion.'

Margaretta strode along the corridor. The walls had paintings now. A newly crafted one of the Queen stood proud above the foot of the stairs. Also dotting the walls were a good mirror and a large round plate of silver, just for display. Margaretta did not care for their silly shows of success. They were going to hear the sharp of her tongue. She did not knock. 'Where is Huw? What have you done with my brother?'

Two startled, then angry, faces turned to her and stared through the light of candles. Angus was mid-chew and spat out his food. 'What the hell are you doing, walking in here to—'

'—to ask what the hell you are doing taking my brother.'

He smirked. Then the usual move of his eyes to her breasts. 'My, my, little sister. You are certainly wide of the mark.' He slid a smile across his face and put another sliver of meat on his tongue, then chewed slowly, staring at her as if looking at a Court fool. 'Dog-boy was glad to come to us.' He looked at his wife. 'Was he not, Susan?'

'Yes.'

'So where is he? If he is so wanted, why is he not sitting eating with you as he sits and eats with me?'

Susan made a spiteful, tinkly little laugh as Angus raised his brow in incredulity and sneered, 'We pay him, we feed him, we give him a roof. He is lucky. He will follow me in the gentleman's wine trade.' He made a hollow laugh. 'There is no good moral or money in log-chopping, dear.'

Damn your soul, Angus McFadden. You see weakness in my anger. Well, I will change my mood. For the one thing you cannot manage is wit. And you cannot manage a cold voice. You are too used to the voices of doxies giving their false praises for your money. You are thinking of papers. What papers?

'It takes a gentleman to create another, Angus. It takes a good merchant to teach trade. And it takes an honest soul to teach morals. So, it seems you have bonded my brother into low-living, loss of money and lewd practice... following you.'

Susan gave a shriek and stood, clattering her chair back into the wall. 'How dare you speak to Angus so.' She was shaking. Then her hand went to her mouth.

Ah. You recall the pox he brought upon you. 'Does your heart feel anything for Huw, sister?' Margaretta made a low chuckle. 'A foolish question. You have no heart.' She dropped her voice and asked low and cold. 'Where... is... Huw? And why do you want him?'

Angus retorted in like voice. 'He is where he should be. Sleeping in The Vintry ready to start his work in the morning.' Susan looked at him, her eyes betraying unease.

Margaretta did not turn to her brother-in-law but kept a steady stare at her sister. 'You put your own flesh and blood to sleep in a shed?' She pursed her mouth and blew out a long breath. 'Your own brother. The little boy who shared your family home. The equal child of Mam and Dada. Your kin... in a shed.' *When I said 'home' you gulped.* She pointed at Susan, her finger close to her face making the other woman blink rapidly. '*Melltith arnat ti.* A curse on you.'

Susan sneered. 'I know nothing of your low tongue.'

'Yes, you do, Susan. You know exactly what I said. I used to say it daily to you as a child. You were vile then as you are now.' She ignored Angus beginning to bluster his objection and raised her voice. 'The difference is, Susan, that then I only said the words of an angry child. This time I use the power of a woman who has learned from England's great conjuror.'

Susan grabbed the table as her eyes widened in alarm. 'What do you mean? What will happen?'

'Your spleen will turn from outward to inward and every cruel thing you have ever done will come back to flay your life with double force.'

'When? What will happen?' Susan's voice was high with panic, cutting through Angus bellowing and banging the table.

Margaretta gave a slow, malign smile. 'Start praying, sister.'

The horse jittered as it picked up on Margaretta's fury. She patted its neck and calmed her voice to soothing. It was not the animal's fault that Susan was hell-sent. Dark was falling and soon the night watchmen would be out and asking questions about a young woman out alone. 'Time to go home. Though the way things are going, it is not my home for long.' *Why do they want Huw? Susan thinks of home. But that home is no more.*

Chapter Twenty-Three

It was a fresh morning with a chill breeze coming up the Thames. Wherries were already making good money and swans pecking at the green river edge. It would be a pretty scene if not for the stinking filth that lapped the shore line. Across the water Margaretta could hear men hailing fares and calling greetings to each other. She sat under the apple tree on the river bank, waiting for Sam in his wherry. She stared at the grass and rocked as the thoughts raced around her mind. *Damn, you. Damn, you. Damn, you. How could you do that? And why?*

'A penny for them.'

Margaretta jumped and looked up to see Sam, holding his oars aloft and grinning at her. 'For what?'

The harshness of her voice wiped the smile from his face. 'Your thoughts, Missy. But from the look on your face and the tart of your tongue, I think I'll keep my money.'

She sighed. 'I'm sorry, Sam. The day weighs heavy on me.'

'Well, jump in and I'll take you to see Lottie. She always lightens your soul. She would make a mad dog wag its tail.'

Oh, the love in your voice when you talk of her. It kills me. I wish, I wish I could forget Christopher Careye... and you. 'Your love of your wife makes my day brighter already, Sam. But I have orders to return to the Doctor this morning.' *I will force a smile.* 'I waited to say we will not need you today.

They loaned me a horse yesterday and I have to take the old nag back. Cecil will provide other transport.'

Sam touched his cap. 'I thank you for telling me, Missy. If I'm not on my retainer I'll spend the day in the building yard and stay close to my Lottie. She felt more quickening this morning.'

'You do that, Sam.' *I feel a break in my heart. If Christopher had remained mine, maybe I would have a little one of my own.*

Margaretta watched as he disappeared into the multitude of wherries and swans on the filthy water. She blinked away tears, straightened her skirts and turned back to the house.

'Is this the residence of Goodwife Constable?' The man was at the back door, sitting on a half barrel.

'It is. Why?'

'I bring this.' He stood and pointed at the barrel, but his eyes were appraising Margaretta. 'He didn't say the maid would be so comely. You walking out with a boy?'

'Who didn't say? Where is this from?'

'Master Angus McFadden, gentleman vintner,' said the lad, evidently repeating the words as he had been taught to say them, for they did not flow from his tongue. 'Told me to bring it here and the same every other Monday morning.'

'What for?'

The lad shrugged so Margaretta pushed him aside and surveyed the oak of the cask. On the side was branded the words *Malmsey. Crete*. She straightened with a gasp. 'Payment. Mistress Constable is paid in barrels.'

'Set your pretty self aside and I'll carry it in for you.' The lad winked and made a big display of heaving the barrel onto his shoulder with one movement and then walked into the kitchen. 'Where do you want it? I'll be a good man and tap it for you.'

I bet flirting will open your mouth. 'So, strong man, do you work for the gentleman vintner?'

He sat himself down, leaning back, thumbs crooked into his belt and fingers pointing direct to his manhood. He glanced down to encourage her to look. 'I do, pretty miss. I plan to be a yard manager by next summer. The one he has is too old to heave the barrel. Not strong like me.'

'Who else works there?'

'Just the barrel boys... new one started yesterday.'

The lad gave a cruel chuckle. 'We're to call him "dog-boy". A strange one. Not able to duck the barrel. Gave him a real bash on the nut this morning we did.' He was laughing loudly now.

'What do you mean?' *I need to smile so you keep talking.*

'We do it with all the new ones. Drop an empty barrel from the top of the stack and see if they can catch it. Went down like a sack of turnips he did. Then howling like a pup and slapping his own head. The master gave him a good kicking 'til he shut his muzzle.' The sniggering continued. 'Then he had another hiding later.'

I must keep calm and stop the scream inside. 'What was that for?'

The lad shrugged. 'Something about a paper. Don't know.' He stood to leave. 'I have to go, pretty miss. When shall we go walking?'

Margaretta showed him to the door and clenched her teeth when two dirty hands clasped her waist and he made another demand to take her walking. 'If I say yes, will you give your master a message from me?'

'I will do.'

'You must repeat it exactly as I give it. Do you promise?'

'I do.' Then a yell as the edge of Margaretta's wooden shoe slammed into his shin. She shut the door on the lad as he hopped into the street shouting that she was 'a fucking mad bitch'. Along the street the beggar man laughed.

The Hampton Court servant told her that she was to go straight to Doctor Dee in Cecil's office. On entry she bobbed a curtsy to the men and asked after Beatrice.

Dee spoke. All his anger of yesterday quite gone. This was usual. His moods came and went like clouds on a windy day. 'She lives and is speaking, but it is garbled. My cousin, Blanche ap Harri is with her. Go and take any notes. Capture all she says.' Dee held out a blank parchment and nodded to the quill and ink horn on Cecil's desk. 'I have these ready for you. Make haste to Beatrice's room.'

'And say nothing on your way nor answer questions,' snapped Cecil. 'These corridors are already humming like a nest of fearful flies.'

Margaretta nodded, picked up her tools and left.

The room smelled of sweat and sickness. Blanche was sitting on a chair by the bed, one hand on Beatrice's arm, the other holding a nosegay to her face. She turned to greet Margaretta in their mother tongue. 'Good morning, Margaretta. The herb woman was with her all night. Left only an hour ago. Said she was through the fever and all we can do now is wait.' She patted the old woman's arm. 'She cried out for David.'

'I think she speaks of her nephew.'

'Ah. We should tell him, but I cannot risk gossip.'

'He is a young lawyer at Lincoln's Inn. I think safe.'

Blanche nodded. 'I will send word.'

I feel a softness in you Blanche, like a mother or sister looking upon a loved one. But also fear. If poison has entered the palace, then your greatest love – Elizabeth – is in danger. You are like a cat ready to pounce on any danger to her kittens.

Beatrice began to stir and the eyelids flickered. Then a whimper. Blanche leaned forward and spoke soft words in Welsh. 'Lie quiet, Beatrice. You are in safe hands. Margaretta is here.'

The eyes opened, rheumy and red as one hand raised a little off the bed to beckon. *'Tyrd ata' i.* Come to me.' Margaretta knelt and put her face close to the old woman refusing to turn from the bitterness of her breath. The words came slowly. 'Black angel.'

Margaretta squeezed Beatrice's hand. 'Did you see the person's face?'

But Beatrice only groaned and shook her head. 'Just black wool, a hood.'

'That suggests a servant,' said Blanche over Margaretta's shoulder. 'Elizabeth expects her gentlefolk to wear nothing less than silk and velvet.'

Beatrice made a sudden intake of breath. 'Black hands.'

Margaretta looked to Blanche who creased her brow and shrugged.

Margaretta persisted. 'Did they speak?'

'No. Just set down the platter.' Her head lolled sideways as her breath deepened.

Blanche touched Margaretta's shoulder. 'Leave her to sleep. We will learn no more.'

Both women rose to their feet and pulled the blankets closer around Beatrice before leaving the room and breathing in the sweeter air outside. Blanche whispered. 'This way. Quiet until I speak.' They walked along the path and through the drying grounds to a seat below an apple tree. 'Speak only in our tongue and low. Tell me everything John Dee has found in connection to this Cygnet Prince.'

Margaretta relayed all she knew – the Cygnet Prince, his claims, the assertions of Catherine Carey and the Duchess of Suffolk. The pattern of the poisonings, first the dog and then the captain and Beatrice, both linked to a figure in black who brought apple cakes – maybe the same figure seen by Margaretta on this very green and in the palace corridor.

'And what did you feel about this figure?' demanded Blanche.

'I do not understand—'

'Don't you hold back from me, girl,' was the sharp rebuke. 'We spoke of this at Hatfield seven years ago. You have the powers of the druids in your veins. I know you feel what others do not see or hear. You feel thoughts.'

Damn. I am commanded to keep this secret. Yet I trust you. If I lie, you will know. If I tell truth, I disobey.

Blanche winked. 'I suggest you disobey.'

Oh, my God. We are not too different you and I. I will trust. 'I feel anger, satisfaction, badness. Doctor Dee says the figure is reacting to what they hear. He also says they are maybe someone who wants the Cygnet Prince on the throne. Or the servant of such a person. Do you know who at Court has such thoughts, mistress?'

'Hah. Such thoughts are held by anyone who fears Master Two-Eyes Dudley becoming their king. And if they like to raise the host at the end of a sermon then their thoughts will be all the more wicked.' Her voice was hard, bitter.

'Why does Her Majesty call Master Dudley Two-Eyes?'

Blanche gave a small, despairing shake of her head. 'Elizabeth's pet name for him due to his insistence that he has only ever had two eyes for her.'

'But he was married to…'

'Poor Amy. May God give her peace in heaven.' Another small shake of the head. 'Cecil described it as a carnal match, so there was once love. But love died in the fire that is Elizabeth.'

'So might he be king one day?'

'No,' snapped the other woman. 'He is the offspring of traitors – who would have ripped the throne from Elizabeth's destiny. Only for the foolery of Kat Astley was he allowed such dreams.'

'Kat Astley again?'

'Indeed. Yet again, she has encouraged the flirtation of an empty-headed rogue to fulfil her own silly romantic dreams.' A sharp sniff. 'Though I suppose when married to John Astley, any man is interesting. He speaks of nothing but fetlocks, saddles and endless lists.' Blanche turned a hard eye on Margaretta. 'You make sure John Dee keeps everything away from Kat. She twitters louder than a sparrow. And she is desperate to get back in favour so will only meddle.'

'She is in trouble again?'

A nod. 'Took it upon herself to write to the Chancellor of Sweden to encourage the marriage negotiations between Elizabeth and their King Erik.' Blanche made a brittle laugh. 'Just like the Seymour Affair, when she realised her foolish encouragement has caused chaos, she swings like a pendulum in a falling clock and creates even more.' She looked into Margaretta's eyes. 'You have kept your promise, haven't you? The one you made to me at Hatfield?'

Margaretta nodded. 'I have, and I always will. You really do not like Kat, do you?'

'Kat Astley is small of stature and even smaller of mind. Did I ever tell you about the handkerchiefs?'

Margaretta shook her head.

'Elizabeth was young. I embroidered her a linen handkerchief for her Christmas present – her name surrounded by primroses as she loved them so very much. I called it *"cwtch sgwâr"* – a square embrace.' She bit her lip. 'I made the mistake of showing my work to Kat and that same day she commissioned the seamstress to embroider six in colours brighter than mine.'

Oh, I feel your pain. Brought to be the mother to baby Elizabeth by your aunt, Lady Troy, I think you fell in love with that little girl. Then Kat took your place. She pushed you aside and away from the child you just wanted to hold. Every day you sit to the side as she is called Mama Kat, as she is forgiven her foolery, as she creates chaos and you have to bring back the calm. But no-one notices that you have the deeper love. You are just old Blanche. You have much power. All you want is the love of a child.

'Though your handkerchief was embroidered with love. I think it the better gift.' Margaretta patted the other woman's arm and had a wan smile in return. Blanche reached out and took her hand, turning it palm up. She traced a line across.

'This is your soul line, Margaretta. See how deep it runs?' She showed her own hand. 'Same as mine.'

Then Blanche sat up straight to break the spell. 'It will be hard to find this person in a woollen cloak. We cannot assume they are a servant. It could be a high-born in disguise.' She turned to look at Margaretta. 'What are John Dee and kinsman Cecil planning.'

'My master intends to speak to a Mrs Gylman and also Margaret Douglas to get confirmation that Anne of Cleves had no child. He hopes they may also know about the missing months in 1541.'

'Missing months?'

'Anne of Cleves was on progress. But there are no records of where she went.'

Blanche groaned and put her hands over her eyes. 'These old eyes may be dulling. Yet still I am not so short-sighted as a man in search of glory.' She stood abruptly. 'Come, Margaretta. Let us lift this veil of arrogance.'

Chapter Twenty-Four

Blanche did not wait for a summons after knocking on the door of Cecil's office. Inside the two men were hunched over the parchment of circles and scribbles.

John Dee straightened up and opened his arms. 'Cousin Blanche, my dear friend. I am so—'

She rounded on him. 'My final warning. You and I are not cousins. Nor are we friends. You are making slow progress. And while you dawdle, a poisoner stalks my lady's palace.'

Dee was crestfallen. 'What have you learned from Beatrice?'

'That she was visited by a cloaked figure who said nothing,' answered Margaretta. 'But one strange thing... she spoke of black hands.'

'Not at all,' sighed Dee as he pointed to Cecil. 'The apple cakes from *The Marianna* have been tested. Poisoned. The killer is simply ensuring they do not get poison on their hands. Beatrice saw gloves.'

Dee glanced at Blanche and shifted in discomfort. 'We are rapidly gathering statements to prove Anne of Cleves was a maid to King Henry. Three already gathered and one more to reach.' He tapped on the paper in his hand. 'I go to see the third today. Margaret Douglas.'

Blanche groaned. 'Do we really have to involve her? If there is gain to be made of it, then she will grab with both hands.'

'I understand she was the one who stayed closest to

Anne of Cleves after the divorce. Her testimony is vital,' insisted Dee.

'Of course she stayed close,' snapped Blanche. 'Anne was both a Catholic and also in favour with Henry. So, when Margaret Douglas decided to have another disgraceful love affair with Charles Howard, being friends with Anne was somewhat helpful.'

Dee raised his eyebrows. 'And did Anne assist her?'

Cecil cut in. 'She likely put in a good word. Margaret was sent to Kenninghall, Norfolk, as a punishment in November, 1541. It should have been the Tower but she requested Kenninghall.'

Dee sighed. 'That puts Margaret in Norfolk in the very period in which the rumours – and this Cygnet Prince – claim Anne of Cleves would have been with the child.' He winced. 'She would have little sight of events.'

Blanche shook her head. 'Wrong. Anne wrote to Elizabeth in March, 1541 saying she was going on a progress to her properties in Norfolk. Would be away for many months.'

'How do you know this?' snapped Cecil.

Blanche bristled. 'I have been responsible for Elizabeth's papers since she was a child – books, letters, journals... I even write her correspondence.' She raised her eyebrows. 'You do not know *everything*, cousin.'

Dee jumped up and looked at Cecil. 'If Margaret Douglas was a neighbour of Anne of Cleves in 1541, then she can vouch better than any living person that she remained a maid.' He assumed a self-satisfied look. 'And with the trouble she is already facing for promoting the marriage of her own son to Mary, Queen of Scots, she is unlikely to help another young man usurp his chances.' He nodded. 'I think Margaret Douglas is our strongest chance of sending this Cygnet away with his wings clipped.' He made a small bow to Blanche and turned. 'Come Margaretta.'

And I feel dread. So do you Blanche.

'Wait,' said Blanche. 'Margaretta says you seek Mrs

Gylman – the limner who lived with Anne to teach her English.' Blanche narrowed her eyes and turned to Cecil. 'You are not keeping abreast of news, cousin William.' She ignored the clouding of John Dee's face as the other man was called cousin again. 'Susanna Hornebolt, who you call Mrs Gylman, was indeed a close friend. She called her son Henry and her daughter was named Anne after Anne of Cleves. But she died a year after Queen Mary ascended the throne.'

Cecil sighed. 'I will have to have the children found and hope their mother talked.'

Blanche rolled her eyes to heaven. 'The children were very young when she died. You need to think, gentlemen. Who would Susanna likely speak to?'

Cecil sat up straight. 'Other women like her. You think of Lavina Teerlinc.'

'Exactly. Elizabeth's miniaturist. She's been at Court since the reign of King Henry and has seen behind many a curtain. She is currently working on a miniature of Robert Dudley.' She looked around. 'Where is Two-Eyes?' Her voice was cynical.

'In the stables, attending a foal,' answered Cecil. He stood. 'Which means Mistress Teerlinc will be free to talk.'

Blanche nodded and turned to Dee. 'Wait here. We will tie up this loose end before you are frayed by Margaret Douglas. I will fetch her. She is a talker. I will need to ensure she does not speak of this.'

Lavinia Teerlinc came into the room like a mouse entering a cage of cats. Her eyes were wide and face pale. She was a woman of about fifty years of age, though only the skin around her eyes had creased. She bobbed a curtsy to Cecil and then looked shyly at John Dee, whispering, 'My Lord, good Doctor. Blanche says I must speak truth and then never say another word of what I say.' She glanced sideways at Blanche. 'I am not sure what I can possibly speak of, sirs.' Her voice was low and still held the vowels of a Flemish accent.

Blanche nudged her towards a chair. 'That is because we cannot speak in the corridors of Court, Lavinia. You know how tapestries grow ears.' The limner frowned, not understanding. Blanche pointed at Cecil. 'Just answer his questions.'

Dee stood, evidently irritated. 'Actually, I am detective. You will answer my questions, Mistress Teerlinc.' He gestured to the chair. 'Pray sit. We want you to feel comfortable.'

The woman sat and began to pick at spots of pigment on her fingers.

'We think you would have known another artist who was a servant to Anne of Cleves. A Mrs—'

'–Gylman. You mean Susanna. Yes. She was a dear friend of mine.' Then a saddening of her face. 'Died when her babes were barely walking.'

'Indeed. Now did you two talk of Anne of Cleves?'

The woman reddened. 'No… no. We are most respectful of privacy.'

No, you were not. You recall sitting in rooms sharing wine and talking behind your hands. Laughing and then gasping at shared stories. You are also thinking of a letter. 'Mae hi'n dweud celwydd. She is lying.'

Blanche turned her head to Margaretta and nodded before turning to the seated woman. 'Come, Lavinia. I was clear that you must tell the truth. We all know that you gossip with your apprentice. Do not claim you did not do the same with a good friend.'

Lavinia blushed further. 'Maybe a few words. Just to know how things fared in our work. What paintings we were crafting.'

Dee stepped closer. 'Let us be very honest, Mistress Teerlinc. If there was gossip about Anne of Cleves, you would know about it.'

And immediately you think of a child. This is not going to go well.

Lavinia looked at Blanche ap Harri, her eyes begging for guidance. The other woman responded. 'Just confirm to

Doctor Dee that you will be witness that Mrs Gylman never spoke of a child born to Anne of Cleves and Henry Tudor.' She made a hard smile. 'Then you can return to your work as limner to Her Majesty.'

Oh, clever, Blanche. You have trapped the woman into never speaking with a veiled threat of losing her position. But why is Lavinia Teerlinc thinking of a letter?

Dee's head barely moved. 'Where were you in 1541?'

'On royal progress. I was charged with making miniatures of the great men who gave their hospitality to King Henry and the queen.'

'And did Mrs Gylman write to you? Maybe she wrote of a child?'

Lavinia rose from her seat. 'Indeed, I cannot bear witness to any such gossip.' She looked at Blanche for reassurance and was rewarded with a smile.

But you are lying and both Blanche and I know it.

Dee looked to Cecil. 'I think that is all we need.'

The other man nodded and gave Lavinia permission to leave. When she had scuttled from the room, he looked at Blanche. 'You led her.'

She pulled back her shoulders and glared. Her voice dropped to a hard hiss. 'I have just secured the witness statement you require to save Elizabeth and put an end to this madness. She is our true and anointed queen. I will not have her brought down by a German prince or a flutter-tongued Flemish painter.' She turned black eyes on John Dee. 'Now go and ensure Margaret Douglas puts her own freedom ahead of slander and treachery.'

With that she turned and walked to the door saying over her shoulder. 'I will try to ensure Lavinia does not speak to her apprentice of this. They are more like mother and daughter. Dangerous.'

John Dee slumped into a chair and picked up his bag. 'Come, Margaretta. Let us away to Sheen and pray Lady Douglas is helpful.'

Cecil huffed and shook his head.

'Fie, William,' said Dee cheerfully. 'She is the strongest nail in the Cygnet's coffin. She was close to Anne of Cleves in Norfolk, and would know her business. And her own business is to advance her son, not a German pretender. She will give us all we need.' He strode out, head high.

Chapter Twenty-Five

Sheen Palace at Richmond was even more beautiful than Hampton Court. Huge towers topped with bell roofs made it look like something from another land. Dee strode up the path from the Thames, his gown flapping in the breeze, towards the gate house. He was subdued, having heard from Margaretta that Lavinia Teerlinc was lying and thought of a letter, but insisted they were within one conversation of success. 'Come Margaretta. We must have our witness signing her troth in half of an hour and tomorrow we travel to Hever to send the Cygnet from making his nest there.'

Well, I can never feel your thoughts, but the speed of your steps and the pitch in your voice tells me all. How you long to march back to Cecil and tell him that all is put to right in less than four days. The fire in your belly is raging and you walk as if going in to smash a foe.

Margaret Douglas walked into the room where Dee and Margaretta were waiting, a small dog cradled in her arms. It growled and bared small, sharp teeth. Her face was set like ice. Cold and giving nothing. 'I understand you seek my testimony, Doctor Dee.' She turned a slow hard stare on Margaretta. 'And who is this?'

'My assistant. She will take notes. Allowing me to give

you my full attention. She will use wax instead of parchment to ensure all can be erased for your privacy.'

'A girl?'

'A woman,' responded Dee tartly. 'Trustworthy and clever too.'

My God. Is that really you speaking?

'I suppose I have little say in who I speak with?' was the response.

'No, madam.' Dee gestured to a chair. 'Please. This will take but a few minutes.'

Margaret Douglas hesitated and glared. Tudor blood was apparent in her appearance. A fair face which would have been beautiful when young was now a little puffed around the eyes and, like all Celts, her jaw was slackening with age. Yet her hair retained its copper sheen only pricked with a few wisps of grey. The eyes were hard, dark and flicked between Dee and Margaretta like a hawk deciding which rabbit to attack. Slowly she stepped across the room in deliberately slow pace and sat. She placed the dog on the floor and then looked out of the window to indicate her irritation and disdain.

What do I feel from you, madam? Worry, yes. Worry at what my Master might know. You also feel frustration and indignation. You rail every day about being holed up in here – though it is hardly a prison to be surrounded by such sumptuous furnishings. You carry yourself like a queen and I feel from you a haughtiness to which you feel entitled. But under that a strange mix. Worry, ambition – you think of a boy and your own power. Also, of a husband with a mix of concern and disdain. And what is this? Revenge. Yes. Revenge and glory all as one.

'I take it that William Cecil is behind this intrusion. Does he send news of when my husband will be released from torment in the Tower and I from wrongful incarceration?'

'No, madam. I only come—'

She stood and shrieked. 'I write every day setting out my innocence. Yet I... Lady Margaret Douglas of the royal blood... am ignored like a peasant in a field.' She pointed at Dee. 'They accuse me of witchcraft and send me a conjuror as jury. How dare they?'

Dee faltered, gulped and gathered himself. 'I do not come in connection with your negotiations with Cecil, madam. But another matter. We are seeking confirmation, going back twenty years. I understand you were close to the Lady Anne of Cleves.'

'As the king's niece, obviously I was chosen to head her house,' was the imperious reply.

'Indeed, and that gave you close insight to the lady's activities.'

'Are you informing me or interrogating me, Doctor Dee?'

Dee cleared his throat and made a wan smile. 'Simply establishing facts, my lady.' He sat opposite her only to get a disapproving raise of her brow. Evidently, she did not approve of people below nobility sitting in her presence. Behind him, Margaretta took a wax tablet and stylus from his bag for taking notes, but stayed standing. Little point in giving her any excuse to divert questions to discussion of manners. 'Now, I wish to take your memory back to the summer of 1541.'

'I recall it well.' Her eyes glazed and her mouth went straight.

You recall a young man. Thomas. Secret meetings. Hushed conversations. Dark corners and the excitement of hidden love. You recall creeping down a path and the joy when he took you in his arms. You are recalling the feel of his hands as he... as he... Oh, my God...

Dee jumped as the wax tablet clattered on the wooden floor and Margaretta, red faced, bent to pick it up, mumbling her apologies.

Margaret Douglas tutted. 'So, she is also a clumsy fool.'

Dee nodded. 'She can be that, yes.'

Clumsy? You have no idea of the carnal things I have just witnessed. This woman was no angel.

Dee continued. 'The king was on progress with Queen

Kathryn Howard and I understand Anne of Cleves was also on progress in Norfolk.'

Margaret made a cynical laugh. 'Not so much progress as pregnancy.' A gloating smile. 'Only a few trusted ladies knew about her son.'

Oh, God's teeth. The Doctor has gone white. This is a disaster.

'What? Are you quite sure? Who knew?' Dee's shock made his voice go up a pitch.

She smoothed her skirts in a deliberate play to make him wait. 'Oh, her servants. Then me... as her only friend in a treacherous Court.' A slow smile.

'Did... did you see this... this claimed child?'

'No. I was on progress to York with King Henry and the new queen.' She glided across the room to a far table where she picked up a book and returned to her seat, holding it up to Dee. 'But I swear on this Holy Bible that Anne of Cleves bore a son in September, 1541.'

Dee blew out his worry and thought. 'But it might have been the son of another...'

'Fie, Doctor. The only man of any standing in Anne's household was Brockhause, her fat cofferer, and his prick was well leashed by his dreadful wife. The other men were mere servants, Anne was a high-born lady, raised to bed kings and nobles, not serfs.' The bile in her voice could almost be tasted.

You recall a conversation with another woman, secret and behind closed doors. '*Pwy ddywedodd wrthi hi?* Who told her?'

Lady Douglas shot a look of concern. 'What did she say?'

'She just mumbles, my lady. A bad habit.' Dee leaned forward. 'If you did not see Lady Anne or the child that summer, who told you?'

'The limner, Lavinia Teerlinc. She sought my advice.'

'Which was?'

'Oh, good Doctor. Many a royal child has been disposed of behind the doors of distant houses.' She paused while the words landed.

You spiteful old crow. You are referring to the story that Elizabeth bore Seymour's child and that she has now born Dudley's. You do not believe these tales – thank the Lord you do not know. But you want to use this as power for your tale.

Margaret continued. 'I advised to have the child hidden in a safe place as the Privy Council would surely investigate. I was right. In November that fool Jane Rattsay and other gossips could not keep their tongues still and there was an investigation. The investigation found no child and all went quiet. The loss of a child is something many of us bear.'

'Did you speak to Anne of Cleves at this time? I understand you also went to Norfolk in November, 1541.'

Margaret Douglas glared. 'I was a prisoner at Kenninghall. I was somewhat indisposed, Doctor. Yet again incarcerated by my own blood family,' was the acid retort. Then a sly smile. 'Having been imprisoned yourself you will know how hard it is to be hospitable.'

'But maybe the Lady Anne visited you, as you were her friend?'

'No. I vaguely recall a fat travelling priest saying he had preached to her… nothing further.' Margaret Douglas suddenly seemed uncomfortable and looked away. 'I moved from royal progress to royal prison, Doctor Dee. I could do little more than eat cake for seventeen whole months until I was released to the household of Queen Katherine Parr in 1543.'

Discomfort. I hear voices… the name Jasper. And you are lying. '*Mae hi'n cuddio rhywbeth.* She is hiding something.'

Dee smiled. 'I think you know more, my lady.'

A hiss from Margaret Douglas and she rose from her chair, banging the Bible onto the table next to it. 'I warn you, Doctor Dee. It is not wise in these days of suspicion and intrigue to accuse a woman of the royal blood of speaking falsity.' She pulled down her mouth in contempt. 'You cannot conjure away a child no matter what dark arts you deploy. If only Elizabeth could see the merit in marrying her two cousins – Mary of Scots and my son – then the Cygnet Prince would glide away. Think on that when you speak to Lord Cecil, Doctor Dee.' She beckoned to the dog. 'Come, my sweet. We will not have our time further wasted.'

Margaret Douglas turned her back and left without another word, her dog trotting behind her.

Dee slumped in his chair and looked to the Bible. 'Oh, dear God. Did she speak truth?'

'Yes, and she knows more than she says. But I heard voices. The name Jasper. She was suddenly uncomfortable when she said she only ate cake.'

'But our strategy is broken.' Dee covered his face with his hands. 'Worse, she will support the claims of the Cygnet Prince to further her own son as husband of Mary, Queen of Scots. My God. We are in trouble.'

As they waited on the bank for the barge to come in from the centre of the river, another boat pulled into the shore. A woman sat in the aft seat, her coif large and flopping over her face. She held it down to stop the wind lifting it. In her lap a basket covered in a linen. She waved to a servant who walked down to the river edge and took the basket, leaning forward as she spoke quietly. The words were faint, but she certainly said 'Lady Douglas'. The servant nodded and reached to his pocket, pulling out a red apple, handing it to the woman, saying, 'And one for you, mistress.'

Margaretta watched as she bent her head and told the wherry man to take her back. Then a gust of wind and Margaretta nearly cried out. The poor woman was disfigured with pock-marks and her mouth eaten away by them. As if sensing she was seen, she twisted away.

The servant walked back towards the palace. As he passed, the linen lifted and revealed a clutch of green apples. Margaretta called out. 'Who was the woman?'

He servant shrugged. 'I don't ask. We just call her the apple woman.' He looked down the river after the wherry.

'Poor thing. Lady Douglas will not have her step foot inside for fear of bringing the pox, though is it well over for her… as is her face.'

John Dee sniffed in disgust and muttered, 'If the apples are for Lady Douglas, then they are better served by a serpent than a poor wretch requiring kindness.'

'I'm not sure you can compare Lady Douglas to Eve, Doctor.'

He raised a brow. 'No? Did Eve not covet the forbidden fruit denied her – just as Lady Douglas covets the rank denied her family?'

Chapter Twenty-Six

Robert Dudley was pacing up and down the office, slapping at his thigh in frustration. Cecil was pinching the bridge of his nose, eyes closed and breathing deeply. Dee was standing, Margaretta's etched wax tablet in his hand. 'I can drop this and her evidence is shattered to pieces…'

'No,' snapped Cecil. 'We cannot silence a woman of the royal blood. And lies will stir the Catholics.'

'Even though that same lying woman seeks to steal the throne from Elizabeth to give to her milksop son?' challenged Dudley. He slammed his hand down on a table making the candlesticks topple in a clatter of falling silver. 'She will do anything to have a Catholic on the throne and her standing raised as high as the host at the end of a sermon.'

Cecil slowly lowered his hand and leaned forward to stare at Robert Dudley, eyes narrowed in fury, his voice dropped to a snarl. 'And that from the man who offered a Catholic throne to further his own ambition… and lust.'

Dudley stopped pacing, turned to glare at Cecil and the two were locked in fury. Dee looked between the two, then at Dudley. 'What is this, Robert?'

'Nothing. Only gossip.'

'Fie,' spat Cecil. 'Francis Yaxley spilled his guts when interrogated in the Tower. When de la Quadra was challenged, he did not deny.'

Dee raised his hands in evident confusion. 'What is all this? If I am to investigate, I suggest you tell me all?'

Dudley turned his back to look out of the window, his shoulders heaving in temper. Cecil spoke slowly. 'Lord Dudley, through his brother-in-law, Henry Sidney, sought the blessing of Philip of Spain, our former queen's Catholic husband. That blessing was sought through Bishop de la Quadra.'

'Blessing?'

'To marry our Queen. And the price of the Spanish blessing was a Court moved back to Catholicism. Back to the very horrors of the pyres, the stopping of which have made Elizabeth so loved by the people.'

The anger in this room is so strong it makes me tremble. Both of you. Joined by love of Elizabeth and cleaved apart by hatred and resentment of each other. But that is the secret I have felt in you, Lord Dudley. You have plotted yourself.

Dee turned slowly towards his former pupil. 'Is this true?'

There was no answer. Robert Dudley stormed from the room, slamming the door behind him.

Cecil sighed and put his hand back to the bridge of his nose. 'Do you see the hornet's nest we have around us, John? No. I should say nests.' He pointed at the door. 'We have the descendant of traitors playing a game of courtly love to gain a kingship and a throne. In Sheen we have a woman of the blood plotting to marry her pretty son to the Scottish Queen – and she *has* been assisted by de la Quadra.' He groaned. 'And now a pretender prince with evidence and now endorsement of being a true son of Henry.'

He stood and pressed his hands down on the oak of his desk. 'And Elizabeth is so blinded with devotion to her horseman that she refuses to look at the hornets, let alone swat them.'

'You mentioned this Francis Yaxley. Another hornet?'

'He was, but his sting is well guarded now. He was in trouble last year for first speaking of a marriage between Robert and Elizabeth and then being fool enough to write in favour of a betrothal to Erik of Sweden.'

'Just like Kat Astley,' said Margaretta.

Cecil looked surprised. 'Indeed. They were all in a flutter because they had promoted Robert and then, when Amy died, they feared being accused of involvement in murder, so swivelled their favour towards Sweden.' He shrugged. 'Anyway, we then found out that Yaxley had moved allegiance again.'

'To who?'

'Margaret Douglas. He was passing messages between Lady Margaret and de la Quadra in the plot to marry Darnley to Mary, Queen of Scots. Two Catholics who, they say, have more claim on the throne than Elizabeth. Their aim is to shift the dynasty from Tudor to Lennox but using the sliver of Tudor blood in Darnley's veins as his lineage.'

Resentment. Deep. But it is more than protection of Elizabeth. When you say Yaxley's name you wince. '*Gofynna am y dyn yn y Tŵr. Mae dicter yma.* Ask about the man in the Tower. There is resentment here.'

Cecil looked at her. 'What did you say?'

Damn. I thought I was quiet. 'I asked to be excused to go to the privy, sir.'

Dee nodded then turned back to Cecil. 'I feel deep resentment towards Yaxley from you.'

Cecil looked surprised. 'Not like you to be so sensitive, John. Yes. I once supported him. Guided even. Helped him in his education, helped him become Member of Parliament for Stamford – my birth place – and supported him becoming clerk of the signet.'

'So, he betrayed you.'

'He did. But he is powerless now.'

'And how did you find out?'

Cecil tapped the side of his nose. 'Money. Borgese Venturini, de la Quadra's secretary, was in high mood claiming he had not been paid for his services. So, I paid him – and received *his* services.'

Dee chuckled and then frowned. 'We need to swat one hornet at a time. Margaret Douglas is in Sheen and her sting limited. Robert is chastened and fearful of being exposed or further falling after Amy's death. So, let us take the sting out of the one who flies.'

Cecil nodded. 'Indeed. I need you to go to Hever Castle and see how strong the sting is. We will have to risk him thinking any attention is support for his cause. You will leave tomorrow.' Then he looked over at Margaretta. 'I thought you wanted the privy?'

Chapter Twenty-Seven

Katherine Constable was up to her cups. She held the edge of a table, her face flushed and eyes dulled. 'You cannot go away for days. How will I manage? Who will cook? Who will tend to the kitchen and the underpots and—'

'Maybe you can bring in help for a few days, mistress.'

'No. No. You cannot go…'

'It is by order of Sir Cecil, mistress. I am instructed to go and scribe for Doctor Dee.' *That's a lie. But I owe you no truth, madam. And the name of Cecil will curb your complaining.*

A short pause, then the set of the mouth. 'But I will have no help in the house. Huw is not here.'

'That's because you sold him for a barrel of Malmsey wine, mistress.' The high-pitched indignation was still flowing from Katherine's mouth when Margaretta slammed the door. *Damn you and you wailing. You have brought this on yourself and I will not bow and crawl to a woman who has sold my brother. If you throw me out, then so be it. I would rather walk the streets than give you subservience. I will make a pottage to see you through a few days and then you will have to dirty your hands with a little toil.*

In the kitchen the cat curled on the seat that was still where Mam used to sit. Margaretta ruffled her ears and told her it was going to be a few days of mice and no cheese. She pulled the pot from the shelf, the clattering ringing out her anger and then started chopping the vegetables and scraggy meat. *I will not even put sweet herbs in it. Only barley. It will be as sour as your heart, mistress.* The door opened. It was Dee.

'Why are you making such a noise, girl?'

'Because I'm angry. Because I'm sad. Because I have no power to change it. And because I have no-one who cares.'

He looked at her, head cocked on one side. 'Mercury still in your twelfth house.' He pointed upstairs. 'I have used the cards. Come and see as soon as you have that pot on the fire.' He turned and the door closed after him.

Damn that stone you call a heart.

'Look at this.' The cards were spread in a circle. 'I took out the cards we know are at play – even if we cannot identify the people they represent. Then I asked the cards to tell us more. Look at the first card to emerge.' He held up the page of wands. 'What did I say a page represents?'

'Usually a messenger or servant.'

'So, we are looking for a messenger or messages.'

'Sir Cecil spoke of messages being passed today.'

Dee shook his head. 'Yaxley is in the Tower and nothing will get past Cecil's spies. No. We are looking for someone able to move freely.' He reached for another three cards. 'I asked the cards to give guidance for Hever Castle. Three cards. Look.'

Margaretta picked them up and turned them over. 'The two of wands – the man holding the world and looking at a mountain. We drew this before.' She picked up the next card and shuddered. 'The Devil again. This is the second time it has come up in connection to the Cygnet Prince.'

'Indeed. There is some evil around the boy. But what? Who? Or is it him?' Dee nodded and tapped on the third card. 'And this fell from the deck. The king of wands… again.' Margaretta frowned. 'And linked to the page… the messenger… again?'

Dee shook his head. 'The cards are giving the same messages. They keep prodding us.' Dee sat back closing his eyes. 'How I hate this part of an investigation. All the clues but the insight yet to arrive.' He sighed. 'We have much to uncover at Hever. Have you sent word to Sam to bring the carriage?'

'I have. As soon as we were home.'

'Good. Well, I suppose I had better pay some attention to our landlady if I am taking you away for a few days.'

Oh, Lord. I had better tell the truth.

'She says I may not go. No-one to work the kitchen. And I... well, I...'

'What have you done?'

'Shouted that it's her own damn fault for selling Huw for a barrel of Malmsey.'

Dee banged the desk. 'God's teeth, girl. You are meant to apprentice not wreck our chances.' He rose. 'I will go and calm Katherine. Explain how your help will rise my rank at Court. Though God knows how I convince her to carry her own wood and underpots for a week.' He made a little frown. 'She is not a bad woman, you know. Just sometimes she does not think clearly.'

'I have an idea. Can you give me a set of breaches and a shirt? An old one is fine. And a pair of old shoes.'

He raised an eyebrow. 'You launder and store them – you know where they are.'

Margaretta crept out of the back door and along the street, ducking under windows to ensure she was not spied by Katherine. She found the crook-nose beggar man hunched in an alley. He smiled when she shook him awake, knowing he was going to get a kind word and a mouthful of bread.

She crouched down and spoke in Welsh. 'I need your help. It means a bath and a haircut. And you will say you are a yard man of Angus McFadden.'

He looked bewildered but nodded, stood and followed her,

chewing on the bread she brought. Half of an hour later, Siôn Jenkins, former archer, man of Conway, was sitting in a bath of hot water, being scrubbed with a hard cloth and grumbling as vinegar was combed through his newly-cut hair with a louse comb. When he refused to stand up, he was given a smack on the shoulder, a linen to cover his manhood and instructions to get dressed ready for meeting the mistress. When marched to Katherine's chamber he played his part better than a mummer on a travelling theatre cart, bowing low, speaking well, asking how bright she liked her fire kept and assuring that he was there to do any bidding she might have. He even spoke with glowing words of Angus McFadden who he had never met. In the corner, Dee kept silent, his eyes bright with pride for his apprentice.

Back in the kitchen, Margaretta started her instructions and was silenced with a raise of his four-fingered hand. '*Hen filwr ydw i*. I'm an old soldier. Survival is my game. My arrow fingers are missing, not my sense.' Then he sat down with a wink. 'And that pottage would smell better with a handful of herbs and some salt.'

Chapter Twenty-Eight

Sam had the carriage outside at dawn. Margaretta was ready, mainly because Siôn Jenkins was up an hour ahead of her, the wood was in from the store, the fires made, the kitchen swept and the bread, which had risen overnight, in the oven. He was a quiet man and asked only a few questions about the Constables and what they would need, then he requested a quill and a paper.

'You write?'

He looked up slowly. 'And why not?'

She shrugged. 'I just thought…'

'That I was a dirty old beggar with nothing to offer this world?' He shook his head. 'My first downfall was having my fingers cut off to take away my standing as an archer. My second was when my back could not be shorn for wool and so my dwelling was burned down and I was replaced by a flock of sheep.' He made a small cynical laugh. 'People look at the dirt and the hunger, Margaretta… and forget that behind the grime is a soul and senses and a life.'

'I am sorry, Siôn. I…'

'Did not think. Seems you have become the true City woman.'

I feel ashamed. You are like my Dada – a soldier. You have saved me, and I have not even asked of your past. Too late. I must go. 'Maybe you can tell me about being an archer when I get back.'

Sam was holding the horses and greeted her with a grin. 'Lottie sends her very best wishes and her love, Missy.' Then his face clouded. 'I worry about being away. She had pains this morning but said I had to go to get the retainer money. How many days will we be?'

'I think two, Sam.' She patted his arm. 'And Lottie is well cared for by Goodwife Tovey.' She took his hand as he helped her into the carriage. 'And be ready to stop. You know how I suffer in these moving things.'

The carriage started with a lurch and Margaretta took a deep breath. 'It is but a few lanes to The Vintry, Doctor. Please can we call in and check on Huw?'

Her master looked up, irritated, then his face softened. 'Yes. We must.'

It was a yell from Sam at the front of the carriage that made Margaretta's heart race. 'Hey, you bastard. He's not a fucking donkey for you to kick.' The carriage juddered as the horses were heaved to a halt and then the sound of Sam jumping down.

Margaretta scrambled to the door and pushed her way out not waiting for her master. 'What's happening? Huw?' She stopped and screamed.

Her brother was bent over double, a keg strapped to his back. His clothes were filthy and one shoe missing. Across his face a red weal as if he had been hit with a stick. His knuckles were grazed. Behind him was a large man, already backing away, his hands raised as Sam ran at him. The punch was hard, making the man gasp and fall back against the barrels. There was a crack as one fell, splitting open and pouring red wine into the gutter. Then a shout from the office and Angus emerged, red in the face, yellow in the eye and mouth open in fury. 'What the hell is going on? Who the fuck are…'

He saw Margaretta, John Dee at her shoulder and stopped. It was her turn to charge and Angus was not fast enough in retreat before she had him by the throat, slamming his head back against the wood and then raining blows to his face. It took two of the Vintry boys to pull her off. Angus pulled himself up, snarling as he brushed the dirt from his clothing. 'What the hell is wrong with you?'

'Wrong with me? And what is wrong with your black soul, Angus, that you use your own kin as a beast of burden – filthy, kicked and abused by your lackies?'

He gave a sneering chuckle and went to turn away. But John Dee stepped forward. 'Master McFadden. I can see no good reason for any Godfearing man to treat a young boy so harshly.'

Angus flicked his hand in dismissal. 'It is none of your business, Conjuror.' He smiled as John Dee bridled at the insult. 'But suffice to say that honest work of trade is harder than contemplating the stars. Huw has to learn how to hold his own on the quays.' He smirked and made a theatre of pretending to remember. 'Did you not once benefit from the skills of a father who worked the quays? Ah, but did he not fall further than the height of a crane into debt due to his foolery? I think he lost all, did he not? Unlike me. We have just won a royal licence to supply Her Majesty. You cannot touch me.' He turned his nasty smile onto Margaretta. 'Not a good idea to attack a favoured merchant of the palace.'

The fury of John Dee was palpable. 'My father may have fallen but he did not rise through brutality. He was a better man than you, sirrah.'

Angus reddened further at being called 'sirrah'. He went to shout, but Margaretta cut in. 'I'm taking Huw with me.'

'You cannot, little sister. I purchased him.' Angus pulled a parchment from his pocket. 'See here.' He jabbed a finger onto a signature. It was Katherine Constable's mark.

'Mistress Constable would never agree to selling Huw into this hell. She had no idea you would abuse him worse than a stray dog. She had no understanding of how low you go to get under your stone, brother-in-law.'

Angus made a loud, forced laugh. 'Ah, she will believe anything through the haze of her Malmsey wine. She has accepted the first payment of a barrel. The deal is sealed.' His face darkened. 'And I think you were less than comely with my delivery man. Now get yourself and your cur dog driver out of my yard.'

'That delivery lad said Huw was beaten over a paper. What did he mean?'

Angus made a sneering chuckle. 'Paper? Foolery. He cannot speak, let alone write.'

Huw can read and write better than you. But I will not tell you until I know why you are thinking of a paper. 'You are scheming something.'

Angus turned his back, went inside his office and slammed the door.

Margaretta stood staring, tears streaming down her face. She felt John Dee's hand on her shoulder, then Sam arrived and wiped her face. 'Come, Missy. I've warned the men that if they touch your brother, I'll be back with a gang of wherry men who will stuff their manhood in their mouths. They promised to stop the beatings.'

She turned to see Huw, stepping from foot to foot, shaking his head in distress. She ran over and stood before him, speaking in Welsh. 'I will get you away from here, Huw. I will speak to Mistress Constable as soon as I am back from Hever.' She tried to smile.

But Huw scowled. 'Angus black. More than before.' He glanced up. 'Margaretta grey.'

'I surely am, Huw. Grey with rage.' She lowered her voice to soothing. 'What is this about a paper?'

Huw started shaking his head. 'Said sign but will not show words. Hit me. Told men to hit me.'

'If they hit you. Hit back. It matters not that Mam told us to always keep our fists in our pockets. Hit as hard as you can. Kick as fast as you can. Can you do that?'

Huw nodded. 'Huw be bad.'

'Not bad, Huw. Just safe until I get you home.' She took his arm and for once he did not pull away. 'And play the fool, Huw. Pretend you cannot read or even write your name. Never sign anything.'

John Dee arrived at her side again and spoke kindly. 'You have done all you can today, my dear. And Sam has certainly quietened their spite. We will attend to this on return.' He took her elbow and guided her to the carriage. Sam climbed up, shouting his final warning to the Vintry boys who stood and scowled but said nothing. They set off, but instead of heading directly back to London Bridge, Sam took the carriage down to Venours Warf where he ran to the river bank. They could see him hailing a group of wherries and then pointing back to The Vintry. He returned and pushed his head through the carriage window. 'There will be a daily check on the McFadden yard, Missy. The Venours boys are a hardy gaggle. One sign of your brother being hard used and the kicking will begin.' He winked. 'Now dry those tears.'

Oh, you are a good man. So was Christopher, but you have a manliness about you that I crave.

Dee was staring at her. 'There is a young man out there somewhere meant for you. Be patient.' He smiled and looked back to his notes.

Chapter Twenty-Nine

Hever Castle was nestled in a small dell, like a jewel in green velvet. Margaretta breathed a sigh of relief, having made Sam stop the carriage many times to empty her aching stomach. She could feel the pinch of it now and craved a glass of small beer to slake her thirst. It had taken all of the day to travel, such were the roads. Three times Sam had to take the carriage into a field to avoid a divot that would have toppled them on their side. Each time he insisted they stepped out and walk as he 'would have no broken bones on my conscience'.

The castle was surrounded by a moat though the drawbridge was down. A servant holding up a pike-staff signalled them to stop. John Dee put his head out of the window. 'We come on Her Majesty's business. I wish to see Widow Waldegrave, owner of this place.' He passed a letter from Cecil out of the window, which earned a raise of the brow and a nod from the guard.

'Widow and Master Waldegrave are away, sir. Only Lord Jasper is in residence.' He waved them on into the central yard. They jumped down onto stone flags. Margaretta looked up at the black and white timbers of the inner buildings. This must be the house of a rich man for nearly every window glistened with glass pane.

Another servant, unweaponed, strode through the entrance of the main building. John Dee handed over the letter again.

They were beckoned forward and Sam told he could take the carriage back over the drawbridge to the stables. Then he pointed to Margaretta, 'You will find the kitchens and servants' quarters to the right of the building. You can get vittles for your master.'

'No, no. She is with me. My scribe,' announced John Dee and turned before the other man could object. 'Come Margaretta. We have questions to ask.' He walked through the door and stepped to the left, down a corridor and through a huge oak door into a receiving room, the servant scuttling after him voicing indignation.

Dee smiled. 'Where is Jasper of Cleves? I will see him now... on Queen's business.' The servant huffed but bowed his head. 'He will be upstairs in the long gallery. He likes it there.'

They ascended the stairs and came out into a small room and beyond that a long gallery, oak-panelled but lit by large windows and further cheered by a lime-whitened ceiling. The sweet smell of rosemary came from the herbed rushes on the wooden floor. At the far end, lounging on a coach, was a young man, dressed in expensive burgundy brocade and holding a book. He was tall, broad, with a fine-turned leg. His hair glowed copper around a fair-skinned face, handsome and well-proportioned with a strong jaw. The sun glinted on a golden chain and locket around his neck. So, this was the Cygnet Prince. He looked up slowly as if expecting a servant and sat up quickly when seeing Dee in his long cloak. 'Who visits me?' The accent was strong, but the words well-formed and the voice clear.

'Greetings, sir. I am Doctor John Dee.' He gestured to Margaretta. 'My scribe.' He sat on a leather chair without waiting to be asked and reached for the decanter. 'Wine?'

The young man looked a little bemused. 'I believe it is called hippocras, sir. Yes, I will join you.' He sat and began to twist a ring on his little finger. It glinted in the sun and Margaretta was stuck by the stone – a dark diamond, flat cut. Unusual.

Dee poured two glasses – his own fuller than the other – and took a deep sip, refilled his glass and sat back as if readying to speak to a friend. 'I come on behalf of Her Majesty's council, sir. But I come in good will.' Dee made an encouraging nod. 'They wish me to understand the basis of your claims.' He turned to Margaretta and nodded at her bag in a signal to start writing. She found a stool and pulled out paper and a quill, balancing the ink horn on her lap.

The man sat up, straightening his back. There was a jut of the chin and one brow raised. 'Claims? Not claims, sir. Simply facts... undeniable facts. I have already set them out to your courtiers.' The voice was self-assured with a twang of arrogance.

Dee smiled. 'Please. Talk me through your... facts... again.'

The Cygnet Prince stood and started to pace to and fro across the gallery, tapping on each wall as he reached it. He made five crossings as if ordering his thoughts. 'I was born in Norfolk in 1541 – September to be precise. My mother was Anne of Cleves and my father was King Henry. I am Jasper Tudor-Cleves, prince of the royal blood.' He turned, smiled, opened his arms in question. 'Do I not look the image of him?'

Dee grunted. 'Indeed, there is a likeness, sir.'

He gave a gracious nod and looked at Margaretta. 'Are you writing all of this?'

'Yes, sir.' *More than that I feel no lie. The only sign of discomfort is how he twists that ring.*

'I was baptised in England and then sent to be raised by my Aunt Amalia in Solingen Castle, in the Duchy of Cleves. My mother sent certain treasures with me to use as proof when the time came.'

'And what would that time be?'

He turned with a raised brow. 'When my country needed me, of course. When England needed a king of the true blood... and faith.' He walked half-way down the gallery and pointed at a painting. It was a map of all England, Wales and the land of the Scots. 'Look at this. A great land which could be greater.' He tapped on it. 'But it needs blood and faith to put the roar back into the lion.' He stepped back. 'Which is what I have been raised to do.'

'And how will you do that?'

'By marriage.' He tapped on Scotland. 'And here I find my bride, Mary, Queen of the Scots. It will be easily arranged and the blood-lines tied.'

John Dee was evidently taken aback by his assurance. 'But, sir. Surely you must first prove you are... if you are... a prince of royal blood.'

'There is no "if", Doctor Dee.' He slipped the locket off his neck and dropped into Dee's hands. 'Look for yourself.'

Dee turned the golden bauble over in his hands. It was heavily engraved. In the centre was the image of a crowned swan. This was surrounded by a wreath of Tudor roses. He clicked up the lid and peered inside. Sure enough, inside was a circle of copper hair plaited with gold hair and, on the inside of the lid, an inscription. Dee read it out. 'God save me well to keep. AoC,' He looked up at the man. 'The inscription on Anne of Cleves'... your mother's wedding ring.'

'Exactly. But there is more.' The man pointed at the hair. 'See the tiny clasp to the side. Pull it.' The twisting of the ring began again.

Dee obeyed and the locket opened to a further tiny chamber. Inside a parchment folded into tiny a square. He took it out carefully and unfolded it. 'I see it is in German. I speak little of that language.'

Jasper smiled. 'Your scribe can copy it for verification, but I can tell you what it says.' He plucked the parchment from John Dee's fingers and read aloud. 'My dearest sister. I send to your loving care my trueborn son, Jasper. Born out of sight, and so he must stay until his father can be safely told of his trueborn son. God send you well to keep him safe and raise him to keep his destiny. Signed. Anne, Lady of Cleves, Regina.'

And all I feel from you is truth. You believe this. There is no fear, no alarm, no hiding. You speak from your heart. Oh, God. We have trouble here.

John Dee raised his brow. 'Kind words indeed. It must give you comfort that the writer was so sure of your future.'

Jasper jerked in reaction. 'I must emphasise, Doctor. The writer was my mother – Anne of Cleves; wedded in body to my father – Henry of England.' He glared defiantly.

'Yes, yes. That is to be verified of course.' Dee smiled. 'I understand you also have letters, sir. Letters you claim are further proof.'

Jasper nodded. 'Indeed, Doctor Dee. Letters which will prove I was raised to be king.' He walked to a small wooden casket on the table and lifted the lid. 'I keep these with me all the time… just in case of theft.' He shot a warning glance, then lifted out two parchments. 'These are the main letters.'

Dee took them and read each one, then placed them side by side on the table. 'These are in very good English, sir. But not written by your… by Anne of Cleves. They are twenty years apart, so she cannot have written the letters after 1557, and the writing is different.'

Jasper shrugged. 'My mother was watched so she had this person send her instructions to my Aunt Amelia.' He smiled. 'She was a clever woman.'

'But surely your aunt knew the letter writer?'

'No. They had to be faceless.'

Dee turned back to the letters and tapped his finger rhythmically between the two signatures. 'The first letter is signed "your friend", but this later letter is signed "your friend, Erand Malas". Does this mean your mother had two friends writing for her?'

Jasper frowned, then put his hand to his neck in discomfort.

'I was never told such a thing. But I have only seen these two letters. Aunt Amelia received other letters but I did not see them. She said I did not need to worry. She would guide me to my destiny.' Jasper was colouring in frustration. 'If they were of import, she would have sent them with me... sir.' Twist, twist. 'She is a clever woman.'

A pang of fear when you said 'clever'. Why?

Jasper shifted in discomfort, then smiled graciously. 'As you say, sir, they are twenty years apart. Age changes a hand. So maybe just one friend.'

A fair answer. But I can tell my master is bothered. He is wondering where to take this questioning for you are speaking true.

Dee's mouth went straight and his eyes narrowed. 'Have you studied Latin, sir?'

Jasper faltered. 'No. In Cleves we have a practical education. I was taught the languages I would need – German for my home country and English for my dynastic country. There was no Latin spoken in Solingen.' Twist, twist, twist of the ring.

Dee shook his head and frowned. 'But Malas means evil or wicked.'

Jasper was quiet, then suddenly smiled. 'But it is only a surname. Erand has no meaning at all. It is just a name. It sounds French, does it not?'

'It is very close to the English word errand which means task or mission, sir.'

Jasper shrugged as if he had not understood the significance, so Dee continued, 'The first letter gives instruction to keep your birthing secret from all people and speaks of a gift to be sent on. The second speaks of "all our tending is now to bear fruit" and instructs your aunt to prepare you for travel to England.' Dee shook the paper. 'What is the tending to which Erand Malas refers?'

Jasper looked thoughtful. 'I think that must be my education. Aunt Amelia has ensured I am well prepared to be your king. I am well versed in English, the Bible, mathematics, money and the Catholic faith.'

Dee looked over to Margaretta, his brows raising in question. She gave a nod. *I sense no lie in you Jasper of Cleves. You believe everything you say. Yet you hide something about your aunt. The doctor is concerned. He knows you speak truth – or you believe it true. But why is he only arriving now? 'Pryd oedd e'n gwybod?* When did he know?'

Dee took in a long breath as if considering his next question. 'Sir, you are a young man, but of age. When did you learn you were the claimed son of Anne of Cleves?'

Jasper made a little frown. 'Just a few weeks before I travelled. Before that I knew only that I was destined for greatness... but Aunt Amalia forbade questions.'

That fear again and look how you twist the ring.

Jasper raised his hand to show the ring. 'I was presented with this last month on the anniversary of my Christening day and my whole destiny laid before me... my true path to be the true king of England under the true faith.'

Dee made a wry smile. 'Many truths, sir.' He turned and traced the grease marks on the first letter, then snapped, 'We understand you had an argument with the captain of *The Mariella*. What was the cause?'

Jasper was evidently surprised. 'It seems this is a land of gossip.' He shrugged and turned away. 'He was an arrogant fellow. I simply explained that as a prince of the blood, I was due his regard.'

No. It was a vicious argument. He threatened you. I see a crucifix being thrown. How do I tell the doctor? A note – in Welsh.

Doctor Dee gave a slight nod as the note was pressed in his hand. Once read, he crumpled it. But Jasper was watching with dark, suspicious eyes. 'What does she write?'

'Just a reminder that we are expected back in Hampton Court this day.' Jasper relaxed and Dee pressed on. 'Now more of the captain. We were told that the argument involved a crucifix. Sailors do talk, you see.'

The other man's face clouded in anger and the ring-twisting sped up. 'How dare they speak of my conversations. I will ensure they are…' He stopped, realising his own foolery. 'The captain and I had different ideas on religion. I am of the true faith and he turned out to be a hidden heretic. I told him that when I am king, he will be called to heel. That is all.'

More than that. He objected when he realised your mission.

'So can you tell us who might be interested in murdering Captain Neerman and his dog with poison?'

There was silence and Jasper put a hand out to the wall to steady himself, colour draining from his face. 'Christ's blood. No. I do not. I… would not…' He just shook his head; mouth open in shock.

'And you would not know about identical poisonings in the palace – another dog and a woman?'

At this the man gave a little cry. 'No. I have been at Hever since speaking with Bishop Alvaro de la Quadra and Sir William Cecil. For the love of God… I am no killer. I am a king. I have no idea…'

Truth. You had no idea at all. Margaretta made a little cough. '*Mae'n wir.* It's true.'

John Dee was quiet a few moments. 'What made you come to Hever, sir? It is far from Court.'

Jasper began to pace again, recovering now that there was no further questioning about poison. 'I wanted to be in my mother's favourite residence. She was happy here. So shall I be… while I await.'

'Await?'

Jasper turned, his face quizzical. 'For the arrangements for my coronation, of course.' He made an expectant smile. 'And the rescuing of England from the hell-sent Protestant whore and that ambitious stable-man of hers.'

Lord, my master bridles. I see the red rising in his face. He is about to shout. 'Gad e yn ei freuddwydion. Mae e'n ddiogel pan mae e yna. Leave him in his dreams. He is safe while there.'

Dee swallowed his words and simply nodded. Then he sat back. 'Will you be meeting Erand Malas while you wait?'

Jasper frowned. 'Aunt Amelia said I would know their face in good time. When the fruit is ripe upon the bough.'

'A strange turn of phrase.'

Another sneer. 'She is a woman with a love of poetry... and destiny.'

And again. You feel uncomfortable – nervous.

Dee made a grim smile. 'I ask that my scribe makes a copy of each letter, sir... as you claim it is evidence. I need to present this to the Privy Council. Jasper nodded eagerly and handed the parchments to Margaretta as Dee moved the conversation to his education in mathematics.

Minutes later, the letters copied, John Dee drained his glass and rose, nodding to Margaretta. He made a polite farewell and they left, with Jasper calling, 'Please inform the whore Queen that I am simply fulfilling destiny as set out by God. Oh, and tell Dudley that next time we walk and talk it will be to discuss his execution.'

So, you think you will be king in weeks. Oh, you are a fool. But you are no liar.

At the bottom of the stairs, John Dee groaned. 'From the look on your face, I think we face difficulties.'

'We do. He speaks truth... or the truth as he believes it. He has the arrogance of a princeling. But there is not a single lie from his tongue.'

Chapter Thirty

As the sun dipped behind the trees, Sam turned the carriage into the yard of a small inn and pulled the horses to still. It was raining hard.

'We must keep going,' snarled Dee out of the window. 'I need to be in Hampton Court by morning.'

Sam jumped down and stood straight, chin jutted in determination. 'I ain't taking half-asleep horses down flooded lanes full of villains so that you can spill your news.'

Dee turned to Margaretta. 'Talk sense into this churl. I have paid my retainer and I will have full service.'

Sam did not wait for Margaretta. 'You retained me for safe and secreted passage, Doctor Dee. Not for a slit throat and no sense.' He pointed along the road. 'We 'ave another twenty miles to go and in pitch dark, through woods. Now if you want to keep going you can have your damn retainer back and keep walking. But I have a family to care for.' He turned and started leading the horses to the stables.

Dee stood outside the Bell Inn glaring after the younger man. Oxted was a mere hamlet, just a few cottages, two barns, a ramshackle church and a green where horses, two goats and a small flock of sheep competed for grass. After a minute of muttering his fury, he snatched up his bag and marched through the door into the fug from a brazier that seemed to give out more smoke than heat. A portly potman came from behind the bar, his rheumy eyes looking delighted at the sight of paying visitors. 'Do you have rooms and clean beds?' demanded the doctor.

'Aye. Also, good ale brewed by my wife and today's bread with a joint of ham, cooked only yesterday.'

'Then we will eat, sleep and be away early. I need the horses fed, brushed and harnessed by crack of dawn.'

The potman nodded, unabashed by Dee's bad mood, and led the way through a dark corridor, up rickety stairs and into two rooms, both with two straw pallets, a blanket on each, a table and a tallow candle. Dee pushed into the first room and beckoned Margaretta inside. 'We will scry while Sam attends to the horses. Then eat, sleep and be ready to run.' He moved to the desk and used the flint to light the candle. 'Jasper was speaking true? No guilt?'

'Yes. He has the arrogance of a cosseted princeling but he is honest,' Margaretta answered. 'There was the twisting of the ring. But no deceit. It was more as if it gave him comfort.'

'And he is the image of Henry. Uncanny.' John Dee grunted, then rummaged in his bag, pulling out his cards. 'I thought these might come in use. As we are trapped in this backwater, we might as well take time to think.'

'God's death, Doctor. What if we are stopped and questioned? This is madness and—'

'Hush, girl. I have told you. They are playing cards to the uneducated... Now look at these.' He shuffled through the pack and pulled the cards he wanted. He pushed the seven of cups card forward. 'What do you see? Do not describe. Interpret.'

'The figure is a young man, dressed in black. So rich. He looks at seven cups each holding a different image. He seems to be looking at the cup that holds a castle. It is high on a hill. Maybe where he is comfortable. His solid base.'

'Good. The next cup?'

'Jewels. Overflowing with abundance. But a chain comes out of the cup. It is as if the chain leads to the riches.'

Margaretta looked up. 'Jasper had his evidence on a chain. If true, that chain and locket lead to riches.' She looked back at the card. 'The third cup holds a laurel wreath, the old crown of victory. So, it suggests he will win.'

'Look at the cup.'

She shuddered. 'There is a face. A skull. So, victory comes from a cup of death.'

'Two people and two dogs poisoned so far,' muttered Dee.

'The fourth cup is a dragon. I don't know the meaning...'

'Evil, danger, threat... and fantasy,' murmured Dee. 'And the dragon is the battle beast of the Tudors.'

'The top left cup holds a head. It looks like an innocent child.'

'Yes, and a darkened face with closed eyes... could represent a child kept in the shadows seeing little. He only learned his status weeks ago.'

Dee tapped on the top right of the card. 'And opposite the child is a snake slithering from a cup – the very symbol of lust, greed and evil. The creature that gave the apple to Eve.'

Margaretta blew out a long breath. 'And the seventh central cup holds an all-powerful, hidden figure. Like a conjuror.'

'A word I despise – but yes. Do you see how the figure, though hidden, holds its hands as in depictions of God and has red power emanating from it?' He did not wait for Margaretta to respond. 'This can mean God – that all before the young man are gifts in the name of God or God-given. And do you see the storm clouds around the cups? That is the maelstrom he brings.'

'And Jasper of Cleves stated he is fulfilling his destiny as set out by God.'

Dee shook his head and sat down heavily on the chair. 'I am convinced this card represents Jasper of Cleves and, when he stepped aboard *The Mariella*, he brought the maelstrom with him.'

'But, Doctor. He does not lie or think himself other than God-designed. The only words that made him uncomfortable were those he spoke of his aunt.'

Dee pondered. 'Hmmm. What did he feel of her?'

'It was a vague fear.'

Dee shrugged. 'A German spinster aunt with designs on his greatness. Little wonder. He will fear disappointing her. But when I spoke of poisoning – what then?'

'He did not know of the poisonings. He has no hand in it.'

'No. That is conjured by another.'

Margaretta looked back at the card and put her finger on the spirit in the centre. 'The God figure?'

'Not God. But maybe someone who believes he works for God… and who thinks Jasper's claim is God's will. The person represented by the king of wands, probably assisted by the page of wands – the cards that hid this one.' He closed his eyes. 'And there is no more ardent killer than one who believes he kills for God.'

Dee quickly shuffled the other cards in his hand and laid down the Devil and the two of wands to the right of Jasper's card. 'These always come up when I ask about Jasper's connections.' He ordered the others and put them to the left. 'The suite of wands. King, knight, page and ten of wands. So, power, ambition, messaging and toil. Working together. These are the players around him – those who further his cause. They seek power… the king always wants power.' He shuffled the deck again and pulled the death card. 'And they want power through destruction of the Tudors.'

Margaretta shuddered. 'But who are they?'

Dee shook his head. 'I know not. But among them are the people who seek Elizabeth's downfall and Jasper's rise… maybe among them are the two authors of the letters… and they will kill anyone who threatens their plot.' He looked up. 'That means you and me.'

Chapter Thirty-One

Seven hours after a dawn start, Sam drove the carriage into the yard of Hampton Court. As servants hurried forward to take the exhausted horses for stabling, he jumped down to open the door. Dee stepped out without a word and made for the side entrance. Margaretta followed with a wink. 'A good decision, Sam. Now go home to Lottie and see she is well. We can get a Court barge back up the river.' She was rewarded with a kiss on her cheek and Sam turned away without seeing the look of sadness on her face. Then the feelings started. *There is fear in this yard. Why do you all look at the Doctor and then to each other. It is too quiet. Danger. Something has happened. You all know it but do not know what. There was screaming. My God. The fear is bristling around me.*

When John Dee and Margaretta entered Cecil's office, he rose from a desk piled high with parchments. He nodded at the scribe at his side to leave and waited for the door to close. He was grey-faced and tight-jawed. 'Thank God you are back. What news?'

Dee sat, reached for the wine decanter and poured a large glass. 'We have a problem.' He took a long quaff and then opened his bag. 'The Cygnet Prince has good evidence and he is the living embodiment of Henry.' He shook his head. 'And he knows nothing of the poisonings. He was quite genuine.'

Cecil slammed a hand on his desk. 'Dear God, John, I charged you with rooting him out.'

Dee bridled. 'You charged me with finding truth. He knows nothing of the poisonings. It seems two people have been instructing his aunt and he absolutely believes himself the trueborn son of Anne of Cleves and Henry and that his claim to the throne is God's will.'

Cecil looked up, his eyes heavy and ringed in dark shadows. 'We have another victim.'

Dee jerked. 'Who?'

'A young woman called Joan Warren. Lavinia Teerlinc's pigment mixer. She was preparing the studio ready for the painting of a new portrait of Robert Dudley and helped herself to wine from a decanter. She was found face down in her own mess.' Cecil grimaced.

'And Lavinia Teerlinc?'

'Alive. Frightened. She was unexpectedly away visiting a client yesterday, so came back to find her apprentice dead.' Cecil sighed. 'Dear God, we could not stop her screaming.'

'So, the poison was meant to for her.'

'Worse. It was probably meant for both Lavinia and Robert Dudley. The killer is closing in on those who give evidence against or who would stand against the Cygnet Prince.'

Dee was silent a moment. 'So why the captain of *The Mariella*? Have you looked at the log?'

Cecil nodded and pulled a paper from a drawer. 'The Dutch translator went through every line of the voyage. The log says little. This is normal. A captain does not want a record of dissent on a private passage. But then we found a strange note at the side.' He passed the paper to John Dee.

'I did not sail a good maid of our realm in life to be made a harlot in death. I will speak out.' Dee looked up. 'What is this?'

'We have checked all the passages of *The Mariella*. We

found one entry for 1541 listing panels of seasoned oak for our Lady Anne of Cleves. But the real link is three years prior.'

John Dee leaned forward. 'Go on.'

'Captain Neerman would have been chosen by the Cygnet's helpers for his safety and sense. It seems he was chosen for the very same reason back in December, 1539. By strange coincidence, Neerman was the captain of the ship that brought Anne of Cleves from Calais to Deal when she came to marry Henry. It was his protection of her which meant that they were late – for he refused to sail in bad weather and put her in danger.'

'So, when the Cygnet Prince, in his arrogance, told Neerman of the plot and argued with him. That is why he threw the crucifix and shouted.'

Cecil nodded. 'Very likely. I also asked the translator about the words "fair gift". He says that is undoubtedly Dutch for poison – "Vergif".'

Dee grimaced. 'So, the poor man knew he was dying.'

Cecil rose and moved to the window, pinching the bridge of his nose. 'Now we know *why* Neerman died. The question is *who* killed him?'

'The same black-cloaked killer who is in plain sight in the palace,' answered Dee. 'What security have you put in place for Elizabeth?'

Cecil glanced at the door. 'Elizabeth is complaining loudly that her food is cold as I have ruled that every morsel is tasted half of an hour before it reaches her table.'

'Giving belladonna time to work on the hapless taster,' said Dee.

Cecil nodded. 'Safer that the elk-horn cup which some fools claim detects poison. And every room is being searched for belladonna. But this palace has many a dark corner. And I have banned all apple cakes.'

You are frightened Sir Cecil. But something else gnaws at you. A deeper fear than that for the Queen. You keep thinking of home. A baby.

Dee put his head in his hands. 'There is something we are missing. Some connection. The Cygnet Prince came to Bishop de la Quadra, the Bishop was linked to Margaret Douglas in a plot, Margaret Douglas was linked to Anne of Cleves.' Dee looked up. 'Every one of them living wants a Catholic to tumble Elizabeth from her throne. Have you challenged de la Quadra again?'

'Yes. This morning. He has not been at Court in days. So, he is not the poisoner. We have also searched his rooms here and in Dudley's house. Nothing. All you get from him is a storm of indignation and he can always prove where he was.'

'There was another name that keeps arising – Yaxley. You said he was passing notes between Bishop de La Quadra and Margaret Douglas. Could he be involved?'

Cecil shook his head as he returned to his desk. 'No. He has only one visitor in the Tower. His wife – and she is not allowed in his cell. They meet on the green, overseen by a guard.' He raised a hand. 'And before you ask, yes, I have had the guard report on their conversations. Apparently, she is a simpleton. Only concerned if he has enjoyed the food she brings in a basket.'

'But there was a connection between de la Quadra, Yaxley and Margaret Douglas.'

'Yes,' snapped Cecil. 'But every one of them is far away from Court. Each imprisoned or limited in their movements – and all watched. None gain from the Cygnet Prince. Margaret Douglas wants her son, Darnley, to marry Mary of Scots. That was their plot. This Cygnet is more a threat to them than anyone. If they were poisoning – he would be the first to fall.' Cecil pinched the bridge of his nose again. 'No, John. The killer is in the palace and clearing away any person who would undermine the claims of this German rogue. Our killer is close… very close… and hiding in full sight.' He slammed his hand on the desk, making Dee and Margaretta jump. 'Do not run down rabbit holes, John. This killer is walking among us and Elizabeth is in mortal danger.'

'Can you move her from Hampton Court?'

Cecil groaned. 'And we move her Court with her. Move Elizabeth and we move the killer. No. We stay here where she is happy and at least out of danger while she spends most of her day galloping the hills with that arrogant bastard, Dudley.' He looked at Margaretta with a wince. 'Excuse my language, my dear.'

Dee stood. 'I should check the body of Joan Warren. Just in case of clues.'

Cecil nodded. 'One of the servants will take you to the outhouse where we have placed her before burial. While you view her, I will think of our next move.'

Chapter Thirty-Two

The room stank of vomit and excrement. The body of Joan Warren was covered in a cloth which, when pulled back, revealed the awfulness of her death. Her undyed, linen smock was stained with yellow bile and, when Dee pulled up her eyelids, the broken veins in her eyes were evidence of a struggle to breathe. He bent down and sniffed near her mouth and grimaced. 'Sweet. Like fruit.' He turned to Margaretta and found her back turned, staring at the wall. 'Turn around and look upon her.'

'No. It makes me ill.'

'I need you to feel. Turn.'

Damn you and your cruelty. You will see me sick to my stomach if it suits you.

She turned. Stepped closer to the body and gazed at the woman's face. It looked peaceful now. Whatever the last terrible contortions of her mouth and cheeks there had been, were now relaxed into a face of just sleep. But the feeling from her was nothing like peace. 'Oh, God. Pain. Terrible. In her stomach and then panic that she cannot reach the privy-bucket. She was screaming at… at…'

'Is there someone there?'

'Yes. A black figure.'

'Look closely.'

'There is no face. They turn. Run. Leave her screaming.

Then... Oh, God. Joan knew she was dying. She is screaming for her mother... please. I need to stop.'

'Yes, yes. Here, sit down.' Dee patted her shoulder. 'Well done, girl.' But there was no time for comforting her. 'We must see the studio. Follow me.'

The studio was cramped. Easels were stood against the wall and in the corner a desk covered in bottles of pigment in every colour that Margaretta could imagine. In the centre, a fallen chair and shards of glass, a broken flagon – the contents spilled on the floor, now dried. Dee kneeled down and peered at the sticky patch. 'Green flecks. It was sweet wine. The belladonna was in the wine – because Cecil has banned the cakes.'

Dee rose and went to the side of the chair. Next to it was a patch of vomit, also drying though the acidic smell still rose. Dee held a hand over his nose as he bent over to inspect. 'I think she was facing the door when she realised. The chair would be pushed over as she got up and it has fallen to the back of the room. He turned and pointed to the door. 'She was looking there. So, they ran away through the door.' Dee stepped quickly across the room and opened the door looking for a likely escape route.

Margaretta followed but something caught her eye. There it was on a shoulder-high splinter in the wood. A black wool thread. 'Look, Doctor.' He came back. 'This is new, not dusty. And Joan was wearing undyed linen.'

'Well observed, girl. Put it in my bag.' He made a small smile. 'We are close to our quarry and our reward. I will insist on another full search and a tear will reveal the killer and my success. But where did they get the wine?' murmured Dee. 'Follow me.'

They walked back through the palace towards the great kitchens and along the corridor leading to the servant stairs and the cellars. Dee walked right in. Inside were stacks of barrels and at the far end tables full of flagons and cups for serving. The smell of wine scented the air and the sound of wood being rolled on stone filled their ears. Dee called to a cellarman. 'You, man. Do you work here every day?'

'I'm a cellarman. They don't want me in the laundry.'

Dee ignored the cheek and strode over. 'I think a flagon may have been filled in here yesterday afternoon. Someone wearing black.'

The man shrugged. 'Every servant in the upper levels wears black – the high-rank servants. The sons of the rich. I have 'em here every damned hour running under my feet for filling of flagons.'

'So, no-one unusual?'

'I was unloading yesterday out in the back yards. We can ask Davy. Mind you, he's as simple as a giddy goat.' He turned and yelled into the room and from behind a large cask emerged a small, freckle-faced lad no older than ten years. He stepped forward, eyes wide. Seeing Dee, he stopped and refused to come further.

You poor thing. You are afraid of your own shadow and you have heard of the Doctor. I hear the word warlock. Someone has been dripping bad words in your ear. She put her hand in Dee's arm in a signal to keep quiet. 'Davy. We want you to tell us who you saw here yesterday afternoon. It is to help Her Majesty.'

The boy looked a little vacant then furrowed his brow. 'I did see Jacob, Master Richard, Master Thomas, Master Gerald, Master Peter, Master Will, Master…'

Margaretta looked to the older man, who shrugged. 'He's listing just about every top-floor servant. I told you they are always down here. The rich don't drink beakers of small beer, miss. It's flagons of wine they want.'

She turned back to Davy. *You are thinking of someone – someone strange.* 'Did you see anyone new or someone unusual?' A slow nod. 'Tell us who it was.' A shrug. 'Tell us what they looked like.'

'Black cloak. No face.'

'Did they speak?'

The boy just shook his head. 'They just came in and filled a small flagon.'

'Anything else, Davy?'

'Black hands.'

Margaretta looked at Dee. 'Gloves. Same as Beatrice. So not a glimpse of skin showing. Nothing to identify them.'

Dee nodded. 'Hiding in full sight. Show me which barrel they used, boy.' He started towards the casks at the back of the cellar. 'Though if the barrel were poisoned, we would surely know by now.'

'It wasn't those.' Davy was shaking his head and pointing to a large cupboard at the side. 'It was the apple wine they did take.'

Dee span round and looked at Margaretta. The both spoke together. 'Apples.'

Chapter Thirty-Three

Cecil was waiting at his door. 'Any clues?'

'The killer is, as you say, hiding in full sight. They move around the palace in a black cloak that covers their face and gloves on their hands.' Dee opened his bag and took out the thread with a satisfied smile. 'That cloak has a small tear or thread-pull in it – at shoulder height. I want another search. Find a torn cloak and we match the thread. That will be our killer. Then I will link the motive to the Cygnet Prince. Every drop of poison is delivered through apples. That is our clue.'

Cecil looked unamused. 'A black thread and apples. That is meagre evidence for days of investigation.'

Dee bridled. 'I ask again. I want to interview the players in the Douglas plot – de la Quadra and Yaxley.'

'For the last time, you are not interviewing either, John,' snapped Cecil. 'The Douglas plot has been strangled and we will not give it further air. De la Quadra is under constant surveillance by my men and Yaxley is under lock and key, and anything he writes intercepted. I will not give him any thought that we have trouble. He will rot in the Tower, thinking he's failed.' He plucked the thread from Dee's fingers. 'I will order the search and we will find the cloaked killer by the time you are back. I will bring in Will Fleetwood for the interrogation.'

'Back? Will Fleetwood?' John Dee rose, his face reddening.

'This is my investigation. I just need to prove the link between the prince and the poisoner and—'

Cecil raise his hand to silence the other man. 'With him in Hever the connection is flimsy even if we can make it. There is only one way to swipe away the claims of this damned Cygnet Prince and prove he was born in Germany before Anne of Cleves arrived in England.'

Dee shook his head, confused. 'And how in God's name do I do that?'

Cecil turned and picked up a parchment from his desk. 'I have here the testimony of Thomas Cromwell. The man who organised the marriage of Anne to Henry and arranged her travel here from Cleves. He had to endure Henry's complaining. Listen to what he states of those discussions. "He plainly mistrusted her to be no maid by reason of the looseness of her belly and breasts and other tokens."'

Cecil put down the paper. 'In another of Cromwell's missives it was claimed Henry thought she "had very evil smells about her", but we will only use that if absolutely necessary.'

Dee looked abashed. 'So, you want me to prove that Jasper of Cleves was a bastard born to Anne of Cleves before her betrothal to Henry.'

'Exactly. Proof of earlier birth and we can put him on a ship back to his aunt. The poisoning will be separated and punished. Then we avoid any diplomatic tensions with Cleves.' He looked straight at Dee. 'You will prove this boy to be a German-born bastard.'

'And how am I going to do that?'

Cecil sat back with a look of satisfaction and then pointed at Dee. 'Your ship sails on Friday. You have four days to prepare to travel to Castle Solingen in Cleves.'

Dee stood abruptly, making the chair scrape on the floor. 'Are you quite mad? I cannot leave my studies…' Then a pause.

Oh, no. Your face has changed. Suddenly your eyes are brightening.

'The *Steganographia* written by Ioannes Trithemius. I can seek the cypher of angelic language.' He turned to Cecil. 'I have spent a year or more learning Hebrew and the Kabbalah. This is like a hand of fate…'

Cecil stood, his face furious. 'No. You will go immediately to Solingen, prove Jasper illegitimate and come back. Nothing else. No wandering the streets of Louvain or any other city looking for your strange tomes.'

'But this is a great opportunity. They told me in Birkmann's bookshop that there might be a copy in—'

'No, John,' shouted Cecil. 'We have a dynasty to save, not a damned angel to cypher.' He took a deep breath and lowered his voice. 'If you do this, I will fund a voyage to Europe to find your *Steganographia*. But for now, your only mission is to save our Queen.'

Chapter Thirty-Four

It was sometime later that Margaretta took a deep breath and wiped the last tear from her cheek. John Dee was in a foul mood and had made it very clear that rescuing Huw would have to wait for another day. He had then loudly bemoaned the 'injustice and malpractice' of Will Fleetwood being given all his evidence for Cecil had demanded every note taken by Margaretta before they left.

Margaretta waited half of the barge journey before daring to break into his thoughts. 'How long will you be away, Doctor?'

He jumped as if she had shouted. 'Will *I* be away? You mean *we*.'

She gulped. 'But I cannot go to Germany, Doctor. What about Huw... and the household?'

Dee sniffed his disapproval. 'I need you with me. With people speaking another tongue your gifts will be all the more essential.'

'But...'

'No arguing, girl. We will just have to placate Mistress Constable.'

'But what about Huw? We will be weeks away,' cried Margaretta, her voice shrill in anxiety.

Dee batted away her complaints. 'No time. Sam will protect

him.' He turned a hard glare on his apprentice in warning not to push the subject further.

You cruel scut. Damn you.

The kitchen was warm, swept and the pots lined in rows like soldiers. There was a loaf of bread wrapped in heavy cloth on the table and a pan of pottage bubbling on the fire. The cat looked up, yawned and dropped its head back on a paw. 'Siôn?' She went to the door leading to the hallway. All was quiet. 'Siôn?'

Then the door to Master Constable's office opened and the old soldier looked out. 'So, you are back.' He nodded sideways into the room. 'I'll be out in a minute.'

Oh, God. Why are you in the office? That's where Master Constable keeps the money. No-one is allowed in there. Not even Mistress Constable. She ran to the door and banged it open. 'What are you doing… Oh.'

Master Constable was in the chair by the window, one eye blackened and a cut across his cheek. His lower lip was swollen and blood crusted on a split. Both hands were bandaged though one still managed to hold a tankard of brew. He nodded at Margaretta and looked back out of the window. Siôn was at the desk, piles of coins before him and linen bags. Each pile was of different coins – half and quarter angels, silver half-crowns, sixpences and even the newly minted three ha'pennies which shone brighter than the others. He made a wry smile. 'I will make the Master's money safe and then be with you in the kitchen, Margaretta.' Then he picked up the half angels, poured them into a bag and tied the ribbon.

You know I was thinking ill of you. I do not need to feel your thoughts – they are written all over your face. I feel shame. Not yours. Mine. 'Yes. I will cut the bread for evening meal.' As she crossed the hallway, a plaintive call came from the mistress' chamber. She opened the door. There was Katherine, slightly askew on her chair, holding a linen she was embroidering.

'Good evening, mistress. We are back.' She entered and closed the door. 'What on earth happened to the Master?'

Katherine groaned and slumped back, taking a glug of wine. 'Vagabonds on the quays. He was out doing business when they jumped upon him and tried to steal all our money. A lad arrived here hammering the door in the middle of the night to tell me.' She pointed towards the next room. 'Thank the Lord that good Vintner McFadden had lent us his man. He was out like a hare from a box and defended the Master. Brought him home on his shoulders. He even chased the villains and retrieved our money.'

'I am surely glad he was here, mistress. You and I could not have been so strong – and the doctor is no fighter.'

Katherine brightened at mention of John Dee. 'No, indeed. He is a man of brilliance rather than brawn.' She smiled. 'Though it seems Vintner McFadden's man is very capable. He has been helping the Master with the accounts and even went to manage a trade for him this morning.' She took another quaff of wine. 'Yes, I will ask Doctor John to write me a letter of thanks to Angus McFadden.'

Oh, hell.

Katherine perked up. 'So, John will be free this evening.'

'I think he will, madam.' *And you can manage the reaction to our going to Germany, Doctor.*

Katherine beamed, sat up, straightened her bodice and pointed at the empty decanter. 'Then he will be in need of Vintner McFadden's superior wine.'

For which you have sold my brother you cumberworld, and I am helpless to get him back for weeks. I hate you for it and could scratch out your eyes. If your eyes were less addled by the wine you would see the look of venom on my face. 'Of course, mistress.'

'*Yli, gwnest ti feddwl mod i'n dwyn.* Look, you thought I was thieving.' Siôn was speaking in his native North Walian, the hard vowels making his accusation all the harsher.

'*Naddo. O'n i ddim ond…* No, I was only—'

'*Paid â dweud celwydd wrtha i, del.* Don't speak lies to me, pretty one.' The look was sad rather than hard.

There was a tense silence, then Margaretta turned to look him in the eye. 'Yes, Siôn Jenkins. You are right… and I was wrong. Very wrong. I think this city has robbed me of trust. I am truly sorry.'

He shrugged and gave a small smile. 'I understand. To be fair, most beggars are driven to steal by the ache in their bellies.' He pointed back towards the hall. 'That man will lose his business if he is not very careful.'

'What happened?'

'It was the day you left. A young lad came yelling that Master Constable was being killed. I arrived to find him face in the gutter, a few villains trying to pull the money from his pockets.' Siôn grinned and held up his hands. 'Good job you fight with fists not fingers.'

'You got the money back.'

'All of it. And made sure they would not attack an old man again. Carried him back and bandaged him up.' He chuckled. 'Though the squawking from the mistress had him begging to go back out.'

Margaretta laughed for the first time in days and sat for the rest of the story. The calming of Mistress Constable, the mugs of wine to quieten her, finding that Master Constable had no idea where his money was or how much he had, how Siôn had ordered his accounts. Then, how Master Constable was too ashamed of his black eye to go to the quays and had sent Siôn thinking he was an experienced man of Angus McFadden's business. Siôn had picked up the general assumption that Master Constable was always too far in his cups to make a good deal and had been on the wrong side of a negotiation for years. 'So, what did you do?'

'I told them the game was over and it would be fair trading hereafter.' Siôn winked. 'I came back with five sovereigns, two angels and a shilling and he nearly fell off his chair – and he hadn't had his first beaker of the day.'

Margaretta sat up. 'You might be the answer to a prayer.'

'I think I am for his coin bags.'

'No. My prayer. If I can keep the lie going for a few weeks, would you stay here?'

'Gladly. The gutter beckons.' He bent his head and his voice lowered to a whisper. 'And here I have felt like a man for the first time in many months.'

'And would you visit The Vintry every day to protect my brother?'

Siôn looked up confused. Minutes later he was angry and vowing to flatten anyone who laid a little finger on Huw. And the deal was made.

Margaretta opened the door to John Dee's office. 'You need to spend time with the mistress tonight.'

He wagged his hands as if batting away a fly. 'No time. We need to prepare for Germany. We have only four days.'

Margaretta's hands went to her hips. 'And you have to convince the mistress she can do without me for a few weeks and also keep your promise to keep Huw safe.'

Dee looked up, angry. 'Do not think you can speak like my mother, girl.'

She held her ground. 'I speak as your apprentice who wishes to help you. Now will you listen to a solution?'

He leaned back with a sigh. 'Speak your mind.' Two minutes later he had agreed to write a letter from Katherine to Angus McFadden thanking him for the loaning of his trusted man, Siôn Jenkins, and requesting if he might be given leave to stay with the Constables to manage their household and any business demands until their servant returns from Germany. Also, that Siôn Jenkins will visit The Vintry every day to ensure he keeps a keen eye on the good mastering of the yard boys. He would get Katherine's mark on it as signature and hand it to Margaretta for delivery.

The cry of Katherine Constable came up the stairs. Margaretta stood. 'Your summons, Doctor. If you get the letter agreed and signed before our evening meal, I will go to Susan straight after and ensure the plan is working by morning.' She walked out, ignoring his blustering at her speaking above her station.

Chapter Thirty-Five

It was after six in the evening when Margaretta arrived at Susan's house. Grace answered the door, her face lighting into a smile. 'Good evening, Miss Margaretta.' She glanced behind her. 'The mistress has been very quiet since your last visit.'

'That gladdens my heart, Grace. For she has a tendency to squawk louder than the chickens she could not count.' Margaretta patted the girl's shoulder. 'Now, is the master back from The Vintry, or have I only one empty skull to speak to?'

Grace sniggered and pointed down the corridor. 'Just one, miss. And you will see the little ones too.'

Margaretta started to make her way towards the door to the main chamber, but a thought stayed her steps and she turned back. 'Grace, you came to assist in the Constable household four years ago. Would you come again?'

'Oh, yes, miss. I truly enjoyed myself.' Her face fell. 'But I will surely miss your mother.'

Oh, little Grace. I miss her every day too, but with a warm heart because of you. 'But you can still keep a flow of wine?'

A loud chortle was the answer. Behind them the door flew open and Susan emerged, her face white. 'I thought I heard your voice. What are you saying to Grace?' She pointed at the girl. 'Back to the kitchens.' Grace ran.

Margaretta pushed past her sister, ignoring the protests.

Inside, Little Maria was on the floor and, seeing her aunt, bounced onto her feet holding up her arms to be picked up. Then the squeaks of joy as she was swept up and swung around in a circle before being pulled close and her forehead kissed. Now nearly four years old she prattled about her toys and ignored her mother's command to leave the room. In the far corner, Little Jack was sitting in a child's chair holding a book but staring at the floor. 'Hello, Jack. Will you come and greet your aunt?' No response. He started rocking. Margaretta walked over. 'Jack. Look at me.' Nothing. More rocking. She bent down. He turned his face to the wall.

'He is shy of strangers. He is only young,' snapped Susan.

'I am not a stranger. And he is seven years old.'

'You have not been here in years, then three times in a week.'

'The last time I saw him he was five. I told you then he was late speaking,' Margaretta turned back to her nephew and bent down again. 'Look at me.' Nothing. *Oh, God. Huw said you had the same colour as him. He was telling me...* 'Susan, open your eyes. You saw this when we were children.'

Susan pointed to the door. 'You need to leave. Angus will be home. After your last attack, he has banned you from the house.'

You are nervous. You are thinking of home.

Margaretta sat down. 'Has he indeed?' Margaretta folded her arms. 'So, he beats your brother in his yard and bans your sister from his house. What a fine family man you found yourself, Susan.'

Susan's chest heaved her fury. 'You cursed us.' Her eyes darted to her son and became fearful.

You are thinking of a fire. Do you fear a fire because I cursed you? God forgive me for being cruel. But I will use this. 'And I will invoke that curse unless you ensure that this has the response I want.' Margaretta pulled out the letter written by John Dee and slammed it on the table.

Susan picked it up. 'This makes no sense. Who is Siôn Jenkins and… why are you going to Germany?'

'It matters not. All you need to know and do is write a letter of agreement.'

'You are wicked.'

'And like knows like.' Margaretta tapped on the letter. 'Now you write what I tell you… and sign Angus' name.'

'I am a good wife. I will not…'

'But he is not a good husband… and you will… or…' Margaretta raised her hands above her head and began to sway. 'Bring upon this house the cur—'

With a panicked shriek, Susan ran to a desk in the corner and snatched up a quill pen. Margaretta walked over and dictated the words in response to Katherine. Then she added that Grace would be sent before Friday to work as a kitchen maid at the full expense of the McFaddens. Susan's attempt to argue was soon quelled with another display of raised arms and swaying. The ink blotted and the signature forged, the parchment was folded, sealed and pocketed. Margaretta walked to the door, turning only to glare at her sister. 'You explain this to Angus in any way you like, but you tell him that a man called Siôn will arrive every day to check on our brother. One bruise. Just one bruise… and I will evoke that curse, quicker than a beat of your black heart.' Then she walked out and slammed the door on her sister's wail.

Back in St Dunstans, Margaretta crept through the kitchen door having skulked along dark streets avoiding the night watchmen. All was dark and quiet. She picked up her mother's cat, pulled it close and slumped into the chair. 'Oh, Cadi, I am frightened. Do you think Mam will look down and think ill of me for upsetting Susan – her little favourite? Have I cursed myself by pretending to curse?'

'Depends on why you did it.'

Margaretta was on her feet with a yell, the cat dropped with an angry yowl. 'Siôn. What are you doing in the shadows?'

There was a chink of flint on metal and the flare of a taper. His face lit up; eyes bright. 'I was trying to sleep until you came clattering in.' He smiled. 'Where did you go tonight? And why so late?'

'To the house of my vile sister and her worse husband.' She pulled out the letter. 'But I have this to secure you a home for a while. And a young girl called Grace will arrive in the coming days to manage the kitchen. Might give you more time to get a name in the business.'

'How the hell did you manage that?'

Margaretta fetched herself a glass of Katherine's Malmsey wine, pulled a blanket over her knees and poured her heart and story out to Siôn Jenkins. The last thing she remembered was being guided to her bed, a blanket put over her and a pat on her head with the words in Welsh, 'An angel you are. And I will be a guardian angel to your brother.' For the first time in days, she slept.

Chapter Thirty-Six

Margaretta was woken by John Dee shaking her shoulder. 'Wake, wake. We are called to Hampton Court.'

She pulled herself upright. 'What time is it?'

'Early. Cecil's carriage is outside. Dress and be outside in five minutes.' He left. She could hear a brief conversation with Siôn. Something about managing all the chores. She pulled on her day dress and stumbled out. Siôn handed her a glass of weak small beer and a hunk of fresh bread. 'Eat this. It will settle you for the journey.'

'What is happening?'

'I don't know. The messenger arrived ten minutes ago and all I heard was the word "poison".'

Oh, God. Not another one.

Margaretta stumbled out in the pre-dawn grey. Further up the road, goodwives were skulking out with piss-pots and buckets of rubbish to slop in the gutters before the city awoke. She clambered into the carriage, still holding her chunk of bread. 'What is the frenzy?'

'Elizabeth is gravely ill. All of Court is in panic. Cecil suspects poison.'

At Hampton Court, John Dee jumped out of the carriage and ran to the side door. Margaretta climbed out slowly. She had been sick three times on the way and earned the fury of her master for making the carriage stop. The stable boys had not swept the yard of dung. And she ran to a corner to vomit again. Then she ran to Cecil's office. As she ran the corridors, the feelings flooded in as wide-eyed servants scurried past, heads bent and mouths pinched. *My God, the fear is everywhere and in everyone. Like animals trapped by a fire.*

Cecil's office buzzed with tension. He was at this desk, face so tense even the moles on his cheek appeared white. He was pinching the top of his nose, with his eyes closed tight. 'This is a disaster.'

John Dee was interrogating a panicked Robert Dudley.

'We rode for hours the day before yesterday. All was well. But it rained.' He stood and started to pace. 'When we arrived back, she was hot. Said she would bathe. Battleaxe Blanche said no, but Elizabeth insisted and Kat organised the ladies to fill her tub. That's the last I saw of her.' He ran his hand through his hair.

'What did she eat?'

Dudley shrugged. 'I was chased away by Kat. I do not know. I have ordered my sister, Lady Sidney, to act as chief nurse.'

Cecil interrupted, 'Doctor Burcot was called here yesterday evening by Henry Carey. The doctor insists it is smallpox, but Elizabeth called him a knave and dismissed him. She has worsened every hour.'

'Burcot? He's a damned engineer and only recently a physician. Why was I not called?' demanded Dee, his indignation making his voice brittle.

'Because Burcot was already close by at Henry Carey's London home and he is trusted by him. I cannot gainsay the Queen's cousin and a member of the Privy Council, John,' snapped Cecil.

You are a muddle of emotions, Sir Cecil. I sense fear, anxiety – like the parent of a sick child. But also anger and hurt. Your eyes keep flicking at Robert Dudley. Something has happened here.

The door opened. It was Blanche ap Harri, her face pale as snow and looking ten years older. She nodded to John Dee and looked to Cecil. 'She has fallen into fever and blemishes rise on her hands. Henry Carey has sent again for Doctor Burcot. But he is taking too long. The messenger says he refuses as Elizabeth called him a knave. The man is a dithering fool.'

Dudley jumped to his feet and shouted across the room at Blanche, 'Then you tell him that the Regent commands his presence. If he refuses, it is the Tower and more.'

Dee's face creased in confusion. 'Regent?'

Dudley raised his chin. 'Elizabeth has made me Regent for the duration of her illness and pensioned my man, Tamworth.' He turned to glare at Cecil. 'Is that not true, Sir Cecil? I control the country.'

Cecil just nodded and looked through the window.

There is the hurt and the anger. Elizabeth chose this man to manage her throne and not you, her trusted and discreet servant. You never flirt, always guide, put her first, protect and advise. She calls you her Spirit. But she chose her horseman over you. You poor man.

Cecil spoke to Blanche and ignored Dudley's question. 'Is she speaking?'

'No. Delirious.'

John Dee rose. 'Can I assist? You may think little of me, cou... Mistress Blanche. But I love our Queen and I have read many works on physik.'

The woman said nothing, but crooked a finger to follow.

The room was cold. Elizabeth was in her bed, her red hair splayed across her pillow, head moving side to side as she muttered senseless words. A sheen on her skin made the redness more vivid. Her ladies were clustered in the far corner, some holding hands. One was weeping. Sitting on the bed was a young woman holding Elizabeth's hand, stroking it and murmuring soft words.

Dee stepped forward and spoke to the woman holding Elizabeth. 'Mistress Sidney, tell me what you have seen. All the symptoms.'

But before the answer, there was a commotion outside and the chamber door slammed open. Through it was bundled a man in a long black gown and behind him, red in the face and holding a knife to his back, a furious Henry Carey. 'Now you get your fucking physik mind working, you knave, and make my cousin well. If you don't, I'll slice off your balls and souse them in vinegar before you eat them.' One of the ladies gasped her shock but only Blanche snapped at Henry to mind his tongue.

John Dee stepped forward. 'Doctor Burcot, can I assist?'

The other man stared, his indignation moving to irritation. 'Who are you?'

Dee introduced himself and came to the side of the bed. 'I see from the sheen and pinking there is fever. Was she raving before she fell into this stupor?'

Anger. Look how you pull your chin back into your neck in a display of indignation. Your desire to be in control is stronger than your fear.

'I am the physician here, sir. Do not question my diagnosis.' Behind him, Henry Carey growled.

Dee looked flummoxed. 'Not questioning – simply seeking to assist. We all want the best for Her Majesty.'

'I am her counsel in health. I do not need interference. Nor do we need conjuring.' He looked back at Elizabeth.

'But did she rave? See things? Did she vomit?'

'Not your business to know of our lady's body,' snapped Kat Astley from the far end of the chamber, then looked at Burcot to be rewarded by a nod.

Margaretta turned to Blanche ap Harri. '*Mae e'n ofnus ac wedi drysu.* He is frightened and confused.'

Blanche nodded and whispered '*Dw i'n gwybod.* I know.'

John Dee stepped further forward. 'I can assist. We need to ensure this is not…'

'I will ensure what needs to be ensured, sir,' was the snapped reply. Burcot turned away and walked towards the far door. 'I will return with a physik to reduce the fever. No blemishes are showing on her face.'

John Dee raised his hands in disbelief. 'For the love of God and Elizabeth, sir…' But Burcot was gone. All was silent except Elizabeth's agitated mumbling and the weeping of a young lady in waiting.

Blanche touched Margaretta's arm and tipped her head towards the door, then did the same to John Dee. Outside, Blanche marched them to a side room. 'Burcot is no fool when it comes to the body, but he is puffed up with his own importance.' Blanche closed her eyes and sighed.

'But does he know about the poisonings?' challenged Dee.

'Yes. And there was no raving, no confusion, no emitting from her stomach or her bowels. She simply started to complain of being hot and it worsened. We tried to give her broth but she turned it away and said she was aching all over and her head was in pain. Then she wanted to sleep. She seemed unable to speak. We thought she was just sleeping and then the murmuring started.' Blanche shook her head. 'That fool of a woman allowing her to bathe.' Then turned to look John Dee in the eye. 'Burcot is frightened but arrogant. He will reject all help from another person or another opinion. That is why he refused to return – because Elizabeth challenged his diagnosis.' She held up her hand to quell Dee's reaction. 'John, I know your standing is important too, but we cannot have Elizabeth saved by a person called a conjuror. I must ask you to assist with no thanks… for Elizabeth's sake.' She turned to Margaretta. 'Where is the woman you both trust? The herb woman?'

'Southwark,' answered Margaretta.

'Then go now, in haste. I will get you a horse.' Blanche left the room, leaving them in silence.

John Dee was staring into the middle distance, angry. 'Is it fair that an honest Christian philosopher be counted and called a conjuror? Shall that man be hugger-mugger condemned as a companion of the hell-hounds and a caller and conjuror of wicked and damned spirits?'

Margaretta laid a gentle hand on his arm. 'It is cruel, Doctor. But today the answer is "yes", and we have to put our Queen above injustice.'

Chapter Thirty-Seven

Clarissa asked questions as she moved around her shelves, pulling out boxes and jars of herbs and flowers and handing them to Simon for packaging, tying and labelling in linen cloths. What started the fever? Did she purge her stomach or suffer the flux? Did she rave? Margaretta answered all except the last question. 'Have you checked inside her mouth?'

When told 'no', or at least it was not reported, Clarissa growled, 'And what kind of physician does not look at a tongue?'

An hour later, the horses clattered into the yard of Hampton Court. Blanche was waiting and led the women quickly down the lower corridors before going up the back staircase to the gallery above. Here she stopped and opened a door to a room where John Dee was waiting, his face clouded. 'Wait here. Sir Cecil will summon the doctor and Kat Astley for a report to get them out of the way. Then I will fetch you.'

The silent minutes seemed to stretch into endless tension. Then Blanche arrived. 'Come. We have cleared the room of all ladies except Lady Sidney, who Robert Dudley insists stays at Elizabeth's side.'

They stepped into the chamber. The temperature was colder still and just Lady Sidney was at the bedside, holding Elizabeth's hand. She looked up at Blanche. 'She has just spoken. I think she is awake just a little.' Then she saw the three behind Blanche and went to object until stayed with a sharp command to 'keep quiet and let me get our lady the help she needs'.

Clarissa stepped forward and put her hand on Elizabeth's forehead. 'High fever.' She looked at Blanche. 'Margaretta said she ached and her head hurt. Was she tired also?'

'Yes. Unable to get to her bed without help. Then stopped speaking.'

Clarissa gently opened the patient's mouth, then took her hands from under the covers to inspect them and sighed.

John Dee stepped forward. 'Pustules?'

She nodded and Blanche gave a little cry.

Oh, God. Fear is rising. You know what this is. You think of death. Panic.

Clarissa turned to Lady Sidney. 'Get the fire made and banked as high as you can.' Then she turned to Blanche. 'Get the physician here but no-one else must enter. And anyone who has touched the Queen must be kept in their rooms.'

Blanche nodded and left quickly, tears gathering in her eyes, Lady Sidney behind her saying she would bank the fire herself.

Elizabeth opened her eyes and frowned at Clarissa but said nothing, then she turned her head towards John Dee and Margaretta. She gave a watery smile and whispered, 'Good Doctor. You are a friend indeed. I fear that I am called to heaven.'

'No, no.' His voice was low, gentle. 'My horoscope says you will reign long and glorious. Be at peace. The angels will protect you.'

Elizabeth's eyes flicked to Margaretta.

Fear. You think of your mother. You thought you saw her. Anne Boleyn. She has been here in the room with you. Telling you to be strong, be brave. 'Gwrandewch ar eich mam, eich Mawrhydi. Listen to your mother, Your Majesty.'

Elizabeth gave a tiny nod and whispered '*Gweddïwch.*

Pray.' Then her head tipped sideways and her breathing went deep.

The door opened behind them and Doctor Burcot entered with Blanche. He was sweating and tense with anxiety. A flash of anger in his eyes when he saw the group but before he could speak, John Dee cut in, 'We do not come to take you place, good Doctor. Only to assist.'

'I need no—'

'Yes, you do,' snapped Blanche. 'And you will not put your station above your knowledge.'

Clarissa stepped forward. 'Her Majesty has all the symptoms of smallpox. You will not expel the evil humours through cold. You need to flush them out with heat.' She pointed at the fire. 'This must be banked and kept burning and you move her to lay before it.'

Burcot gave a small mew and stepped back. 'I was right. This could run through the palace and touch us all.'

'It may. But your duty is here,' replied Dee. He looked at Margaretta. 'Your mother used a red blanket on me to break a fever.' Clarissa nodded agreement.

Lady Sidney returned quietly. 'I am here, Elizabeth. At your side.' She looked towards Blanche. 'I have promised Robert to stay. We all know what this means.'

Clarissa looked at her. 'You will surely be in danger here, madam.' The only answer was a nod of her head.

Clarissa opened her bag and pulled out two linen pouches. 'One is wormwood, the other is a mix of comfrey, marigold and lavender.' She strode over to Burcot. 'Make the wormwood into a tisane. When the lady rouses, get her to sip as much as possible to cleanse her bloods. The pustules will rise in two days. Do not burst them. They will scab and weep. When each is empty cover it with an ointment made of the flowers ground into honey to make a paste.' She turned back to look at Elizabeth. 'The only other remedy is prayer.'

Both Cecil and Dudley rose as Dee and Margaretta entered the office. 'Are our worst fears confirmed?'

Dee nodded. 'Smallpox.'

Dudley slumped into his chair. 'I hoped my sister was wrong. Oh, God help us… and Elizabeth.' He put his head in his hands and tried to hide the tears.

The fear in here is making my innards tremble. Look at my hands shake. I look around. You all quiver too. Outside, the palace is silent as servants walk, eyes down, mouths straight and faces full of worry. It feels like the end of days.

Cecil sat behind his desk with a sigh that was close to almost a moan. 'We have to suppress all news of this. If it reaches the Cygnet Prince or, God forbid, the schemers around Margaret Douglas, it will only fire their plotting.' He picked at the moles on his cheek and stared out of the window. 'We need Jasper of Cleves off our shores urgently.' He pointed to a seat. 'Sit, John. Your mission has just become all the more important.' He pulled out a parchment, rolled and tied with a black ribbon. 'I have the plans here.' The paper was unrolled and spread across the desk. 'You will be met in Antwerp by one Peter Albrecht. He is a Hungarian noble but well-travelled in Germany and a scholar of languages. He will accompany you to Solingen and act as a translator as the family of Anne of Cleves knows little English. Peter has already received finance to pay for a wagon and horses to transport you.' He handed another roll of paper to Dee. 'This is a list of the people who accompanied Anne of Cleves across Germany to Calais, or at least the important people.'

'There must be twenty names here.'

'There were actually more than two hundred. I have listed those noted by the English ambassador, Nicholas Wooton. We have no knowledge of who is alive. You need to find out.'

'Why is this one underlined?' asked Dee, pointing to the top name.

'Otto van Wylich. He was mentioned by Nicholas Wooton in a letter to Thomas Cromwell. He was significant in her entourage but unfortunately fell ill in a place called Revensteyn and had to be left behind. He was described as very able and close to Anne of Cleves. He was also an advisor to her father and from a district close to Solingen. He must have known Anne well, for his bastard son, Otho, was sent some years later to live in her household.' Cecil made a small frown. 'Wooton said he was very alike to King Henry.'

'Is the son still in England?'

'Unfortunately, not. The year before Anne of Cleves died there was some dispute in her household over expenditure. Her cousin stirred trouble and Otho, along with Anne's cofferer, Brockhause, was forced to leave England by the Privy Council. There is no trace of him after 1556.'

'Do you know the whereabouts of the father, Otto Van Wylich?'

'No, but his closeness to the family suggests he may be in or near Cleves. He will be an old man if he lives, but he may be able to give us the information we need.' Cecil opened a drawer and took out a pouch, which clinked with coin. 'This might loosen his tongue.'

Dee took the pouch and put it in his bag. 'I will prepare our questions and we will be at St Katherine's dock on Friday morning.'

Cecil looked up. 'We? Peter Albrecht will take your notes.'

'Margaretta is coming too. She will scribe for me.'

Cecil looked incredulous. 'You do not need a servant, John. You will be staying in inns and a castle.'

'She takes my evidence... how I like them written.' Dee picked up his bag. 'And she understands my methods. Like the cards.'

And I just stand here in the corner while you both talk as if I were not here. Just a woman. Invisible. But what I have come to realise is that is my power, no matter how I resent it. You are both ruled by a woman, you were born of women, you have sisters and you, Sir Cecil, have a wife who is more than your match in intelligence. But do you acknowledge the power of woman? No. Pray God, the Doctor is not going to show Cecil his cards. Surely, he is not carrying them.

John Dee pulled the pewter casket out of his bag and placed it on the desk in front of Cecil. 'See. These are powerful in helping me identify and analyse.' He opened the casket and pulled out a card. 'Queen of Swords. This is—'

Cecil reached over and slammed the casket shut. 'What the hell are you doing with these? I warned you before. This is conjuring'

Dee looked indignant and put the Queen of Swords back into the casket. 'You do not have to worry. They are simply playing cards from Europe. Only I understand the messages. They are linked to the Kabbalah I have been studying and...'

'I have warned you before about bringing your dark arts into my office,' shouted Cecil.

John Dee went still. 'Yet you are interested enough when you come to *my* office, William.'

'Your office is not in Court. We cannot risk any sniff of gossip around Elizabeth.' He picked up a file and began to open it. 'I have papers to attend to. Please go and prepare for your journey.' He pointed at Margaretta. 'If your servant is going, you pay for her.'

Chapter Thirty-Eight

'Grace. It is good to see you here.' Margaretta sat heavily in her mother's old chair having tipped the cat onto the floor. 'What was my sister like when you left?'

The girl grinned. 'Angry, miss. So, all is as normal.'

Margaretta smiled. 'Grace, is Little Jack shy?'

The girl looked up from the bread she was kneading. 'No, miss. He is special like your brother.'

Oh my God. I was right. The poor child.

Siôn came through the door, wearing a doublet. He nodded at Grace and spoke in English to Margaretta. 'Well, you were away before the birds had risen this morning. Is all well?'

'We have done as required.' Then she made a slight shake of her head to indicate to ask no more in front of Grace. 'You have a new coat.'

'An old coat of Master Constable. He wants me looking smarter in the yard.' He pointed at Grace. 'I am grateful to have this young lady helping in the kitchens. Master Constable has requested I spend each morning in his business, managing the morning trades.'

My word. If this does not make me even more ashamed at how I thought of you. All you needed was a shirt, breeches, a bath and scissors to your hair. You are no gutter-rat. You are a man of intelligence and ability. 'I am glad indeed, Siôn.' *You look at Grace and a sudden surge of sadness. You think of a child. A little girl. I hear the name Eleri. She was small like Grace. You mourn. I think you were a good father and husband like my dada. And I looked down upon you.*

Grace had started to chatter about what to buy from the Cheap in the morning. Then a cry from the hall. Siôn suppressed a grin and pointed to the barrel of Malmsey. 'Off you go, girl. And don't fill the beaker. I can't carry both of them to bed.' Grace jumped to her task with a giggle.

With her gone, Siôn sat at the table and turned to Welsh. 'I went to The Vintry today. My first visit. They call your brother "dog-boy" but stay away from him. He is already showing them for the fools they are by his ability. Apparently, he can look at a cargo and give the number of barrels without counting.'

'He is special, Siôn. But easily hurt and frightened.'

Siôn nodded. 'And what have you said to your sister? That low churl Angus McFadden seemed frightened of me. Was very keen to say Huw was happy.'

'Good. I might have been a little foolish in frightening Susan with a curse.'

Siôn smiled. 'There is nothing foolish in doing anything to protect the people you love, *del*.' He stood. 'Now let's get the wood in for the evening meal.'

I vow to help you Siôn Jenkins. You will not go back to the gutter.

Katherine Constable was in her room and saw Margaretta passing through the hallway. 'Margaretta, come.'

'Yes, mistress.'

'You and John will not be back for weeks.' She was at a slight angle and the words blurred. But there was not the usual frustration in her face or the hard bitter voice that was usual after several beakers of Malmsey. She suddenly looked as if she would weep.

'What troubles you, mistress?'

'Is this my punishment?'

'For what are you punished?'

'For sending Huw to Angus McFadden.' She pointed to the door. 'I heard that good man tell Master Constable that Merchant McFadden is not a kind man nor clever.' She gulped. 'I thought I was giving Huw a trade… I thought…' Her eyes moved to the beaker at her side.

Reality is you thought you could have it all, madam. A trade for Huw and a reward for doing it. You allowed yourself to be blinded. Now you are beginning to see the truth. You are not a bad woman, but you are so desperate to be liked you do not think. 'May I sit a minute with you, mistress?'

Katherine nodded though her brow was creasing in confusion. Margaretta sat on the seat next to her and turned to look into her unfocused eyes. 'It is true, mistress, that I was very troubled by Huw being sent to work with Vintner McFadden, though I cannot blame you. Angus and my sister are practised in the art of deception.'

Katherine made a little mew and her hand flew to her mouth. 'Oh. Lord.'

'But Siôn Jenkins is a good man and will watch over Huw until I return from Europe with the doctor. And then we can put things to rights.'

'How? I have put my mark on a contract.' Her eyes flicked to the beaker again.

Margaretta leaned in conspiratorially. 'You and I worked together seven years ago to save a good man,' She pointed towards the stair and the door of John Dee's office. 'Mayhap when I am back, you and I can help two good men or even three.'

Katherine's face creased in confusion.

'A contract can be changed. Siôn Jenkins would be happier working for an honest master like Merchant Constable. Your husband would be a more successful man if he had a trusted manager in his business. Huw would be happier in a household with two other good men.' Margaretta winked. 'Think, madam, how we can help three good men.'

Katherine took a deep breath. 'But how can two women effect such change?'

'You plant the idea in your husband's mind, mistress. And when I am back, I will deal with Angus and my sister.'

'But Angus is powerful. He has contracts with Court.'

'Oh, I think when we return, Doctor John will have more power at Court than a mere wine merchant.'

Katherine brightened. 'Indeed?'

'Indeed. Now why don't I work with Grace to make the meal and then you should spend some time with Doctor John before he travels.'

Katherine Constable nodded and sat back, a smile on her face.

I can almost hear your mind working out how to influence your husband. Good. Now I pray I can keep my side of the promise.

Part Two

Chapter Thirty-Nine

St Katherine's Dock was teeming with sailors carrying canvas bags, wharf-men with barrows shouting to be given clear passage to ships, captains shouting at crews from upper decks, hawkers calling their wares and small boys darting between legs being screamed at for trying to pick pockets or steal apples from baskets. Margaretta clung to Doctor Dee's sleeve and put her head down as he jostled them both through the melee. The Christina was rafted three ships out and so they had to climb across another two decks, ducking hoisted bales of wool and the elbows of the sailors as they filled their cargo holds to the top. The air was thick with noise and the smell of oily fleeces and fish.

'You must be Doctor Dee.' The captain walked forward. A tall man, bright blue eyes in a grizzled face. He held out two strong arms to take John Dee's bag and frowned at the weight. 'Are you carrying stones?'

'No. Books.'

The captain looked askance and pointed to Margaretta. 'You need to send the lady ashore, sir. We sail in half of an hour on the ebbing tide.'

'She is my servant. She sails too.'

The captain rounded, blue eyes narrowing. 'I've not been paid for two passengers and certainly not a woman. This is a working ship, sir. We don't bring bad luck aboard.'

Damn you and your foolish superstition. I am no more bad luck than a drunken sailor. In fact, less. I will hold your gaze and damn your words.

'I will pay her fare.'

'No. I will not have a woman on my ship.'

'If this were your Queen, would you refuse?'

The other man paused. 'Well, no. Of course, I would not. I—'

'Well, Her Majesty is not travelling today and so Margaretta will have her place. Come, girl.' John Dee marched along the deck and down the steps into the lower deck. Behind them the shouts of the captain that she was not to leave their cabin.

On docking in Antwerp, Margaretta walked down a gangplank thanking God she was alive after days of sickness. John Dee had been kind, but he could not stop the thoughts in her head – first that she might die, then that she was definitely going to die and for the last day praying she *would* die. Her stomach ached from heaving and her throat was tight. Again, she was clinging to Dee's sleeve trying to keep her footing on cobbles as he pushed through a crowd. This time the voices were a different mix. More French and other accents than in the London docks. Suddenly he stopped and called out. 'Are you Peter Albrecht?'

Margaretta looked up. He was a little taller than her, though shorter than Dee, solid in stature with early evidence of good living around his girth. She was struck by his face: square, strong, with a full mouth. But it was his eyes that held her gaze. She had never seen such kind eyes. He bowed to John Dee and proffered his hand. 'It is my great pleasure to meet you, Doctor Dee. I have heard much of your work in Louvain and as a young man I was one of those listening through the window when you lectured on Euclid's *Elements*.'

Dee puffed up like a bantam cock. 'You studied in Paris?'

'Yes, sir.'

Oh, hell's teeth. Not only do I want to lie down and die, but I have to endure another story of how you filled every lecture hall in Paris. Why does the ground feel as though it is moving? My ears are muffled. I feel...

'Madam Dee, are you unwell?'

I can see those brown eyes looking at me. So gentle. Worried. But I cannot speak. I worry I will be sick on my dress – again. I think I must smell. You are taking my arm, a hand on my back, being pushed forward. I can hear you telling people to stand aside. I can hear John Dee explaining that I am just his servant not his wife. I stumble. You hold me up and I hear gentle words. Now through a door. I am put on a seat, a blanket wraps around my shoulders and a beaker is put to my mouth. I drink. It tastes of honey. I take a breath. Those kind eyes looking into mine. 'Thank you, sir.'

'You must call me Peter.'

Sleep had been deep. Margaretta woke with the birds and looked out of the window onto the streets of Antwerp, like London but so different too. The calls of the early traders were loud but in in French, Flemish and Dutch. Other things were the same. The gutters holding drunks who had not made it home, the smell of piss rising from dark alleys, filth on the streets and the grease from unsold hawkers' pies tossed on the ground. But the dogs were happy. She pulled on her dress, sniffing the front to see if the washing she did last night had taken out the smell of sick. The mistress of the inn had been kind and given her lavender water to sweeten it. Only a slight acrid tang remained. A day in fresh air and she would put that sea voyage behind her.

At the bottom of the narrow wooden stairs, she stepped into the eating area. Dee was already at a table, pen in hand, writing on a parchment. 'Doing our investigation list again.'

'Why again?'

'You wiped your mouth with the first one before I could wrestle it from your hand.'

To her relief, Peter arrived at their side. He spoke first to Margaretta. 'I hope you are feeling stronger today, mistress.'

'I am... and please call me Margaretta.'

Why do you smile as if I have kissed you?

Peter turned to John Dee. 'Our wagon is ready, sir. I suggest we start early before the streets fill. I have brought extra blankets as Margaretta evidently does not like movement. She will have an easier journey if she sits with the wagon driver.'

Oh, my. Such kindness. I cannot remember this since Christopher held me in the carriage to Wolf Hall. I want to cry. I so miss care. There is so little these days. 'Thank you, Peter. I will go and get the bags.' *And run upstairs before the tears fall.*

The journey to Solingen was four days. On the first three days it had rained and Margaretta had been wrapped in an oiled cloth to keep her dry. The wagon driver did not speak, and so she was left to her own thoughts. From inside the wagon, she could hear the drone of the two men discussing every kind of intellect – mathematics, the stars, the planets, something called trigonometry. Sometimes the conversation was in a strange, harsh language. Doctor Dee was practicing his Hebrew on Peter. On the second day there had been a shout from the wagon and she had called back to ask Dee what was wrong. Nothing – he was simply yelping in delight, for Peter had told him he might know of a copy of the *Steganographia*. Conversation over dinner that evening was taken up with it. No matter how many times Peter tried to turn the conversation to include her, Dee returned to his obsession like a ball on a string.

Every evening I sense the growing warmth from you, Peter. By the third evening you were looking into my eyes when you talked to me and you kept touching my arm as we walked around the town to stretch our legs. You ask of Wales and my language. You have learned to say 'bore da – *good morning'*, 'pnawn da – *good afternoon', and* 'nos da – *good night'. This morning you asked me the words for beautiful and love. You had an innocent look on your face, but you did not know I felt far from innocent thoughts from you. Oh, Peter. Do not fall for me, for my heart is truly hardened. I will not be hurt again.*

Chapter Forty

On the fourth day they rounded a corner and the wagon driver nudged her and nodded into the distance. At the end of the long, wooded valley rose a great cliff and atop it a grey castle, with a glimpse of red roofs and a high tower. The wagon-man laughed and pointed to his own eyes. He was telling her they would already have been seen by the people of Solingen Castle.

The great entrance arch was guarded by men in livery. Unlike Elizabeth's green velveted and richly-decorated servants, here, the guards were in dark cloths, the only colour a russet jerkin. Their faces were obscured with iron helmets and on their feet, great boots, laced to the knee. One stepped forward and held a halberd towards them with a harsh shout to 'halt'. Peter jumped down from the wagon and produced a rolled parchment, richly decorated and written in a fine hand. The guards surveyed it, looked inside the wagon at Dee and then up at Margaretta. With a terse nod, they were admitted. The wagon rolled into a yard at the back of the castle. The grey walls rose four stories high with small lookouts across the valley. Other buildings in the yard were black-timbered and brown-plastered.

They followed another guard up a flight of stone steps and through a huge door carved with a wheel of eight spokes. 'The wheel is the ducal badge of Cleves,' explained Peter as they progressed into an inner courtyard, centred by a tower even higher than the main castle. At the very top a balcony jutted out. Margaretta noticed that a strange round cage swung in the breeze from a great beam jutting out of the tower. Servants were everywhere, carrying baskets and joints of meat. They stared at the visitors. The guard spoke to Peter in German and beckoned them forward to a set of steps rising in the corner of the yard. Margaretta stopped to look at the fountain with water tumbling from a lion's head but was hurried along by John Dee.

Inside the smell was of a clean rushed floor, polished wood, dust and also the sweet smell of baking. They moved through a square hall and even Dee was moved to stop and study the frieze around the wall depicting people, plants, coats of arms, castles and animals – all connected by a single vine branch. Through another door and they emerged into a great hall. Huge, coloured-glass windows cast a rainbow of lights and the polished wooden pillars gleamed below a wooden, ornately carved ceiling. The dark wooden floor was soft with a heavy covering of rushes and a fire burned in a grate large enough to stand in. Beside it was a woman, sitting with needlework in her lap. She stood, smiled and held out her hands as she stepped forward to greet her guests. In heavily accented English she bade them welcome before turning to German and Peter stepped forward to translate.

'This is Lady Amalia, sister to Anne of Cleves as you call her in England, sister to Wilhelm von Cleves and aunt to Jasper of Cleves.'

Amalia smiled sweetly and beckoned them forward to sit around the fire. She clapped her hands and servants jumped forward to clear a table of a chess set carved from ivory and lay it instead with glasses, a decanter of wine, baskets of bread, cheeses and cakes. 'Please eat and warm yourself.' She patted a chair next to her. 'Mistress Dee. Sit.'

Margaretta looked to Peter who explained that she was a scribe for John Dee and was trusted with taking notes but keeping confidences. Amalia's brow furrowed for a second and then gave way to another gracious smile. Margaretta pulled out a paper and a pen, placing the ink horn on a small table at her side.

She was a tall woman, apparently sturdily built but it was hard to tell with the layers of heavy cream-coloured velvet and damask that made up her gown. Over greying, fair hair she wore a square headdress, richly decorated with brocade, pearls and small embroidered flowers. She had once been a pretty woman, though a long nose detracted from the large blue eyes now circled with the creases of age. Her voice was clear and that of a younger woman. Her gaze was steady, direct, never faltering, straight into the eyes of Doctor Dee.

John Dee asked about the castle and complimented her on the strong structure and excellent design, only enhanced by such exquisite wall paintings and wood carving. She kept up the smile and explained that this was the favourite castle-palace of her parents and so it had been made comfortable for the raising of their family. She went on to speak of her happy childhood with Anne and then dabbed her eyes, stating the loss of her sister still weighed heavy on her heart.

Strange. I see your feelings but sense not a thing. When I came in, I felt satisfaction, even a little pleasure. Now nothing. God's teeth. What if my gifts only work for my own people? What if I am of no use here? Doctor Dee will be furious. Maybe if I look at you carefully. Concentrate. Nothing. Yet you weep openly. Oh, God.

The conversation stayed on Anne, Amalia smiling and speaking through Peter but her eyes never leaving Dee. 'My younger sister was the sweetest of girls. We had such love. We sat together for hours with mother learning our needlework, playing chess and then learning how to bake. Anne was always the better cook and made the best honey-carraway cakes that have ever been tasted.' Then her face fell. 'I remember the day the men came from England. A man called Wooton and another. They kept asking to see us, though my mother did not like them trying to view our faces. You see, women were veiled in those days.'

'I think, madam, these were the men who came to negotiate the marriage contract.'

'Yes. Then a painter came to us.'

'Hans Holbein.'

'A very good man. It was so much easier when he was here as he spoke German. He made us laugh when he painted.' She sighed and raised her hands as if in prayer. 'I recall our mother looking at the little pictures and saying, "which one will the great Henry choose?"' A sweet smile. 'Of course, it would be Anne. Just as it should be. She was the prettier sister.'

Oh, my. A sudden surge of anger. Yet you smile. I can almost taste your bitterness in my throat. It is like being back on the ship. Peter and the doctor are smiling at you. You sound so sweet. How do you act so well? And how do you stare but never blink?

Dee leaned forward. 'I must ask, my lady. Was your sister happy to go to England? I understand she had previously been betrothed to a French prince.'

'Francis, Duke of Bar, son of the Duke of Lorraine. Yes, but they never even met, and Anne never agreed. It was nothing.' Her face suddenly went solemn. 'Which is why my mother was distraught when your king, Henry, tried to say his marriage to my sister was invalid.'

'Yes, my lady. An unfortunate statement… but any prior… how can I say… connections… would be of interest.'

I feel fury. You are thinking of slicing his face with your nails. I need to keep my face down in case I show the alarm I feel.

Amalia smiled sweetly. 'Good Doctor Dee. My sister was a woman of virtue and honour. She only ever had one… as you say… connection. That was to your own king – Henry.'

Dee gulped. 'What can you tell me of the man who calls himself Jasper of Cleves?'

Amalia sat back and smiled again. 'He is son of my sister

and Henry and the most princely of young men. He arrived here as a tiny baby, still in swaddling, for his own protection and to be raised in readiness for his destiny.'

'Yes, I have met him, madam. Tell me about his arrival here.'

'He arrived with a trusted servant. Anne sent him with a golden locket and the letter inside.'

'It must have been a great surprise.'

'Yes. But we knew by then that Henry was remarried. We understood why Anne was protecting her... their little boy.' Another gracious smile. 'And I was more than happy to add him to our nursery, for I had his cousins here – Marie, Anna, Sibylle and Elisabeth, God rest her little soul. It was good for them to have a brother – just as Anne and I had been so blessed with our brother, Wilhelm.'

So why do I have an image of a man running at you with a sword, screaming that he would kill your dark thoughts and heresy?

'And you have raised him all these years? Alone?'

'Yes. Exactly as requested – in the education and languages required to meet his destiny as a king. He had an English tutor from the age of four, though sadly that man died three years ago. With Jasper's own mother gone to her maker...' Amalia paused, dabbed at her eyes and made a little sob. 'I will be proud to continue to act as his mother.'

You weep. But I feel nothing.

Dee looked sympathetic. 'I am sorry to distress you. You said "as requested". Who was instructing?'

Amalia shrugged and glanced over at a heavily carved chest on the far side of the room. 'I do not know. But a dear friend and supporter of Anne and her son.'

'We have seen two letters. By different hands. Were there two friends?'

Amalia breathed out slowly. 'I suppose there were.' She smiled and nodded.

'We have seen only one name – Erand Malas. Is that a true name?'

A little shrug. 'I suppose.'

Irritation. You resent these questions.

'Jasper said there were more letters. May we see the others?'

'There were very few.' Amalia stood and walked across the room to the chest. She lifted her top skirt and pulled a chain from under it which jangled with keys on a ring. She selected one and unlocked the chest. After a few seconds of rummaging in papers, she pulled out a browning letter. 'Here is one. It broke my heart.' She locked the chest and gave the letter to Dee, dabbing at her eyes again.

Dee took the letter and read it aloud. 'My dearest Amalia. I write with the gravest of news. Anne, mother of Jasper, lies in Chelsea Manor preparing to meet her maker. She will have been dead some days when this reaches your hand. She has this day written her will and has ensured that all those who she has loved will be given tokens of her esteem. Jasper will receive his sign of her love and his parentage. Break the news kindly such that he feels well of his future. Erand Malas.'

She thinks of a ring. He kept twisting his ring.

Amalia stepped forward and plucked the letter from John Dee's fingers, put it back in the box and turned the key.

'It would assist us to see all the letters, my lady.'

'As I said, she sent few.'

Margaretta touched his arm and whispered. '*Dywedodd hi "hi"*. She said "she".'

John Dee did not even nod but kept staring at Amalia. 'And how do you know Erand Malas is a woman?'

Amalia's steady gaze hardened. 'For only a woman would have shown such tenderness, Doctor.' A strained smile. 'And you saw the writing. They are by a delicate hand.' She clapped again and a servant opened the door. She turned back to her visitors. 'You must be tired. You will be taken to your rooms.'

They rose and prepared to leave. Amalia turned suddenly

to Dee. 'Do you play chess, sir? It is my favourite game – so good for the mind.'

'I do not, my lady. I regret…'

Her face went hard. 'A shame. It is a good game to understand the mind of another.' She walked out.

Anger. Irritation. You wanted to dominate him.

Margaretta spoke quickly to John Dee as they were taken along the corridor, keeping to their Welsh language to ensure nothing was overheard. 'Doctor, I am getting strange senses from the lady. When she weeps, she looks genuine in her feelings, but nothing comes from her. No sadness, no fear.'

'Any feelings at all?'

'Anger. And when you spoke of Anne's connections it was violent. She thought of a ring when the letter said Jasper would have a sign of his mother's love. Then irritation when you said you did not play chess. She wanted to beat you.'

Dee raised an eyebrow. 'Interesting. We must learn more of her. Keep watching, girl.'

Chapter Forty-One

Margaretta looked out onto the courtyard below. There were baskets of bread, meats, vegetables and herbs being carried from the tower to a door below her, all loudly organised by an elderly woman. She was dressed in a long brown smock to cover her dress and an apron stretched over a well-rounded stomach. The stoop of her back showed her age. There was a knock at the door.

'Peter. Is the doctor looking for me?'

'No. No. I wondered if I might show you around the castle. It will be very different to the castles in England.'

I can feel your nervousness. Your eyes are wide and you blink too often. 'That would be nice. Shall we ask the doctor? He loves anything by which he can learn.'

And how your face falls in disappointment.

'I think he is busy, Miss Margaretta. I will show him around later.'

You are a good man. What harm can there be? 'I will get my cloak.'

They had walked slowly around the castle three times, Peter teaching her about the defences, the history, the politics and the people of Cleves, and how the land was the bread-basket of Germany with great farms for wheat, beef and dairy. 'That is why everyone here is very round. Have you noticed?' He nodded at a servant passing with a basket of cakes resting on his belly. 'Tradition here is to feast every night on rich food and listen to music. All washed down with wine from the Rhineland.' Then he turned to look at her. 'You should be careful, Miss Margaretta. That tiny waist of yours will strain at your dress if you eat like these people.'

And you are thinking of reaching out and putting your hands on that waist. Time to move. 'Then lets us walk faster, Peter, and make room for our feasting.' *Oh, I have disappointed you. But better than hurt you. For I will never let a man take my heart again.*

They walked back into the central yard. The old woman who had been organising the servants earlier was sitting on a stone bench, a cake in her hand. She nodded and smiled, showing a broken row of brown teeth like old tombstones and called out to Peter. He laughed and told Margaretta that the lady was concerned by her slenderness and that she should ensure to eat her cakes. She made a small bow and asked Peter to thank her and say that if the smell from the bakery were true, then she would be eating cakes all day. Through Peter's translation she learned that she was called Gilda and had been the baker for more than thirty years. She spoke with the loudness of old people whose ears are failing – more shouting than speaking. She put her hand to her ear when Peter was speaking and obviously snapped at him to speak up as he started to raise his voice. When asked if she recalled the Lady Anne, her face lit up. Yes, she did recall her and the castle had been darker since the day she left.

Strange words, but maybe it is your way of speaking. I feel your sadness. You recall tears on the steps over there. A mother weeping. But also, another girl staring, angry.

'Peter, would you ask Mistress Gilda if she would speak with Doctor Dee?'

The woman answered that she would speak all day about

her beloved Anne and it was agreed to meet after she had baked the cakes for this evening's feast.

Dee was at a table in his room, the cards spread in front of him. 'Look at this.' He picked up a card and turned it to Margaretta. 'This fell from the pack. If ever we need proof that the cards speak true, this is it.'

'The three of cups. Three women in a dance together in celebration and abundance.' Margaretta frowned. 'I thought this was a good card, of friendship, kindness.'

Dee nodded. 'When I pulled the card, it was reversed. So, three woman working together but maybe not for such good. And one has her face hidden.'

'So, are you saying that the people we are looking for are all women?'

'I do not know. We cannot be too literal with the cards. We think Erand Malas is a woman – though we only have Amalia's slip of tongue as proof. But something else made me worry about this card and what it is telling us.' He held it up again. 'Look at the ground.'

Margaretta gave a little yelp. 'Apples. They are dancing in apples. The poisoner used apples.'

'And has no face.'

'Did you ask for more information?'

Dee nodded and turned over the next card.

'Oh, my God. The Tower. They are trying to bring about destruction and turmoil.' Margaretta took the card and surveyed it closely. 'A crown is falling from the top of the tower and the woman falling from the tower wears a crown. This can only mean Elizabeth.'

'Precisely. It means we are dealing with three people bent on throwing our Queen from her throne.'

'Who is the man who falls?'

Dee shrugged. 'Mayhap me if I cannot stop this fate. Or maybe Cecil or Dudley.'

There was a heavy silence. Margaretta hoped the chance of speaking with Gilda would hearten her master, but he was deep in a dark mood. He nodded agreement and sent Margaretta away to let him think. She closed the door and gulped down her anxiety.

John Dee, Margaretta and Peter waited on the stone seat. Gilda arrived exactly as promised carrying three golden cakes. The cakes were heavy, sweet with honey and spiced with carraway. She said they were Anne's favourites and that she had taught the young princess to bake them when she was just seven years old. Then she announced, with great pride, that she was in her seventy-fifth year and was as strong as when she was twenty. Only her teeth had gone to their maker. She slapped her thigh laughing and nudged John Dee with a wink. Good humour made her voice even louder.

You are a truly kind woman. Brimming with warmth and laughter. I feel so many memories coming from you. 'Mistress Gilda. We have heard that Lady Anne was a good-natured woman. Tell us about her.'

'She was sweeter than the honey in the cake you eat. So gentle. As a little girl she was surely shy and never left her mother's side. Her sisters Sibylla and Amalia too, though they were rowdier. Oh, I remember the day Sibylla threw the cutting shears at Amalia. She missed and poor little Anne was hit on the face.' A wan smile. 'She sobbed and sobbed until I picked her up and gave her a special honey cake.' The old lady leaned her back on the stone wall, plump hands across her belly and talked through her memories. She recalled the day the English men came to see old Duke John to enquire about his daughters. A man called Wooton who was charming and another man called Christopher Mont who had annoyed Duchess Maria by asking for Anne's veil to be lifted. Gilda chortled. 'He was soon told he was not here to check her teeth like a brood mare.' Then she frowned.

'Though Lady Amalia was quite happy to lift her veil for the gentlemen.'

Dee looked at Margaretta and nodded to make sure she noted that down.

I feel interest and anger. But from the old woman only warmth. It cannot be you, Doctor, for I cannot reach your senses. Why would Peter be angry? Up. Look up. There is the balcony. But it is empty. No, a shadow. Someone is hiding.

Gilda continued her cheery monologue through Peter. The painter, Holbein, had been a good man. Very polite. He was always down in the kitchens stealing cakes for he said they reminded him of his mother. He had painted Gilda a tiny picture of her little dog. She still had it in her room. Every night she said goodnight to it though it has been in heaven now seventeen years. Then the letter came to say that Henry had chosen Anne as his bride. Gilda suddenly frowned.

Sadness but also anger. You are recalling loud voices. You are recalling Amalia shouting. 'Mistress. It must have been very difficult for Lady Amalia to know she would lose her sister to another land.'

The woman looked suddenly uncomfortable. 'Oh, any disappointment was soon taken up with all the preparations. We had to make Anne a whole new wardrobe.' She laughed. 'But she was eating so many cakes because she had heard English cooking was terrible. We had to have the dresses taken out three times.'

Margaretta glanced at Dee who had also picked this up. *The testimony of King Henry said she was loose of the belly. This does not fit with being plump.*

Dee leaned towards the woman. 'Do you recall a Mrs Gylman arriving?'

'Why, yes. A kind lady but, oh, did she talk? Every morning she would teach Anne English and then she was down here in the yard painting and talking to everyone who passed. She drove us mad with her chattering.'

With encouragement Gilda continued. 'I recall the day

Anne left. She had been made a gilded wagon and I had filled another with breads and cakes and food for their journey. Her ladies-in-waiting were all assembled – fifteen of them, including Mother Lowe and Mrs Gylman, the trumpeters who would herald her way, other nobles, wagon-men. More than two hundred were readied to go. And Count Otto van Wylich, who was to ride at her side every mile of the journey.' She shook her head. 'Her mother wept. I have never heard such sadness. It was worse since Anne's father was only nine months dead. So, Duchess Maria and Amalia would be left alone here.' The old woman sighed deeply. 'My son lives but three leagues away and still I miss him.'

'Did Lady Amalia weep too?' asked Margaretta. *I think she did not.*

Gilda shrugged and said she could not recall. *And you are lying. You are recalling anger and bitterness. But your mind is going back to Wylich.* 'Mistress, the Count you call Wylich. He must have been important to be trusted with the safety of Lady Anne.'

'Yes. Yes, he was.' She looked down at the floor with a furrowed brow.

'Yet, you look sad when you speak of him.'

Gilda shrugged again. 'I never understood. He was a trusted friend of Anne's father – a neighbour living but four leagues away. He came back after leaving Anne in Calais and was so kind in telling Duchess Maria that she was well and safely in England. Then he came again to report she was happy even though your king had thrown her aside for a child-bride. He came directly from Antwerp to tell us what a wonderful time they had had and a true German celebration for the New Year. The next winter, Lady Amalia told us he was to be shot if he arrived at our gates.'

Fury. I feel fury.

Dee looked confused. 'What had he done?'

Gilda shrugged. 'We never knew.' Then she leaned towards

Dee and whispered very loudly. 'But I refuse to believe my sweet lady Anne tried to have him poisoned.'

'What?'

Gilda raised her plump hands. 'That was the story. They said she sent poisoned linens. But I do not believe it. She did not have a cruel bone in her body.'

Margaretta noted everything down. *There is something in this. I feel it. So does Doctor Dee. I can see in his face he suspects a connection.* 'Mistress, what year was this?'

'Late in fifteen forty-one. The year little Jasper arrived.'

'Was Count van Wylich injured?' asked Dee.

'No, but his servant died.'

'And where is the count now?'

'Dead and buried, sir. The same month as our dear Anne.' Tears gathered in her eyes.

Dee winced his disappointment. Another line of enquiry blocked by time and death. 'That is a shame. We hoped to make his acquaintance while here and learn more of her.'

The old woman brightened. 'Well, his son is now lord of their lands.' She leaned forward and put her hand to her mouth as if it would cover her loud words. 'Born the wrong side of the sheets, but the count left the home to Otho. He lived with Anne in England so can tell you of her goodness.' She waved a hand towards the valley. 'He is only four leagues away in Witzhelden. But you will have to travel there, for he is banished like his father.'

Dee's eyes brightened and he nodded at Margaretta before turning back to Gilda. 'Tell us about the baby Jasper, Gilda.'

'Oh, a dear little thing. Only weeks old when he arrived with two servants from Anne's household in England.' She grinned. 'And he has never refused a cake from me.'

'And were you told of his parents?'

Gilda shook her head. 'No-one ever said. Just that he was a child who needed a good home. Anne was always a girl to protect the abandoned and unwanted. She was always sending me to the gate with food for the town orphans.' She looked around and lowered her voice to what she thought was a whisper. 'Though the way he has been raised, I would say he is the child of a noble woman born out of wedlock. It does happen you know. And what better place to raise a child out of sight than this castle?' She made a little laugh. 'But she must have loved him, for letters arrived every year.'

'Was he a good child?' asked Margaretta.

'The sweetest. He reminded me of Anne. The only time I ever heard him being arrogant was the day he left here last month. He said, "Gilda, next time I see you I will make you curtsy." The silly pup. He was strutting like a little king.'

There was a shout from a door and Gilda was off her seat like a greyhound, calling something over her shoulder. Peter looked at Dee. 'Her cakes are ready in the oven. She was saying farewell and eat well.' He looked after her. 'That was a strange story.'

Dee nodded. 'Very strange. But at last, some luck. Tomorrow, we travel to visit Otho van Wylich.'

There was a noise above them. The sound of footsteps and a door closing. Margaretta looked up. 'Someone was listening.'

Chapter Forty-Two

The tables were groaning with food. Huge roasts of meat, breads of all kinds, pastries, marchpane fancies and cakes with seeds, honey and spices. People had arrived from all the surrounding great houses and eyed the guests from England with interest. Some bade them greetings in broken English and smiled kindly before turning to each other to make a comment. Margaretta was seated next to Peter who kept handing her delights as if tempting a child. Dee had been seated further up the table between a scholar from Cologne University and a church minister in a long black robe. They were conversing in Latin and were engrossed in a debate. Dee had sent Margaretta to get a wax tablet and stylus such that he could write his formulae. She had heard the word 'Steganographia' again and it was evident the scholar was being quizzed about his knowledge of the tome.

Amalia sat at the top of the table keeping a keen eye on all the guests and clapping her hands to servants as soon as she saw an empty plate.

Peter handed Margaretta another morsel and pulled his chair closer so that his arm was touching hers. 'Do you like the food, Margaretta? I hope it is not too rich for you.'

You are trying to impress me, but I am soon to be like a stuffed piglet. 'I think I cannot manage another mouthful,

Peter.' *Oh, now you look hurt.* 'As you said, I am not used to such a quantity of food. *I glance at your belly. You are. But those kind eyes compensate for anything.* 'Tell me about Hungary, Peter.' *I will keep you talking of facts and not feelings. Safer.*

It was some hours of eating, followed by music from a group of minstrels before the guests started to depart. Slowly they ebbed away, all making a point of coming to say farewell to John Dee. The scholar from Cologne was reluctant to go and kept shaking Dee's hand. Again, the word 'Steganographia' and a smile.

The hall quiet, Amalia asked if they had sufficient food, would they like another drink. Her face was calm, smiling. Then the question, 'I saw you talking to Gilda. Why?' The change in her tone was evident. Peter looked uncomfortable.

Anger. What are you worried about?

'A gracious lady,' responded Dee. 'She spoke so kindly about your sister, Anne. And also, the joy of having little Jasper here.'

Calming. But your eyes are still narrow.

'What else did she say?'

'Little. But tomorrow I wish to travel to visit a certain Otho van Wylich, who was in Anne's household.'

Oh, my God. You want to hit my master. I see your hand twitch.

'No. I forbid it.' Seeing Dee's incredulity, Amalia changed tack. 'The roads are dangerous this time of year. Vagabonds and wild boar.'

'But we arrived here with no incident, my lady. So, with a good wagon we will be safe. Otho van Wylich must be interviewed as part of our investigation.'

Your eyes are like a wild-cat. Black.

'It is a waste of your time. He was a mere servant. Nothing.' The voice was almost the growl of a feral dog.

That hard stare, no blinking. Fury.

Amalia snarled on. 'He is the bastard son of a traitor and so born with evil in his soul. His father is the reason my mother died screaming, and Anne only hated him for the journey she endured.'

There was a stony silence. Amalia glared. Dee tried to calm her by using a kind voice. 'I am sorry to cause distress, my lady. But we must investigate every factor. The claims of Jasper have huge implications for our country.' He made an encouraging smile. 'You surely understand that we already have a queen on the throne.'

Amalia kept her steady stare and her voice went to low anger. 'Jasper is the son of your king and my sister. He has the royal bloodline in his veins. He has the old and true religion in his heart and has been raised for his destiny… our destiny.'

Dee jerked in surprise. 'True religion? Madam, you must remember I have just dined with your Minister – a man of the reformed religion. This house is Lutheran.'

For a second, Amalia looked alarmed. Then her face settled. 'I may need to keep to the religion of my country, sir. But I have raised Jasper to take his country back to the true faith.'

You do not feel that. It is a lie.

Dee was holding strong. 'To take a country to a new king and a religion held by a minority would require significant proof of rights, my lady.'

She raised a finger at John Dee. 'You have the proof. The only travel you need to arrange, Doctor, is my travel to England to take up my rightful place.'

'*Your* rightful place?'

'Mother to a king. He will need me to support him in negotiation with the Queen of Scots.'

Why do you keep looking at the chest? 'My lady, Gilda mentioned many letters arriving for Jasper. Do you have more in the chest?'

Amalia turned with a sharp intake of breath as if insulted at being questioned by a servant. 'I told you. No. There is nothing else of Jasper's or of Anne's in the chest. Only my private papers.'

I feel tension. You are lying. Though you are a very good liar. You look me in the eye and never falter.

Then Amalia turned to Peter and spoke directly to him before turning on her heel and leaving the room. He looked shaken. 'She says that any attempt to speak with van Wylich will only bring danger to us. She says he is evil personified.'

Chapter Forty-Three

They rounded a corner on the wooded road and the hunting lodge loomed above them. Peter had spent the journey explaining the geography, the politics and the local families as they went. All Margaretta could remember was that they had crossed the River Wupper and were now in a place called Witzhelden. She sighed her relief at the motion soon stopping.

Grey stone, tall towers with rounded roofs, narrow windows. Every roof tilted at a sharp angle to stop the snow from gathering. Around the top of the main building were stones made to look like battlements. Steps led up to a black painted double door. Carved on each was a lion's head.

The door opened slowly to reveal an old woman who peered out into the sharp light of the day. Peter explained their visit and they were beckoned inside and shown two hard benches either side of a large stone-flagged hallway. At the far end, a dark wood staircase led up to the balconied floor above. They waited some time and then a call from above. A smiling man looked down and John Dee gasped. 'He looks just like Jasper and King Henry.'

'Greetings.' The accent was that of an English noble. 'I was not expecting guests from England.'

They trooped up the stairs into a large room, well-lit and warmed by a great fire. The walls were draped with tapestries, and the floor covered with a carpet made of woven rushes. Margaretta marvelled at how soft it felt below her feet.

Otho van Wylich was a big man. Tall, red-haired, a beard still well-coloured though streaked with grey below dark eyes. His shoulders were broad, square and his chest the size of a barrel. *No wonder my master gasped when he saw you. You look like the paintings of old King Henry of England. You could be his brother. But there is a sadness about you. A gentleness. This is not the man Amalia of Cleves described.*

John Dee was flowing with diplomacy. Bowing to Otho, he exclaimed, 'You surprised me, sir, looking so much like our old King Henry.'

Otho nodded. 'They said the very same of my father, whose looks I follow. Now, what brings me the pleasure of your visit?'

Dee explained he was on a mission from England to understand the story of Anne of Cleves. The man went quiet, his face falling into sadness and he gestured for his guests to sit. Then a bell was rung and a servant arrived. Though in German, it was evident that refreshments were being ordered. Minutes later, hot wine, bread, cheese and a basket of red-ripe plums were brought in and set on the table before them.

The small talk over and the servants departed, Otho van Wylich put two hands on the table. 'Why are you really here? Your Privy Council dismissed me from the household of Anne of Cleves in 1556 and told me to never return to England. So why do I get a visit from England's great Conjuror six years later?' His voice was now quiet, bitter.

But you are not cruel or harsh. You are a gentleman in every way. We bring you sad memories, but my master cannot afford to be resentful. 'Bydd yn dawel. Mae e ond yn drist. Be silent. He is only sad.'

Otho turned to Margaretta with a frown.

Dee batted a hand. 'She is a woman of Wales. Very hard to understand. They speak in half-words. Only a few of us understand her. But she takes adequate notes.' He pointed to the bag.

Damn you. Be careful. Peter has just shot you a look of derision. But I will play the game and pull out the paper and pen.

'I think we share experience of the cruelty of Queen Mary's Privy Council, sir. They banished you from the land and me from my position at Court.'

Otho softened instantly and sat in a throne-like chair. Margaretta noticed the lion carved into the high back, which appeared to stare over his head. 'I am sorry, Doctor Dee. My words were harsh and unfair. What do you want of me?'

'You must know Jasper of Cleves, raised in Solingen Castle.'

Otho's face clouded further. 'I do not. My father was banished from that place more than twenty years ago and I have never sought to visit.'

'Ah. Yes. Can you tell us why Lady Amalia became so... hostile?'

Otho shrugged. 'No. Nor did my father understand. He was called a traitor to their family, later blamed for Duchess Maria going mad and was ordered never to darken their door again. Admittedly, he did not agree with Anne's brother, Wilhelm, going to war with the Holy Roman Emperor, but he was no traitor.' Otho raised one eyebrow. 'My father called Amalia the dark to Anne's light.'

Dee nodded but made no comment. 'We understand your father accompanied Anne on her journey to Calais in 1539. Were you in that train?'

A wry smile. 'It is a little delicate, Doctor Dee. I was my father's son but not the son of his wife. I would not be tolerated. But he did tell me of it when he returned.'

'Please, tell us what you can.'

'My father was chosen as Anne's chief outrider as he had been well favoured by her father who had died months earlier. He was determined to see her safely through the hostile territories. He was at her side every day.'

'But we have seen a letter from the English ambassador saying he fell ill at a place called Revensteyn.'

Otho nodded. 'True. Bad fish. Then he rode like the wind to catch up, such was his concern over her fear.'

'Fear? Pray, why? You mentioned hostile territory.'

Otho shook his head. 'No. Anne was granted safe passage through Imperial lands and the nobles kept to their word. It was that damn foolish woman, Mrs Gylman. She had been sent over weeks before to teach English to Lady Anne. My God, she prattled. She was the same in Anne's household in England. We used to joke that the sight of her had us running for moss to put in our ears.'

Dee frowned. 'Prattling caused fear?'

'Ah – but such terrible prattles, Doctor. Endless talking to the Ambassador from England – he was called Nicholas Wooton. A good man, but he failed to keep her quiet.' He paused seeing Dee's confusion. 'She told terrible tales of Henry's Court. Anne had believed King Henry to be good and kind. But Mrs Gylman talked only of a first wife poisoned, a second beheaded and the third torn apart in childbed to save a prince. The husband Anne thought she was going to love was, in fact, a monster. She was terrified and had stopped eating by the time she left Hoogstraten, and there was a long hard journey ahead.'

Peter leaned in. 'I thought Anne of Cleves spoke no English. How did she understand?'

Otho made a cynical laugh. 'Mrs Gylman had spent seven weeks teaching Anne English. Like so many people learning a second language, she could hear the words but stuttered to utter them. So, she had to endure the dark tales of her future husband. She faded away.'

'She lost weight?' asked Dee.

'My father said she looked like a skinned cat.'

Dee turned to Margaretta and nodded to make sure the note was captured.

Otho continued. 'At Calais it was worse. A whole

entourage of English men staring at her and in the middle of them that braggart, Thomas Seymour.'

John Dee groaned. 'What did he do?'

'Anne asked him and the other men of the English reception party to teach her the card game Cent to please Henry when she arrived. Seymour drank too much and said, "Pray, Madam, you do not get with child, for you may find yourself ripped in two like my sister." The drunken fool.'

Peter's face creased in confusion. 'Who is Thomas Seymour?'

Dee turned to Peter. 'Thomas Seymour was the older brother of Jane Seymour, Henry's third wife who bore his son and then died.' He turned back to Otho. 'That was cruel, but Thomas Seymour was always a man with a mouth larger than his mind.'

'Maybe. But Anne was terrified. My father said he tried to comfort her but…'

And I am sensing more than comfort. Something happened between them. I feel love and I think you suspect it too, Count Otho.

'We understand your father visited her for New Year celebrations in 1541.'

'He did indeed. I think he was still concerned for her welfare. Henry had cast her aside by then and taken little Kathryn Howard as his bride. Lady Anne was alone in a strange land as so many of her ladies had been sent back to Cleves.'

'Did he tell you anything of that visit?'

Otho thought for a moment. 'No. Not a word. But he arrived back in good cheer. He went first to report to Anne's mother and sister in Solingen that she was well and then returned here. He was the happiest I ever saw him.'

I feel love again. Not you for your father. You are as suspicious as me. 'It sounds as if he had great fondness for Lady Anne, sir.'

Otho winked at Margaretta and replied. 'I think if my

father was a younger man and not bound to my step-mother he would have run to Anne of Cleves.' His face clouded. 'Then in the November of that same year it all changed. Happiness died. First Lady Amalia accused my father of treachery and then there was the letter. My God. I only saw my father cry twice and that was the first time – when they said the letter was from Anne.'

'You were here?' asked Dee.

'Yes. On holiday from university. I was out hunting with my father.' Otho took a long quaff of wine and poured another beaker to the brim. 'A messenger arrived with a basket of linens as a gift from Anne. They were finely sewn and so likely by her hand. As was normal, they were given to the laundress for freshening and pressing. She found a letter sewn into one kerchief and gave it to the comptroller for opening. The next thing…' He put his hand to his mouth. 'Dear God, what a way to go.'

'Go on,' encouraged Dee.

'Apparently, he opened the letter and a cloud of white dust went into his face. He started screaming and scratching at his eyes and throat. Fifteen minutes later he gasped his last breath.'

'Was the powder analysed?'

'Good God, no. They threw water over the poor man to try and stop the burning.'

'And the letter? What did it say?'

Otho shrugged. 'The ink was washed away. Then the letter was burned by the comptroller's wife. The poor woman. She was with child and widowed.'

'Is she here? She might remember something.'

Otho frowned. 'Of course, she is. Father would not send a woman into the world when her husband was a good servant of his.'

That is because he was, and you are, truly good men.

'Then may we speak to her?'

Otho shook his head. 'Widow Kleinman is a frail and frightened woman. Has been ever since. I will not have her bothered.'

Margaretta spoke up. 'I can speak to her, sir. Another woman will know how to be gentle.' She pointed at Peter. 'And this gentleman is as kind as you are.' *And I will smile as now you see I am not as ignorant as my master suggested.*

It was agreed. Peter and Margaretta were directed to the dairy beyond the cow fields. As they rose, Otho gestured to Dee. 'I remember you are a man of learning, sir. Come to my library.'

Oh, no. I hope your books are on chains.

As they walked, Peter tried to take Margaretta's hand. 'Do you really think me kind, Margaretta? It made me happy when you said that.'

'I do, Peter. But let us do our work.'

He finally grasped her hand and swung her round to look at him. 'I can work and wish at the same time, Margaretta. Wish that you would just give me a chance to show you what a good man I can be.'

Oh, God. No. No. I like you and that terrifies me. 'We can talk another time, Peter.' *And I feel your hurt as I turn away. Damn this.*

Widow Kleinman was wary but was soon soothed by Peter. When they took her back to that fateful day, tears flowed and she put her face in her hands as if that would stop the memories. Margaretta patted her arm and spoke softly, asking what she had seen in the letter. At last, a shuddering breath and she looked up. '*Drei Wörter. Unser kleiner Löwe.*'

Margaretta looked at Peter who was frowning. 'Three words. Our little lion.'

Back in the lodge, John Dee was waiting alone in the library, bent over a book. 'This is a great writing. It is of immense value to our thinking about the planets.' He grinned. 'Otho gave it to me.'

Oh no, you don't. 'I think you meant – gave it to you to read while you waited, master.'

Dee scowled. 'I could not tell the exact words but I certainly heard the library servant say, '*für Sie.*' That means—'

'For you to look at while you wait,' snapped Margaretta. 'But back to the purpose of our visit. Widow Kleinman saw three words: "Our little lion".'

Dee sat back with a gasp. 'And where did we see the lion?'

'On the scrying card representing Anne of Cleves. So, there was more than one lion in her life – Henry and another.' She sat by Dee. 'Or, maybe we were wrong and Henry was not her lion.'

Dee raised his eyebrows. 'This is a good lesson for you. What is another possibility? Think of the timing.'

Margaretta's eyes widened. 'Count Otto visited in January and the child… if there was a child in 1541… was seen in September. Jasper arrived here in November when the rumours began in England. Otho sits on a chair carved with a lion.' She shook her head. 'You don't think…'

Dee shook his head. 'Very unlikely. Anne would have sent the boy here and not to her sister.' He smiled. 'But would that not have made a sweeter story?'

The door opened and Otho came back in asking if they had the information they needed. His eyes were red rimmed. *You have been thinking of your father and Anne of Cleves. You poor man.* 'Before we go, sir, can you tell us of Anne of Cleves? What was she like?'

A sad smile. 'The dearest lady you could ever imagine. My father never believed she was guilty of the letter and so sent me there in 1542. It was a good solution – my father's wife did not have to see me and I could watch over Lady Anne. I recall his words so well. "If I cannot give her the world, then I give her my son." Then he said, "God save you well to keep her safe."'

'And did she speak of him… mention the letter?' asked Dee.

Otho shook his head slowly. 'Never. If I ever mentioned his name, she just looked sad and walked away. But even though she never contacted him again, she did not send a poisoned letter. She was the kindest, most gracious woman I ever served and I was sad to leave her.' He stood straight and smiled. 'But when your Privy Council forced me back here, they maybe did a good thing. At least I had a year with my father. We could not close the years apart, but we had many months to close the gap between us. And I was here to comfort him the second time he cried.'

Oh, God, I hear a terrible wailing like an animal. It is unbearable.

Otho has reddened and looked out of the window, his hands balled. 'It was July, 1557 and word reached us that Lady Anne had passed away due to a malady in her breast. My father screamed and wept the whole day.' Otho's shoulders shook and a small sob escaped him. 'He died the following day and, when we laid him out, there was a locket in his hand – inside, a tiny painting of Anne.'

There was no more to ask. Dee pointed to a painting with questions as he did the buckle on his bags and then handed it to Peter to carry. When the wagon arrived, Peter handed the bag to Margaretta so that he could open the door for her.

Damn this. It is heavy. And the doctor is avoiding my gaze. She turned to Otho. 'I am sorry to ask. But may I use the privy-chamber before we journey?'

The response was a kindly 'of course', and she walked quickly, ignoring Dee's shrill insistence to leave the bag with Peter. She ran back to the panelled room, placed the book on the table and looked around. *Lions. Not only carved into the chair in which the count sat, but into the panels as well. Lions everywhere.*

Back outside, she nodded thanks and asked, 'I saw many lions on your wall. What do they mean?'

He laughed. 'The animal in our family crest. Though sometimes I feel more of a kitten in this cruel world.'

Margaretta put her hand on his arm. 'I think you and your dear father made the world less cruel for Lady Anne of Cleves.'

Chapter Forty-Four

The return to Solingen was tense. Dee was furious that Margaretta had 'robbed' him of the book, which he insisted was a genuine gift.

'So, why did you secret it into your bag and not give generous thanks when we left?'

Dee had huffed and batted his hands as if she were an annoying fly. 'You are getting above yourself, girl. I am master and not to be questioned – and certainly not to be wilfully disobeyed.'

'Even if I save you from yourself?'

The wagon was stopped and she was told to sit with the driver as her bile was sure to make her sick in her stomach. She had stomped out leaving Dee angry and Peter bewildered.

It was evening when they rolled back through the gates of Solingen castle. The first thing Margaretta noticed was the quiet. In the far corner a young girl was being comforted as she wept. *Something has happened here. There is terrible sadness.* She called down through the wagon window. 'There is something wrong.'

Peter stepped out and went to speak to a man carrying a basket of meat who shook his head and pointed towards the main buildings. When Peter returned, he looked pale. 'Gilda died this morning.'

Oh no, no, no, no, no.

'What happened, my lady?'

Amalia shrugged. 'She was old. She sat on her chair with a cake and then fell over. Dead. Such a shame. But a good life and a mercifully quick end doing what she loved. Eating cake.' She raised her hands as if in prayer. They were gloved in white lace.

Surely you feel something? You are cold to it all. Yet you look straight into the doctor's eyes. Even Doctor Dee is stunned by your calm, and he is not a man of emotion. I look at Peter and he is horrified. 'My lady, will her family come to take her for burial? What is the tradition here?'

Amalia looked irritated at being questioned by a servant. 'She is already nailed in her coffin. There is no family.' She glanced across the room at the carved chest.

I see the colour red.

'But she has a son just three leagues away. She spoke of him,' argued Dee.

'She does not. The burial is set for the morning.'

You lie. But I feel no discomfort. Yet I feel horror. Violence. I keep seeing the colour red.

Amalia was glaring. Then a sudden turn to sweetness. 'Let us not think of death. We will feast tonight and celebrate the new king of England.' Another swivel of her eyes to the chest.

Dee was looking confused. 'Are you not interested in our visit to Otho?'

Her face hardened into a look of pure malice. 'I do not want his name mentioned in our home. He is nothing. My sister hated his father. I hate him. My mother died hating the whole family. He is the bastard of a viper and should be skinned as one.'

'He speaks of poison which killed a man. They said it was in linens sent by your sister, Anne.'

She shrugged. 'Who would blame her?'

Dee frowned. 'But everyone speaks of Anne's sweet nature. It seems strange.'

'Hah.' Amalia smiled. 'Then more likely he had the letter poisoned himself.'

Your first mistake. My master did not mention a letter. He has noticed too.

The woman left the room, saying that the guests would be arriving in the hour. Dee turned to Margaretta, his face worried. 'What do you feel?'

'Violence.'

'We need to look in that coffin.'

Peter spoke to servants and learned that the cook's coffin was in the basement below the kitchen. He looked horrified when John Dee asked him to get an iron bar from the blacksmith so that they could open the coffin and a hammer to put the nails back. Behind him, Margaretta was gulping air in panic. 'Be quick,' ordered Dee. 'We need to go down while everybody is busy preparing food and Amalia is greeting her guests.'

Peter trembled as he watched the door of the dank basement. The coffin was made of rough wood as if it had been put together quickly. 'Give me the bar,' commanded Dee and in seconds he was prising up the lid. 'Bring the lamp close, Margaretta. And before you complain – stop. I will not tolerate this feebleness with bodies any longer. It is just a shell with the soul gone.'

The wood came up with a creak as some of the iron nails gripped. The body was wrapped in a linen cloth which Dee pulled back. The face was white, bloated with dark spots that looked like ink-blots around the mouth and jaw. Dee frowned. 'Come and look.'

Margaretta took a deep breath and stepped forward trying

to stop the lamp shaking. Peter stayed back in the shadows averting his face from the scene.

Dee took the head and moved it. 'Stiffness. So, it was certainly this morning.' He frowned. 'But the bloating should not start for another half day.' He pulled open one eye. 'Bloodshot.' He looked up at Margaretta. 'What does that tell us?'

'Maybe poison... again.' She held her breath and bent over further, making herself study the face. 'Her neck is swollen too. Look, it bulges in the front. I don't recall her having a lump there when we spoke yesterday.'

Dee frowned. 'No. Indeed.' He pulled up the top lip. The blackened teeth were caked in food. It was yellow. 'That's honey cake.' He looked up at Margaretta. 'This will not be pleasant. The stiffness always starts with the face and so the muscles are taut.'

Oh, no. If he is being kind then it is going to be dreadful.

'Get me a knife from somewhere.'

Peter came over with a knife from his belt and darted back to the shadows. Dee lifted the lip again and slipped the knife into a gap in Gilda's teeth. Then a swift movement as if shucking an oyster. There was a sickening crack that made Margaretta cry out. He hushed her and peered into the cavity. 'Oh my God, she was stuffed like a goose. This woman choked on her own cakes.' He pointed to the red blotches. 'She was held.' He tugged at the linen cloth and exposed her hands. 'Look. This is another lesson for you, Margaretta. Always look for the next clue. See here. The nails are ragged and this one has blood under it. She was held down and struggled.' He stepped back. 'This poor woman was choked to death on her own cakes. And it was violent.'

And I sense red again. What is it?

Chapter Forty-Five

The coffin lid back in place and the nails tapped back in with as little sound as possible, they had managed to leave the basement without being seen. Dee and Margaretta were standing on a balcony overlooking the main yard, discussing the findings of the day when Peter arrived at their side, sweating. 'I think we must keep quiet about what we know.'

Dee huffed. 'Why? The woman was murdered.'

Peter pointed across the yard to the tower. 'Do you see that cage hanging at the side of the great tower? That is an execution chamber.'

Dee rolled his eyes to heaven. 'You are being fanciful, Peter. It looks like a cage for hoisting goods to the upper floors.'

'No, Doctor. Look again. The chain does not lead to a door. It is just a hoist to raise the cage.' Peter glanced over his shoulder. 'The servants have been told that if they speak of Gilda's death to any one of us, they will suffer death by bees.' He was breathing quickly, rivulets of sweat now running down his face and throat. 'They smear the cage with honey and then lock the person inside. When the bees come, they are stung to death.'

Margaretta grabbed the handrail of the balcony to steady herself. 'Oh, Lord. Please can we go?'

Dee cocked his head on one side. 'If they are not to speak of it, how do you know all this?'

'I overheard the blacksmith warning his apprentice when I took the hammer back. He said he was told when they took the coffin to the great hall and he had to nail it shut.'

Dee was silent a second. 'Why the hell would they take the coffin of a servant to the great hall when she died in the kitchens? Or did she?' He looked at Margaretta. 'Did you feel anything when we spoke to Amalia? Any lies?'

She shook her head. 'No lies. I feel nothing from her. But she keeps looking at that chest. And why is she suddenly wearing gloves?' She turned to Peter. 'Take me to the blacksmith. As if you are just showing a girl around.' *I cannot tell you of my abilities. So, I must be unkind and give you hope.* 'Come. I will take your arm and they will think nothing of it.'

Peter beamed, wiped the perspiration from his face and led her away.

The blacksmith was sitting in the corner, quenching his thirst from a large tankard. Next to him, his apprentice, already scarred on the face and his skin blackened by their furnace. Peter led Margaretta in and spoke to the older man, then whispered that he has asked to show her the skilled work he did. The man stood and picked up an iron horse-shoe for Margaretta to inspect. 'Peter. Ask if he is upset by the death of poor Gilda.'

The blacksmith flinched at the question and shook his head. Peter persisted in German and each question had the man moving from words to grunts.

You think of the coffin. Something red. Amalia was there. She frightened you. Scratched hands. You were in the great hall. Why were you told only to look ahead when you put the body inside? You knew something was wrong. Then the banging. You were made to hammer the lid down. Then a threat. You think of the cage. You look at the boy and say something. He nods and puts his head down. You have told him to be silent.

Margaretta plucked at Peter's sleeve. 'Please tell the blacksmith we do not see such fine work in England. Thank him for his time.' She handed back the shoe with a smile.

The blacksmith visibly slumped in relief when they walked out.

Dee was waiting on the balcony. 'What did you feel?' he whispered.

'They were in the great hall. He was commanded to look ahead when they put the body in the coffin. Fear. Something red. Scratched hands. He had to nail it down quickly.'

Peter looked confused. 'How do you know this?'

Dee was suddenly distracted by the arrival of guests in the courtyard. 'The priest and scholar from last night. Good.'

Thank goodness. I can escape Peter's questions.

The great hall was full when they entered. Amalia was walking around, proffering her gloved hand and greeting all guests with the sweetest of smiles. She seemed all the more radiant tonight, like a queen in white and gold brocade. Seeing John Dee, she pushed through the crowd. 'Doctor Dee. I have a special event for you.'

'Event?'

'Please stay at the end of the meal.'

The evening continued. Talk, music, tables groaning with food. Margaretta sat again with Peter who spent the evening trying to impress her with his noble parentage in Hungary and how he would inherit a fortune, though he was still nervous. She smiled and listened and wondered how to escape. The clock in the courtyard struck eleven and the guests rose. One by one they left, though the priest was asked to remain. Eventually only the priest, Amalia and her visitors remained. 'Good Doctor, I thought I should put your troubled mind to rest,' purred Amalia. She walked to the chest and lifted her outer skirt to obtain the key. Then turned. 'Do you really need your servant here?'

Dee nodded to Margaretta. 'Only because she will write the report of the event, my lady.'

Amalia fixed her gaze on Margaretta and made a smile that did not reach her eyes. 'Very well.' She lifted the lid of the box. 'You were concerned that I had more papers from my sister. I want to prove I have only the two letters I showed you.' She nodded to the nervous priest. 'Witnessed by a man of God.' She lifted out the two letters and handed them to the priest. 'Father Beitel has seen these and can verify.' As she stretched her hands forward, the sleeve slipped – revealing a deep red scratch on her wrist.

The old priest trembles. His eyes flick and I sense his discomfort. It is not a lie, but nor is it the truth.

Amalia continued. 'If you look inside, Doctor, you will find only two more pouches, one with my will and the other with letters from my brother. She stepped back and held her hand towards the chest. Please. Look for yourself.'

Dee stepped forward and lifted the first pouch. From it he pulled a scroll.

That pouch is red-oiled linen.

He opened it and beckoned Peter who stepped forward nervously and took the scroll. He untied the red ribbon and started to read. Only seconds later he looked up at Dee. 'This is indeed a last will and testament.'

'Take the other pouch, Doctor,' urged Amalia.

Red cloth again.

Peter was given the contents and flicked through them. 'These are letters from Wilhelm of Cleves. They are varied but mainly about family, news and also the education of his daughters.' He turned to Amalia. 'I think you disagreed, my lady?'

A sudden flash of a man with a sword. Chasing you. The slam of a door. Screaming of children.

Amalia smiled sweetly. 'Brothers and sisters. Is it not always the same?

No, madam. Your brother tried to kill you in rage.

Dee looked inside the chest again and took out a small book bound with tooled leather. Amalia bridled. 'My poetry. Private.' She looked at Peter and snapped, 'Open any page and confirm – but only one verse.'

Peter obliged and opened the book in the middle, read silently, shifted on his feet as if embarrassed, then moved to another page and nodded. 'Poetry and very heartfelt.' He reddened as he passed the book back to Amalia.

I hear the name Katharina.

Amalia snatched the book away.

Dee put his hands in to test the bottom of the chest. It was empty.

The priest again. Eyes flicking. He is confused. He knows there was more in there. She is lying. He thinks of a book. Now he wants to escape. See how he looks at the door. But Amalia is turning to him.

'Father, please swear that these documents have been in the chest each time you saw it opened.'

The old churchman nodded and looked like a mouse facing a cat.

Amalia took the crimson pouches, put them in the chest and slammed it shut. 'I hope that has satisfied your curiosity, Doctor Dee.' She turned with dark eyes. 'Do sleep well.' She turned to the priest. 'I will see you tomorrow for the burial, Father.' She left. The frightened priest walked out in silence.

Dee turned to Margaretta and Peter, who was beginning to sweat again. They were in the dim light of candles as shadows danced across the walls. 'Red,' whispered Margaretta. 'I felt the colour red. The blacksmith saw red. And that priest has seen much more in that chest.'

'The coffin,' muttered Dee.

Chapter Forty-Six

'Sir, I was hired as a translator and you are making a grave robber of me.' Peter was trembling as he held the lamp under a cloth to dim the beam. 'I was nearly caught stealing this bar and the sacks from the blacksmith. And the sentries saw me talking to the wagon driver in the village.'

'Stop bleating, man. We have to find the papers.'

'But I think—'

'Well, stop your damned thinking and give that lamp to Margaretta. I need your strength to heave the body.'

Margaretta took the lamp and said quietly. 'Excuse the cussing. It is a sign of his concern.' *I mean fear, but I do not want you to sweat more, Peter.*

They looked like three shadows in the half-light. Each one wearing all their clothes and their shoes muffled with sackcloth ripped into strips by Margaretta. Readied by the door was Doctor Dee's bag of papers, pens and his box of books.

Dee grabbed the iron bar from Peter and worked around the coffin lid, again easing up the nails one at a time to ensure no noise. Margaretta stood at the door of the cellar, holding her breath and listening for any footsteps. There was a soft clunk as the lid came loose and then a scratch as Dee pulled it off the coffin. 'I should have realised when I saw the depth of this. I know she is big, but this is the depth of my arm.' He beckoned to Peter. 'Come here. The body will be fully stiff by now. We will need to heave it sideways in the coffin.'

The other man hesitated.

'God's teeth. Help me,' hissed Dee.

The two men grabbed the white cloth covering Gilda and with one big pull, tipped her onto one side. There was a terrible groan from Gilda and Peter jumped back with a muffled yelp. 'She is alive.' He was gasping in fear.

'Find your metal, sir. The body expels air after death. She is quite dead. Now come back and hold her while we look.' Peter reluctantly obeyed, though he closed his eyes. Dee peered inside. 'Margaretta, bring that lamp. Look under the body.'

There was no time for arguing. She stepped over, shone the lamp. 'A whole layer of red wrappings. Hold the body up.' One by one, she tugged them from under Gilda. Some were flat, others bulky. Then under Gilda's head she put her hands on a larger package, square and hard. 'A book.' Satisfied the coffin was empty, she nodded to Dee and the body thumped back onto its back. Peter looked as if he were about to be sick.

'Get the sack,' ordered Dee. In seconds, the red pouches were collected together and they could go. 'Now let's get this lid back on. We will not nail it closed. The noise would be too loud. They will not notice the nails are missing until morning.' He turned to Peter. 'Where did you tell the wagon to wait?'

'At the end of the road, around the bend. But how do we get past the sentry on the gate?' Peter's voice wavered with worry.

'You will go and tell him you saw someone in the yard walking towards the cellar,' commanded Dee.

Peter shook his head. 'Why bring attention to this place?'

'Because when he sees nothing amiss it gives us more time to get away. Also, when they move the coffin in the morning and find the items gone, they will think we are only recently departed.' Dee tapped his own head. 'You have to think as they will. Now hide those coffin nails.'

They crept out into the dark of the yard, their lamp extinguished. Only a cloud-covered moon gave a sliver of light. Keeping to the shadows, they skirted the walls to the alley which led to the outer yard and the main entrance. The sentry was standing with his back to them. Dee nudged Peter and tipped his head in a command.

Peter steadied himself, then walked forward. His words were muffled, but they saw him point back towards the inner yard. In seconds, the sentry was saying 'danke' and running into the castle. Dee grabbed the sack, Margaretta their bags and Peter the box of books and they ran. The wagon was there, the driver waiting on his seat. Inside the carriage, Dee was firm. 'Tell him to go in the opposite direction. Away from Antwerp.'

Peter shook his head. 'We need to get out of Germany. Antwerp is the closest port.'

'And exactly where Amalia will send her posse as soon as she realises the papers are not under the body.' He pointed at the roof. 'Tell him to run to Cologne. It is but twenty miles in the wrong direction and easier to hide in a city. We will go to the house of Caspar Vopel.'

'The mathematician?'

'Mathematician, cartographer, great scholar of the stars. Yes.'

'I heard he was very ill.'

'No matter. He will hide us. And he has a good library.'

Hours later the wagon entered the outer walls of Cologne. Just as in London, the air changed from fresh to sour. The smell of piss pots, rotting vegetables, a dead dog and of too many people pushed into dark alleys and small houses assaulted their senses. Margaretta, who had already had to ask the wagon to stop twice, groaned and covered her nose. Peter reached out and then pulled his hand back, unsure.

Houses were still in darkness, and they went down a few

streets before they found one with a light burning in the window. Peter jumped out to ask directions, though the sad look on the woman's face told a story. Peter sat back in his seat. 'Doktor Vopel died at the end of last year. Only his daughter remains in his house on the Heumarkt.' He looked at Dee. 'So where do we hide now?'

'With the daughter,' snapped Dee. 'Give direction to the wagon-man.'

Peter shook his head but called out to the driver.

They pulled up outside a tall, narrow-timbered house. Dee knocked on the door while Peter gave the driver extra money and instructions to take his wagon and keep going. Eventually, a dishevelled woman came to the door, scowling beneath a hastily pulled on coif, a blanket around her thin shoulders. Peter took some minutes to explain that they were visiting scholars and were so very sorry to arrive at such an early hour. Reluctantly she stepped aside for them to enter and the conversation, though terse, continued with John Dee and Margaretta standing in the corner simply looking between the two. Eventually, Peter explained. 'This is Doktor Vopel's daughter, Ursula. She says you are not expected. You see, in Germany is it customary to—'

Dee nodded. 'Tell her I am a great admirer of her father's work and a mathematician myself. Say I want to know more of her father's work so that I can speak of his brilliance in the great houses of England. Ask if we might simply stay a few days and look at his books. We will pay for our keep and work silently in his office. No disturbance.' He pointed at Margaretta. 'Tell her my servant is a good cook and can clean.'

What? Damn you. I am no cook and I hate cleaning. Seven years on and you repeat history by offering me as a chattel in order to get your own way. And why do you think it is acceptable to invade this poor woman's grief to fill your mind with what you crave – more knowledge than anyone else? I hate you.

Peter relayed the message and slowly the daughter nodded. Then she turned to Margaretta and pointed upstairs, making gestures to mimic making up beds.

I will never forgive you for this, John Dee.

Dee grunted and asked for entry to Vopel's office.

Half an hour later, the women descended the stairs, the beds made and water put in each room. Ursula seemed a kind woman and had helped. She gestured to the kitchen and made the motion of cutting bread then upturned her hands in question. Margaretta nodded and opened the office door where Dee was already hunched over a book and, in the corner, Peter was reading another by candlelight. 'We need to buy bread.'

Dee looked up, red eyed from having had so little sleep in the wagon. He nodded to Peter. 'Your task, I think.'

Peter rose and left looking less than comfortable with the situation. Margaretta waited until the door was closed. 'Have you looked in those pouches yet, Doctor?'

He glowered. 'No. We will do it together.'

'Good. Then let us start now while Peter is out.'

Dee huffed. 'Very well, but soften your tongue.' He looked up sharp-eyed and pointed at her. 'Roof.' Then he pointed the finger back at himself. 'Recognition.'

There were no fewer than twenty letters. Amalia was evidently an efficient organiser of her papers, for they were in exact order. Dee read through each one and then handed it to Margaretta with instruction to read and feel.

When all were read, he sat back in the chair. 'So, we have a picture. We know the first letter – the one held by Jasper – simply says to hide the child.' He thumped the desk. 'Damn

Cecil, taking my notes. Those words might be significant. Do you remember the date?'

'I think it was November, 1541.'

Margaretta kept reading. 'The second letter – and the first in Amalia's chest – is dated December, 1541. This is from the person signing "Your friend". It says, "The arrow of early death has pierced the mother's heart. The secret nearly secure".' She looked up at Dee and then grasped the next letter. 'Something else sad happened in that winter. This is dated February, 1542.'

'Who signs it?' demanded Dee.

'It is the friend again. It says, "Your words of coldness have landed. The mother weeps once more but her heart must break for the destiny of England".'

Dee frowned. 'Coldness? Odd words. Maybe the coldness which led to Wilhelm's war and prevented Anne from returning home. No wonder she wept. Maybe that is why Otto sent his son.'

Margaretta kept working through the papers. 'There is a long gap. The next letter is dated April, 1545.' She held the paper out to Dee. 'No grease marks and the hand has changed.'

Dee looked at it and turned the parchment to show her the bottom. 'And this is the first letter signed by Erand Malas. Keep reading.'

'Erand Malas assured Amalia that she would rise with Jasper. Listen to this. "Forsooth I understand your yearning and your righteous anger that the negotiations with the Margraviate of Baden have left you bereft. Though, mayhap, your brother has been kind in refusing to place you in a marriage which would bring you a husband either low in good living or low in age. God works in his own way and so brought to you Jasper, who will bring to your life the love of a child and the right place as the mother of a king".' Margaretta looked up. 'This tallies with Amalia stating you should be organising her travel to England and claiming her destiny as dowager queen.'

Dee nodded. 'Sad really. But whoever Erand Malas may be, they believe themselves powerful enough to make such assertions.' He shot a glance at Margaretta. 'Or made such promises in order to keep Amalia doing all their bidding. And they know of Amalia's situation.'

Margaretta scanned the next letter again. 'This one says he must be a king that brings England back into the heart of Rome and the true faith. That she is to raise him and select a priest to instruct him, even though Amalia may follow a different path. It says he must be like his uncle and not his aunt.' She sat back. 'Peter picked up a dispute between brother and sister in the letters he read – and I kept getting images of a man with a sword, screaming.'

Dee looked up and scowled. 'You didn't tell me. You should have learned before, girl. Keep nothing from me. Nothing. You have already made that mistake with the black cloaked figure and we still do not know who they are. God be begged that Cecil has found the torn cloak by the time we return.' He pointed at the papers with a sharp command to continue.

'Every other letter focuses on Jasper's education and what needs to be covered. The House of Tudor, the English parliament, our currency, courtly manners. Also, a list of Catholic martyrs. In this one it advises that Jasper is taught certain dances and also enquires after his English tutoring.' She went to another letter. 'This one sends regret that the English teacher has died – so Amalia was telling the truth about that.'

'Go to the last letter.'

'This is evidently prior to the last letter Jasper is holding. It says "Time is drawing near. The English heretic has shown her base nature and the people will soon rise. Court despairs at her lying with a stable hand and making England the mirth of Europe." It goes on to say that the stable man is a low fool who thinks our Bishop of Spain will gain him favour with Philip. Then it says, "A fool and traitor so combined will be the downing of the bastard usurper".'

John Dee was sitting back in the chair, his eyes closed. 'So

Erand Malas is not only a Catholic plotter but close enough to have the gossip of Court.' His eyes snapped open. 'And they know that Robert Dudley was a fool who sought the help of de la Quadra in gaining Philip's support for a marriage with Elizabeth.' He sat up and began tapping the table. 'Amalia revealed Erand Malas is a woman. Which woman would be close enough to know the secrets of de la Quadra?'

Margaretta nodded. 'Sir Cecil spoke of the link between de la Quadra and Margaret Douglas.'

Dee sighed. 'Yes, but Margaret Douglas would want this child hidden forever. He threatens the chances of her darling son, Darnley.' He put his head in his hands and growled. 'I feel we are so close. So much evidence and yet nothing makes sense.'

Margaretta was opening the next pouch that held a book. It was leatherbound and embossed with gilt. On the front, the initials 'AC' bound together with a gold thread and below that of a crowned swan. She opened it carefully and inside the front cover was a short letter in English. She gasped. 'Doctor. Look at this.'

Dee took the paper and read it through. 'Oh my God. "Herein is sent to you the diary of Anne of Cleves, the King's sister for the years 1541 to 1542. Pray keep this close and forever hidden, for true destiny is hidden in its pages. The jewel is, by command of EM, to be given to Jasper of Cleves in memory of his mother.'

'My God. I think that jewel was meant for the Duchess of Suffolk. Look at the sender.'

His eyes went to the bottom of the page and opened wide. 'Francis Yaxley, Clerk of the Office of Signet.' He looked up at Margaretta. 'The man in the Tower accused of passing messages between de la Quadra and Margaret Douglas also passed information under instruction of Erand Malas.' Dee jabbed at the book. 'Open it.'

'It is written in German.'

Chapter Forty-Seven

Peter seemed to be hours in returning. At last, he came through the door with a linen bag. 'Bread, cheese and good German ham.' He smiled and those kind eyes softened. 'I hope I have what you need, dear Margaretta.'

She nodded and pointed to the office door. 'I will make up the meal. The doctor needs you to translate for him.' *You hoped for kind words. I cannot let you have any.*

Dee was up and pacing when Margaretta re-entered the office with a tray of food. He was trembling with excitement. 'The diary gives us clues.' He turned and pointed to the other man. 'Read them out to Margaretta.'

Peter turned back the pages. 'The first passage of interest to Doctor Dee is December, 1540. Lady Anne has made a list of the foods she has ordered for the New Year celebrations. She says, "My great Lion will have everything that home would provide. I pray to God every day for his release to true love." The days after that are simply small notes about the servants and the baking she was doing. Though three days later, four new gowns are delivered with French hoods. The following week, starting January 1st, 1541, each entry has only one sentence – the same words – every day. God send me well to keep our joy.'

Margaretta looked at Dee. 'So, is the great lion the source of joy?' He nodded and she knew they were both thinking of the lions in a carved panel in Witzhelden.

Peter turned the pages forward. 'The months of February and March are lists again – and small notes about money she has given to poor families. She mentions a warm gap left by the lion. Then, at the end of March, she states she "must away from the lights of London and seek solitude". She lists two women – a Frances Lilgrave and an Elyn Tyrpyn – who will attend for their confidence.' He looked up. 'These woman were timid?'

'No,' muttered Dee. 'They kept a confidence. The English language has many meanings unlike German.'

'There is little in the month of April. But here, in May she refers to a lion again. She says "our lion's cub quickens".' Peter looked up confused.

'That's it,' shouted Dee. 'She was with child. "Quickening" is the word used when the babe is felt to move in the womb.'

Peter was still peering and flicking through the pages. 'She was being advised. She refers to a friend. See here, she writes two weeks later. "Our friend writes to hide the cub from the lion. Joy is better revealed when thriving."'

'Anne was told not to tell the father,' growled Dee. 'But who was telling her? And is it the same friend as in the letters?'

Peter went on. 'Then in September: "Today our cub is born." Then the next day: "Joy thrives. Joy eats. Joy grows. Joy to be baptised."'

'Does she give a name?'

Peter nodded and read on. 'There is an entry. September 26th. "Our cub is baptised Jasper. Our friend sends a name of high fortune, as begetter of the Tudors."'

Margaretta looked to Dee. 'Why would Anne name her child after Jasper Tudor, the man who raised Henry the Seventh – the first Tudor King?'

'I do not know – but there was a reason and the reason lies in the identity of the friend.'

Dee came to Peter's shoulder. 'Go on to November.'

Peter did as asked, reading through each day, saying they were just lists. Then he stopped. 'The Apple-Cake Man of name and nature—'

'Stop!' barked Dee and looked at Margaretta. 'What was that name?'

'The Apple-Cake Man of name and nature,' repeated Peter. 'You English have strange names.'

'Apples again,' said Dee. 'Write that down Margaretta. Go on, Peter.'

'"Our friend has told us uncovered and our little cub must away. God send me well to keep him safe".' Peter went through the following pages. 'There are more lists but not of money and people this time. Now she writes of a ship, of caskets, clothes and instructions to "those who will guard our little cub". This is like a journey being planned.'

Dee was looking grim. 'I think she was planning the shipment of a child... her little cub. The great lion's son. Keep going.'

They waited for Peter to read through more weeks. 'In November she writes of the Apple-Cake Man again and "Our friend commands my cub to a sister's care so to gently tell great lion. God speed you well to safety my sweet. Mama will follow."'

Dee groaned. 'So, Anne was told to send her child to Amalia and not the father.'

'Because Otto van Wylich was married and already had one illegitimate son,' said Margaretta. 'So, to tell him gently was sensible.'

'We have evidence but no proof of paternity,' snapped Dee and gestured to Peter to continue.

Peter kept reading and the tension rose. Then he shook his head. 'Oh, no. Oh, no.' He looked to his companions. '"Apple-Cake Man. God speed me well to keep my faith, for little lions die and mothers weep." Look at this.' He held the page towards Margaretta. 'It is stained with tears.'

Oh Lord, I cannot stem my weeping. That poor, poor woman. I look at my master. He pats my hand. His eyes are red. That heart does beat.

'Go into early 1542,' commanded Dee. 'Look for something about coldness.'

Peter bent to the diary again. 'Yes, here. She writes, "I learn the great lion's care has died. No lion, no cub, no love."'

Margaretta moved to the desk and sorted through the letters. 'It marries with this one sent by the friend early in February, 1542. "Your words of coldness have landed. The Lady Anne weeps once more. We must let her heart break for the destiny of England".' She looked up at John Dee. 'So, this friend let that poor woman believe her little child had died and then that the father had grown cold towards her.'

John Dee nodded. 'And she never tried to leave England again. A cruel friend.'

My God. I see tears in your eyes.

Dee shook his head. 'Tragedy. And another scheme of Cecil's has failed. Jasper Tudor was certainly not German-born.' He blew a long, slow breath. 'But I am failing to get to the heart of this web and explain what has been done by who or why. Cecil will punish me.' He banged his hand on the table. 'And we have no absolute proof of anything. Just a raggle-taggle of events and ambitions, an Apple-Cake Man, whoever that is, and a diary. Nothing is clear.'

Margaretta pointed at his bag. 'Then we need to look at the players.'

Dee looked up slowly, nodded, then turned to Peter. 'I need you to translate the whole diary. Ask Vopel's daughter for paper and a pen, then find a quiet space.'

Peter looked confused. 'That will take days, Doctor Dee.'

'Indeed. We need to lie low here for several days until Amalia's posse returns with no news of us.' Dee smiled. 'You have all the time you need.' He pointed to the door. 'But now Margaretta and I need to work alone.'

Peter tried to argue but was barked down by Dee and so

left the room crestfallen at being excluded. As soon as the door shut, Dee was opening his bag, pulling out the casket and sorting through the cards. 'We will look at each one we have pulled. We need to start naming the players in this tragedy. Maybe there are clues we have missed.'

The cards already seen were laid out in the line. He picked up the first two. 'These we know. The queen of swords is Elizabeth and the strength card is Anne of Cleves.'

Margaretta leaned over and picked up the death card and the tower. Dee contemplated. 'The death card does not mean physical death. It means death of an era or maybe a dynasty.' He sighed. 'Though, God knows, we have witnessed three deaths and a near death. But in two different countries. So, we have more than one killer around this drama, but we know only one – Amalia.'

Margaretta picked up the other cards and lay them out in a line, looking at each one. *Speak to me. There are messages here. Tell me.* 'Look.' She snapped up the two of wands. 'A man, alone, staring over water at somewhere in the distance. The background has a high hill. I think that is Otto van Wylich. Everything in the card links to him.' She responded to John Dee's nod to continue. 'A man alone on a high balcony wall – the hunting lodge at Witzhelden had a high balcony with low battlements. He stares across water towards a high hill. Solingen Castle is on a high cliff across the River Wupper.' She held up the card to Dee. 'This man holds a world. He said to his son, "If I cannot give her the world, I give her my son." He was offering Anne of Cleves a son without knowing he had already given her a child.'

Dee looked at Margaretta with a smile. 'You are learning well, my dear. Very good. Not absolute proof – but very close.'

Oh, these little moments when you are proud of me make my heart sing. It is like being with my dada again, when he taught me letters and numbers and the ways of the land.

Dee was buoyed with enthusiasm. He was staring at the Devil card. 'Each time I pulled this card, it hid other cards, including the two of wands.'

'Lady Amalia,' said Margaretta. 'She is surely evil. She tried to stop us seeing Otho, to learn of his father, Otto. She killed a servant who assisted us and threatened the others with death by bees. That sounds like a devil to me even though I could not feel her. Also, the murderous letter – she let slip that she knew the poison was in the letter within the linens sent to Otto.'

'The intention is obvious. Otto was meant to read about the little lion and then die badly within seconds.' Dee looked aghast. 'But could the nature of a woman actually be the Devil? There is one terrible nature in which a person seems good and fair but they hide a soul of no feeling. They stare into your eyes with no care for your soul. They seek only for themselves.'

'Doctor, I told you I sensed violence from her. And an old woman was held down and stuffed like a goose in her great hall. That's why the coffin had to be taken up there. When she said Gilda was dead, I felt violence, but no sorrow. Her arm was scratched. And she could lie with no feeling – nothing.' *You just cannot imagine a woman would be so evil.* 'If you want to consider the dark potential of a woman, Doctor, just think of my sister. As we sit here, she has my brother acting as a beaten slave in her husband's yard.'

'You are right. I just cannot believe.' He sat up straight. 'We will try another method. I have been practicing this. I did not want to show you before I was sure…' He pointed to the bag. 'Take out the garnet crystal. Then we need string.'

A few minutes later, the garnet orb was swinging on a thread tightly wound around its centre. Dee held it in his right hand above the oak of the table and told Margaretta to be silent and focus only on the crystal. She was to clear her mind in case she sent energy to the stone. He steadied it to absolute still, then whispered, 'Show me "yes".' They waited, holding their breath, and the garnet began to move, slowly at first, then in ever increasing circles. 'Clockwise,' said Dee. He repeated the process but whispering, 'Show me "no".' Again, a pause before the stone moved. This time the circles went in the other direction.

'What is it doing?'

'The stones have an energy which is connected to our soul. Our soul is dictated by angels. So, the stone is allowing angels to answer us.'

Margaretta sat back, bewildered. 'How do you know?'

'I don't. I need proof. But the evidence is that my hypothesis is working. Every time I ask a question the garnet gives the right answer.'

'But if you already know the answer, then maybe your hand is guiding the jewel and not your angel.'

Dee glared. 'Do not go above yourself, girl. This is a perfect test. Give me the card.' He took the Devil card from Margaretta and lay it on the desk, then held the crystal above the card, steadied it and whispered, 'Is this Amalia of Cleves?'

The room seemed to close in and go cold as they waited. The stone began to move. Tiny movements at first were hard to understand, then the back and fro started to transform into a circle.

Margaretta gulped. 'Clockwise. It is saying "yes".'

There was a bang, which made Margaretta scream and Dee drop the garnet, sending it rolling across the desk onto the floor. They looked round to see a book on the floor.

'It fell from the shelf,' said Margaretta. She walked over and looked up at John Dee, eyes wide with fear. 'It is a Bible, Doctor. I think you are getting a warning not to take your conjuring too far.'

Chapter Forty-Eight

The knock on the door was a welcome interruption to the tension. Peter entered holding a scrap of paper. 'Doctor, I have found something else. It makes no sense but this was pushed into the back of the diary.'

John Dee was like a squirrel gathering the cards and putting them in his lap out of sight. 'Show me, Peter. Bring it here.'

Peter put the paper down on the table and pulled the candle closer. 'You can see here the paper is different, and the date here is July, 1542.' He moved his finger across the words as he read. 'It says, "Young Otho arrived today. If not holding ours, then yours."'

Dee glanced over to Margaretta, his head shaking slowly. 'I think we have our proof. If only there were a formal record.'

Peter looked between the two, confused. 'What is happening?'

'Nothing we can share at this moment. But this is most helpful.' Dee paused. 'You read the poetry of Amalia. What was it saying?'

'It was very sad. Every verse I read was about the loneliness of life with no companionship or love.' Peter reddened.

You are embarrassed. I feel your discomfort. Why do you think of a woman?

'One of the letters referred to her disappointment over a marriage negotiation. Was that her sadness?'

Peter reddened further.

The poems embarrass you. You keep looking away from me. Better the doctor probes. 'Cywilydd. Embarrassment.'

'Is there something in the poems which tells us more of Amalia? Maybe her nature?'

Peter gulped and glanced at Margaretta. 'I… well… maybe best not…'

'Out with it, sir.'

Peter cleared his throat, his face now nearing puce. 'The poems are not written to a man, doctor.'

I hear the name Katharina again. You poor man. You want the ground to swallow you.

'Interesting,' said Dee, apparently not shocked by this revelation. 'So, a heart living with no love – or maybe a hidden love that others would never accept – seeks another road – glory.'

You are a strange one. Our church would have that woman flogged, but you just accept it as part of nature. I like you for that. God made us one and all, and in all shapes and forms.

Dee pointed to the door. 'Please continue your translating.'

A crestfallen Peter looked at Margaretta and left.

Dee pulled the cards from his lap. 'We are breaking the code.' He pointed to the Bible. 'Maybe that was a message that we are doing right.'

Oh, you will twist anything to be right. But I am scared. You are talking of angels again.

Dee spread the remaining cards on the desk. He tapped on three. 'The king, knight and page of wands. Then the ten. All in the same suit and so likely connected. Name these and we have our players.' He beckoned Margaretta. 'Study them carefully. Start with the king as that is the power card in this group. And it has hidden the others.'

She picked up the cards and studied. 'A king. Power. A man, though the face is soft like a woman… a woman? He holds a budding staff. A focus on new beginnings.'

Dee jumped up, snatched the card and stared. 'Like a

woman. Amalia let slip that Erand Malas is a woman. A king sees Court and the letters reveal sight of Court – as does the letter writer. Could this be Erand Malas?'

Margaretta picked up the page of wands. 'You said before that this card means a messenger. We know Francis Yaxley was a messenger between Bishop de la Quadra and Lady Margaret Douglas. Now we know he was also a messenger taking instructions from Erand Malas while he was a clerk in the Office of the Signet.'

Dee nodded. 'On death, royal chattels become Crown property and that office has power. Not only would he be in charge of listing Anne's assets, but he had access to a royal signet seal which would give any package safe passage.' He growled and put his head in his hands. 'Cecil's need to bury a plot has limited us. The fool.'

Margaretta stood. 'Come, Doctor. We are making progress. We know Jasper was born in England. We have good evidence that his father was Otto van Wylich – so we can name the two of wands. We think we have identified the page of wands – the messenger – as Yaxley. We are sure that the king of wands is Erand Malas – a woman with sight of Court.'

'Your excitement is groundless Margaretta. We have a diary and letters. But we do not know the true identity of Erand Malas. We have no formal record of Otto being Jasper's father. Yaxley was a messenger in 1557 – but we have no evidence of his involvement in 1541.' He tapped on the other two cards. 'And we have no insight into the knight of wands or the ten of wands – the fighter and the hidden-faced worker. There is the mysterious apple-cake man. The only thing we absolutely know is that hidden plotters seek to put Jasper on the throne and they will poison the people who stand in the way. We are in trouble.' Dee rubbed his eyes and groaned. 'Dear God. The cards are screaming all the players and all the clues and still we have no firm answers or proof. The only thing of which I am sure is that Jasper was born in England. Cecil will despair.'

'But Lady Anne's diary and the letters are strong evidence that Jasper is the son of Otto. All the dates match. They look alike. The lions.' Margaretta smiled her encouragement.

'Do not use childish hope, Margaretta. Cecil is a lawyer. He will want absolute proof. And he will want names.'

'So, what do we do?'

Dee turned to his apprentice. 'If you were with child, where would you go?'

Oh, that hurts my heart. I yearn for love and a babe to hold as my own. 'I would go where I felt safe – home.'

'We know Jasper was baptised. There is a church record somewhere with his name. If we find that record, then we maybe name the father. We know Otto loved Anne. Can we prove she loved him?' Dee stood and started jabbing at the air. 'Good, good. Nicholas Wooton was in Anne's retinue to Calais in 1539. If anyone can attest to love growing, it is him.'

'There is the little issue of the poisoned letter and Otto being told Anne hated him.'

Dee leaned forward. 'The first letter – the one Jasper showed us in Hever – mentioned a gift to be sent on.' They looked at each other and said in unison, 'Amalia. The Devil.'

Margaretta shuddered. 'I think we were in the presence of pure evil, Doctor. She helped break her sister's heart, she used Jasper to pave her path to power and only she could be the killer of old Gilda.'

'Yes. I will write to Cecil. We need interviews with Yaxley and Wooton and also a list of Anne's homes,' said Dee snatching up a pen. 'We are not beaten yet.'

Margaretta nodded. 'Peter can get the letter sent. And there is one more mystery. She picked up the card with three women dancing. 'Three women, one with their face hidden – just like the ten of wands – dancing among apples. We do not know what this card is telling us. But my hand tingles when I pick it up. It is telling us something.'

Chapter Forty-Nine

They were four days in the house of Caspar Vopel. Peter translated the diary, Margaretta wordlessly helped the daughter and Doctor Dee barely left the office but spent hours studying the many books of the dead scholar. Every day, Peter went out for food and drink. He had told the local people he was a traveller from Bruges and was careful to always take a different route when returning to the house and come in through the back door. His travelling companions were never mentioned and, luckily, never asked about.

On the fifth day he hired a local man with a wagon to take them to Antwerp. More than that, he went to the university and swapped his own cloak and that of Doctor Dee with the cloaks of two students on the promise that they would never say how they were suddenly attired in cloaks they could never afford. Caspar Vopel's daughter was paid a good price for a smock and a bonnet for Margaretta to wear. She tried to refuse the money, telling Peter that she would give all her clothes in gratitude for Margaretta's kindness, but the money was pressed into her hand.

It was dark when they left and they did not stop until night had fallen. Margaretta had to sit above with the wagon-man but could hear the constant dialogue of the two men discussing planets, numbers, the ideas of Caspar Vopel. She ached when they arrived at an inn but jumped down and reached up for the bags that were being passed down. Dee's was heavier than before. She looked inside and stormed over to where he was stepping out and stretching his back. 'You thief.'

'What is this, girl?'

She opened the bag. 'Four books. Four.' She pointed back down the road. 'You took these from the office of that dead man.'

Dee sniffed and looked away. 'Well, he will not use them.'

You old magpie. 'That is no reason for pocketing them like a gutter-imp cutting purses.'

Dee reddened and raised a warning finger. 'Enough, Margaretta. I am building the biggest library of knowledge in the world. It will be my legacy. Caspar Vopel would have approved of my choices.'

'You mean you took the most valuable of the books. You are dreadful.'

Dee walked away, leaving Margaretta shouting after him that he should be ashamed. Peter stood silent, looking as if he wished he were anywhere but here. He tried to calm Margaretta who only snapped that he was just as bad. His kind eyes clouded in pain. She took a deep breath. 'I am sorry, Peter. You did not deserve that.' She pointed after Dee. 'But it is sometimes too much to work for a man who you so often want to push under a cart.' She started to cry. Peter stepped forward and held her close, rocking her slowly while murmuring comfort. Then he led her inside and asked the landlord for a beaker of their best-spiced wine.

The following four days were tense. Dee gave only curt instructions to Margaretta and Peter struggled to keep the atmosphere light. Margaretta thanked the Lord for her sickness and sat next to the wagon-man, churning her fury, mile after mile. At last, they reached Antwerp. No one had stopped them.

That evening, Peter was gone for some hours. Margaretta stayed in her room while Dee sat in the chamber next door.

She could hear him mumbling to himself. That meant he was reading and making notes. It only made her angry again.

Then footsteps on the stairs and a knock on his door. Voices and then a yell. She heard a chair overturn.

Oh, God. What is happening? Have they found us? You need me. She picked her food knife and ran to his door, bursting in, the blade held high. She stopped dead. It was only Doctor Dee and Peter, their smiles fading as they stared at the weapon.

'What on earth are you doing, girl?'

'I came to save you.' She lowered the knife, face reddening.

Dee pointed at Peter. 'Wonderful news. This young man has secured a loan of the *Steganographia* here in Antwerp. I must return and study it.' Beaming delight, he took Peter's hand. 'You are a good man, Peter Albrecht. A good man and a good scholar.'

Margaretta was then told they sailed in the morning. Dee had written an advance letter to inform Cecil and it had been lodged on a ship leaving that very night. With luck, he would be waiting for them.

The ship was bustling when they arrived on the quayside. Peter took them to the gangplank. 'I have written your names as Master and Mistress Smythe.' He looked at Dee. 'If they ask, you are a wool merchant.' He looked a little uncomfortable. 'I think you mentioned that was your father's profession and so you will know the language. I have said Margaretta is your sister and likely to be unwell. She will need you to care for her, so neither of you are likely to leave your cabins. That will limit any questions.'

Dee took his hand. 'I say again, Peter. You are a good man. I will see you when I return.' He picked up the bag and walked up the gangplank.

Margaretta paused before following and made a weak smile. 'He is surely right, Peter. You are a very good man.'

He reached out and took her hand. 'Will you return with Doctor Dee? I really only arranged the loan of the *Steganographia* so that I might see you again.' He began to sweat. 'Maybe you could learn to like it here. I can teach you the language. I could make you happy if you just gave me a…'

She put her fingers to his lips. 'Stop, Peter. I am not what you think.'

'But I know what you are… I saw what an angel you are in the house of Caspar Vopel.'

'No. My heart is harder than you think, and I have to be harsher when I return to England. I have to give all my energy and love to one man… my brother. For if I do not… well, my soul will die.'

Please do not look at me with those kind eyes. They are filling with tears and your chin trembles. You are such a very good man. But I have loved two men before and they have broken my heart. I need a whole heart in order to love again and so I must go. I will reach out and squeeze your hand just once and then turn away. Turn away to a life alone. I want to cry. Is it regret or guilt?

Three days later, during which Dee had nursed, comforted and cleaned his apprentice, they stepped off the ship onto the quay in St Katherine's Dock. Waiting for them was William Cecil.

Part Three

Chapter Fifty

When underway, Cecil spoke in a low voice. 'Our Queen is recovering. But we have no time for relief. Her sickness had the Catholics rising in the North. It is turning into a succession crisis.' He turned a hard stare on Dee. 'I hope you have answers, John. The letters demanding information suggest you have not reached the conclusions we need.'

Dee took in a deep breath. 'Anne of Cleves left Solingen a maid and we are sure Jasper was born in England.'

Cecil groaned.

I feel your despair, Sir Cecil. Yet there is something else. That feeling of hope I felt before. It is stronger. Your thoughts keep shifting to Lady Mildred. I think you love her more every year that goes by. It makes me think of Peter. Was I fool to refuse him? Maybe he was the one good, kind man that God was going to offer me – and I pushed him away.

John Dee seemed unperturbed by the atmosphere. 'First tell me of our Majesty.'

'She strengthens every day. Thanks to you.'

Oh, look at you puff up, Doctor. Every little snippet of being above others is like giving a worm to a bird. You are just delighted that Doctor Burcot needed your guidance. I bet you will not mention the help of Clarissa.

'I am glad my advice on treatment has served her well.'

As predicted. And are you going to tell Sir Cecil about your magpie activities – snaffling the goods of a dying man?

'When she is fully well, I will tell Her Majesty of the important books I managed to purchase on my travels.' Seeing Cecil bridle, he raised his hand in placation. 'Fear not, William. We did not go in search of books. Fate intervened as we focused only on the assignment.'

You are quite dreadful.

Cecil raised an eyebrow. 'It will be some weeks before Elizabeth is able to peruse any books, John. She strengthens every day. But Lady Sidney… Oh, God.'

I feel horror from you. I see a face, red and weeping with pustules. A woman is screaming. 'No, no…'

Cecil and Dee turned to look at Margaretta who was clasping her hand over her mouth with her eyes closed trying to stop the images. Dee, evidently understanding, called to the carriage man to stop and instructed Margaretta to wrap in her cloak and sit aloft so that her sickness did not slow them. As she jumped out of the carriage, she heard Cecil say, 'Mary Dudley – Lady Sidney – is so terribly scarred by the smallpox that even her husband calls her "as foul a lady as the smallpox could make her". So cruel.'

When the carriage pulled into the rear yard of Cannon House all was quiet. Most of the servants had now departed to Cecil's new home on The Strand. Cecil had chosen to come here as there were, 'eyes and ears to worry about'. Margaretta looked across the great yard at the stables that were built for twenty horses but were now clean and silent. *I wonder if there is still a beam with the name Jonas carved into it. The poor child. Is it really seven years? He would have been a young man by now. And over there is the door to the basement kitchens where Lottie greeted me with delight and Goodwife Barker with disdain. Who would think they would almost feel like family to me now?*

Led inside by a liveried servant, they entered a large room, sparse of furniture but lit by windows higher than the height of a man. Seated below one pane was Lady Mildred, her face serene and one hand resting on her stomacher. The man with her was old and bent with white hair and a straggling beard. The sinking of his cheeks was like shadows. A long nose descended from two dark eyes, which seemed to hold much sadness. He struggled to rise from his chair and was told by Mildred to 'sit easy, Father. You are with friends who have no need for pomp.' He slumped back with a grateful sigh.

Mildred came immediately to her husband and planted a kiss on his cheek before turning to John Dee. 'Welcome, John. It is good to have your presence. Still handsome and yet no Goodwife Dee.' Then she laughed as he blushed and grunted something about being too busy with the mind to worry about marriage. Then it was Margaretta's turn. Over the years, they had created a strange friendship. A lady of Court and a strangely-gifted farmgirl from Wales. Yet they shared a love of books, a keen mind and many encounters through Doctor Dee's investigations. Mildred took Margaretta's hands. 'It does me well to see you back safe, my dear.'

I feel your hope. It is like your husband's. For the past few years, it has been nothing but sadness and grief. You ask me about Lottie and Goodwife Tovey. I tell her the last I heard was that Lottie was about to have her second child. Your hand swiftly goes to your stomacher. That hope again. I glance down and you give a tiny nod. Who thought I would ever look straight into the eye of a lady and know she sees me as a friend? I squeeze your hand and we both know. 'I feel all will be well this time, my lady.'

Dee was pulling a chair over to sit by Nicolas Wooton as Cecil was asking a servant to bring victuals. The two men exchanged some small-talk and then Margaretta was instructed to take notes. Wooton was immediately confused and looked to Cecil who raised a hand and assured him all was in order.

Your weariness is to your bones, Master Wooton. You have

seen so much and faced so many challenges. You are tired of life. Worry, too. You think of Anne of Cleves, so Cecil has evidently informed you of the doctor's interest. You recall a young woman, soft, gentle... frightened.

Dee went straight to the point. 'You negotiated the marriage contract of Anne of Cleves to Henry Tudor in 1539 and then accompanied her to Calais from Solingen and then by ship to England.' The old man nodded. 'It was a long journey and so you would have become acquainted by all in her entourage. You wrote to Thomas Cromwell, the king's advisor, about them.' Another nod.

Wooton cleared his throat – a wet, phlegmy sound – and then swallowed. 'Do you have questions, Doctor Dee, or do I just nod at everything we already know?'

Ooh, the doctor flinches. He did not assume an old head would hold such sharp tongue. He is swallowing. Now shifting in his seat. He does that when uncomfortable.

Dee made a tight smile. 'Indeed. Pardon me. In your letter to Thomas Cromwell, you spoke of a good man called Otto van Wylich. What can you tell us of him?'

Tension. You do not need my skills to see it. Your eyes widened. Your jaw tightened. A slight flinch under your left eye.

Wooton looked towards the window. 'Yes. An advisor to her father. Local landowner and noble. He became ill at Ravensteyn. We had to leave him behind.'

Clever. You are trying to put my master off the scent by saying a truth.

Dee was like a hawk spying a running mouse. 'And he caught up with the entourage before Calais... please do not try to hide anything, sir. We have spoken to his son, Otho van Wylich.'

Old Wotton tensed and looked to Cecil. 'I did not come here to be interrogated about irrelevancies of the past. They are all dead and gone.'

Dee cut in before Cecil could speak. 'Maybe not. Now tell me about Lady Anne on her journey.'

'She was happy. Well-cared for by her ladies. We could only make headway of five miles a day and the going was cold and hard, but she bore it like a strong and true queen.'

You are lying again. You are recalling distress. 'Ofnus. Frightened.'

Dee did not even look around, but made a tiny nod. 'We heard she became frightened. Why?'

Nicholas Wooton started to object and then went to struggle from his chair, saying he would not be questioned by a young churl. But Cecil stepped forward, his voice moving to the flint-like quality he only used when determined to alarm. 'Father Wooton. It is not sensible to withhold information that could be necessary to secure our Queen's safety.' A heavy pause. 'You are too old a man to be carving your initials on the walls of the Tower.'

Wooton mewed and even Lady Mildred looked across the room with a look of alarm, though she did nothing to curb her husband.

Dee changed tactics to being the friend. 'Come, sir. Just tell us the truth… the full truth… and you can return to the comfort of Canterbury.'

Wotton seemed to be chewing his bottom lip for an age.

It is all coming back – the fear, the sadness, your concern.

Eventually he spoke. 'Yes. Otto van Wylich did rejoin our entourage. I must say I was glad, for Lady Anne of Cleves was bereft when he became ill. He had ridden alongside her carriage every day looking over her and trying to raise her mood.' He frowned. 'The poor lady was becoming anxious. That damned Gylman woman would never shut her mouth and was telling terrible tales of Court. Lady Anne stopped eating. Dear God, she climbed into the carriage in Solingen a comely maid and by the time we reached England she was skin and bone.' He reached for the goblet of wine on the table and Dee moved quickly to pass it to him. 'When Otto van Wylich caught up, she seemed so much happier.'

'And what happened in Calais?'

'We waited. The ship's captain – a man called Neerman – refused to leave until the weather improved.' He stopped, hoping it would be enough. Then sighed. 'That fool Seymour. He drank too much and claimed his sister, Queen Jane, had been ripped in two. Poor Anne of Cleves ran from the room. She understood more English than we realised.'

'And what happened?'

'Sometime later, Mrs Gylman found her in the arms of Otto van Wylich, weeping and begging to go home.' The old man dropped his head. 'I was the one who had to tell her she could not return with him. That the treaty was signed. It felt like announcing a death sentence.' He made the sign of the cross over his chest. 'May God forgive me.'

You are recalling more than weeping. You are recalling your alarm at their feelings. 'Teimladau. Feelings.'

Those dark eyes darted to Margaretta. 'She keeps muttering. Who is she? What is she saying?'

Dee flicked a hand towards Margaretta without even looking at her. 'She is a simple scribe. Born with an unfortunate tick. Makes her utter strange sounds. I only keep her as a charity.'

Sometimes I hate you. But Lady Mildred is glaring at you. I think you might get the end of a sharp tongue later. I hope so.

Dee continued. 'Master Wooton. You have said that she had his constant company when he was well, that he gladdened her heart, that she was relieved when he returned, that she ran to his arms when frightened.' A long and deliberate pause. 'What were the true feelings between Otto van Wylich and Lady Anne of Cleves?'

Wooton drained his goblet and held out a hand for it to be refilled. Dee obliged. The old man's voice was now low and trembling and he kept shaking his head as if in despair. 'As a man of the church I tried to turn away from any suggestion of sin. But as God is my witness, despite his age being that of her father, I saw love grow between them. Passion.' He bent his head. 'Anne was weeping like a child when we cast off from Calais. I was almost relieved when she became sick and had to be taken to her cabin.'

Dee cocked his head on one side. 'She was seasick?'

'Terribly. We feared for her.'

Dee turned to Margaretta. 'Make sure you note that.'

Cecil looked perplexed.

Dee turned back to Nicholas Wooton. 'Sir, it must have been a great concern to you – knowing the lady was sailing away from a man she loved to a man she feared.' Wooton nodded sadly. 'What happened in the following years?'

'The unfortunate first meeting with Henry. The marriage. Henry's fury that put us all in fear and ended in the death of Thomas Cromwell. The divorce.' The old man frowned. 'But you know all this.'

Dee persisted. 'I want you to tell us about 1541 and the rumour of Anne of Cleves having Henry's son.'

Old Wooton gulped more wine, his hand shaking violently and making some spill on his coat. 'I saw her only once that year. It was New Year in Court. Anne was in high spirits and charmed everyone by dancing with little Queen Kathryn. We were admiring of her grace. Then I was appointed Dean of Canterbury Cathedral in the April and I heard nothing more until those foolish rumours in November.' Another quaff of wine. 'But that was soon dismissed.'

'Over those New Year celebrations, did King Henry visit Anne in her household?'

A hard cackle came from Nicholas Wooton's sinewy throat. 'What foolery. He was like a lovesick boy with his new bride and planning their progress in the spring. Anyway, Anne had visitors from Germany staying with her in Richmond.' He made a little laugh. 'Anne was a good host. We heard it was a better place to be than Court. Food, festivities, Anne's company. There was more than one courtier hoping to be invited.'

'And was Otto van Wylich one of those visitors?'

Wotton gulped and Dee filled his goblet. No word. Just a nod.

'Having spent so much time in his company, did you not seek to visit?'

A shake of that white head. 'I am a man of God and must speak truth, Doctor Dee. But what a man does not see he cannot speak. I stayed away.'

Chapter Fifty-One

Dee's face, which had been filled with satisfaction when they said farewell to Nicholas Wooton, was like a thundercloud when he climbed into the carriage and slammed the door. 'I only make little of you in order to protect you – so that no-one will guess what you are.'

Ah, Lady Mildred has chastised you for the way you speak to me, and you could not tell her the truth because to reveal my gifts only diminishes your own. 'Maybe if you appeared a little kinder, you would not be chastened for your sharp tongue.'

A flash of anger in his eyes. 'I have *not* been chastened.'

Liar. Old Scut. Thief. 'Yes, Doctor.'

Dee slammed his bag on the seat. 'And to make it worse, I am prevented from speaking to Yaxley – again. Cecil refuses.' He sat heavily and shook a pouch of coins. 'He was tight-fisted with payment too.'

Grace was busy in the kitchen when Margaretta returned. She had left Dee with an agreement that he would spend an hour charming Mistress Constable with tales of Germany. They would meet in his office later. 'My word, Grace. You have this kitchen gleaming.' She gave the girl a hug and pushed Cadi the cat off Mam's chair to sit.

'Oh, I have so enjoyed myself, miss.' Grace poured them

both a beaker of small beer and sat down to chatter. She widened her eyes. 'A gangly-legged youth brought another barrel of Malmsey and said he would not bring it in, in case the mad-kicky woman were here. I think he meant you.' She shook her head. 'I told him straight there were no mad women here but he said he wanted no broken leg and ran away. Siôn had to carry it in and tap it for me.' She took a breath. 'I have kept Mistress Constable happy and warm, but she starts to cry the more she drinks and keeps asking if Huw is well.'

'Good. And has Siôn been checking on Huw?'

Grace nodded. 'Every day before he starts with Master Constable he gets the logs in for me, lifts the pots on the stove and then goes to The Vintry. I think he is a very good man.'

'What has he said of Huw? Is he well?'

Grace's face clouded. 'Well, but not happy. Siôn insisted he has a day of rest on Sunday and brings him here for his meal. He tells me they do not hit him, but words do cut deeper.' The girl looked angry. 'He says he wants to come back here, but Master McFadden says he is bonded until the land is in rightful hands.'

'Land?'

Grace shrugged. 'I didn't understand and Siôn told Huw to keep it quiet until you are back.' She smiled. 'So, Huw and I just talk about all our dreams. He sees colours, you know. Then Mistress Constable comes down and cries.'

What the hell has been going on? Siôn running the business, land and Huw talking. 'Is Siôn here?'

She shook her head. 'He is with Master Constable who seems to keep him busy all day.' She leaned towards Margaretta like a little conspirator. 'He tells me in the evenings what he is doing. He has cleaned out the merchant shed, counted the money, thrown away the rotten cloth and goods. Every morning he does the trading. Then last week he chased away two rogues who have been cheating Master Constable for years. Frenchmen they were.' She lowered her voice to a whisper. 'I heard Mistress Constable tell the Master that Siôn was sent by God.'

Well, actually, he was sent by greedy, Godless landowners

who want their fields for the gold that is sheep wool. 'I think Mistress Constable is right. Though I think God was thinking of Siôn.'

Mistress Constable was upright and alert, though her words a little slurred. 'The doctor has told me all his adventures – castles, the cities, hunting lodges. I understand a great scholar has honoured him with important books for his collection.

Dear God, if he says it often enough, he will start to believe his own lies. 'Yes, indeed, Mistress.'

'John is going to tell me more after our meal. You need to tell Grace to make sure there is a clean goblet here and I would like some marchpane. The poor man has been at the mercy of German food for weeks. All that honeyed bread. Ugh.'

'Have Grace and Siôn been to your liking, Mistress?'

'Yes. Indeed, yes.' She put out a hand. 'I have been thinking as you suggested. Is Siôn fully bonded to Vintner McFadden?'

'I do not know, Mistress.' *I cross my fingers to cut out the lie.* 'Let me enquire gently.'

Dee was bent over his desk, studying a list. 'What is that, Doctor?'

'The list I requested. It gives every house and parcel of land granted to Anne of Cleves upon her divorce from Henry.' He took in a deep breath and straightened up. 'No wonder she was the richest and most important woman in England after the new queen.'

Margaretta leaned over and looked at the line of names. 'Hever Castle, Richmond Palace. Then Breamore Priory, Southwick Priory. Bletchingley Palace.' She pointed to the smaller list at the bottom of the parchment. 'A house in Lewes, another three in Norfolk. What are these?'

Dee nodded. 'Likely they are all smaller manor houses or

hunting houses. Each will have land and a tenant from which Anne would have had an income.' He picked up the paper and studied it. 'Blanche ap Harri confirmed she was in Norfolk, so in here hides the summer home of Anne of Cleves in 1541.'

'But which one?'

'That is what you are going to find out tonight.' Dee pointed at the window. 'It is a full moon tonight and you… are going to be guided by angels.'

Oh, no.

Margaretta returned to the kitchen. Siôn was warming his feet on the hearthstones as Grace fussed around, getting him bread, cheese and a small beer. He grinned and stood up. 'It is good to see you back, *del*.' He offered the chair. 'Tell us all about Germany.'

'I will Siôn, but first tell me of Huw.'

'Your brother is well of the body. They do not touch him, throw barrels or other brutality, but they bother him with their words. I have told him that every harsh word will make him stronger, which seemed to work as now he has started counting them.'

She looked at Siôn through tearful eyes. 'Damn that man Angus. Why does he want Huw? He can get a hundred strong men to carry barrels.'

Siôn glanced at Grace and turned to Welsh. 'He has asked your brother to sign something. Told him he can be freed if he signs it.'

'What is it?'

The man shrugged. 'It is related to land. Huw keeps insisting he needs to show you. That it is for both of you. He has let Angus think he cannot read.' He frowned. 'But Angus is so keen on a signing he has even tried to become my friend and asked me to convince Huw to give his mark before you return.' He pointed at her. 'Go there tomorrow, *del*. There is something bad brewing in the mind of Angus McFadden.'

Chapter Fifty-Two

'I do not want to do this.'

'You have no choice. We have to bring this investigation to conclusion. Cecil has told me that the Catholics are rising and Margaret Douglas is talking openly about Darnley marrying Mary of Scots. They are fuelled as news of the Cygnet Prince spreads. Elizabeth is in danger.'

Dee looked at the door. 'Is all quiet in the household?'

'It is nearly midnight. All god-fearing people are in their beds.'

He grunted. 'The moon is at the peak of the sky at midnight. We will scry then.'

'How will the cards tell us the house?'

'They will not. You are going to channel the angels and dowse.' Dee pulled a velvet pouch from a drawer of his desk. 'This is our tool.' It was a silver chain and at the end a violet crystal shaped like a teardrop. He held it up into the moonlight and whispered. 'We will leave it in the moonlight to cleanse until we are ready.' He crossed the room to place it on the windowsill, then turned back, stepping over the parchments and various implements he had scattered across the floor. 'We need to get our choices ready. Bring a parchment.'

She brought one to the desk and lay it before him.

He made three crosses on the parchment, evenly spread and covering the whole paper. 'Read out the names of the

Norfolk houses, one at a time.' He laid the paper flat on the desk and moved to ensure the light of the moon was sending its beams across every name. 'A few minutes and we are at full moonlight.' He picked up the crystal and placed it in Margaretta's hand. You will start with determining "yes" and "no". Hold it above this sill with the light shining through. Steady the crystal to still and then ask the angels to give you "yes".'

'It tingles. It makes me feel strange.'

'Do it,' he snapped.

She held the crystal a few fingers above the sill, making violet beams shoot into the room. 'Angels give me "yes".' Slowly the crystal began to sway and then arced into a circle. 'It goes the direction of the clock. As it did for you.'

'Do the same for "no".'

She did and the crystal swung anti-clockwise. She breathed out and put her hand to her stomach. 'It is as if the angels are shaking my insides.'

'No matter. It simply means they can divine through you.' He pointed at the desk. 'Get ready.' With her in position, she was instructed to hold the crystal over each house and ask the angels to say if Anne of Cleves was in that house in 1541. Then he watched the window. Suddenly he tensed. 'The moon is high. Start.'

Margaretta asked the question and held her breath.

'Anti-clockwise. No.' Dee leaned across and scored out the writing. 'Move to the next and stay your crystal.'

'Anti-clockwise. No.'

Another scored out. 'Move to the third.'

Margaretta moved to a house named Manor House, Saxlingham Nethergate, Norfolk. She took a deep breath, stayed her crystal and asked. At first there was no movement, then the tingle in her hand almost made her drop the gemstone.

'Clockwise,' shouted Dee. 'Look. And the circle is strong.'

Dee handed her a glass of sweet wine. 'You have done well, girl. Now we need the map.' He strode across the room and started rummaging in a wooden chest. 'I know it is here.' He ordered Margaretta to bring a candle, ignoring the pallor of her face. Minutes later he pulled out a rolled parchment, took it to the desk and spread it out, weighted with candles at each corner.

'A painting of all England,' murmured Margaretta. 'It is beautiful.'

'It is a map. This was the map delivered by John Rudd to Cecil two years ago.'

'Who is John Rudd?'

'A vicar from Dewsbury in Yorkshire with a passion for mapping the land. He has a young apprentice called Sexton. To be honest, it is the lad who has the real skill. He brought this to Cecil in 1561 and was given two years' leave to make a detailed map of the whole of England.'

'So why do you have this?'

Silence.

'You stole it, didn't you?' Her voice was high in indignation.

Dee turned with a glare. 'Stop whining about thieving and look for Saxlingham Nethergate.'

I hate you again. If I am sick from angel energy, I shall aim my mouth at you.

They scoured the map. There it was. A tiny hamlet. Dee jabbed at the paper, his face lighting with excitement. 'There. And the map has a church indicated too.' He moved his finger south-west on the map. 'Kenninghall. Margaret Douglas' prison. And the two places can only be fifteen miles distant. Half a day's ride on a horse.' He straightened with a satisfied grin. 'Get word to Sam. We go to Norfolk tomorrow.'

'I want to see Huw before we leave. I will not go unless I see him.'

Dee scowled. 'A passing check. No more.'

Chapter Fifty-Three

The carriage arrived at dawn. Sam jumped down to hug Margaretta. 'A strong, healthy boy, Missy. We have called him Ralph after my father.' He stepped back. 'Lottie has asked me to bring you to see us.'

'I will, Sam. As soon as we are back. And is Lottie well?'

'She is like a flower in spring, Missy.' He frowned. 'I cried to hear her in pain, but she were as brave as a warrior and Goodwife Tovey did not leave her side. Lottie told me I was being a fusskin.'

Margaretta patted his arm. 'A fine fusskin you are, Sam. Lottie is a lucky girl... and so is little Ralph a lucky boy.'

Their conversation was interrupted by Doctor Dee coming through the front door, pursued by Mistress Constable who was demanding to know when he might be back. 'In a day or so, Mistress. When my important work is complete.'

'But you have been weeks away. The house has been so empty.' A little huff. 'I have had no company.'

'You have had Grace and Siôn to speak with. He is an intelligent man.'

Katherine Constable looked indignant. 'He may be, John. But he is all day organising my husband... and a good thing too.'

'What about Grace? She is a sweet child.'

Katherine's face fell into a look of anguish. 'She keeps

asking why Huw is not at home. Chirrups about him all day. It makes me feel...'

Guilty. And serve you right, mistress. You sold my brother for a barrel of Malmsey and never questioned why Angus wanted him. 'We are going to see Huw this very morning, mistress.' Margaretta shot a look at Doctor Dee before he tried to wriggle out of his promise of last night. 'I will enquire about release from your contract... or you will only have me when Grace and Siôn leave.'

'Leave?'

'They are on loan, mistress. Not sold like...'

'Margaretta,' cut in John Dee. 'Let us go.' He pointed at the carriage door with a look of warning to say no more.

The Vintry was bustling as a ship had just arrived at the quayside. Huw was at the crane counting in the barrels. Hearing Margaretta he turned, ran to her and, for the first time since Mam died, threw his arm around her in a clumsy hug. 'You're back, you're back, you're back. Four hundred and seventy-three bad words.'

His sister held him close but avoided his eyes. 'Yes, Huw. We are going to Norfolk, but only a few days more.' She pulled him to the side, out of line of sight from Angus' office. 'Has Siôn looked after you?'

'Yes, and wherrymen. They come twice a day. I had one kick and they battered the boy.'

'Who kicked you?'

'Tall lanky one. Said you had kicked him.'

'I did, but he was meant to pass that to Angus not you.'

Huw grinned. 'Siôn takes me for Sunday meals with Grace.'

Are you blushing brother? I feel a warmth from you. Margaretta whispered, 'Siôn said you are asked to sign something.'

Huw frowned. 'Uncle Dewi is dead.' He began to step. 'Lawyer said house is mine and fields. Angus says Susan must have them. Wants me to sign. Hits me.'

Margaretta frowned. 'But Uncle Dewi would leave the farm to his son, our cousin Maldwyn. Are you sure, Huw?'

The boy shook his head in distress. 'I read it. Maldwyn died same time. Fire in barn.'

'God rest their souls. Have you seen the papers of ownership?'

More shaking of the head and stepping. 'Angus will not give them to me. Puts a pen in my hand and hits me, saying to sign them.'

'Alright. Just a few days more, Huw. Can you manage that?'

Huw nodded, though his face creased in disappointment. 'Margaretta grey.'

'I am worried, little brother. But when I return, we will get back to our happy colours.'

'Another hundred bad words,' said Huw.

Margaretta climbed into the carriage after thanking Sam for the help of the wherrymen. 'We are going back to the house.'

'No, indeed. We have not the time,' protested Dee, almost sputtering his indignation.

She leaned forward. 'Well, your precious time will have to stretch as I am not going to lose Huw's inheritance.' Dee was silent. She called out of the carriage window. 'Sam. Back to St Dunstans.'

Siôn was just leaving the house with Master Constable who was rheumy eyed from a night in the taverns. Margaretta spoke to Siôn in Welsh. 'I think Huw has inherited land in Wales. There will be a letter from a lawyer and papers of ownership. Can you act like a snake and say you will work on Huw to sign them over?'

Siôn looked indignant. 'I'm not sure I can act as a snake.'

Margaretta raised her brow. 'You did well acting as a poor, ignorant beggar when you have the brain of a scholar.' She returned his grin. 'Act like the louts you have been chasing away from Master Constable's trade.'

A slow nod. 'I can do that. And I'll ask for money to get the signature he wants. That's the sly dealing Angus McFadden will understand.'

The agreement made, Margaretta climbed onto the carriage by Sam. 'Norfolk, Sam. As fast as you can.'

Three days later in the mid-afternoon, they trundled into the small village of Saxlingham Nethergate. The house was visible a mile away, grander than the other houses and cottages, on high ground and surrounded by a narrow moat. No sentries guarded the bridge, just a chained dog that started barking as they approached. By the time they arrived in the yard, a man was standing at the front door.

He was a short, rounded man with cheeks rosy and apple-like. Wisps of dark hair sprouted from a bald pate and flesh folded from his chin to his chest. There was no suspicion in his face. If anything, he seemed pleased to have visitors.

Dee climbed down, putting on his charming face. 'I come on Her Majesty's instruction. Your name, sir?'

In a second the man's face dropped to concern. 'Tom Chapman, but we have done no wrong. I am just a farming man. I...'

Dee smiled more warmly. 'Have no concern, Master Chapman. We simply come for information.' Dee was already walking up the steps as Margaretta pulled down the luggage and Sam put the nose bags on the horses. 'I think this house was once owned by the Lady Anne of Cleves.'

The man was puffing up the steps behind Dee. 'Why, yes. But we did buy it fair and square in 1557. My brother and I did give a good price—'

'Yes, yes. No question of that,' answered Dee as he walked through the front door. Silence. Then a shout. 'Margaretta. Come here.'

She walked through the door and stopped dead. She was in a square room, panelled all around in oak. Each panel was carved and in the centre of each an oval raised motif. Three in a repeat pattern. The first was A and C entwined. In the second, a wheel with eight spokes. 'The ducal badge of Cleves,' Dee murmured. Margaretta walked to the third and traced her fingers over the carving of a lion's head before turning to John Dee. 'This is exactly the same as the lion carvings in the hunting lodge of van Wylich.'

The portly householder was now by their side looking one to another and then to the carvings. 'Why do you stare at these?'

'Because they hold the answer to our Majesty's throne and the safety of our realm.'

The man gulped. 'They were put here by Lady Anne of Cleves.' He made a small smile. 'I kept them for I had much affection for that lady. I think she was a good queen... while she was our queen.'

Dee nodded. 'Is there anything else here belonging to Lady Anne?'

A shake of the rosy-cheeked head. 'When she died, everything was removed from the house by the Crown agents. My brother and I bought it quite empty.' He put his head on one side. 'Though if you like the panels, you will find more in our church of St Mary. It seems she was much grateful to the place, for she furnished it well for the local people.'

Dee was already heading for the door. 'We will go now. We will be back, sir, to make a drawing of your panels.'

Margaretta ran after him and helped Sam turn the horses, though he was complaining they had pulled enough for a day. It took only a quarter of an hour to reach the small church, nestled in a ring of trees. Dee jumped out of the carriage and was walking up the path, his cloak billowing in the breeze before Sam even reigned up.

Chapter Fifty-Four

It was quiet inside the church. The usual smell of rushes, polished wood and stale incense filled the air and everything echoed as they walked down the aisle to the alter.

'There they are,' exclaimed Dee. 'Exactly the same. Anne's initials, the ducal badge of Cleves and the lion of van Wylich.' He knelt down and ran his hand over the motifs. 'Draw these, Margaretta. Then we will go back and draw those in the Manor House as proof.'

'Can I help you?' The thin, high voice from the shadows made them jump. Dee span round assuming his charm-smile. He faced a tall, skinny man. He was wearing the heavy cloth of a clergyman, but the sharpness of his shoulders was evident and the sinews on his clasped hands were raised like tracks on a road. Blue veins showed through milk-white skin. Pale blue eyes surveyed Dee, then looked to Margaretta and back to Dee. 'I am William Pudding. Priest here.'

Dee and Margaretta looked to one another and he mouthed, 'The Apple-Cake Man of name and nature.' Then, before the priest could question his words, he made a polite bow. 'Good evening, Father. We are here from London... from Court.'

The pale blue eyes widened. 'Why would Court be interested in a little town like this? We are good living, God fearing—'

'Be not alarmed, Father. We seek information about the

visit of Anne of Cleves in 1541.' A calming smile. 'But from the freshness of your face I think another priest would have looked after the flock of Saxlingham Nethergate.'

The thin man nodded. 'My father. Also William Pudding. Priest here for twenty years until… until he departed this life. I was but a child at the time.' He looked abashed. 'Your name, sir? And why your interest of events so long ago?'

'I am Doctor John Dee, scholar of—'

William Pudding gave a little yelp. 'The great conjuror of England?' He started to walk backwards, bumping into the end of a settle as he went.

Oh, dear. Now the fury. Your face goes white, master. And those grey eyes go black. 'Fie, Father. My master is no conjuror. That is a cruel rumour set about by those who are not able to keep up with the speed of his mind.' She smiled. 'Do you not see in your flock that people of small mind always belittle that which they do not understand?' She waited for a hesitant nod. 'You look to me like a man who would meet my master's scholarly mind.'

William Pudding took in a deep breath and looked between Dee and Margaretta. 'Very well,' was the tremulous answer. 'But I prefer to stay within the sanctum.'

Dee looked up at the carved oak beams of the roof and then to the painted walls depicting stories from the Bible. 'As do I. Let God assist our thinking.'

Hah. You might be an ordained priest but I never see your Godly side. I believe you took ordination from old Bishop Bonner all those years ago to save yourself from the pyre… and keep yourself in his household to spy. You still have not explained why letters to Cecil are always marked with 007 at the bottom of the page. But at least you took my lead and played the game.

Dee was smiling again. 'Did your father keep church records?'

William Pudding brightened. 'Indeed, he did. A most fastidious administrator in every way with a neat hand.

I have learned from him and do the same. Every birth, marriage, conflict, death and also parish notes and dates of his home visits.'

'Good, good,' replied Dee, pointing to the door behind the alter. 'I assume they must be in the vestry.'

Pudding nodded and then trotted after Dee who was striding ahead without waiting for agreement. In seconds, they were in a dark, oak-panelled room and the priest opened a heavily carved cupboard to reveal rows of books. 'Here I keep our records and also our precious books.' A musty smell of old paper and dust floated out.

Dee was immediately animated and twitching to reach out. But Pudding was ahead of him. 'Now, let me see.' He tapped across the spines of the books, talking to himself as he calculated the years covered in each book. 'The book for now, fifty-five to sixty, fifty to fifty-five…' He pulled the sixth book out of the row, slowly walked it to a desk and stool at the side of the room and opened it with reverence. 'Yes, my father was indeed diligent.' He sat on the stool and started turning the pages, muttering the name of every person recorded. Dee and Margaretta stared over his shoulder. He turned the page until 'September, 1541' showed at the top of the page. He traced down with his finger. 'It was not a busy month. Who are you looking for?'

There was a gasp from John Dee. 'There she is.' He stood to the side of Pudding and slid the book across. 'Look at this, Margaretta.' His eyes were wide. 'My God.'

She came to his side and read the entry for September 26th, 1541.

Today the baptism of Jasper of Cleves. Mother – Lady Anne, residing in Saxlingham Nethergate. Father – Otto van Wylich of Cleves, Germany. In attendance, Mompesson, representing Lady

Margaret Douglas, Godmother. Elyn Tyrpyn, witness. Frances Lilgrove, witness.

There was silence as they took it all in. Then Dee whispered, 'Our absolute proof. A child born and hidden for more than twenty years.' He shook his head. 'Raised just four leagues from a father he has never known.'

You look so very sad. These are the times I like you. When you show you have a heart; that you feel the pain of others. Those few times when a person is more important than your reputation. It will not last, but better a little heart-feeling than none at all.

Margaretta tapped on the name Lady Margaret Douglas. 'She lied.'

'No,' said John Dee. 'Margaret Douglas confirmed a child was born in September, 1541 and that it could only be the child of a noble. She tricked us with half-truth.'

'But she is listed as Godmother. Yet she said she did not see the child. She was—'

Dee raised his hand to silence her. 'She was still on Henry's progress in September, 1541 and so represented at the baptism. Very common for high-born godparents to send a trusted servant. In the November, she was taken straight to Kenninghall under house arrest, so unlikely had visitors for entertainment. Only official visitors…'

I feel something from the priest. He recalls cake. His father returning. 'Sir, did your father go as far as Kenninghall in his capacity as priest?'

The thin man nodded, wide eyed. 'Y… Y… yes. But I do not want any trouble or stain on his reputation.'

'Nor will there be if you assist,' purred Dee as he flicked through the pages. 'You said your father kept records of visits.' He opened the pages for late November and tapped on an entry. 'Here. November 25th. Kenninghall. Cake presented to be delivered to AoC. The babe must be secreted by a sister's love.' Dee looked up at the priest. 'Did your father ever speak of his visits?'

'N... n... no. I was just a child. All I knew was that if he went, the Lady Anne sent me a slice of apple cake.'

Apple cake. The diary said name and nature. 'Sir, you mentioned you are like your father in making fastidious notes. Are you like him in looks?'

Pudding chuckled. 'No, indeed. I follow my mother in looks. My father was as round as the apples in the cakes he loved.'

The fat priest Margaret Douglas mentioned.

Dee nodded at Margaretta and looked back to the ledger to flick through the pages. 'December 20th. Kenninghall. Cake for AoC. Saddest news. Death of the infant Jasper. Mother grieves most pitiful.'

Oh God. I can feel the horror coming off the page. I want to weep.

Dee turned again until he reached February 14th, 1542. 'Kenninghall. Cake delivered to AoC. Lady appraised of coldness in Cleves. May God stand by her.' He sighed and moved on through the pages. 'February 28th. AoC left this day for Richmond. Ague rising and heart heavy.'

He looked at William Pudding who was wide-eyed and worried. 'We must take this book away for submission to Sir William Cecil.' He put a hand on the other man's shoulder. 'Do not be alarmed, sir. Your book will be returned – and with the gratitude of Her Majesty.'

Pudding made a little mew. 'The Queen?'

'Indeed.' Dee closed the book and handed it to Margaretta. 'Your father's excellent administration has just saved a dynasty.' He instructed Margaretta to draw the panels on the altar and turned to leave. But he stopped at the open cupboard and surveyed the books. 'You have the book *Lamentations of a Sinner* by Catherine Parr. A treaties on the reformed faith.' The other man nodded and looked wary. 'I expect you had to keep this well concealed when Queen Mary was on the throne.' Another nervous nod. Dee shook his head. 'This would be safer in the royal library. Not sensible to have books that have been proclaimed as sinful... even in these more tolerant times.' He smiled at the frightened face of the priest as he handed the book to Margaretta with instruction to put it in the bag. Then he walked out, along the aisle and into the light, leaving William Pudding staring after him open-mouthed.

You old magpie. Shame on you.

Chapter Fifty-Five

Tom Chapman was in his yard when the carriage arrived back. 'Did you get the information you required?'

'We did, sir,' chirped Dee. 'May we entreat you for a room to write my notes and also hospitality for the night?' He pulled out his pouch of coins. 'And stabling for our horses.'

Dee lit a candle and spread the contents of his bag across the table. 'We still have many questions, Margaretta.' He picked up the pewter casket which was wrapped in linen and tied with a red ribbon.

'I wish you would not travel with those, Doctor.'

He batted away her words. 'I have told you they are merely playing cards in the lands of Europe. People have yet to understand their power.'

'But if we are stopped and they find you with these and a book on lamentations which is not safe for a priest to hold... a stolen book of lamentations—'

Dee turned to face her. 'I have told you about getting above your station, girl. You are an apprentice. Nothing more yet.'

'An apprentice thief?'

'Curb your tongue, girl.' The voice was more of a snarl than a command. He pointed to the papers and books on the desk. 'We have a spider's web to untangle. Now organise everything into piles – letter, notes, drawings... everything.'

Margaretta bit her tongue and got to work.

Minutes later, they sat with beakers of small beer and manchet bread with cheese delivered by a shy house maid. Dee sat back in his seat. 'We know that Anne of Cleves fell in love with Otto van Wylich. They had a child and that child was sent to Solingen in Cleves to be raised by her sister. We know she believed the child dead by the end of the year and thought her lover's feelings also dead in February of the following year.' He paused. 'That poor young woman.'

Margaretta scanned the notes. 'We know Margaret Douglas knew of the child and was close enough to be godmother. She arrived close by in Kenninghall in November, 1541 – two months after Jasper's birth and baptism. William Pudding – the man Margaret Douglas dismissed as a fat priest, and whom Anne called "the Apple-Cake Man of name and nature", visited both Margaret and Anne. He was passing messages.'

'Of course,' murmured Dee. 'Get the letters and give me that priest's ledger. Read me the dates of the early letters.'

Margaretta jumped to the table. 'The first letters in Amalia's chest are dated November 25th, December 20th and then February 14th in the next year, 1542. Then nothing until 1545 and that is when the hand changes and Erand Malas becomes the writer.'

Dee turned the pages of the ledger with a grim smile on his face. 'The dates of each letter are the dates of his visits to Kenninghall and look at the hand. The same.'

'Margaret Douglas is the friend, but the priest was writing the letters?'

'Margaret Douglas was under house arrest and anything she wrote would be intercepted. So, the fat priest was the scribe and...' He tapped on a grease stain. '...hid the missives under the apple cake so kindly sent to Anne of Cleves until he could send them to Amalia.'

'But why would Margaret Douglas want the child sent away? Was she protecting Anne?'

'Hah.' Dee tapped his head. 'Your next lesson, Margaretta. Learn to get into the mind of the players in life's great games.'

'But I do that all the time for you. Without me you would not know—'

He raised a finger and spoke sharply. 'No, girl. You need to go beyond what they feel in the moment. You need to progress to thinking as they do… seeing the world through the lens of their ambitions, fears, beliefs and dreams.'

Margaretta huffed. 'Well, at least I have given you enough to tell Sir Cecil that the mystery is solved and the Cygnet Prince can be sent back to his nest.' She banged the letters down on the desk.

'No, girl. And curb your tongue,' snapped Dee. 'Breaking the puzzle of a pretender is only half our challenge. We still have the shadowy figure or Erand Malas who today plots Elizabeth's downfall and a poisoner bent on killing anyone in the way of that plot. We must uncover them. Only then is Elizabeth safe.'

Dee picked up the cards again, ignoring Margaretta who stared out of the window, lips pursed in fury. He spread left to right the king, knight, page and ten of wands. Next to them the three of cups with three women dancing in apples. 'Five cards. Right in the middle is the messenger.'

'Yaxley,' growled Dee. 'Two times a messenger.'

Margaretta looked back to the table. 'Do you think Yaxley can reveal Erand Malas?'

Dee picked up a paper and started writing. 'I will send Sam ahead on horseback tomorrow to make sure Cecil has him readied for questioning. I will be hindered by his foolery no more.'

Margaretta stared at the cards while he wrote and picked up the three of cups. 'We have never made sense of this one. Three women in a dance. One with her face hidden.'

Dee stared. 'I would lay a bet that the two women we see

are Amalia and Erand Malas who Amalia said was a woman. They have certainly been dancing together since 1545. But who is the third?'

'They dance among apples,' said Margaretta. 'Letters in apple cakes. Poison in apple sweetmeats and wine.' She looked up. 'When we were at Sheen, a woman with a large coif brought apples.'

Dee chuckled. 'You are learning well, girl, but do not let your imagination run away. A simple woman delivering apples is not whom we seek. We seek someone with designs on greatness. You will be searching for Adam and Eve next.' He winked. 'But your apprenticeship is working.'

I like you again... for a minute, anyway.

She gazed again at the cards. *Come, speak to me. Where is the clue? What is the message? The king draws me. My hand tingles.* 'What's this?' She pointed to a creature at the feet of the king. 'It looks like a lizard.' She stared again. 'And there is a lizard on the throne and in the king's cloak.' She pulled the other cards towards her. 'The same lizard is in the clothing of the knight and the page.'

Dee frowned. 'That is not a lizard. It is a salamander.' He put down his pen and sat back.

You are staring at nothing and your eyes make little winces. I know there is something forming in that great mind of yours. But, damn it, I cannot feel it.

The door opened and Tom Chapman entered, announcing that he and his brother would like their company for evening meal. Margaretta jumped on the table to sit on their cards. Scrying was over for the night.

Chapter Fifty-Six

Sam settled into the saddle and pulled on his hat before bending down to take the oilcloth-bound letter from Dee. 'Straight to Sir Cecil as you ask, Doctor. The house on Cannon Row not The Strand. Reckon I can do it in a day and a half on this horse.' Then he turned to Margaretta. 'You go careful, Missy. I've told the gentleman's carriage driver that you are better sitting with him but he must wrap you well to keep out any chills.' He grinned. 'Don't want you getting an ague before you see my boy and Lottie.'

This is like a dagger to my heart. I do not want to look on your happiness. 'I look forward to that, Sam. You give them both a hug from me.' She waved and watched him ride into the early morning mist.

Dee patted her arm. 'I think that young man still makes a flutter in your heart, girl. A flutter not even Christopher could smooth.' He looked at her with kind eyes. 'But the day you pushed him to your friend you made two other people very happy.'

'But I did love Christopher, Doctor. Truly I did.'

He nodded slowly. 'I could see it. And he loved you. But the first love leaves a little flame in your breast.'

'You sound as if you have felt it, master.'

He made a slight smile. 'I did... I do.' A chuckle. 'You think this heart is a stone. But it beats.'

Do you feel my thoughts? Did you feel me hate you? Be kind. 'Is there no chance, Doctor?'

He shook his head. 'She is married.' Then he pointed after Sam. 'But we are all going through our own life journey. Sometimes a path crosses twice.'

A married woman? Who are you thinking of?

Inside, Margaretta gathered up their evidence into the leather bag. Dee sat at the window staring out into the yard where the carriage was being readied with a driver loaned by Tom Chapman. He drummed his fingers lightly on the table. 'I have been pondering the three of cups card. Who is the third woman?'

'The one with a hidden face?'

He nodded. 'Pull that card out. We have a few minutes before we go.' He took the card from Margaretta and placed it on the table. 'Look carefully. What do you see? It will speak to us if there is a message to take.'

'One is in white, usually the symbol of a virgin, and her hair is dressed which is usually of a higher-born woman.' *I think of Amalia.* 'Amalia has never married and is high-born. She wore cream damask. It fits with it being her.'

'Good. Now look at the other whose face we can see.'

'Dressed in a golden tunic and crowned.' Margaretta looked at Dee. 'Like a monarch. That fits with the king of wands who we are sure is Erand Malas?'

'Excellent. You are thinking well. But focus on the third.'

'Bare headed and dressed in brown, usually the colour of lower-born… like me. But she has a red cloak. Red is a colour of wealth. Our sumptuary law says no-one below a knight may wear crimson.'

'Yes. Now think again. Look, girl. What is the cloak doing?'

Think, think, think. 'It covers her.' Margaretta span round to look at Dee. 'She is poor but covered or concealed by someone rich.'

Dee nodded. 'The cards are not always literal. But the poisoner is hidden, faceless, and has walked within Elizabeth's Court.' He picked up the card. 'This just might be the figure in a black cloak. A person of lower birth could easily move unseen in the corridors of Hampton Court Palace or the quays of St Katherine's dock. Just as you can move unseen pretending to be my servant.'

'You think the poisoner is a woman?'

'That is where the connection ends. Margaret Douglas last meddled back in 1542. Amalia is in Cleves. There is no other woman in this spider's web.'

'A man in disguise?'

'Quite possibly.' Dee pulled the ten of wands. 'Maybe this man – also with a hidden face. He holds ten staffs – so he toils unseen.'

Sometimes I just cannot understand how your mind works. But when it does, you are the cleverest man beneath the stars and planets you love.

Tom Chapman came in to say the carriage was ready.

Chapter Fifty-Seven

You could smell London before the walls of the city were clear in your eye. Though Margaretta was grateful for the driver loaned by Tom Chapman, he had chattered every inch of every mile of the way. Margaretta had to choose between the pain of her ears and the agony of her stomach, which would surely have turned sick if she had sat inside the carriage. Three days of wittering and she was ready to weep.

They entered through Aldgate and immediately the stench hit them. Dung, rotting vegetables, unclean people. In the distance the baying from the slaughterhouses. Sailors weaved out of taverns and the poor gathered around the door or St Botolph's, filthy hands begging for food. The carriage had to stop several times as cattle were herded across the road to be pressed on to the killing yards. Suddenly, the sweet air of Norfolk was an age away.

It was only midday and so Dee insisted they went directly to the house of Cecil in the hope he was in residence. They were lucky and the servants announced he had been waiting for them since the letter arrived. As ever he was behind the polished desk, surrounded by papers and files, each neatly placed and the scroll bound with ribbon. 'Give me your news, John,' instructed Cecil, his voice weary. 'Is it what we need?'

'It is good and bad. First, we... I... can confirm that Jasper, your Cygnet Prince, was the son of Anne of Cleves and Otto van Wylich. The love found on the journey to Calais progressed in the New Year celebrations of 1541. Jasper was born and baptised the following September.' Dee turned to Margaretta. 'Show William the records from St Mary's Church.' He sat back. 'So, we can dismiss the Cygnet's claims.'

Cecil studied the records and then stood and went to the window, his hand going to pinch the top of his nose. 'And how does this relate to the poisonings?'

'That is the last part of the puzzle and I mean to uncover it,' announced Dee. 'I take it you did not find a torn cloak or you would not ask that question.'

Cecil nodded, still staring out of the window. 'We have searched every room in Hampton Court and even the houses of people who visit Court. Nothing. Many cloaks but none torn or recently darned.'

'You have read my letter. I wish to see Yaxley. You prevented me before – it was a mistake.'

Cecil span round, his face angry. 'We do not want to stir the pride of a Catholic plotter, John. And the connection to de la Quadra gives us a diplomatic problem. Tensions with Spain are already too high.'

Dee shrugged. 'As I said, it was a mistake.'

'Why? Give me your reasoning?'

Dee shook his head. 'You asked me to investigate. To do that I need to be given freedom to ask the questions and to use my intelligence to bring all the facts together and present the picture. I cannot be encumbered with half-explanations, explaining half-thoughts, justifying half-formed questions. There is no time.'

The worry in the air was palpable. Cecil's mouth stiffened into a straight line and, without another word, he scribbled on a small parchment, then dripped wax and stamped his seal into it. 'Take this to the Tower.' But as Dee reached out to take it, Cecil snatched it back. 'Ensure your half-thinking is made whole.' The voice dropped to a warning growl. 'And make sure I am never in the dark, John, no matter how dark the reaches of your mind become.'

This is uncomfortable. I feel nothing from the doctor though he has bridled. From you, Sir Cecil, I feel not anger but alarm. You feel out of control. A fear of looking foolish. Your fury is growing and you are beginning to think of how you control my master. 'May I ask after Lady Mildred?'

Cecil jerked as if he had forgotten she was there. Then a smile. 'She is well, Margaretta. You may look into the library before you leave. She is still organising our books for moving them to The Strand.' Dee sat up straight and Cecil turned to him. 'Not you, John. You are not to be trusted in a room of books.'

Lady Mildred Cecil was sitting at a small desk, her paper lit by an oil lamp. She looked up as the servant announced Margaretta's presence. 'My dear child.' She beckoned. 'Come in and sit.' She rose and put her hands on her stomacher as if protecting a kitten. 'You look tired, my dear.'

'I am indeed, my lady. We have travelled more than six days and I do not travel well. It makes me so sick.'

A slight smile. 'Something we share these days.'

Oh, I feel your joy and yet fear. Will this one survive? Will you have a babe to hold or will God snatch it away from you? 'I have heard that lemon water is a good calming drink for a sickness of the morning.'

Mildred's eyes shone and a smile brightened her face. She reached out and took Margaretta's hand. 'I will be sure to try that.' She nodded to the door. 'Tell me of John. Is he making progress on this mystery?'

'We... he is, madam.'

A small laugh. 'I think *we* was the correct term, my dear.' She winked. 'I know very well where the real brilliance lies.' She gazed around the room. 'I was raised in a house of learning, full of books and tutors and encouragement. I can write in languages of the philosophers and understand their thoughts and claims. But many years from now, people will not enquire of the mind of Mildred Cecil or the part she plays at Court. No. They will write of my husband, the Queen's great advisor. No-one will ever ask who advised, calmed, guided and contained the man himself.'

Margaretta squeezed Mildred's hand back. 'But one thing time will never take from you, my lady.' She glanced at the other woman's stomach.

Mildred smiled, a tear in her eye. 'God be begged.'

Chapter Fifty-Eight

The Tower sentry looked at the paper from Cecil and nodded them through. Margaretta stared through the carriage window, swallowing down the bile and trying to stop her heart from beating out of her chest. It was just as last time, cobbled roads between great stone buildings, bustling with soldiers, servants, men delivering hay, rushes, food, flagons. Carts rattling along, laden with stinking rubbish, pulled by miserable looking mules who slipped on the stones slick with grease. Above the din of people shouting came a roar from the menagerie.

Inside the warder's office the guard looked up from a filthy beaker. 'Who are you here to see?'

Oh no. It's you. I remember your rough tongue when I was here seven years ago. But will you know me without the dress and affected voice? I will stay silent and look down.

'Francis Yaxley. And I want a visit of an hour... at least.'

'Prisoners have fifteen minutes. That's all we give his mad wife.'

You are thinking of apples. Cecil mentioned the apples. '*Gofynnwch am yr afalau?* Ask about the apples.'

The guard shot a look at her. 'What she saying?' Then the narrow-eyed stare. 'Do I know you?'

I will exaggerate the accent of my homeland. 'No. I's never been 'ere before.' *Thank the Lord the Doctor has the sense to put a look of blank indifference on his face.*

'Fucking Welsh,' growled the warder. 'Too many of 'em around.' The smell of onions and beer drenched in the pungency of a rotten tooth floated from his mouth.

Dee leaned forward, his face close to the stinking guard. 'You might well remember that your Queen has Welsh Tudor blood in her veins.' A wry smile. 'As I am on Court business, I will take an hour.'

The other man looked away, nodded and said no more.

They were led by a young guard to the Beaufort Tower. 'Why did you not ask about the apples?' demanded Margaretta.

'In time, girl,' was the response. 'I want to get a measure of the man first. Then we will look at this love of apples.'

Francis Yaxley was a man in his middle thirties, though his thinning hair made him look older. He had a pallid face and blue eyes so light they looked the colour of sky. A blue vein was visible between his brows.

Well, that vein in your centre forehead means you will die by water, and Mam used to insist that light blue eyes were a sign of madness. Let us see the colour of your mind, Mr Yaxley.

He stood nervously fingering the edge of his jerkin. The cell was small, cold, meagrely furnished with only a trestle bed, a desk and a stool. Though the desk did hold a Bible. The smell of rats' piss floated up from the floor.

Dee held out his hand. 'My name is Doctor John Dee. I have come to ask some questions of you, sir.'

Yaxley squinted at him. 'The John Dee who conjured the Queen's horoscope?' The voice was high, sneering, self-important.

Dee was silent a second, then spat, 'the John Dee who was ordained a Catholic priest by Bishop Bonner in 1555, sir.'

Hah. So, you use that dubious ordination when it suits. Yet you have never explained how you managed to study and pass all your ordinations in three short months. Or why you did it when you have little faith in any religion.

Yaxley relaxed. 'Forgive me. I see we are of same mind.' A slight, arrogant smile.

You are not, but this is useful to my master.

Dee nodded to Margaretta to start her notes and sat on the trestle bed. 'I understand you are here for knowing much.'

Yaxley sniffed and raised an eyebrow. 'It has been much exaggerated. When you are a man of Court with knowledge of certain events it is only a mere duty to ensure the right people are informed.'

Oh dear. A little pigeon in peacock feathers.

Dee smiled benignly. 'I understand you have the ear of many a high noble. I am told the Bishop de la Quadra, Lady Margareta Douglas and, some time back, Sir William Cecil has had you in their confidence?'

Yaxley began to strut. 'Yes, indeed, I have held many a high office – secretary, clerk of the signet office, member of Parliament. I am confidante to the powerful – entrusted with their thoughts.'

All I can feel is foolish pride. This man is a fopdoodle, fluffed up with his own importance.

'To be entrusted with their thoughts on Robert Dudley, the benefits of our Queen marrying the King of Sweden and other matters close to our faith is merit indeed.'

You are reeling him in like a fish on a pole.

Dee leaned forward conspiratorially. 'But being in these thick walls you will not know of the pretender.'

Yaxley smiled. 'Actually, I know all.'

Dee feigned amazement. 'Heavens, sir.' He glanced towards the door as if checking they could not be heard. 'But what is to be done?'

Yaxley continued his strutting. 'It is simple. Jasper has a true claim. The only way to keep England from Germany is to bolster the English monarchy.'

Dee leaned back, assuming a look of confusion. He said nothing and it worked.

Yaxley bent to his ear. 'Marry Scotland to England, Doctor Dee, and we have a monarchy of union and the true faith.'

Dee frowned as if he was puzzling with Yaxley's words.
This is like a cat playing with a very stupid mouse.

Then Dee opened his eyes wide in feigned realisation. 'Darnley?'

A pompous smile slid onto Yaxley's face. 'Indeed. A rightful king of unity and faith.'

That is what Lady Margaret Douglas hinted at. You have remembered too, Doctor. I see that glint of delight in your face.

Dee smiled. 'I see no erand malas in that.'

Yaxley looked confused. 'You see no what?'

Clever words, Doctor. So, this man did not know about the scheming of the letter writer to Amalia.

Dee stood. 'Most illuminating, Master Yaxley. I thank you.' He nodded to Margaretta to get the bag ready to leave. 'I understand your wife brings you apples.'

Silence. Yaxley opened his mouth to speak and then snapped his mouth shut. A nod.

Panic. I feel it and see it. You are blinking as if the doctor has spat in your eye. Your fear is so great, I feel my own heart race.

'Is it true she brings you fruit?'

Yaxley nodded and then stammered. 'Y... yes. But we only ever meet outside on the green.'

Dee looked around. 'I see no apples in here.'

'Eaten. All eaten.' The voice was a squeak now.

Dee bowed and turned to the door. 'Thank you, Master Yaxley.'

'But you have not questioned me.'

Dee turned with an unreadable smile. 'Oh, but I have. Good day.'

Yaxley was stammering his bewilderment as they shut the oak door and the guard turned the key. They moved quickly down the spiral stairs, Margaretta on her master's heels. 'Why did you not ask him the main questions? You ignored the diary and letter he sent to Solingen. You forgot to ask about Erand Malas.'

'I did not.' He stopped and turned with that same smile and tapped his head. 'All in good time, Margaretta.'

The guard was slumped back and snoring, his black-haired belly rising with every snorting intake. Dee picked up his pen and jabbed him in the chest only to create a huge snore and a shout as he came back into the waking world. He rubbed his eyes. 'Just a short sleep. This work is tiring.'

Dee ignored the grumbling. 'I understand prisoner Yaxley is visited by his wife.'

The other man took a large slurp of beer. 'The only visitor allowed. We call her Black Mouse Meg. Mad bitch.'

'We are told she brings apples.'

The warden shrugged. ''Tis no problem. She pays us a penny to bring him a basket and he picks the fruit he wants.' A frown. 'Then they pass a few words about life and she goes.'

Why did you frown? I see a red apple. '*Afal coch.* Red apple.'

'And does he have a favourite type of apple?'

'Red. She always has just one red in that basket. Every time he picks it up, shines it on his sleeve and puts it back saying it is for her. Strange couple if you ask me. Him full of importance, her full of timidity and hiding.'

'Hiding?'

'Always in a veil. Someone said she is ugly from the smallpox.' Another loud slurp of beer. 'Fucking strange I say. Like a mouse in black cloak.'

Outside the Tower, Margaretta pulled at Dee's arm. 'Do you think Yaxley's wife is part of this?'

'I am not sure and we dare not present a false or partial solution or Cecil will hand everything to Will Fleetwood. Tonight, we scry.' He pointed along the riverbank. 'I will walk awhile and think. You go home.'

Chapter Fifty-Nine

The kitchen was warm and full of the smell of newly baked bread. Grace was scrubbing the oak table and chattering to the cat. The smile on her face when Margaretta entered was like sunshine. 'You is back, miss.' She pushed Cadi off the chair. 'Did you have a good trip with the doctor?'

'A fruitful trip, Grace. But tell me what has been happening here.'

'Well, I do not know what it is all about, miss, but Siôn brought papers from Vintner McFadden and showed them to Mistress Constable.' Grace lowered her voice. 'Whatever she saw has put her off the Malmsey, something terrible. Not a drop has passed her lips in two days.'

'Mistress, I am back.'

Katherine Constable looked up from her stitching. 'Have you seen Siôn?'

'No. Grace says he is out on business with Master Constable.'

The older woman nodded and then looked to the window. 'I thought I was doing right.'

Margaretta walked around to be in line of sight. 'Grace says Siôn has brought papers. That you are upset. What has happened?'

Katherine pressed her mouth together and bent her head as the tears flowed. 'I did not know about the land.' She looked up. 'I really did not know and I cannot read.'

As if a prayer was answered, the front door opened and the voices of Master Constable and Siôn came from the entry hall. Margaretta ran to them. They both fell quiet and Master Constable looked worried. 'You have spoken to my wife?'

Margaretta nodded. 'I do not know what is happening, master.'

Master Constable turned to Siôn. 'Get the papers.' He took Margaretta by the arm and gently led her back into the Mistress' chamber. 'We have a terrible dilemma, my dear. Come and let us talk it through.'

Siôn returned and spread three papers across the table in the middle of the room. He picked up the first one and looked at Margaretta. 'I did as you asked and played the vile-rogue. Seems Vintner McFadden feels some empathy with such fellows.' He winked. 'My next role just might be a mummer he believed me so well.' Then his face went back to serious and he waved the paper. 'It seems your uncle owned a farm in Brecon.'

'A small farm. But Huw said my uncle died, and with him my cousin.' She looked down. 'We had little contact after I brought Mam and Huw to London.' *And I feel shame at that.*

'Well, your uncle left a will, stating that the land goes to his son and thereafter his brother... your father. As your father is passed, the next inheritor is his son... Huw.'

'Huw has inherited land?' Margaretta jumped up. 'But this is good news indeed.'

Siôn held up his hand and Katherine made a little whimper. 'The lawyer wrote to Angus McFadden as the eldest living male relative of your family. And Angus saw money.'

'It is Huw's money.'

'But Angus saw a scheme.' Siôn nodded to Katherine Constable who was chewing on her bottom lip and dabbing her eyes with a linen. 'He came to Mistress Katherine with an offer to give Huw a trade if she signed a contract passing his bond of employment to him.' Siôn picked up the next paper. 'But he inserted a clause in this contract, which says that the bond includes all of Huw's worldly assets.'

Margaretta turned on Katherine Constable, pointing to the kitchen, her voice high. 'You sold Huw and his inheritance… all we had… for a barrel of Malmsey wine?'

In seconds, Master Constable was on his feet telling her to mind her manners. Siôn stepped forward, his voice strong and determined. 'We will not solve this by adopting the venom of McFadden. We need to find an answer.' He picked up the third paper. 'This contract closes the circle. It is a release from bond. If Huw signs this, then he is released from the McFadden yard… and all its cruelty… but he leaves the McFadden's with his inheritance. This is what Angus wants signed.'

Margaretta sat down hard and put her head in her hands. From the side drifted Katherine's weeping. Siôn put a hand on her shoulder. 'My fists, though they twitch, will not solve this, *del*. We need proper help.'

Oh, God. What do I do? This is a chance for Huw. A chance for both of us. A chance for freedom. But Angus is clever, connected, monied. He holds the cards. He holds the legal power to stealing all we have. She looked up. 'The legal power… we need a lawyer.'

Master Constable made a hard laugh. 'Do you know how much they cost?'

Margaretta stood. 'I know a woman called Beatrice. Her nephew is a pupil at Lincoln's Inn. I will beg on my knees for help.'

Master Constable put his head on one side. 'And I will pay what I can to counter my wife's foolery.' He looked to Siôn. 'Thank God you are working our business, so I have a little spare.'

This only made Katherine wail that she could not read and had been sorely tricked.

My anger and fear made me cruel. You are a poor fool who

has been duped. For the second time in seven years, Margaretta joined with her and stepped to her side. 'My mistress is not to blame, sir. She is a good woman who would never assume such evil in another. She thought she did her best for Huw.' She felt Katherine's hand slip into hers and suddenly they were as they were before. Two women with a man to save. Last time it had been John Dee. Now it was Huw Morgan.

Chapter Sixty

'The moon is new tonight. Not much light but it is the best for the cleansing of the stones.' Dee handed Margaretta a bag. 'You know what to do.'

The crystals dipped in fresh water and placed on the sill, she returned to his desk. The cards were out. This time the doctor had put them in clusters. The cards of wands were together, the tower and death which indicated the events were side by side. Elizabeth as queen of swords was separate as was the three of cups which showed the three women dancing among apples. John Dee kept picking it up peering at it.

'You have not mentioned the Duchess of Suffolk or Catherine Carey since seeing them,' suggested Margaretta. 'Though I felt no malice in either.'

Dee grunted. 'Both Protestant, both allies of Elizabeth and both close to Cecil. Unlikely, unless our scrying tells us something. Make sure Sam is ready early in the morning in case we have much travel.'

'First he must take me to Lincoln's Inn with Mistress Constable.'

'What? No. Whatever it is must wait,' snapped Dee. 'You cannot let fripperies stand in the way of my reputation—'

Margaretta stood, hands flying to her hips. 'My brother is no frippery... nor is the land he has inherited which Angus is trying to steal.'

Dee looked askance. 'For the love of angels what are you talking about?'

The plot explained, Dee looked thoughtful. 'Are you sure this David Owens will assist?'

'We saved his aunt – Beatrice.' She swiped a tear away. 'And I've already said that if needs be, I will get on my knees and beg.'

Dee made a small smile. 'I have a few savings. You will have those in your pocket. But try to be back here by nine of the clock.' He did not wait for thanks. Instead, he gestured to the crystals. 'Come. If we have less time tomorrow, we need to make sure we are asking all the right questions.'

Another glimpse of a man that does have a heart. How can I move from hating you to caring much for you?

Dee carefully placed the large garnet in the centre of his piles of cards, then handed the amethyst on a chain to Margaretta. 'I know you do not like the feeling but we need the angels to speak. By using two powerful stones we will help them.' He beckoned her forward. 'Hold the amethyst over the garnet and ask for a "yes".'

Once again, the purple stone began to circle clockwise.

'Now ask for "no".'

Almost instantly the stone circled the other way.

'Now ask for a connection.'

Margaretta obeyed and the stone began to swing to and fro like a pendulum.

'Good, good. This is very clear.' He looked to the window. 'A few minutes and the light of the new moon will help us.' He blew out the candle and moments later a faint, blue glow started to cast across the desk. 'Put the amethyst above the page of wands and ask if this messenger is Yaxley. We must be sure.'

'Clockwise. Yes. So, he still works for Erand Malas.'

'Now go to the three of cups and ask if we have correctly identified Erand Malas and Amalia.'

'Clockwise. Yes.'

'Ask if we have seen the third dancer – the hidden one.'

'It is doing a figure of eight. Yes and No. What the hell…' Margaretta swayed a little. 'I am feeling weak, Doctor. I feel…'

'Stay strong, girl. We cannot stop.' His voice was excited, hard. 'We have to find the connections.' He looked up at her. 'Just ask the angels to show you who is connected.'

She held the purple stone over the garnet again. It stayed still. 'It's not speaking, Doctor.'

'Concentrate. Keep asking. They will tell us.'

As he spoke his last word a sudden breeze came through the window, lifting papers and snuffing the candle. Margaretta yelped. They were in the dark save the single line of moonlight. 'The cards have moved, Doctor. The card with the three women has moved to the centre.'

Dee lowered his voice to a whisper. 'Show us the connection.'

The amethyst began to swing. In seconds it was connecting the three of cups with the ten of wands that depicted the person toiling, face turned away. Margaretta whimpered. 'My hand is tingling. It is beginning to hurt.'

'Keep strong, girl. It is telling us they are connected. Look at how the direction is changing.' He stood and leaned in, eyes bright with excitement. 'It is connecting the page of wands – Yaxley – with the dancing women.'

Then another cry from Margaretta. 'Look at the card of three women, master.'

The moonlight had struck the garnet and a red light flowed out. The three women in the three of cups were bathed in red light and the cloak of the hidden face woman glowed. In an instant, Margaretta dropped the crystal and grasped her hand. 'It is like a knife in my palm.'

Dee looked up at his apprentice. 'We have our answer. Who is connected to Yaxley and also apples?'

Margaretta was shaking. 'Yaxley's wife.'

'Who covers her face and wears a cloak – her husband was a messenger.'

'Yaxley's wife.'

Dee sat back. 'Now it makes sense. The ten of wands – who toils for the page of wands – hides their face. The third woman in the three of cups, who dances with those who dance around the Cygnet Prince also hides their face. This is the same person. The cards were telling us.'

'Yaxley's wife?'

Dee nodded. 'But we need proof. Tomorrow, we find the mouse in black.'

'But we still do not know the identity of Erand Malas.'

Dee smiled and told Margaretta to clear and hide away their tools. As she busied herself, he sat back with a sigh. 'You said Katherine was much distressed.'

'She was.'

'I will ensure to comfort her in the morning.'

Chapter Sixty-One

It was only half of an hour after a messenger was sent for Sam that the carriage trundled to a halt in front of the Constable's house. He jumped down with a smile to Margaretta who was waiting on the road. 'Good morning, Missy. How are you this fine day?'

'A little fearful, Sam. We go first to Lincoln's Inn. Angus McFadden is trying to take inheritance from Huw.'

Immediately, two strong arms crossed Sam's chest. 'Do my lads need to go ashore and give that bastard Vintner a kicking? We can make him squeak like a rat if you like.'

Margaretta laughed. 'No, Sam. Let us try a legal kicking and then if it doesn't work…'

Five minutes later, Katherine Constable was heaving herself into the carriage, helped by John Dee who patted her hand with words of encouragement. 'Tell only the truth, my friend, and shame the Devil.' He was rewarded with a delighted smile and a promise to do just that.

Lincoln's Inn was bustling with young men, all wearing dark tunics, some cloaked but on their heads white coifs tied under their chin. Many were bent under the weight of books and others had arms so full of scrolls they looked like farmers carrying hay. Margaretta stopped a young lad and asked for David Owens.

'You will find him in Old Hall, ladies.' He made a small bow. 'Ask anyone there. They all know David.'

David Owens emerged, red faced and smiling, from a throng of young men all shouting at each other and beating their hands on various books and papers. A mop of dark curls fell above blue eyes and an open face. 'I understand you seek me.' He pointed back at the gaggle of men. 'I was debating a legal question.'

'My name is Margaretta Morgan. I recently tended Beatrice ap Rhys and—'

He clasped her hands. 'She has spoken of you.' He grinned. 'How do I repay your kindness?'

Thank the Lord for that. I can feel Katherine Constable relax at my side. Margaretta asked to step away from the noise of the students and explained the dilemma. David listened intently and asked Katherine to repeat exactly what she recalled of her conversations with Angus. 'You need Will Fleetwood. He is a good lawyer but is also rising, well connected at Court and has the power of the Merchant Taylors behind him. It would take a very brave vintner to challenge him.'

And how am I going to tell my master that I have consulted with the investigator he most resents? What did he say? Forgiveness is easier gained than permission. 'Thank you, Master Owens. But we have limited means.'

A smile. 'We can but ask.'

Everything about Will Fleetwood was large – his body, his face, his smile, his voice, his energy and his hands as he beckoned the two women through the door. 'Come, come. Now what can I do for you? Please sit.' He squeezed himself into a chair behind a desk and grinned. 'Well, well. I hear you are connected to Doctor Dee. How is that?'

'Servant, sir. And I also take notes for him,' answered Margaretta. *You know more than you say. You are smiling.* 'Mistress Constable is his landlady.'

They sat as he read through the papers. Then the questions. What had Angus offered? Did he talk Mistress Constable through the contract? What promises had he made about Huw's employment? And just how many barrels of Malmsey wine had been delivered? Katherine Constable answered, often in such a high-pitched voice and at length that Fleetwood winced and held up his hand to silence her. It did not always work and Margaretta would need to tap her arm for quiet.

The interview over, he sat back to contemplate, pressing huge palms together. 'This is a clear case of acquisition by deception. Unjust and simply wrong.' He looked at Margaretta. 'I think your brother-in-law is more wily than favoured by wit.'

With that, he boomed out into the next room, where David Owens was waiting, making both women jump. 'Pupil Owens. We have a letter to write. Good practice in inheritance law and fraud for you.' The other man came in, sat with a cheerful grin and the letter warning Angus was dictated, signed, sealed and handed to Katherine. 'You deliver this, Mistress, along with replacements of the three barrels of Malmsey wine. You do not leave without the boy, Huw. If Angus argues, you come back to me and we will send a few lads to assert your message.' Behind him David Owens raised his fist. Will Fleetwood turned to Margaretta. 'The law is for the good, Margaretta. And you and your brother are on the right side of good.'

'Thank you, sir. And the payment?'

A shake of the head. 'Do me one favour. Tell John Dee that we are fellows not foes.'

So, you knew. 'I will surely do that, sir.'

Oh, you good man. If only the world had more of such men. You remind me of Christopher in your kindness, but you are stronger.

Chapter Sixty-Two

Back at St Dunstan's they found Dee in the road, waiting impatiently. 'No wonder lawyers are so rich. Charging every minute and every word. You have been two hours. How much has it cost you?'

'Nothing,' trilled Katherine. 'Master Fleetwood was most generous… and charming.' She breezed into the house, calling to Siôn that he needed to procure three barrels of Malmsey, so she did not see her lodger's face twist to fury.

He turned on Margaretta. 'Did you go and see that—'

'Good man? Yes. And I will be forever thankful.' Margaretta took the bag off her master's shoulder and put it in the carriage. 'He asked me to send his good wishes. Said you were fellows not foes.'

Dee glowered. 'And how would he know what I thought of him?'

Margaretta put up two palms in question. 'Because you cannot say his name without a scowl? People talk.'

Hampton Court seemed to be less anxious than at their last visit. Dee beamed when servants bowed as he swept up the steps to Cecil's office. When they reached the door there was a shout from the end of the corridor. 'Doctor Dee. What news?' It was Robert Dudley, running along the stone floor towards them. 'Cecil will not tell me anything. Have you undermined the Cygnet?'

'Yes. But we have a few strings to tie together. Do not worry. My mind has all but solved the case.'

Your mind? And one string called Erand Malas is far from being tied. You tell lies like truth.

Cecil was at his desk and gestured to them to shut the door. 'Did I hear Dudley outside?'

Dee nodded. 'He is anxious for news.'

Cecil raised his brows. 'As am I.' He glanced at Margaretta and told her to pull up a chair, so she might take notes comfortably.

More warmth. I hear your wife's voice. She has told you... no, instructed you... to be kind to me.

Cecil turned back to Dee. 'Catholics in the North are clamouring to have Margaret Douglas released from Sheen.'

Dee reached for a glass, poured himself a generous wine and looked defiantly at Cecil. 'I need you to find Yaxley's wife and if she has links to Court. My analysis says she may be involved.'

'How? What analysis?'

And how do you manage this, my master? How do you tell the great Sir Cecil that we have arrived here through your conjuring cards and a swinging crystal? You are wincing your discomfort and the silence is deafening.

'I will tell you how when I have interviewed her. Before that it is but theory.'

Cecil shook his head. 'Meg Yaxley is no more than a mouse. She will only set her eyes on a cross. She shuns all other Court servants, probably for shame of having a husband who has fallen from grace and languishes in the Tower.'

'Court servants?' Dee yelped. 'She is here?'

Cecil frowned. 'It was only charitable... and safer.'

'Safer?' snapped Dee, his voice rising.

'Yes, John. Safer to have the wife of a plotter where we could watch and control her.'

Dee stood and started towards the door. 'Well, it may be that you have failed to control a poisoner. Where will we find her?'

Cecil paled. 'Likely picking apples. It is the season.'

'We will go...'

John Dee started down the corridor but was halted by a bark from Cecil. 'She will not speak to any man. Believes it is a sin to her marriage.' He turned to Margaretta. 'We all know you are more than a servant in these investigations. I will call Blanche and you will both manage this madness.' He took her arm and marched her off, leaving John Dee standing.

There was a fine drizzle outside as they walked towards the orchards, Margaretta explaining everything to Blanche. In the orchard, a figure was bent over, picking apples into her apron, a veil tied under her chin to stop it falling from her face. 'Meg,' called Blanche. 'I want you to meet a friend of mine.'

The woman stood upright and just looked. As they approached, Margaretta could see she was a small woman, tiny in frame. Through the veil it was just possible to see a face, distorted and red. 'Good, morning, Mrs Yaxley.' No answer.

Meg turned to a basket and started to unload the apples, all green, from her apron. The hands were red, pocked and the side of every nail raw from being bitten.

The same hands that delivered apples to Margaret Douglas. 'Tell me about your apples, Mistress. What variety do you have?'

'God's food to remind us of sin,' was the muffled reply.

Margaretta smiled. 'But I see they are all green. I think Eve was tempted with a red apple.' *That was the trigger. I feel your panic. You are looking around. But no red apples. So where are you getting them? You are thinking of a dark room. A cross on the wall.*

'I hear your husband gives you a red apple each time you—'

Meg Yaxley started to wail and sway, beating her hands against her face. 'Thy will be done. Thy will be done.'

Blanche gasped at her sudden distress and stepped forward telling her to calm. But Meg howled like a trapped animal and slapped her hands away. She snatched up her skirts and started to run towards the palace. Blanche turned, white faced, to Margaretta. 'What in God's name…?'

'She is thinking of a dark room with a cross on the wall.'

The other woman's brow furrowed. 'The chapel is light. But she is of the old faith. They kept crosses on all walls.'

'Her room. We need to move quickly.'

The door to Meg Yaxley's room was locked and no amount of hammering would get her out. Cecil commanded the guards to force it and within minutes the oak was splintering under an axe. They went in first and grabbed a screaming Meg Yaxley who was trying to climb from a stool to a high window. She kicked and squirmed like a wildcat, shrieking that they were the servants of Satan and that the true faith would rise. One pulled her down as the other grabbed her wrists. As he did, two red apples fell from under her skirt and rattled across the floor. She suddenly went still and stared at the floor, repeating over and over in a high-pitched chant, 'Thy will be done. Thy will be done.'

Margaretta stepped in and pulled up the veil. Despite gentle words to calm her, Meg spat in her face and screamed. Margaretta turned to Dee. 'This is the same woman who delivers apples to Lady Margaret Douglas… where she was given a red apple.' She bent over and picked up one of the red apples which had fallen to the floor. It was smooth, glossy, perfect. She handed it to John Dee. 'It is not an apple.'

Cecil and Dudley gathered around. He lifted it and turned it in the light. 'It is carved of wood.'

Apple. Thy will be done. 'What says the Bible about Eve's apple?' asked Margaretta.

Blanche stepped forward. 'When the woman saw that the fruit of the tree was good for food and that it was a delight to the eyes, she took of the fruit and did eat. And she gave also one to her husband. The eyes of both of them were opened.'

'The apple opens,' whispered Margaretta.

Only Dee heard her. He took the perfectly carved stalk with a bend at the end and green-painted leaf. He twisted then pulled. With a tiny scrape it came away revealing a chamber containing three rolled slivers of parchment. He plucked them out. He read the first. 'This is from the Book of Genesis. "From dust you are, to dust he shall return". Neerman.' He unrolled the second. 'The same verse of Genesis and the name Beatrice ap Rhys.'

Before he read out the third, Dudley cut in. 'It says Dudley and Teerlinc, does it not?'

Dee nodded.

Margaretta picked up the other apple as Dee turned to Cecil. 'Did this woman visit her husband yesterday afternoon?' He was answered with a nod. 'Then that apple will name me.'

Margaretta pulled out the parchment. 'From dust you are, to dust he shall return. Dee.'

Meg let out another animal wail and started her ranting of 'Thy will be done.' Cecil nodded to the guards who dragged her out screaming.

Cecil sat on the stool and pinched the top of his nose. 'Dear God. She was hiding in plain sight. But how did she hide the apples? I instructed that every basket be checked when she left and returned. We have been waiting for Yaxley to use her.'

Dee nodded. 'I will explain that later. More important, where is the cloak?'

Margaretta looked around. *Under. It is under something. Hidden. Apples. They have hidden everything.* In the corner was a large basket of apples. She stepped across and tipped them out. Below was a thin black cloak looking like a cloth to stop the bruising. She shook it out. There, on the shoulder, was a tear. Under the cloak was a pair of black gloves.

Cecil gasped and closed his eyes. 'My God.' He looked to Dee. 'You have done well, John.'

All I feel is relief – that we do not have to mention that all this was uncovered by a swinging stone.

Dee was already squaring his shoulders. 'I want all the players gathered. It will take a few days to bring the Cygnet Prince, but he must attend. That gives me time to construct my summing up.' He pointed at Cecil. 'I want all the papers you demanded for Will Fleetwood and also access to your files.'

'What files?'

'The files you secret away on every person of note.' He walked out calling over his shoulder, 'Margaretta, get your brother home and tomorrow evening we prepare to reveal the sad story of a Cygnet Prince.'

Chapter Sixty-Three

The Vintry was clearing up for the day as the sun sank to the horizon. Angus was slouched on a barrel, drinking wine, his lips stained red and eyes rheumy. He stood with a leer when Margaretta stepped out of the carriage, and then looked surprised to see Siôn follow her. When Katherine Constable squeezed through the door, his expression turned to concern. Then he spied the three barrels strapped to the top of the carriage and it turned to alarm, though he tried to hide it with a sly grin. 'I am indeed honoured by such a gathering.'

'We are not here to honour, brother-in-law. We are here to get my brother... and he will bring with him his inheritance.' She waved the letter from Will Fleetwood. 'It is all explained in here.'

Angus forced a laugh so harsh it made the yard lads stop and stare. From the waterside, Huw ran up towards them. 'Have you come for me?'

'Yes, Huw,' said Katherine. 'Get in the carriage.'

'I warn you against breaking a contract, mistress,' snarled Angus. 'It will have you in Newgate.' He went to grab at Huw, who jumped sideways making Angus lose his footing and stumble. He pulled himself up and went to grab him again. Huw ran and so Angus turned on Margaretta, bending down to put his face so close, his spittle hit her cheeks. 'You think dog-boy deserves land, do you? He can hardly fasten his breeches let alone manage land.'

Margaretta smiled. 'As least he fastens them, brother-in-law. Unlike you. You are lower than the worm beneath the stone and my sister is plastered in dirt just like you.' She ducked as Angus' hand flew up to slap her.

Then a yell and a thud as Siôn threw his arm around Angus' neck and yanked him back, before slamming him against the wall and pinning him by the arms. 'There are a few things I don't like in a man. One is cruelty, another is violence towards a woman, the third is deceit. But most of all I dislike the stupidity of not knowing how stupid you are.' He shoved again, making Angus splutter and a dribble of red wine flowed from his mouth. 'So, it seems there is nothing to like about you, Vintner McFadden.'

'I have my rights,' squeaked Angus. 'I will have my rights.'

Siôn nodded towards the carriage. 'Your rights are swilling in barrels on that wagon. As thin and weak as your mind.' He nodded to Margaretta. 'Huw's rights are in the letter she holds.' Another shove and Angus squealed. 'So, I suggest you drink your rights while reading about the legal hell which will descend if you continue this deception.'

Angus bared his teeth and looked to Katherine who was clinging to Margaretta. 'I will have you in Newgate, bitch.'

Siôn lifted Angus off his feet, slammed him again. 'One more insult to a woman and I will have you in the fucking water, boy.' He dropped Angus who simply crumpled. Siôn nodded to the women. 'Margaretta, throw that letter into the man's lap and both of you get in the carriage.'

Margaretta saw that Sam was standing on the top, unstrapping the barrels. She clambered in, shoving Katherine ahead of her as Angus got to his feet and started after them. She turned to keep the door open for Siôn, but he shut the door and climbed onto the roof with Sam.

Angus screamed, 'Lower my goods.'

Then Sam's voice. 'I hear your favourite game is to drop barrels on the weakest lad to see if he can jump fast enough.' A scrape, a crash, a yell from Angus and the first barrel exploded on the ground. Angus wiped the wine from his eyes just as the second barrel shattered into staves and hoops. 'You better jump, vintner. This one is for you.' Angus fell backwards as the third barrel blasted its contents on the ground. He was lying, snarling in a lake of Malmsey wine.

Katherine Constable was white faced and wide eyed, just staring ahead. Margaretta took a deep breath and went to comfort Huw, but he was sitting looking out of the window, grinning. She looked down. He was holding Katherine's hand.

They arrived back at St Dunstan's within a quarter of an hour. Master Constable was outside, thumbs crooked into his belt. He opened the carriage door. 'The news is already abroad. I hear the vintner sits in his own juice.' He reached to assist his wife out and bid Huw welcome. Then he looked up at Siôn, who was laughing with Sam. 'I think the vintner will not be renewing your bond of employment.'

There was a silence. *Oh, Siôn. I feel your sudden worry through the roof of this carriage. You think of the streets, the dirt, the shame. But I look at Master Constable and hold my breath.*

Master Constable stretched up his hand. 'If you would consider it, sir. I think my business is all the better for having you in it.'

A hand reached down from the roof of the carriage and Siôn Jenkins had hope and a future again.

Huw was stepping side to side repeating, 'Thank you, thank you, thank you.' Sam looked down with a grin. 'You have just given me the best evening since my babe did arrive.' Huw laughed and ran inside.

The agreement made for Sam to arrive early in two days' time, along with the carriage, for the last journey of his retainer, Margaretta and Siôn turned to the house. She felt a squeeze of her arm. '*Diolch, del. Diolch o waelod fy nghalon.* Thank you, pretty one. Thank you from the bottom of my heart.'

In the kitchen, Grace was bending over Huw, chattering her fury at the cuts on his face as she dabbed them with a linen. The cat was in his lap, but he was not looking at Cadi.

Oh, my God. Huw is looking into Grace's eyes.

Chapter Sixty-Four

The carriage was waiting outside. Sam had even put on a good coat and brushed his hair. 'Last journey, Doctor Dee. Thought I would make an effort.'

Dee chuckled. He was in high spirits and eager to make his display. Margaretta settled in. 'You have been closeted away in Cecil's offices for two days, Doctor. But there remain huge flaws in your investigation. Why would Lady Margaret Douglas lie to her friend Anne of Cleves? Why hide a child? And who is Erand Malas?'

Dee smiled. 'Your gifts are invaluable, Margaretta, and you have done well. But you are still the apprentice.' He tapped his head. 'And this mind is ahead of you.'

'Why did you make me bring Huw's wooden letters?'

He grinned. 'Theatre.' He then pulled out his notes and the rest of the journey was in silence.

Cecil was waiting in his reception room. 'All are assembled. I have Henry Carey representing his sister as she is still in deep mourning. Meg Yaxley is raving in chains. But come to my office first.'

When they went in, five red apples were in a row on his desk. He pointed to one at a time. 'This was in Yaxley's cell secreted in his bed straw. This was in Margaret Douglas' bedroom. This one in de la Quadra's office in Dudley's house. The last two are from Meg Yaxley's room.' He picked up the first apple and took out a paper. 'Only this one, from Yaxley's cell, had a message in it. It has Genesis again – "From dust you are, to dust ye shall return". But no name.'

Dee took the fruit. 'That is because you found the apple before he wrote the name, Cecil.' The room went cold.

Dee raised his eyebrow. 'Good thing you have me and not Will Fleetwood investigating.' He picked up one apple.

Cecil grunted and pointed to the door and led the way.

There was a strange silence. Every person was sat, staring ahead, saying nothing, like a circle of puppets waiting for the strings to be pulled. From the far corner was a clink. It was Francis Yaxley, manacled and a guard either side. In the middle, on a carved chair was Margaret Douglas, her face set like granite. Next to her was Bishop de la Quadra, his hands clasped together as if in prayer. On the longer couch sat the Duchess of Suffolk, her eyes betraying alarm, and Henry Carey glowering. At the back was Blanche ap Harri and Lavinia Teerlinc. Next to them, Nicholas Wooton. Under the window, seated on cushioned chairs, were Robert Dudley and the Cygnet Prince assiduously looking away from each other.

Cecil showed Dee to his seat and then took Margaretta to a small desk in the corner well-stocked with paper, pen and ink. 'I will rely on you to make a full record. For my eyes only.' She nodded and prepared her pens in the ink horn. She also, as instructed by Dee the evening before, took out all the evidence. Cecil turned to Dee. 'Your floor, Doctor Dee.'

Dee stood, smoothed his gown, raised his chin and slowly surveyed the gathering.

Look at you. On stage and in your very element. This is where you display your brilliance, make them gasp, let them wonder at the mechanics of your mind... and I sit in the corner out of sight and out of mind again. Your secret weapon in the game of crime. But to them just a woman who can write.

Dee raised one apple and looked to the German prince.

'Jasper of Cleves. You came here in good faith, believing yourself the true and rightful heir to our throne.'

Jasper stood and bowed. 'I will truly do my duty – unite your lands and bring your people to the salvation of the true faith. I will reign with love.' He looked around smiling, though it faded as no-one looked at him. He frowned. 'I thought you were here to confirm.'

'No, sir.' Dee's voice was gentle. 'I am here to tell you how people around you have stolen your life for their own benefit.' He gestured to the young man to sit and he gazed around again. 'There are three parts to this sad story – *what* has happened, *who* are the players and *why* they did what they did. It is a sad and sinister tale of deception, deceit, distress, dynasty and death – and you have all played your part in it.' He turned to Cecil, though pointing at Jasper. 'Your first instruction was to prove that this child was not born to Anne of Cleves and Henry. And we almost managed that.'

Dee went to stand in front of the Duchess of Suffolk and Henry Carey. 'The mission started with a launderess stating that no child of Henry's was born to Anne of Cleves.' At the back of the room, Blanche ap Harri nodded her agreement. 'There was no official record of a birth or any papers relating to Anne of Cleves in the year 1541, and the Court limner also stated that she could not attest to a child.' Lavinia Teerlinc nodded nervously. Dee bent towards the Duchess. 'You stated, my lady, "Anne did not birth a Tudor prince."' The woman also nodded, her face tense. Dee looked to Henry, 'Your sister said, "I did not see any sign of Anne bearing a Tudor prince." The same message.'

Henry Carey rose to his feet, a finger pointing at Dee. 'If my sister said there was no fucking Tudor prince, then there was no fucking—'

Dee raised a hand. 'The ladies did not lie. But neither did they tell the truth. Nor did the limner. They acted as true friends and protected the name of a woman they truly admired.' Ignoring Henry Carey's look of incredulity, Dee walked over to Margaret Douglas. 'Then you, madam, broke the chain and insisted that Anne of Cleves did bear a child in September, 1541, stating it could only be King Henry's child.'

'It is true. A child was born – a royal child.'

'And you were the godmother.'

Margaret Douglas went pale. 'How do you know? I did not tell you.' Then she smirked. 'I told you I never set eyes on the child.'

'True, Madam. Because you were on progress with King Henry and Queen Kathryn Howard when Jasper was born.' He turned to Lavinia Teerlinc. 'You were on that progress too.' He waited for a nod. 'And when your gossiping friend, Mrs Gylman, wrote saying Anne was with child, you told Lady Margaret Douglas.'

Lavinia stared ahead until she was nudged by a hatchet-faced Blanche. She gave a little sob and nodded.

Dee turned back to Margaret Douglas. 'You decided to act the friend, the advisor, the apparent protector but out of sight. So, the records of St Mary's Church in Saxlingham Nethergate show that you sent your servant, Mompesson, to Jasper's baptism to stand as godparent in your stead.'

For the first time, Margaret Douglas looked alarmed. Then a sneer spread across her face. 'It seems, Doctor Dee, you have only been able to show the truth of my words.' She turned and smiled at Jasper.

He rose to his feet. 'If this is true... if I was born and baptised here... why are you not just arresting your false Queen and declaring my birthright?' At this, Dudley sprang up and started shouting, only to be barked at by Cecil. Jasper continued. 'If I have the blood of your king and his queen, I am your rightful king.'

Dee smiled. 'That brings us to the first *who* of this sad tale, sir. I had to discover exactly *who* you are.' He pointed to Cecil. 'Your next strategy was to defame the Lady Anne and prove she had given birth before her marriage to Henry. You used the cruel words of Henry that she was of loose belly and breast and had strange smells. A cruel ploy, but the only one you had to hand.'

Cecil looked uncomfortable and glanced at Jasper who was staring at him, horrified. 'They were not my words,' muttered Cecil. 'Get on with this, John.'

Dee nodded. 'I went to Cleves to see if I could, indeed, besmirch Anne's reputation.' He made a short bow to Jasper. 'I failed, sir – and I am glad to tell you that. Instead, we uncovered a story which would break the most hardened of hearts. Your story does not start in 1541 – the year of your birth. It began in 1539 when a young, innocent, much-loved princess was chosen to be the fourth bride of England's King Henry.'

Henry Carey started to growl. 'Where are you going with this, Dee? My sister had no part in any—'

Dee raised a hand to silence Carey and turned to Nicholas Wooton. 'You then escorted the young princess across Germany, Austria and the lowlands to Calais. Her belief was that she was going to marry a golden king and be queen of England. Her only preparation was the little English taught her by Mrs Gylman. But on that journey, hope soon turned to horror – because Mrs Gylman took delight in recanting terrible tales of Henry having poisoned one wife, beheaded the next and had a third ripped in childbirth. Only one was true, but Anne was not to know. Then Thomas Seymour, in the reception party in Calais, furthered Anne's terror. Anne had stopped eating in Hoogstraten. The pretty round-faced girl painted by Hans Holbein lost all the weight she had gained in eating the cakes of baker Gilda and was down to skin and bone.'

Jasper smiles at the name of the baker who has fed him all his life. Oh, you poor man. You have yet to hear the worst.

Dee looked up to Cecil. 'A human body which loses so much weight so quickly has loose skin – the looseness of belly and breast so cruelly mentioned by our former king. As for the smell.' Dee looked at the Duchess of Suffolk. 'When you met the Lady Anne from her ship, did she have a strange, sweet smell about her and harshness of breath?'

A nod. 'She looked as if she had been in prison.'

'Well, she was certainly feeling she faced a prison. But when a person stops eating, the body feeds on itself and the effect is to create the so-called "strange smells" that repulsed Henry. If you go to Newgate, you will smell it on every prisoner.'

The Duchess looked up. 'Which is why when she calmed in London and started eating, she was sweet of breath as well as nature.'

'Exactly, my lady.'

Jasper stood, flushed in the face and his eyes glassy with suppressed tears. 'My mother was cruelly treated.'

'She was indeed. But there was one light in her life. On the road to Calais, she had fallen in love with one Otto van Wylich.' Dee beckoned to the Canterbury priest. 'Tell us about him, Master Wooton.'

The old man stood. 'He was a fine man. I wrote to Thomas Cromwell of his goodness and also his likeness to Henry. If they had stood side by side, you would have thought them brothers. Same build, same colour, same face.' He looked around the room. 'The love I saw was true. And God forgive me I have kept it secret for twenty-three years. May I be forgiven.'

'You thought you were doing right, Master Wotton,' said Cecil. 'Be at peace.'

Dee looked at the Duchess of Suffolk. 'Six months later, your friend was divorced from Henry and life changed. She started to laugh, she changed her dress, she began to bake her German cakes. She began to plan.' He turned to Margaretta. 'Bring the translation of the diary.'

In the far corner, Yaxley made a small cry. Dee turned with a smile. 'You are right to show concern, Master Yaxley. Your dealing in this sorry affair began in 1557, when you were in the Office of the Signet and responsible for auditing the papers and belongings of Anne of Cleves when she died. Under instruction you sent this diary, which contained the truth, to Solingen for it all to be hidden. You also sent a diamond ring as a dead mother's keepsake for Jasper.'

Dee looked back to the Duchess. 'Please describe the ring you were to inherit from Anne of Cleves, my lady.'

'A large table-cut diamond, set in gold.'

Jasper made a small cry and held up his hand before looking at the Duchess. She stared at his hand, wide-eyed, before moving her glare to Yaxley who began to shake.

Dee tipped his head to the frightened man. 'I will return to you, sir. For you are up to your neck in this sorry tale.' Yaxley opened his mouth, then snapped it shut and shook more.

Dee fluttered the papers. 'In here we can follow the story of Anne of Cleves and her child. In December, 1540, she excitedly plans New Year for her German guests – one of whom was Otto Van Wylich.' He asked the Duchess. 'What was Anne like that Christmas and New Year?'

'Full of joy. It was wonderful to see.'

'She was indeed full of joy because she was full of love… for Otto van Wylich. And from that love, a child was conceived.'

Jasper jumped up. 'This is foolery. Otto van Wylich is an enemy to our family. He is banned.'

Dee nodded. 'Which is part of the cruelty to which I must expose you.' He gestured for Jasper to sit. 'Anne found she was with child in spring 1541. Luckily, Henry was planning progress with his new bride, so she could disappear to the country unnoticed. She fled to one of her divorce-settlement houses in Norfolk. A small, secluded hamlet called Saxlingham Nethergate.'

Dee looked to Jasper. 'You were born in a house which your mother made a homage to your father. Still, there are panels of her crest, the wheel of Cleves and his emblem – a lion's head. The same was gifted to the church where you were baptised on September 26th, 1541.' Dee spoke over his shoulder to Margaretta. 'Please show Jasper the German written diary, the church records and your drawings of the panels.'

She walked over and put them in his hands. He stared, shook his head and tears fell. He looked at Margaret Douglas. 'You really are my godmother? But your name has never been given to me.'

By now, Dee was standing in front of Margaret Douglas who refused to meet his gaze. 'Because your godmother wanted to do as all godmothers do and shape your life, but she would do that from the shadows. In the November after your birth, in disgrace herself, she asked to be taken to Kenninghall, which she knew was only a half day's journey from your mother and you. From there she would start to shape your future. In that diary you will find references to a friend. That friend was the prisoner of Kenninghall.'

'Lies,' spat Margaret Douglas. 'Everything I wrote was intercepted.'

'But your guards would not question the visits of the fat priest.' Dee raised his voice over Margaret who was snarling her refute. 'Every time Anne reports advice from her friend it is linked to the visit of a man she calls Apple-Cake Man of name and nature. His name was William Pudding. He scribed your letters, hid them under apple cake, took the instructions or messages to Anne of Cleves in his parish and then sent the letters to Amalia in Solingen.'

Henry Carey growled again. 'This is surely a fancy. You have lost your mind, Dee.'

'No, sir. The son of William Pudding confirmed the visits. The records of St Mary's Church give further evidence. The dates of the visits match dates of letters sent to Solingen in Cleves. Those letters are grease stained from being hidden under a cake and the hand is the same.'

The room was in silence, all staring at Margaret Douglas. She stood and turned to leave, but Cecil commanded her to sit and face the truth. Then he nodded at Dee to continue.

'You were meticulous in your shaping of Jasper's life.

You even advised the name Jasper. A clever move, my lady.' He picked up the translation of the diary. 'Anne says you advised the name as it would make it easier for her babe to come back to Court. Why? Because Jasper Tudor was the man who guided Henry the Seventh, the first Tudor King, onto the throne. The name is held in great esteem in the house of Tudor. Clever.'

I look at Jasper. Oh, you poor, poor boy.

Dee lifted the translated diary again. 'That same November, a rumour began that Anne had birthed a fair child. With a heavy heart, advised by her friend, she sends her little babe to be kept safe in the castle of her childhood – in Solingen – to be cared for by her sister, Amalia. Anne planned to follow, and that is when the real cruelty begins.' He pointed at Margaret Douglas. 'Within a few months you broke the heart of Anne of Cleves with the lies that her baby was dead and that the father had no love for her. She never tried to go to Germany again.'

Everyone was staring at Margaret Douglas, except Bishop de la Quadra who looked at the window, his normal arrogance moving to sadness. Jasper rose to his feet. 'Why? Why did you have me sent away?'

Margaret Douglas almost spat. 'It was for your safety and your mother's reputation.'

'Untrue, madam, and it brings us to the first *why*,' shouted Dee. 'The reason was ambition. You think yourself rightful heir to the English throne through your mother – King Henry's sister. With Henry's daughters declared illegitimate, you believed that the only person between you and the throne was Henry's sickly son – Edward. You knew Henry craved a second son – even one born out of wedlock. He had already raised and lost one bastard – Henry Fitzroy – and had considered putting that boy in the succession line. If Henry thought there was a healthy son and people believed it his – he might just take that boy to be his own – and push you further from the throne.'

Margaret Douglas made a forced laugh. 'Hah. Henry was seeking to sire a boy with his new queen.'

'And on that progress, Queen Kathryn was taking young Thomas Culpepper to her bed. All her ladies saw it. You knew, madam, that she was not long for this world. And a grieving Henry would be even more interested in Anne's child. So, you quickly had that child removed and hidden from all who could have loved him.'

Cecil snarled into the silence. 'I think you cannot deny it, Lady Margaret.'

She shrugged. 'It was for Anne's reputation. I did nothing else.'

Dee span round, holding up his arms for effect. 'Untrue. Four years later another advisor started sending letters to Solingen: a certain Erand Malas who had been manipulating the lives of the players in this tragedy since 1545. Living their Latin name – a wicked errand.' He clicked a finger at Margaretta. 'The letters.'

You old scut. Back to treating me like a minion again. Damn you. 'Yes, master.'

'Sent every year of Jasper's life, these letters have dictated his education, his language, his understanding, his destiny.'

Jasper was on his feet again. 'No. Aunt Amalia knew who I am. She raised me for my destiny.'

'I am sorry, Jasper. But your Aunt Amalia is a bitter woman who has been tricked for years into believing that she would share your future in England. Forced into the life of an old maid, she dedicated her efforts to you believing that she would, one day, be recognised as a mother of a king. Sadly, she shared the same greed for power as Erand Malas, which is why she sent poison to your father to make him think that Anne hated him and then banned him from your castle under a false claim of treachery. When she faced our questions, she killed again – this time an old woman who spoke too loudly in her deafness and too honestly.'

Jasper looked puzzled. 'Who?'

'The woman who has made your honey cakes since you were a child. Gilda. She was killed by her own baking and her coffin used to hide all the evidence before you. Every witness threatened with death by bees.'

Jasper bent over, put his head in his hands and groaned.

'For fuck's sake, Dee. Who is this Erand Malas?' shouted Henry Carey. 'A minute ago, you were accusing Margaret Douglas. Now it is Erand Malas. Get to the fucking point.'

Dee tapped on the name at the bottom of the letter. 'It took much thought and investigation. But I put all the strange factors together and twisted my mind into that of a woman bent on her own gain.'

Liar. I did that. I guided you to uncover the name. Oh, but as a woman I have to sit here mute and weak and let you cover yourself in vain glory. I should have said yes to Peter.

Dee turned to Margaretta. 'The wooden letters which spell Erand Malas.' He tipped them out onto the floor in front of the gathering.

'The name Erand Malas is a muddle of...' He slowly put the letters together as everyone stared. '"Salamander", the emblem creature of the Douglas family.' He gave a satisfied grin. 'A creature revered by the Catholic Knights Templar for they believed it could live through fire and rise again. And you did rise again, my lady, from the ashes of three people's lives – Anne of Cleves who thought her baby dead and her lover cold, a father who lived heartbroken only four leagues from his own son but never knew him, and a child who never knew the love of his parents and became a puppet for your ambition.'

The only sound was Lavinia Teerlinc who began to sob, Blanche patting her shoulder. Then Cecil rose. 'John, this cannot be. We all know the true ambition of Lady Douglas is to put her own son on the throne. Why would she—'

'A good question – and it brings us to the second *why*. The clue is the date. 1545.' He turned to face Margaret Douglas. 'In that year you birthed and then grieved the loss of your first son. The Tudors were known for bearing few children. But there was a boy in Solingen, your godson, who could be manipulated as a future, Catholic claimant on the throne. You began the long game.'

'I later had my own son – Darnley. Then Charles,' spat Margaret Douglas.

'Yes. But having lost one, you kept shaping Anne's child as a reserve. A child to be used for your ambitions. And in bringing him here you unleashed a storm of death.'

The room seemed to go cold as every face turned to Margaret Douglas. She stared ahead, face hard, then snarled. 'I have not killed anyone.'

'Not directly, madam. But that brings me to the third *who* of this tragedy – who is the poisoner of every person who has spoken against Jasper being our future king? The captain of *The Mariella*, the old launderess, the limner's assistant,' Dee turned to Robert Dudley. 'Though that poison was meant for you, Robert. I would wager that when you had the conversation with Jasper of Cleves, telling him to leave England, you were walking in the Court orchard.'

Dudley jerked in surprise. 'How do you know? There was no-one there except...'

'...the veiled apple woman,' finished Dee. 'And the next day the Queen's dog went mad and attacked.' Dudley nodded mutely as Dee walked across the room. 'Because that was the first belladonna poisoning of many. It was probably practice though it acted as a terrible prophesy of what was to come. We assumed it was a man. Surely only a man would kill so cruelly?'

He stopped before Yaxley who was now looking nervous. 'The messenger fool. So determined to be important that you thought you would continue passing instructions and smoothing the desired path of your mistress – Margaret Douglas.' Yaxley began to shake his head and rock to and fro. 'You could do little from the Tower, but you had a wife who was obsessively Catholic and who has always depended on you for instruction. Scarred to the point of hiding her face and hands behind a veil and black gloves, she was the perfect poisoner. Kept in Court as a charity when your foolery had you imprisoned. She could hear, she could move unnoticed and she could find her victims.'

Blanche stepped forward. 'I cannot believe such a timid woman as Meg Yaxley would plan to kill, John. You must be wrong.'

'Oh, she did not plan, cousin.' He smiled as she frowned at being called cousin. 'She did what she has done all her married life. She followed instruction. She delivered apparently innocent baskets of apples. But in every basket was a red apple. And every time she brought apples, she was given one back with the message, "This for you."'

Dee walked to the desk and picked up one wooden apple, plucked the stem and revealed the hidden chamber. 'She took messages from one person to another and when given the command, like Eve doing Satan's work, she poisoned with the apples she picked.'

'She is not Eve,' screamed Yaxley. 'She is my wife.'

'Yes. And like the serpent in Eden, you have used her, just as your mistress used Jasper of Cleves to try and mould destiny.'

Cecil barked again. 'These apple baskets were checked every time she left and returned. It is impossible that she hid anything.'

Dee smiled, put the apple together and raised it to Cecil. He then span round and faced Cecil again, hands raised, empty. After a dramatic pause he opened his cloak to show the apple hanging by the stalk. 'Clever carving of the stalk makes a hook. No guard would approach Meg Yaxley as they fear her scars will give them the smallpox they dread. The secret apples came and went in the black cloak.'

There was a silence, then a wail from Yaxley as the guards grabbed his shoulders.

Dee looked around. 'There is one more person. You,

Bishop de la Quadra. We have no evidence of wrongdoing and yet you have knowingly meddled against our Queen. You have received apples, you have listened at doors, you have dabbled in our destiny in a pursuit of Spanish power.' Dee pointed. 'Shame on you.'

Dudley shouted, 'They should all go to the Tower for trying to depose Elizabeth and take us back to Rome.'

Bishop de la Quadra span round. 'Hypocrisy, sir.'

Dudley sprang to his feet, hand going to the knife in his belt, making the Duchess yelp her fear.

Cecil stood and barked at the men to desist, and Henry Carey grabbed Dudley, pushing him back into the seat.

Silence fell and Dee looked around. 'This brings us to the third *why*. Why did a woman of Court with such personal ambitions promote the false claim of a German prince?'

Cecil stood. 'Exactly. This makes no sense, John.'

Dee smiled. 'Oh, but it does.' He moved again to stand before Margaret Douglas. 'Why would you encourage Jasper to propose to the Scottish Queen when you had been plotting to marry your own son to Mary, Queen of Scots, joining the bloodline and two people of the Catholic faith? Why, when you believe yourself to have more right to the throne than Elizabeth, did you summon a pretender? Why risk your own freedom and...' He pointed at Yaxley. 'Let your own messengers moulder in the Tower and...' He pointed at de la Quadra, 'let ambassadors meddle in our Court?'

Silence.

'It is because Jasper of Cleves has been your pawn for more than twenty-one years. Both you and your imprisoned messenger leaked your dark scheme by saying that Elizabeth should approve a marriage. Jasper of Cleves started as your long game to have a ready pretender to the English throne – your own godson. But when you had your own son, that babe in Cleves became your ammunition rather than your ambition. His arrival here would be used to force Elizabeth to secure the throne in English hands by agreeing to a marriage between your son, Darnley, and the Scottish Queen. Or maybe Jasper was a back-up if your son was not successful. For even a German Catholic would be better than a Protestant Tudor. Is that not true, madam?'

There was a gasp and then a long silence before the Duchess of Suffolk turned to Margaret Douglas. 'Damn you,' she growled.

And this is why they admire you. The most learned man in Europe and the most brilliant of minds.

Eyes turned to Jasper and Dee walked over to put his hand on his shoulder, which was shaking as he gave way to tears. 'Jasper of Cleves. You were born of love into this cruel world. The tragedy of your life is that greed and naked ambition has kept you from a mother who loved you and a good man who was your father. She never stopped loving him or you, and he never stopped loving her.'

Jasper looked up; pain etched on his face. 'How do you know?'

'Because when he could not give her the world, he sent her his own son – your half-brother – a man called Otho van Wylich. He is as good a man as your father was. Go back to Cleves and find him – and start to heal this cruelty.'

You do have a heart. A good, kind heart, Doctor Dee.

As they filed out, Katherine Willoughby walked over to Jasper and put her arms around him. They heard her whisper, 'She loved you more than life itself. She would have given you the world. Now I give to you, her ring.'

Chapter Sixty-Five

'Robert is right. She should go to the Tower.' Dee was facing Cecil in his office. Dudley sat in the corner. He and Margaretta have been summoned two days after the unravelling of the story of the Cygnet Prince.

'Margaret Douglas is of the blood, John. Elizabeth will only gain enemies if she incarcerates the woman who is at the centre of the Catholic faction. It will make her a martyr and only fuel their love of Mary, Queen of Scots.' Cecil sat heavily. 'I share your fury, but we need to contain this. Margaret Douglas will remain in Sheen under close supervision.'

'What of the other players in this sad drama?'

'Jasper of Cleves was greeted as an ambassador by Elizabeth yesterday.'

'And I was not invited?' The voice was high, indignant.

Dudley broke in, much to Cecil's annoyance. 'We thought it best to keep it quiet, John. Elizabeth was kind and has sent Jasper back to his lands with a handsome reward.'

'You have paid him to keep quiet,' snapped Dee, glaring at Cecil.

'We have given him encouragement to repair his life in Cleves... with his brother.' Cecil kept his eyes on the desk, leaking his discomfort.

'The Yaxleys? De la Quadra?'

'The bishop has been ordered to remain in his Westminster

residence and refrain from any dabbling in our country. He will not even use the privy-chamber without eyes upon him. He is no longer welcome at Court, which will cause him considerable problems in Spain. As for the Yaxleys...' Cecil pinched his nose. 'Francis Yaxley is a helpful fool. Such is his desire to be seen as a great seer of Court affairs, he actually gives us information. It was his bleating that led us to the plot earlier this year to marry Darnley to Mary, Queen of Scots. Our decision is to keep him under close watch in the Tower and interrogate him further when he thinks all has settled. We will play him.'

I sense horror. You are not saying something. Something worries you, Sir Cecil. 'Sir, what about Meg Yaxley?'

Cecil frowned. 'That is not for you to worry about, Margaretta. Nor is it for you to question me.'

Dee snapped at Cecil. 'Margaretta asks the same question as me. What of Meg Yaxley? Two dead and one still recovering.'

Cecil winced. 'The normal punishment for poisoning is to be boiled alive, though it has not been used for years.' He swallowed as Margaretta let out a little cry.

Dee shook his head. 'But she was a puppet to other people's plotting. A simpleton doing as her husband bid her do. Surely—'

'And she brought poison into Court,' shouted Dudley. 'If we had not stopped her, she would have poisoned Elizabeth.'

Cecil stood and rounded on Robert Dudley. 'We cannot say that, Master Dudley. And is not treason a form of poison? If so, your forefathers would have boiled at Smithfield.'

Dudley jumped up, making his chair clatter to the ground, and put his hand to the knife in his belt. His face was red with fury. 'How dare you...'

Dee stepped forward, putting his hand on Dudley's shoulder. 'Calm yourself, Robert.' He turned to Cecil. 'I think the enmity in this room is poisonous enough, William.'

Cecil sat again. 'I will try to have her sentence reduced to hanging. It is, at least, quicker.'

'And me?' asked Dee.

Cecil frowned. 'What about you?'

Dee angered, his face beginning to flush. 'I expect an audience to tell Her Majesty about the investigation and then we will discuss my reward.'

Cecil raised an eyebrow. 'What have you not understood, John? We have spent two days planning how to keep this sorry tale out of public knowledge. This place has a hundred ears in every room. We cannot tell the world how close they were to losing their Queen.'

Dee bristled. 'And you expect me to hide away? Say nothing? Have my efforts and intellect ignored?' He walked towards Cecil's desk. 'You will try to cover me when I should be at Court?'

Cecil raised a hand in placation. 'You will be rewarded, John. In a way most fitting to your position as a scholar to Court.'

Dee calmed. 'Go on.'

'You mentioned a Hungarian noble who can access a copy of the *Steganographia*.'

Dee seemed to grow two inches. 'Peter Albrecht. Our… my interpreter in Germany. Yes, he can.'

'And Her Majesty will fund an excursion for you to travel to Cologne to study the book. You should start making your arrangements immediately. It may take some months in planning.'

Well done, Sir Cecil. My master is happy. And I think it better we leave the enmity between you and Dudley. There will be no cheer in this room, for you both want to be favourite of the same woman.

As they waited for the barge to take them back up the Thames to St Dunstan's, they heard a woman's call. Blanche ap Harri was walking across the grass towards the waving. Dee pulled himself tall. Before he could greet her, she raised a hand. 'Do not call me cousin, John Dee.' He deflated.

You are putting on a serious face, though I feel the warmth beneath. You are a good woman, Blanche ap Harri, but as protective as a tiger to her cub.

She spoke to Dee first. 'I know Cecil said you were not to have an audience. But you should know, John, that Elizabeth knows all of your work and your loyalty. When things are a little calmed, you should come to show her some of your ideas.' She made a small smile at the excitement in his face.

Then she turned to Margaretta. 'And you, my dear. Elizabeth knows of the help you have given.' She pressed something into Margaretta's hand. 'She asked me to make one of these for you too so that you would know you are looked over with care.'

Margaretta looked down. It was a white handkerchief, perfectly embroidered with E in one corner and M in the other. Tears filled her eyes. 'As I said, Mistress Blanche, Elizabeth was much graced with the care of the hand who made this. And I am graced with the square embrace you have given me in this linen.'

Epilogue

In February, 1563, John Dee boarded a ship in London bound for the continent. He made his way to Cologne, where he was given ten days in an inn called the Golden Angel and a copy of the *Steganographia* to transcribe, organised for him by a Hungarian noble, Peter Albrecht.

Back in St Dunstans, Siôn Jenkins had already risen to master of accounts in the business of Master Constable. He was a regular visitor at the merchant's house where he would insist on eating with Margaretta and Dee so that they used their own language. In early summer, he introduced a young woman called Delyth Williams, a seamstress from Nefyn in North Wales, and Margaretta sensed that a broken heart was mending.

Grace reluctantly returned to the house of Susan McFadden, though she always found reason to travel to St Dunstan's on her free Sundays. She and Huw would walk the riverbank – looking at each other.

The machinations of Court went on and the rumours of Elizabeth's love affair with Robert Dudley continued throughout the year. But in the house of Cecil, in June, a baby boy was born. Mildred feared for months but eventually believed her babe would survive to be a man. Cecil poured love into him, but every time he saw the boy, he remembered the curse of a mummer in the garden of Hatfield House. The dwarf, Petit Pierre, had screamed, 'I curse you, that any son you have will be stunted like me.' Robert Cecil was born with a twisted back and the physicians said that he would never grow more than the height of a child.

Susan and Angus McFadden did not contact Margaretta about Huw's inheritance. The letter written by William Fleetwood had done its job. Early in 1563, Siôn Jenkins went to Brecon to survey the small farm and found a farmer who was given a five-year tenancy. For the first time in his life, Huw had an income. He was a man in his own right. But all he said of it? 'Huw look after Margaretta. Keep Margaretta pink.'

Historical Facts

The characters

Anne of Cleves

Born in 1515, Anne was the third daughter of Johan and Maria of Julich. She was raised in Solingen Castle which is as described in the novel. She was a good-natured child and very close to her mother. It is true she was hit by a pair of scissors thrown by her sister, Sybilla.

In 1538 she was identified as a fourth bride for Henry VIII who was recently widowed after Jane Seymour, sister of Thomas Seymour, died soon after childbirth. Nicholas Wooton was sent to negotiate the marriage, and in late 1539 Anne started the five-week journey to Calais. It was certainly a long and arduous one, sometimes only making five miles in a day due to the roads. Her retinue was over two-hundred people and she was accompanied by Nicholas Wooton, Mrs Gylman and Otto van Wylich (See below).

In Calais, Anne was met by a huge welcoming party of English nobles, one of whom was Thomas Seymour, and she did ask them to teach her the card name, Cent. The depiction of Thomas Seymour getting drunk and terrifying her is fiction – though in line with his loud-mouth persona.

She was delayed ten days in Calais due to bad weather and eventually crossed the channel in late December. Some reports say the crossing was rough and she was sea-sick.

When she arrived in England, she was met by Katherine Willoughby, who later became Duchess of Suffolk. They remained life-long friends and the Duchess was left the table diamond ring in Anne's will. Margaret Douglas was made head of her household.

Henry, having fallen in love with the portrait painted by Hans Holbein, was horrified by Anne's appearance, shouting 'I like her not', and claiming she was loose of belly and breast with evil smells around her. The painting of Anne by Hans Holbein shows a pretty round-faced girl with full cheeks. But when Anne arrived in England, the French ambassador, Marillac, described her as 'thin' and of 'medium beauty'. I have no firm evidence that she had lost weight en-route to her new home, but it is true that rapid weight loss creates ketosis in the human body which leads to sweet smelling sweat and bad breath.

Anne was divorced by Henry in July 1540. He used the excuse that she had previously been betrothed to Henry Duke of Bar, son of the Duke of Lorraine. Her agreement to the divorce was rewarded with great wealth and many properties – including Hever, Lewes and properties in Norfolk. One of those properties was the Anne of Cleves house in Saxlingham Nethergate described in the novel. Granted to her for life as part of the divorce settlement, this house in the time of Anne Cleves was U shaped and moated. The house on the site today is an eighteenth-century rebuild. The property was in the ownership of Thomas Chapman in 1558 immediately after the death of Anne of Cleves.

William Pudding was a licenced preacher in Saxlingham Nethergate in the 1600s but it was too good a name to reject on the basis of time – and who says he was not one of a line of William Puddings who preached in St Mary's?

The panels described are the Anne of Cleves panels discovered and researched by Sarah Morris and Jonathan

Foyle. My placing of the panels in St Mary's Church is fictitious – though no-one knows where Anne actually placed her panels.

After the divorce, Anne went into a period of great gaiety. She bought new clothes, entertained – apparently she loved a party, gambled and was a great cook. She did attend Court and danced with Catherine Howard (which I have spelled Kathryn in the book as this was such a widely used name and I had to create some differentiation) and was much praised by the King and others for her grace. Anne was loved by all who met her – including Elizabeth and Mary, the royal princesses. She was known for her kindness to all servants and put them in her will. Elyn Tyrpyn was indeed her old laundress.

The rumour of Anne giving birth to Henry's child in 1541 is a fact. It is also true that she went on progress in 1540 and there is no record of where she was. Jane Rattsay was questioned; Frances Lilegrave and a Richard Taverner were arrested and questioned in the Tower and the Privy Council investigated. No child was found and Anne's reputation was restored. She did want to go back to Germany but stopped planning for that around 1542 as her brother's war against the Emperor made it impossible.

As set out in the novel, Anne re-appeared in March 1542 in Richmond and was unwell. King Henry put his physicians at her disposal.

Anne lived the rest of her life in England. Otho van Wylich, illegitimate son of Otto van Wylich, did join her household and stayed with her until 1556 when he, along with Anne's cofferer, Jasper Brokehause, was forced to leave by the Privy Council when her cousin stirred resentment towards them. She was evidently very fond of Otho as she fought to keep him with her.

Anne died in July 1557 with a malady of the breast – through Alison Wier has suggested it was an infection which ended her life. Her assets and chattels were indeed indexed and auctioned – and yes, Mildred Cecil paid over £100 for her clothes – about £23,000 in today's money.

Amalia of Cleves

Little is known of this lady – through it is known she was Lutheran and had arguments with her brother Wilhelm. The scene felt by Margaretta in which he chases her with a sword after a row about religion is true. She did raise her nieces and nephews but never married. She was also considered as a bride for Henry – but the ambassadors opted for Anne. There was another marriage discussed – to the Margravitate of Baden – but her brother refused to agree terms as the man was depraved.

We know that Amalia was a good needlewoman, liked playing chess and did write poetry. One love poem she wrote is evidently to a woman and she was so close to one lady, Katharina, that people commented on their inappropriate behaviour.

That said, the portrayal of Amalia as a sociopathic killer is fiction.

Margaret Douglas

Margaret Douglas was a constant thorn in the side of the Tudor monarchy. A direct descendent of Mary Tudor, King Henry's much-loved sister, she believed herself to have a right to the throne above that of Elizabeth. As a staunch friend and supporter of Queen Mary Tudor (Bloody Mary) she saw Elizabeth to be both illegitimate and also a protestant heretic.

As well as being an outspoken critic and plotter, she also had a bad habit of having affairs with men of whom the monarch disapproved. In 1541 she did go on the progress of Henry and his new bride, Katherine Howard, where she started an affair with Queen Katherine's brother, Charles Howard. She was punished by being sent under house arrest to Kenninghall in Norfolk – which is seventeen miles from

Saxlingham Nethergate. She was held in Kenninghall from November 1540 until 1543 when she was released to the household of Katherine Parr, Henry's last wife.

In 1561, Margaret started her strategy to have her son Darnley married to Mary, Queen of Scots who had arrived in Scotland in August that year. She had been in communication with Bishop de la Quadra through Francis Yaxley, his secretary, and so they were certainly involved. She was brought from her Catholic stronghold in Yorkshire to Sheen where she was held under house arrest again. Her son, Darnley, did slip the net in York and is thought to have fled to France until safe to return. Her husband was put in the Tower and was badly psychologically affected by his incarceration. It is true that Margaret was accused of witchcraft – though by a biased, bitter servant – and she did bombard Sir William Cecil with demands for her and her husband to be released.

Margaret Douglas did have a long-serving servant called Mompesson who was named in her will.

Francis Yaxley

Francis had been an up-and-coming man of court – entering the Office of the Signet which gave him power. He was clerk of the signet in 1557 when Anne of Cleves died. He also became MP for Stamford – William Cecil's birthplace. As secretary to Bishop de la Quadra he became embroiled in the intrigues to marry Darnley to Mary, Queen of Scots. He was exposed by Borgese Venturini who was, indeed, angry with de la Quadra over lack of payments and informed William Cecil. Yaxley was caught, interrogated, confessed, and put into the Tower early in 1562. There he stayed until 1563 when he was released. But his plotting did not stop. On release, he became a go-between for Margaret Douglas and Philip II, travelling back and forth from Edinburgh and Flanders and Segovia. He came to a watery end in 1565 when his ship was wrecked in the North Sea and he was washed up in Northumberland.

Bishop de la Quadra

He was ambassador to the English Court in the early years of Elizabeth's reign and he was certainly involved in intrigues. It is correct that Robert Dudley tried to befriend him and did try to scheme to get the support of Philp II of Spain by promising to return England to Catholicism. The Bishop also schemed with Margaret Douglas using Yaxley as the messenger.

After 1562, he was under constant watch and ordered to stay in his residence. He was resentful at his lack of power and died a frustrated man in 1565.

Robert Dudley

Robert Dudley was certainly a high-risen favourite in 1562. He had cemented his friendship with Elizabeth after they were both in the Tower at the time of the Wyatt rebellion, though it is not known if they actually met there. The day after she was declared queen, Robert was made Master of the Horse which ensured he was in Elizabeth's company daily, either hunting, travelling or discussing her stables. Her passion for him and his for her became the talk of Court. Such was the rumour that she would make him King were he not married to Amy Dudley that the gossip reached Europe through the loose-tongued ambassadors. In September 1560, just a year after Elizabeth became queen, a messenger arrived in Court to announce that Amy Dudley had been found dead at the foot of two stairs, her neck broken. Immediately, the shadow of suspicion fell on Robert Dudley. This was not helped by the previous comments of William Cecil who in his resentment of Dudley had told Bishop de la Quadra that Amy might be found dead one day. Dudley set up an enquiry immediately and Elizabeth had no choice but to send him from Court while the officials made their investigations. Within weeks Dudley was exonerated and returned to Court, but the stain of suspicion lingered.

Dudley was handsome, quick-witted, talkative and loved his food. But he was also arrogant, puffed-up and determined to be king. He was disliked and resented by many – especially William Cecil, who almost resigned in frustration at Dudley's influence over Elizabeth. It is true that Elizabeth called him Sweet Robin and Two Eyes – and she danced with him. When she fell ill with smallpox in October 1562, she made him regent and gave his man, Tamworth, a large pension.

Sir William Cecil

In 1562, William Cecil was Elizabeth's trusted advisor though having to navigate her relationship with Dudley. He was very concerned about the succession issue as Elizabeth refused to marry. He was closely involved in the arrest and imprisonment of Margaret Douglas and her husband, and also that of Yaxley.

In his personal life, he was grieving the loss of two baby boys – both called Willliam. But Mildred Cecil would have found she was pregnant in the autumn of 1562 as their son, Robert, was born in June 1563.

Catherine Carey and her brother, Henry Carey

Catherine Carey did have sixteen children. The last, called Dudley, was born in May 1562 and died in the June. He was the only child to die a baby. She was a maid of honour to Anne of Cleves but was taken into the Court of Henry when he married Katherine Howard a day after his divorce from Anne. She was well-trusted all her life – through had to flee in 1554 when Mary Tudor ascended the throne and, as a protestant, Catherine and her family faced threat of treason. They lived in Germany until Mary died and Elizabeth became queen and return was safe. There as much speculation that Catherine and her brother, Henry, were the children of Henry VIII with Mary Boleyn – Sister to Anne Boleyne and aunt to Elizabeth. Their likeness to their cousin was remarkable; they were favoured and protected as close relatives, but whether King Henry was their father was never discussed. Henry Carey was certainly a significant figure at Court, and loved by Elizabeth. He was well dressed and swore like a trouper.

It is true that Dr Burcott, who attended Elizabeth, was brought by Henry Carey, and when he refused to come a second time because Elizabeth had called him a knave, he was dragged back at knifepoint.

The Duchess of Suffolk

Katherine Willoughby met Anne when she arrived in England and accompanied her first to Deal and then on to Rochester. She was present when Anne first met Henry and the trouble began before the marriage was made.

In 1562 Katherine Willoughby, now Duchess of Suffolk, was still in the mire of settling a will and her inheritance, and was assisted by William Cecil. They were firm friends. She was a renowned sharp-tongued and witty woman who did, indeed, have a dog called Gardiner named after the Bishop she detested, and she took pleasure in 'calling it to heel.' To be honest, the dog was probably long gone by 1561, but it was a detail too lovely to exclude – and maybe she called all her dogs Gardiner.

She was a life-long friend of Anne of Cleves and was bequeathed a table-cut diamond ring in her will.

Nicholas Wooton and Otto van Wylich

Nicholas Wooton was one of the ambassadors sent to first view Anne and Amalia of Cleves and then pursue the marriage negotiations. It is true that they requested that Anne and Amalia raise their veils in order to see their faces, though their mother, Maria, objected.

He was in the retinue which accompanied Anne of Cleves from her home to Calais. He sent letter to Thomas Cromwell appraising him of his progress. In a letter of December 4th 1539 he wrote '*Hovemester Willik, one of the greatest men about the Duke, is left sick at Ravesteyn...*

He is not unlike the King in height and face, and of good knowledge and experience'.

Otto van Wylich (different texts have varying spelling – I landed on this one) did have an illegitimate son called Otho, who was sent to stay in the household of Anne of Cleves after her divorce. He stayed in her company until 1556 when he was forced to leave after Anne's cousin, Waldeck, stirred up trouble over accounts being limited and manipulated Anne's brother, Wilhelm, to demand Otho's expulsion by the Privy Council.

Nicholas Wooton did not stay close to London after bringing Anne of Cleves. He was made dean of Canterbury Cathedral in April 1541.

John Dee

In 1562 John Dee had been travelling Europe in search of books and he was studying Hebrew in order to better understand the Kabbala. It is quite true that he heard of the book – The *Steganographia* – in Birkmann's bookshop and became obsessed with finding it. We know that in February 1563, he was in the Angel Inn in Cologne copying the book which had been sourced as a ten-day loan to him by a Hungarian noble.

In 1562, he was still battling the reputation earned by conjuring the queen's horoscope in 1555 and was frustrated by this slur. The quote at the end of Chapter 36 is a true quote.

Queen Elizabeth

Elizabeth was wooed by Erik of Sweden in the early years of her reign and she dangled him along, with no intentions to wed him. In 1562, Kat Astley and her husband – along with Francis Yaxley – did get into trouble by writing to the Ambassador of Sweden and encouraging Erik in his pursuit of Elizabeth. This interference put them both out of favour. But Elizabeth's love of Kat ensure this was a short period. Erik died insane.

In 1561, Elizabeth had been presented with a pair of silk stockings which her silk maker, Mistress Alice Montague, had spent six years making. The queen was immediately smitten and declared 'I will wear no more cloth stockings.' A year later she was being brought black silk stockings from Europe.

In 1562, Elizabeth was in her third year of her reign and her passion for Robert Dudley was causing an ongoing scandal. It is true that Kat Astley begged her to show more restraint having originally encouraged them.

The reference to a pearl-encrusted looking glass is true. It was in Elizabeth's chambers. She also was constantly mislaying her precious things.

In October of that year, there was an outbreak of smallpox causing panic in the City. On October 10th 1562, she had been out hunting and insisted on taking a bath. She then appeared to have a chill but it rapidly worsened. Her cousin, Henry Carey, sent for his personal physician, Burcott, who left in a rage when she called him a knave. Elizabeth became week and unable to speak. A day later the classic pustules of smallpox began to appear. Burcott was summoned but refused as Elizabeth had offended him. Henry Carey stepped in and the hapless doctor was bundled back to Court at the end of a knife. Burcott insisted she was moved to lie before a fire wrapped in a red blanket. Her key nurse was Mary Dudley, Lady Sidney, sister to Robert Dudley, the Queen's favourite. Mary Dudley contracted smallpox from Elizabeth and was terribly scarred. It is quite true that her husband who had been travelling during the illness stated that *"When I went to Newhaven [Le Havre] I left her a full fair Lady, in mine eye at least the fairest, and when I returned I found her as foul a lady as the smallpox could make her, which she did take by continual attendance of Her Majesty's most precious person (sick of the same disease). The scars of which (to her resolute discomfort) ever since hath done and doth remain in her face, so as she liveth solitarily sicut Nicticorax in domicilio suo [like a night-raven in the house] more to my charge then if we had boarded together as we did before that evil accident happened."*

Blanche ap Harri and Kat Astley

Blanche ap Harri – a wonderful woman, so wrongly in the shadow of Kat Astley – was a fierce protector of her cherished queen, who she had rocked in her baby cradle. She had been brought to Elizabeth's household by her aunt and the princess' first nanny, Lady Troy. We can be sure that Blanche was brought with intent to become governess, but Thomas Cromwell wanted the more biddable Kat Astley. We know that Kat was domineering of Elizabeth and pushed her other ladies away – stating that she could not abide anyone else sleeping with the little girl. The event of the handkerchiefs is documented and maybe a good insight into the character of Kat – determined to be 'mother figure' for Elizabeth and jealously blocking all the other women who also loved the little girl.

Blanche did manage all the paper and books for Elizabeth and was trusted with her jewels.

Kat Astley and her husband, John Astley, were in trouble in 1562 for writing to the Ambassador for Sweden. But she was soon back in favour.

FACTS OF THE PERIOD

On June 4th 1561, the eve of Corpus Christie, London was hit by a huge thunder storm. Lightning hit the oak and led steeple of St Paul's Cathedral causing a furious fire which consumed both the steeple and the church roof. Molten lead poured down paving the streets with metal. The Bishop's Palace was saved by five hundred people rushing to bring water – but the Cathedral was destroyed all but the communion table. Rumours abounded about foul play – but most rumours blamed Popery. It soon became a warning of a great plague to follow if life did not change. Elizabeth ordered immediate repair and gave one-thousand marks from her own purse and oak from her own woods. But the steeple was never rebuilt. The Cathedral was useable within months – but still the belief remained that God was punishing London.

In the years 1561–1562 there was several reports of strange births. Henry Machyn wrote of the body of a still-born child being presented at court. It has a strange ruff of skin and hands and feet which looked like those of a toad. It is also true that the prophesies of Nostradamus in Europe and Prestall here in England were causing concern and fear.

The Bell Inn in Oxted is its oldest inn and was there in 1562.

Hever Castle was in the hands of the Waldegrave family, which was strongly Catholic. The father had died the year before leaving the property to his widow and son, Charles.

The royal barges were managed by Will Scarlett.

Casper Vogel, cartographer, mathematician and astrologer, did live in Cologne and died in 1561.

John Rudd did deliver a map to William Cecil in 1561 and was given a two-year commission to map the whole of the British Isles. His assistant, Sexton, was actually the skilled cartographer.

References

As ever with a historical novel, your inspiration and comfort comes from the work of others who do the real research and bring to life the times of your characters.

My reading list would fill many pages, but if you want to read further into the lovely Anne of Cleves and the characters who are pulled into this novel, I would recommend:

Anne of Cleves

While maybe the most gracious and endearing of Henry's wives, Anne was the shortest in duration and seems to be the least favoured in books dedicated to her. But take a look at these:

You will never go wrong with Alison Wier. Her novel **'Anna of Kleve'**, was the novel that inspired my interest in Anne of Cleves (as she is generally named). Alison Wier has a different take to me and presents the possibility that Anne did have a child before leaving her parents' home. Alison Wier's ability to use her incredible research and convert it into an empathic story is quite brilliant.

For strong factual history, I relied on **'Anne of Cleves – Henry VIII's Discarded Bride'** by Elizabeth Norton who always gets under the skin of her subjects.

Also **'Duchess of Cleves'** and **'Children of the House of Cleves'** by Heather R. Darsie gives a huge amount of detail about both Anne, her siblings and the political web in which she was living.

John Dee

The excellent research by Glynn Parry in **'The Arch Conjuror of England'** and Bejamin Woolley in **'The Queen's Conjuror'**, will give you in-depth insights into John Dee, his life and his achievements. For this book, I also looked at a much older biography **'John Dee 1527–1608'** by Charlotte Fell-Smith, which though very much in Edwardian style, is full of rich detail. The work of John Dee on his Propaedeumata Aphoristica could only be skirted on in this book as every writer has to focus on story more than research. However, if you want an insight into the depth of thinking this man had, take a look at the excerpts in **'John Dee'** by Gerald Suster.

Elizabeth

For this novel I needed the detail around Elizabeth's relationship with Dudley and the smallpox episode. Yet again, Alison Wier is at the top of the pile with **'Elizabeth the Queen'**. Also excellent in detail and insight is **'Elizabeth's Bedfellows'** by Anna Whitelock, and **'Elizabeth's Women'** by Tracy Borman.

Margaret Douglas

I used many references for this interesting woman – but if you want absolutely everything in one book, you cannot go wrong with Alison Wier's **'The Lost Tudor Princess'**.

Blanche ap Harri or Blanche Parry

Until 2007, little had been uncovered about this elegant and loyal woman – maybe because she was eclipsed by the self-promoting and indiscreet Kat Astley. However, Ruth Elizabeth Richardson's book, **'Mistress Blanche: Queen Elizabeth's Confidante'**, righted this with an in-depth account of her loyalty, influence and power at court. It was from this book that I created the persona of Blanche ap Harri. As Richardson says – she was 'an elegant lady'.

The Cecils

So much has been written on the Cecils – maybe because they were so influential. David Loads' **'The Cecils'** will give a detailed account of their influence. For an in-depth biography of William Cecil, read **'Burghley'** by Stephen Alford.

Robert Dudley

A good first read into this man who became such a force in Elizabeth's life is **'Elizabeth's Robert Dudley'** by Robert Stedall.

Life at the time

We must never forget the society, sounds and smells in which John Dee and Margaretta moved.

Ian Mortimer in **'The Time Travellers Guide to Elizabethan England'** transports you back into the sights, sounds, sensibilities and terrible smells which surrounded John Dee and Margaretta.

'Tudor London' by Stephen Porter is a well-researched book on the capital in which this tale takes place, as is **'Elizabeth's London'** by Liza Picard.

Acknowledgements

As ever – where do I start? A book is never delivered by one person. It takes a team of advisors, friends, guides, challengers, critics, helpers and educators.

This book is in your hands because of the excellent team at Legend Press. Editing by Lauren Wolf-Jones sharpened the story and then the team delivered everything required to get my words on a shelf. I am constantly impressed by the skill and enthusiasm of this dream team. Linked to them is the very talented Sarah Whittaker who creates covers which make me very proud to say, 'that's my book.'

I am also blessed by friends who remain interested, positive, uplifting and who are willing to give me a kick when I go into the doldrums of creativity. Nicky, Ceri, Sharon, Liz, Gabriel, Peter, Rhiannon, Josh, Sarah, Nigel, Barbara, Jean, Pat, all 'The Village Damsels', and of course, Millie. You make a writer's life better in so many ways.

Then there are the wise heads whose research and brilliant writing educate me in the history, the progress, the adventure, the scandals, the religion, the gossip, the characters, the smells, the fun, the ferocity, the wonderment and everything else which made such a magnificent melee that was Tudor times. For this book, I must shout out the incredible knowledge of Cevin Conrad at Solingen Castle whose knowledge of the castle, the history, the people and the area was a joy to absorb.

Finally, my Beta readers – the people who give their time and intellect to read, consider, critique and give their honest opinion. They pick up detail, point out mistakes, guide me to be clear and tell me when I need to cut and cut again. Annie Lewis, Mair Morgan, Vicki Davies, Elizabeth Pritchard, Kathie Wareham, Kate Jones, Melanie Edwards, and Elena Kelsall – thank you. This book is better for having had your eyes on it.

Love to all.
GJ